Children of the DARK

Jonathan Janz

Sinister Grin Press

Austin, TX

www.sinistergrinpress.com

March 2016

Cover Art by Matthew Revert

Book Design by Travis Tarpley

ISBN: 978-1-944044-14-5

Acknowledgments

I could write a novel thanking all the people who deserve to be thanked, but I'm going to single out just a few and give my apologies to the rest.

First and always, I want to thank my family. My wife, my son, and my two daughters are my reason for doing everything I do. You four love me, support me, and keep me smiling through fun times and challenges. I love you four more than you'll ever know, and I'll try for the rest of my life to be the husband and father that you deserve.

Next, I want to thank my grandparents and my mom for their continued support. You three are amazing and have always believed in me.

I want to thank my four pre-readers on this book: Tim Slauter, Tod Clark, Louise Fury (my agent), and my son. Tim, you helped me feel confident in the direction the book was headed. Tod, your enthusiasm for the project was invaluable. Louise, your advice and effort helped me a great deal. And Jack, though I left out the profanity and some of the violence when I read this to you, your feedback was crucial in shaping this narrative. You're the smartest ten-year-old I know.

Though Don D'Auria didn't work on this book, Don's fingerprints are all over my career. Don, your support and belief in my work has wrought wonders for my self-confidence. Thank you.

And lastly, I want to thank Brian Keene. No writer has been as supportive of me and my writing as you have, Brian. You haven't done all these things for me for any reward or recognition; you've done them because that's the kind of person you are. People who don't know you might only see the entertaining stories, the staggering sales, and the prestigious awards. What I see—in addition to an incredible writer—is a loving, devoted father; a generous helper of those in need; a tireless champion of new voices in the field; an artist who bleeds for his craft; and a genre scholar who refuses to let people forget horror's astonishing history and heritage. For all these reasons and more, Brian, I thank you.

And I'm proud to call you my friend.

Now, if you've read these Acknowledgments, I'd like to tell you a story.

Take my hand and come this way...

Dedication

Jack, this one's for you. The ten years I've spent being your father have been the best of my life. I've never seen a son who is more supportive of his dad, and I want you to know it means the world to me. *You* mean the world to me. I love you, Bubba.

"And men do love sin, Will, oh how they love it, never doubt, in all shapes, colors, sizes, and smells."

Ray Bradbury
Something Wicked This Way Comes

"Love isn't soft, like those poets say. Love has teeth which bite and the wounds never close."

Stephen King
The Body

PART ONE

LEGENDS

Chapter One

The Championship and the Grudge

The week I saw seventeen people die didn't begin with blood, monsters, or a sadistic serial killer.

It all began with a baseball game.

Looking back, I wonder if things would have been different had we lost that night. You'd think that winning the league championship would have kicked off the best summer of my life.

But it didn't. That summer was my worst, and that's saying something. Despite only being fifteen-years-old, I'd already had some shitty ones.

I think that was part of it, our age. My best friend Chris Watkins and I had just completed our freshman year at Shadeland High, but despite our inexperience, we were two of the best baseball players in the school.

That didn't sit well with Brad Ralston or Kurt Fisher, who were two years older and had been the starting varsity pitcher and shortstop until Chris and I came along. On the night I'm talking about, the third evening of June, our head coach was in the stands watching. It made me nervous; Coach Aldrich was an enormous, bearlike man with tiny black eyes, a thick Hitler mustache, and though he hardly ever spoke, when he did, you listened. Like a temperamental Grizzly bear, I was always afraid he'd maul me.

Coach Aldrich's eyes were riveted on me as I stepped to the plate in the top of the ninth inning with two outs, my team trailing by one, and runners on second and third base. Mia Samuels was watching me too, and as much as I feared Coach Aldrich, Mia's opinion counted for far more. Her striking blue eyes and black, punkish hair were a part of that—as was her body, if I'm being totally honest—but even more importantly, she made me feel like I was something other than a loser.

There were maybe two hundred people in the stands, and the temperature was pushing ninety. But I tried to block out the crowd and the heat because Brad Ralston—Mia's asshole boyfriend—was on the mound, and whatever flaws the guy had, he was a flamethrower of a pitcher. He'd already beaned me twice that game—a hard slider to the ribs and a screaming fastball in the hip—and I knew he wouldn't hesitate to obliterate me again.

I dug in, told myself to be brave.

But when the first pitch howled in and nearly tore my head off, whatever bravery I had evaporated.

Trembling, I stumbled out of the batter's box to dust myself off. A voice behind me said, "Relax, Will. If he hits you, it might improve your looks."

I turned and saw my best friend waiting in the on-deck circle, his yellow aluminum bat resting on his shoulder.

"Big words coming from someone as disfigured as you."

It was a lie, of course. Every girl in the school wanted to date Chris Watkins.

He grinned his lopsided grin. "The longer you wait, the more your balls will shrink."

"You're a prick, Watkins," I said under my breath.

"Want a hug?"

"Piss off," I muttered, and reentered the batter's box.

Ralston was grinning at me, clearly relishing how terrified I was.

Don't worry about that, I told myself. *Don't worry about Brad, don't worry about Coach Aldrich. Don't even think about Mia, who by the way is looking extraordinarily hot tonight.*

I glanced toward the stands, spotted Mia, and felt my cheeks and temples burn. Then, I brushed away several impure thoughts and readied myself for the pitch. As I did I saw Brad scuffing a cleat into the reddish dirt of the pitcher's mound, the ball looking no larger than a hard-boiled egg in his massive hand. I caught a glimpse of the ugly, worm-colored scar on his wrist, remembered how he'd supposedly sliced it by punching through his bedroom window while in the throes of an ungovernable rage.

Brad was still grinning, but I fancied I could distinguish the same maniacal rage in his eyes now as he stepped onto the pitching rubber.

I raised my bat, blinked sweat out of my eyes.

Brad checked the runners. I waited, bat aloft, and took a quivering breath. Brad started his motion. I tensed, expecting another fastball at my helmet.

It blazed right down the middle.

I swung.

And smashed a fierce grounder at Kurt Fisher, the shortstop and Brad's best buddy. I ran like crazy thinking I was out for sure. I was a fast runner, but Kurt was built like a tank, had a cannon for an arm, and he was almost always accurate.

I glanced to my left to see if the ball was traveling to first base already, but that's when the night took its first surreal turn. Rather than fielding it cleanly, the ball rocketed under Kurt's glove and skittered into the outfield. It was a routine play, one I'd seen him make a hundred times. But this time he didn't. We plated two runs and seized the lead.

Chris popped out, and we entered the bottom half of the ninth inning up by a run. Chris was pitching, so I liked our chances. He had an even better arm than Brad, which was why he was on the verge of overtaking Brad as the number one pitcher on the varsity team. No one had to say it, but if Chris out-dueled Brad that night, with Coach Aldrich in attendance, Chris might very well start the following year ahead of Brad on the depth chart.

But Chris got into trouble. There were two outs, but the bases were loaded, and we were clinging to a one-run lead.

Brad stepped into the batter's box, a manchild who already stood six-foot-four and had homered eleven times that season.

Chris's first two pitches were out of the strike zone, the sweltering heat and the pressure maybe getting to my best friend a little. I hustled in from my shortstop position to calm him down.

I said in a low voice, "Why do squirrels swim on their backs?"

He shot me a look. "What the hell are you talking about?"

"Why do squirrels swim on their backs?" I repeated.

His glare began to relax. "I know you're gonna tell me whether I want to hear it or not."

I stared at him, eyebrows raised.

"Jesus," he muttered, taking off his hat and mopping his brow with a forearm. "Okay, why do squirrels swim on their backs?"

"To keep their nuts dry."

He shook his head but let out a small chuckle. "You're a dumbass, Burgess."

"Uh-uh. I'm just fascinated by animal genitalia."

He was still shaking his head, but he looked like he'd relaxed about five ticks. "So what would you throw him here?" Chris asked.

"Brad's not gonna be swinging. Just throw a strike."

Chris cocked an eyebrow at me. "And if he hits it?"

I shrugged. "I'll field it."

The umpire appeared at my side. "You two done swapping recipes?"

I nodded at Chris. "We were talking about the new Stephen King book. It's about a pitcher who stalks an umpire because he kept making bad calls."

"Very bloody," Chris put in.

The umpire grinned. "Morons. Let's play ball."

I nodded, tapped Chris on the back with my glove, and returned to my position.

Chris's next two pitches were pure gas, scorching fastballs that Brad could only watch as they zinged by. The next pitch was a change-up that Brad swung out of his cleats trying to hit.

Strike three.

The championship was ours.

Chris and I and the rest of our team exploded with jubilation. It's a wonder none of us got killed in the scrum on the pitcher's mound. At one point Chris was hoisted onto a couple guys' shoulders, but their balance sucked, and he ended up facedown in the dirt.

But he never stopped grinning.

Neither did I. I spotted Mia and Rebecca gazing at us from the other side of the fence, and though their boyfriends had just lost the championship, they were applauding along with the rest of the crowd. I didn't dare read too much into that—sports can bring out weird emotions in people—but I won't lie. It made me feel even better.

My good spirits lasted for about three minutes. I wanted to keep celebrating, but I had to take a piss. If I jumped around on the pitcher's mound any longer, I was going to have an accident, and then I'd be known as the guy who couldn't control his bladder rather than the one who drove in the game-winning run. So I slipped away from my teammates, exited the field, and scurried around to the dingy cinderblock bathroom. I jerked on the door handle, but just my luck, the damn thing was locked. I was about to dash into the adjacent woods so I could relieve myself when I heard a raised voice that made me forget all about urination.

I paused and stared at the gray bathroom door, the dented metal rusting in several places.

"...didn't concentrate!" a man's voice shouted.

A muffled answer, the voice belonging to someone younger.

"Don't give me that! You *choked*, plain and simple."

Another response, this one something about being nervous.

A harsh bark of a laugh. "You want me to feel *sorry* for you? You were nervous, so now that little Burgess bastard is gonna start at shortstop instead of you. Jesus Christ Almighty."

My stomach muscles contracted. I realized who this was and why this was happening. Kurt Fisher's dad—an overzealous drill sergeant of a father if ever there was one—was berating his son for making an error. As if Kurt didn't already feel lousy enough.

"I'm sorry," Kurt muttered.

"I am too!" his dad answered, a biting edge to his voice. "I'm sorry your coach had to watch you forget everything he taught you. Everything *I've* taught you. Hell, I don't know why I even bother."

Kurt said something I couldn't make out. Then I heard a sniff.

"*Ohhh*," his dad said. "You're gonna cry now. Sure, that's gonna make everything better. For God's sake, how old are you?"

Kurt didn't bother to answer. I didn't blame him. I felt like crying myself.

"Get yourself together," Kurt's dad growled. I heard a rustling sound within the bathroom, a couple footsteps. "I wanna get the hell out of here."

I bolted toward the woods before Kurt or his dad could emerge. I didn't want Kurt to know I'd heard the exchange, didn't want him to feel any worse than he already did. It was funny—he'd been an asshole to me for as long as I could remember, but it wasn't until that moment that I gave a thought to why.

If I had a dad like that, maybe I'd be an asshole too. Of course, I'd never had a dad at all, and for once, I was thankful for that.

I remained hidden several feet from the forest's edge, peering at the bathroom door. A moment or two later, Kurt exited, followed closely by his father. This time Mr. Fisher wasn't speaking at all, but he was glaring at the back of his son's head as though he wished Kurt would die. I wondered how sad he'd be if something actually did happen to his son.

My hands shaking, I unzipped my baseball pants and peed on a maple tree.

◆

When I finished my business in the woods, I found Chris behind our dugout stowing his bat and batting helmet. I was opening my mouth to tell him about Kurt, but soft footfalls from my left stopped me.

Mia and Rebecca.

In the combined glare of the overhead ballpark lights and the softer glow of the full moon, Mia's spiky hair looked glossier than ever, her stunning blue eyes a bit feline. She wore an electric blue tank top that showed a strip of brown skin above her jean shorts. And though the tight clothes weren't skimpy, they certainly didn't hide much.

Not that I was complaining.

Mia had on pink flip-flops. I noticed her toenails were painted the same blue as her eyes and wondered if that was something girls did. My only knowledge of female behavior came from my mom, who never put effort into her appearance; my six-year-old sister, who was too young to know anything; and the Internet, which I only got to use at Chris's house. Needless to say, I was mystified by girls.

Rebecca was smiling at Chris, and though I'd always been obsessed with Mia, I completely understood why Chris wanted so badly to date Brad Ralston's kid sister. She had long blond hair, light blue eyes, and though she didn't display as much flesh as Mia, she definitely had a nice body.

"You sore?" Rebecca asked me, and because I was so transfixed by the sight of Mia, it took me a moment to register her meaning.

I played it cool. "Brad doesn't throw *that* hard."

"The hell he doesn't," Chris said. "Coach clocked him at eighty-five this spring."

Rebecca tilted her head. "I bet your fastball is better."

Chris blushed violently. I restrained the urge to laugh at him. Though Chris had a slew of girls pursuing him on a regular basis, Rebecca was the one he really pined for. Seeing him act so shyly was something I wasn't accustomed to. I made a mental note to tease him about it later.

Mia stepped closer to me. "*Are* you okay? I think I heard your ribs break on one of those pitches."

It was my turn to feel awkward. My throat was so dry I could hardly avoid coughing, but I managed to say, "I shook it off."

One corner of her mouth turned up. "Because you're a big tough man?"

Chris snickered. "Will doesn't even have armpit hair."

I glared at him but couldn't summon a good comeback. Truth was, he was right. I didn't have armpit hair yet.

Maybe sensing my embarrassment, Rebecca asked, "How's Peach?"

"A pain in the ass," I said.

"Be nice to her."

"You kidding?" Chris said. "Will's practically her dad."

I shifted uncomfortably, but Rebecca gave me an approving look. She always asked after my little sister, probably because Rebecca had a caring heart. But there might've been another reason, one I didn't want to think about. For a moment, I wondered what kind of pain Rebecca might be feeling…

She said, "You know, you two made my life miserable by winning tonight."

"Think Brad's gonna be in an ugly mood when you get home?" Chris asked.

"How could you tell the difference?" I asked. "Isn't he always in an ugly mood?"

"Not always," Mia said.

My insides shriveled, and I stared bleakly toward the empty baseball diamond. Why did Mia have to be dating Brad?

Rebecca frowned. "He'll act like it's my fault he lost. And he'll probably yell at me for talking to you two."

"How's Kurt taking it?" Chris asked Rebecca.

"What the hell do you care?" a voice snapped.

We all turned and saw Kurt Fisher stalking toward us with Brad Ralston in tow. *Oh hell.*

Both of them sported expensive baseball backpacks, their helmets and bats and gloves jutting out in all directions. Kurt had stowed his hat, so that his square black crew cut glistened in the ballpark lights. Brad wore his green cap backward.

Both of them looked absolutely murderous.

"Mom and dad are waiting on you," Brad said.

"We were just saying hi," Rebecca answered.

Brad jerked a thumb toward the parking lot. "Get your asses in gear."

The words were out of my mouth before I knew it. "Don't talk to them like that."

"Yeah," Mia said, her blue eyes glittering. "Don't talk to us like that."

"What's wrong with you?" Kurt asked Rebecca. His eyes were red from crying, but to Rebecca I'm sure it just looked like he was pissed. "You ever heard of loyalty?"

Rebecca gave him an incredulous look. "*Loyalty?* Kurt, this isn't life or death. It's a baseball game, for God's sakes."

"*Coach Aldrich was there*," Kurt nearly shouted, and I was instantly reminded of Kurt's dad, who'd used almost the same tone of voice, only harsher and deeper, back in the bathroom. Kurt jabbed a finger in Rebecca's direction. "Don't tell me it doesn't matter!"

"Hey, look," I said to Mia. "It's okay. You guys should probably go."

She turned her fierce look on me. "I'll go when I'm ready."

Kurt stepped closer to me. "You think just because you got lucky tonight you can tell our girlfriends what to do?"

I put my hands up. "I didn't mean—"

Kurt shoved me. Hard.

Though Chris and I had begun to lift weights that winter, Kurt's muscles were twice the size of ours. I went flying back and only just avoided sprawling in the grass. Rebecca stepped toward Kurt and swatted him on the chest. "Don't take it out on him."

"I'm gonna say this one more time," Brad said in a low, dangerous voice. "Get. In. The *car*."

Mia stood her ground. "We're not your property."

"It's because we lost, isn't it?" Kurt asked. "You'll chase after anybody as long as they're on the winning team."

Rebecca scowled at him. "That has nothing to do with it, and you know it. Stop being so stupid."

Brad pushed Rebecca in the shoulder. Not hard, but harder than any guy should push a girl, even if he is her brother.

"Now wait a minute," Chris started, but Kurt headed him off, got right in Chris's face.

"Jesus, Watkins. I can't believe you're still slumming with Burgess," Kurt said. "Next thing you know, you'll be buying your clothes from Goodwill too."

"Shut your mouth, Kurt," Rebecca said, her lips a thin white line. Mia too looked like she was ready to punch Kurt in the nose.

But Kurt wasn't to be put off. He gestured at me. "You loan Burgess those shoes, Watkins? I know he's too poor to afford them on his own."

I clenched my fists, my body thrumming with rage.

Remember Kurt's dad, I told myself. *You'd be in a bad mood too if you'd just been berated by the person who's supposed to support you the most.*

Brad surveyed me, his eyes deadly cold. "Mad, Burgess? I'd be angry too if I had a drug addict for a mom."

I forgot how big Brad was, how strong. I rushed at him.

But Mia beat me there. She'd buried her hands in Brad's green baseball jersey, was attempting to shake him, but he was so big, he just laughed at her.

We all turned at the blat of a car horn.

Rebecca's parents. They'd driven up along the road bordering the ballpark, were idling in their white BMW maybe twenty yards away. Rebecca's mom rolled her window down, called for the girls to come on.

Mia released Brad, but I could tell it cost an effort. Rebecca looked almost as furious as Mia. She glowered at her brother. "You two need to leave Will and Chris alone."

"Don't worry," Brad said with mock cheer. "We're just gonna celebrate their victory with them, aren't we, Kurt?"

Kurt shrugged. "Absolutely."

The car horn sounded again, three blasts in quick succession.

"Come on," Rebecca said. "I don't want to get grounded." She looked at Chris. "I'm sorry my brother sucks."

She set off, and after a lingering glance at me, Mia followed. Frowning, I watched them motor away into the night.

Kurt gave Brad a backhanded tap on the chest. "Look at that. Burgess and Watkins need girls to protect them. What are you two gonna do now?"

"We don't need anybody—" I started, but then Chris broke in.

"We'll fight you right here."

I glanced at Chris, suspecting I'd heard him wrong. But he didn't look scared at all. He looked eager for a brawl.

"*Outstanding,*" Brad said, but it was Kurt who strode forward, looking ready to knock Chris's head off.

I said, "You don't have to prove you're tough."

Kurt froze. "What the hell are you trying to say?"

I took a breath. "I was outside the bathroom."

He turned and looked at me with narrowed eyes. "So?"

"Do you really want me to say it?"

I could see the doubt in his gaze. "You don't know anything," he muttered.

I opened my mouth, but the memory of his father's bullying voice stopped me. Kurt was a jerk, but he wasn't *born* a jerk. His dad had transformed him into one through years of careful training. I didn't want to humiliate him, but what could I say to defuse the situation? Like Kurt, Brad looked ready to crush our bones to powder.

Brad smiled uncertainly at Kurt. "What's this dickhead talking about?"

Kurt appraised me in silence. I could feel Chris's confusion wafting out of him in waves, but I didn't dare look away now. If I could stare Kurt down, maybe he'd see I really had been privy to the incident with his father. Maybe he'd even realize I felt bad for him.

All the fury seemed to leave him. His gaze dropped to the dewy grass. I glanced at Brad, who was glaring at his friend in puzzlement.

Then Brad shrugged off the straps of his backpack and knifed toward me with his fists raised.

"There you two are!" a woman's voice called.

Brad stopped, his cocked fist lowering to his side.

I turned and saw Chris's mom approaching from the road, her arms crossed despite the mugginess of the night. Like my best friend, she had straw-colored hair and an infectious smile. I'd never been so happy to see her.

Brad grunted. "Second time you've been saved by someone's parents."

"We don't need saving," Chris said.

"Chris?" his mom asked. "Do I need to get your father?" A nod at Brad and Kurt. "Or one of their dads?"

Yeah, I thought. *Like that's gonna help.*

"Come on," Kurt muttered. "I'm tired of Burgess's stench."

Kurt set off without a backward glance.

Brad lingered another moment, his gaze fixed on me. "I catch you talking to my girlfriend again, I'll make you hurt a lot worse than you did tonight."

As if in answer, I felt a sharp pang in my ribs. Man, Brad could throw hard.

Chris's mom raised her eyebrows at Brad. "Do you want me to tell your parents you're threatening people?"

Brad made a scoffing sound. "You do what you want, Mrs. Watkins." He winked at me. "See you soon."

And with that, he moved toward the parking lot and Kurt's red pick-up truck.

"Poor losers," Chris's mom said. She ventured a smile. "All right, boys, time to go. Congratulations, by the way."

"Thanks," I said, though I didn't feel much like celebrating.

Chris and his mom moved toward the road, where their shiny black Escalade was parked. Chris's mother stopped and called after me. "Come on, Will. Your mom will want to hear about the game."

The hell she will, I thought. *She'll be passed out cold. If Mom had any interest in the game, she would've come.*

But I didn't say any of that. I didn't say anything at all as Chris's mom drove me to my house. Looking back, I don't think any words would have mattered.

Nearly everyone I talked to that night wound up dead anyway.

Chapter Two

Peach, Barley, and the Treehouse

Peach said, "I don't want shredded wheat."

I didn't say anything, only poured the milk and carried the bowl over to where my sister sat. This morning she looked even younger than her six years. The way she was slouching, only her eyes were visible above the rim of the bowl.

I tapped my fingers on the counter. "What do you want?"

"Nerds."

I squinted at her. "The candy?"

She watched me with big brown eyes.

"You want candy for breakfast," I said.

She nodded.

"Well, you can't eat candy for breakfast."

"Why not?"

"Because it's crap."

"That's a bad word."

"You'll be three feet tall for the rest of your life if you eat that stuff."

Peach paused, tilted her head. "How tall is that?"

I held my hand up near my belt.

"I'm already taller than that," she said, smiling.

I grabbed a banana from the counter. "And you're going to *keep* growing. So stop arguing and eat your food."

"Meanie," she muttered, but she spooned a chunk of frosted wheat into her mouth.

I went to the fridge, opened it, and noticed there was hardly anything inside. As usual.

Sighing, I slid open the meat drawer and discovered a plastic sack of honey ham. Unable to recall when mom had bought the ham, I eyed it suspiciously, then sniffed it.

It didn't smell rancid, but I still wasn't reassured. But it was either that or frosted wheat, and I'd eaten the cereal the last five mornings. I carried my potentially fatal package of honey ham to the table and plopped down across from Peach. I opened the sack and fished out some stringy ham.

"Barley called this morning," she said around her mouthful of shredded wheat. "You were asleep."

"He didn't talk about anything scary, did he?"

Peach's eyes widened a fraction. "Like what?"

"Never mind," I muttered and stuffed some ham into my mouth.

"How can you eat that by itself?" Peach asked, milk dribbling down her chin.

"Chew your food."

"Mom still asleep?" she asked.

"I guess. What time did she go to bed?"

She shrugged. "Seven? It was still light out."

I shook my head. "Perfect."

"Barley wants to meet at the treehouse."

"He say what time?"

"Uh-uh. He said morning."

"That's pretty vague."

"What does 'vague' mean?"

"Unclear. Unspecific."

"What's pacific mean?"

I made a face. The ham tasted like a rubber rain slicker someone had dipped in motor oil.

I could feel Peach's gaze on me. "You look like you just ate a worm," she said.

Wordlessly, I got up and dropped the rest of the ham in the trash.

"You can have my banana," she said.

"Nice try," I answered, toweling off my tongue and spitting into the sink.

"*Wiiii-illlll*," she moaned, drawing my name out to about fifteen syllables. "I hate bananas."

"You hate anything that isn't coated in sugar. Your teeth'll fall out."

"You said I'd stop growing."

"That too. You'll be a toothless dwarf."

I moved toward the back door.

"Where're you going?" she asked quickly.

I stopped and gazed down at her. I noticed she'd done her own hair. She'd attempted a ponytail that jutted from the top of her head, but the red rubber band had only been looped around her rope of brown hair twice. As a result, it was already coming loose, a good deal of it dangling over her left eye.

"Hold still," I said.

She squirmed a little as I redid the ponytail. As I manipulated the red band, I noticed how greasy her hair was. "When's the last time you took a bath?"

She grinned. "Do I stink?"

"Probably. Take a bath as soon as you're done eating."

"Why?"

"And put your bowl in the sink."

"I can't turn the water on in the bathtub," she said, frowning.

"Come on. It's not that difficult."

"I'm not strong enough."

I realized with alarm she had tears in her eyes.

"Fine," I breathed. "At least tell me you brushed your teeth before bed last night."

In a small voice, she said, "I forgot."

I glanced at the clock over the stove. 9:15.

"Damn it," I grumbled. Barley might already be at the treehouse. The guy stayed up until three in the morning every night, but somehow he was always awake before anyone else.

"You shouldn't say that," Peach reminded me.

"Cut me some slack. I had a rough night."

She followed me through the kitchen, into the living room, and into the hallway leading to the bathroom.

The whole trip took about ten paces.

"You won last night?" she asked.

"Yep."

"Chris struck out that big kid?"

I gazed down at her. Automatically lowering my voice so as not to wake up Mom, who was snoring on the other side of the bedroom door, I said, "How'd you know about that? Did Chris call this morning too?"

She shook her head. "Barley told me. His little brother was at the game. Barley's brother said you hit it really hard and that Chris struck the last guy out."

I cocked an eyebrow. "How long did you and Barley talk?"

"Not long."

"Then how do you know so much?"

"Barley talks really fast."

I couldn't argue with that. I twisted on the bath water. I pushed up on the lever to close the drain, then remembered it was broken, like a hundred other things in the house. I went over to the sink and found a washcloth, which I balled up and shoved into the drain for a stopper.

Peach started to peel off her pajama top. "Will you stay with me?" she asked.

"Come on, Peach. You're old enough to take a bath by yourself."

"But what if the water's too hot?"

"Then turn it down."

I moved toward the door.

"What if I mess it up?"

I stopped, my back to her. "Mess *what* up?"

"The dials."

"Peach, the *H* is for hot and the *C* is for cold. You know your letters." I made to leave.

"*Please*, Will?"

Her voice was oddly muffled. I turned back to her and realized her purple pajama top was tangled on her head and her elbow. She looked like a corpse someone had started to mummify but lost interest in before he could finish the job.

"Seriously?" I said, but I chuckled a little and helped her disentangle herself from her shirt. Then I slumped on the closed toilet lid and found an old *Sports Illustrated* from the cabinet.

Peach climbed into the bathtub and began to sing a song from *Frozen*. I thought of telling her to keep it down, that Mom was still sleeping. Then I decided I didn't much care if she woke Mom up.

Soon I was humming along with her.

♦

My walk through the forest served as a kind of therapy for me. While home was a cauldron of bad memories and conflict with my mom, Savage Hollow was a place that reminded me of my friends, Chris most of all. Not only had we built a kickass treehouse in the Hollow with the help of Barley and his dad, we'd also engaged in numerous other activities in these woods:

hide-and-seek, mushroom hunting, dirty magazine gazing, even BB gun wars. There were steep hills we pretended were mountains, marshy places we imagined were full of quicksand. On the west side of the Hollow lay the rusting hulk of an abandoned baby blue Studebaker from the 1950s. How it had gotten there we had no idea, but on several occasions Chris and I had sat in the front seat pretending we were racing the Indy 500 or even eluding the cops in a high-speed chase.

Yes, the Hollow was as happy a place as I could imagine.

At least, it was happy until everything went to hell.

When I neared the treehouse I heard a sharp *snick*ing noise emanating from the plywood structure. The forest had greened out over the past few weeks, and I made the mistake of taking my eyes off the path to glance up at the treehouse. Immediately, my legs were besieged by the thwacking of nettles and other plants, some of which might have been poison ivy. I hated poison ivy, somehow managed to get it every damned summer. Already my legs were beginning to itch.

The snicking sound got louder the closer I got to the treehouse.

"That you, Barley?" I called.

The sound ceased for a moment, and I knew right away it was Barley. Chris would have answered me immediately, but not Barley. No, my bespectacled friend had to turn everything into a movie scene. I could imagine him up there listening tensely to my footfalls. He'd be holding his breath, as if his life depended on it, and waiting for me to identify myself. Like we were in a war, or some situation involving espionage.

Or even better, I reflected as I mounted the first couple wooden rungs we'd hammered into the huge oak tree, he'd be imagining himself in a horror movie. Something involving a killer in a hockey mask, or maybe even a zombie. I loved horror movies—we all three did—but neither me nor Chris took them as seriously as Barley.

"Who is it?" he asked when I was halfway up the crooked column of rungs.

"Carl Padgett," I said. "I've come to devour your small intestine."

Barley's face appeared in the opening above me, his slightly magnified gaze stern behind his thick spectacles. "That's not funny, Will. That guy is worse than Jeffrey Dahmer. A total nutcase. They say he used to eat his victims while they were still alive. That he liked to watch their faces while he chewed on their body parts."

I climbed through the aperture as Barley moved aside. "So I've heard."

And I had. In addition to horror movies, Barley had a morbid interest in true crime, the more lurid, the better. Carl Padgett—also known as Padgett the Blade, The Bedford Cannibal, or The Moonlight Killer—was one of the sickest individuals in the annals of serial killer history. He preyed mainly on children.

"I hope he never gets out," Barley said. "If he does, he's only two hours away from here. I bet he'd head straight for Shadeland. With all these trees, it's the perfect place to hide." He plopped down in front of the barrel we'd sawn in half for a table.

"So you're an expert on serial killer psychology?"

Barley was clutching a hatchet and a sharpened stick about three feet long. He continued to shave off curls of wood with rough, jerky movements. I sat down on a five-gallon bucket like the one on which Barley sat. Only mine contained a whole lot of kerosene, which we'd somehow lugged all the way up here to fuel the lamp we used at night.

Barley's dark brown hair was longer and shaggier than mine or Chris's. He had a belly on him, but he wasn't too overweight. He just looked like he played more video games than outdoor games, which was pretty much the case. He'd begun to get some acne in the past year or so, and though I had some too, Barley wasn't as self-conscious about it as I was. In fact, he claimed it was a sign of maturity.

"Padgett's family is from Bedford," Barley pointed out.

"So?"

"*Soooo*," Barley said, shoving the blade down the stick's length with a little more force, "Bedford is in a direct line between here and Chicago."

"But no highway comes near here," I said, scooting away from Barley and his makeshift spear. The way he was handling that hatchet of his, one of us was going to get impaled. "The chances of him getting out of jail are somewhere south of zero anyway."

Barley stopped and stared at me. "Are you really that dense? We're talking about a criminal mastermind here. The fact that this town is out of the way is exactly why he'd come here."

"Padgett's not that clever, Barley. He's a lunatic."

"It comes to the same thing. Remember *Halloween*? How Michael Myers returned to his childhood home and slaughtered all those babysitters?"

"He didn't slaughter them all," a voice called from below, making us both jump.

Chris's head poked through the ladder hole. "He only killed two of them, plus one of their boyfriends. Oh, and a dog."

"He killed his sister too," Barley pointed out. "Strapped on that clown mask and hacked her to pieces."

I had a sudden thought of Peach and pushed it away, shivering. I hoped Mom would be up by now. Otherwise my little sister would be sitting in front of the TV watching cartoons all morning. I told myself the hollow feeling in my belly was just the spoiled ham and the hunger, but deep down I knew it was guilt.

Chris was riffling through the shelves of the medicine cabinet we'd installed, the one Barley had found by the curb.

"What're you looking for?" Barley asked.

"Tampon?" I suggested.

"I need one, I'll just borrow yours," Chris replied. I watched him rummage through all the junk we'd brought up here over the years. A sturdy length of rope. Several pencils and pens. Batteries, most of them dead. A hooked blade affixed to a thick wooden handle, a tool Barley claimed was for cutting carpets. A padlock with a key inside. We never used it, but we had bolted a fastener to the trapdoor in case we ever wanted to.

Chris cursed. "I know I didn't—ah, here it is." He plucked something from the cabinet and joined us around the table. "I thought I'd lost it."

"Please tell me I'm hallucinating," Barley said.

But he wasn't. Chris let the silver chain dangle; a green stone pendulumed from the bottom of the chain.

"I can't believe you still have that," I said.

Chris studied the necklace. "Pretty, right?"

"You said you threw it away."

Chris grinned and fingered the green stone. "I guess I lied."

I exchanged a glance with Barley, who rolled his eyes.

35

"Look," Barley said, "you bought that for Rebecca three years ago, right?"

Chris shrugged. "So?"

I said, "So it probably stinks by now."

Chris sniffed it. "Not really," he said, but he was frowning.

"Dude," Barley said, snatching the necklace from Chris. "You really think this is going to impress her? It's ugly as hell. She's gonna laugh in your face."

Chris made a grab for it, but Barley yanked it away. "Give me the goddamn chain," Chris demanded.

Barley held it at arm's length. "I'm just saving you from yourself. You're not thinking clearly, man. Kurt's gonna total you for sure if you give this to his girlfriend." He held the necklace out the window and let it dangle forty feet above the forest floor.

"*Hey*," Chris growled. "Give it back."

"It's insane," Barley said. "Rebecca's got a boyfriend, right? She's not breaking up with him, especially after you give her some stupid green rock."

"It's a peridot."

"You should be embarrassed to know that," I said.

"Give it *back*," Chris said and before I realized what was happening, he'd gripped Barley with both hands and wrenched him toward the middle of the treehouse. Barley landed awkwardly on the half-barrel table, then flipped over sideways against Chris's bucket, which overturned with an angry clatter.

"Jeez, man!" Barley shouted. "I was only trying to help. You could've broken my arm or something."

"I warned you," Chris said, snatching the necklace from where it had fallen.

I helped Barley to his feet, dusted him off. "Love makes people do weird things," he muttered.

I eyed Chris uneasily. There were livid spots on his cheeks, the edges of his blond hair darkened with sweat.

He pocketed the necklace. "Okay, if Barley is done giving relationship advice, I'd like to talk about tonight's plan."

"I didn't know we had a plan," I said.

Chris righted his bucket, folded his arms, and leaned back with his feet crossed on the table. "Mia is spending the night with Rebecca."

Barley glared at him. "How do you know that?" It was a point of pride for Barley to know every piece of Shadeland gossip first.

"So what?" I said.

Chris's smile broadened. "So we're going over there at midnight."

Chapter Three

Crashing Rebecca's Party and The Moonlight Killer

Chris's plan was simple. So simple that Barley thought it was asinine.

I was inclined to agree.

"I don't see the issue," Chris said. "You sneak out by eleven-thirty, and we're there by midnight."

"Okay, fine," Barley said. "Let's pretend we're all three able to sneak out without anybody knowing it, despite the fact that my mom's a light sleeper and Will here is afraid of the dark."

"You're the one with the *Harry Potter* nightlight," I said.

"It was *Star Wars*, and I haven't used it for over a year. So let's say we actually make it all the way to the Ralstons without being seen. What if the cops discover us outside that late? We're underage. They could seriously bust us."

"First of all," Chris said, "the Shadeland cops are idiots. They're not gonna bust anybody. And you act like it's in another state or something. Rebecca only lives a few blocks from me."

Barley nodded. "In the richest neighborhood in town."

"What does that—"

"It means there'll be security systems to deal with," Barley interrupted. "Guard dogs, fences. Maybe even neighborhood security guards."

"Security guards? The only thing our neighborhood has is a pool, and it's been broken since last summer."

"So let's say everything works out and we get to her house. What then? Do we just knock on the door and say to her parents, 'Hey, I know Chris beat your son's team last night, but he wants to give your daughter a necklace that smells like an old man's ass?"

"You pretty experienced with old men's asses?" I asked.

"We won't be using the front door," Chris said.

"What then, we throw rocks at her window?" Barley said. "Serenade her by moonlight?"

"They're staying in a tent."

Barley glanced at Chris in dismay. "And how the hell do you know that? You have her under surveillance or something?"

Chris plunked his feet down and leaned forward. "I rode my bike past there before I joined you two morons. Rebecca was outside putting up a tent."

Barley shrugged. "That could mean anything. Maybe she was—"

"She told me."

Barley and I stared at him.

Barley's entire demeanor changed, as if Chris had communicated with some alien species. "What do you mean, she told you? You're saying you just went up and *talked* to her?"

I could tell Chris had been waiting to share this news. He donned a nonchalant expression. "I waved at her, and she told me to hold on. I pulled into her driveway—no armed guards or Rotweilers—and she told me she enjoyed watching me pitch."

"No way," Barley said, but he was grinning a little.

"I swear," Chris said. "Then I asked her if she was camping tonight, and she said she was."

"Whoa," Barley said and looked at me. "You believe that?"

"Astounding," I said.

"Furthermore," Chris said, "she said Brad would be staying over at Kurt's house tonight. Which means we're all clear."

My stomach fluttered at the ramifications of this.

Barley frowned. "Hold on. This still sucks for me. If Rebecca and Mia are camping out, what am I going to do? Make s'mores while you four sit around declaring your love for each other?"

"Actually," Chris said, "Rebecca is having *two* friends stay the night. Mia and Kylie Ann Lubeck."

Barley gaped at Chris. Kylie Ann Lubeck was one of the prettiest—and iciest—girls in Shadeland. She was also a year older than us.

"Since when does Kylie Ann hang out with Rebecca and Mia?" I asked.

"I don't know," Chris said. "But it gives us a nice even number, doesn't it?" He turned to Barley. "So?"

Barley scowled at him. "So *what?*"

Chris cocked an eyebrow. "So you're out of excuses."

Barley rose and retrieved his spear from the floor. He heaved it out the window dejectedly. It landed with a muffled thump. "I think you're forgetting something."

"Like?"

"Like—" Barley faced us and used both hands to gesture down the length of his body. "—*this.*"

Chris waved him off. "Don't underestimate yourself."

Barley gave him a flat look. "Under*estimate* myself? Seriously? Have you checked my skin lately? It's like a relief map of the Himalayas."

"You said that was a sign of maturity," I pointed out.

"And what about this?" He grabbed the roll of pudge hanging over the waistband of his shorts. "I'm sure Kylie Ann will be smitten by the sight of this pale layer of blubber."

"Some girls like a guy with meat on his bones," Chris said.

"Sure, *you* can say that. Mr. I'm-So-Handsome-and-Athletic-and-My-Parents-Are-Millionaires."

"Screw you," Chris answered. "You're just scared."

"Darn right I'm scared," Barley said, his voice going hoarse. "Kylie Ann Lubeck is a goddess—in every sense of the word. Every time a guy tries to talk to her she looks at him like he emitted a bad smell."

"Listen, guys," I said. "Are we sure we want to go over there?"

"Yes," Chris said immediately.

"No way," Barley said at the same time.

"So I guess it's up to me to decide," I said.

Chris and Barley looked at each other. They shrugged and turned to me.

I nodded. "We go over there."

Barley whimpered.

◆

I got to the Marleys' house by a quarter past eleven.

I felt terrible sneaking out that late, not because I was betraying my mom's trust—what trust there'd been between us had long since dissolved—but because I was leaving my little sister with an irresponsible parent. At least Peach had been asleep when I'd left our room—she slept on a single bed beside mine—and my mom had seemed fairly coherent before she'd headed to her room for the night. I estimated she'd only downed two or three pills, which was less than half of her normal nightly intake.

Pedaling my bike as quickly as I could, I arrived at Barley's house. Like the night before, it looked like the moon and stars would be smothered by ominous-looking clouds. I parked my bike at the end of Barley's driveway and tried not to think about Mia.

I guess I should explain why we call him Barley.

His real first name is Dale, which he hates. His last name is Marley.

But our fourth grade swimming instructor didn't know that. The girl was some horse-faced college student who looked about as interested in teaching us how to swim as she did in quantum physics. She asked us our names, and Barley happened to have a cold that day. Which made his name sound like Bale Barley rather than Dale Marley.

She repeated it, her expression disbelieving: "Bale Barley?"

"*Bale Barley*," he said, trying and failing to pronounce his Ds through the mucus clogging his nostrils.

"Well, go get a Kleenex, Barley," she'd said. "You've got snot all over your lip."

And since then we'd called him Barley.

He came schlepping down the driveway a minute or two later, and when he reached my ten-speed, he made to sling a leg over the seat behind me.

"What the hell are you doing?" I asked in alarm.

He stared at me. "Getting on. What else?"

"Ride your own bike."

He hooked a thumb over his shoulder. "It's in the garage."

"So get it."

"I can't," he said as though I were an idiot. "The garage door will wake my parents up."

"You should've thought of that earlier."

"What's the big deal? We can both fit." He made to get on again.

"The big *deal*," I said, blocking him, "is we'll look like douchebags."

He glanced around the dark street. "Who's gonna see us? Raccoons? The possums?"

"No, it's just..." I gestured feebly.

Something dawned in his face. "Wait a minute. This is about Mia, isn't it? You're afraid she's gonna think I'm your boyfriend."

"Jesus," I said. "Shut up and get on."

Most of the way there Barley acted like a pain in the ass. Telling me to go faster. Criticizing the route I was taking. And all of it breathed into my ears in a sweaty cloud of the onion rings he'd eaten for supper that night.

Don't ask me how, but we arrived at Chris's huge house about ten minutes later. They lived in Connor Creek, the fanciest neighborhood in town. It was nestled between the golf course and Savage Hollow and featured properties that looked like something in a magazine.

Chris laughed as we wobbled up his drive. "You should see yourselves," he said. "I've never wanted an iPhone as badly as I do now."

"I'd kill you if you took a picture of this," I muttered.

Chris walked his bike up next to ours. "You're sweating."

"My legs are on fire," I grunted. "You try pedaling up a hill with two people."

"Is that a crack about my weight?" Barley said.

"No," I answered. "It's a crack about how dumb you were to forget your bike." I turned to Chris. "We ready?"

"Totally," he said, and set off on his bicycle, which was the fancy hybrid kind that could adapt to either trails or roads. I felt a familiar surge of jealousy and fought to suppress it.

In another couple minutes, we reached the Ralstons' house.

It wasn't quite as impressive as Chris's, but it was in the same league. There were four columns out front, three garage stalls attached to the house, and three more unattached. I recalled seeing Dr. Ralston driving, at different times, a red Porsche Boxster, a vintage yellow Corvette, and, when he wanted to slum it, a white BMW.

"There's the promised land," Chris said, nodding at the tent.

My mouth went dry. Was Mia in there now?

"You ready?" Chris asked.

I shook my head. "I'm gonna pass out."

"What about you, Barley?"

Barley gulped. "Hell no. My balls are clinging to my undercarriage."

I looked at him. "I'm didn't think you had testicles."

Chris said, "Me either. Come on."

He propped his bike against one of the many trees rimming the estate and crept into the darkness beside the long, curving driveway. Looking like a man preparing to pitch himself off a mountain cliff, Barley drifted after him.

44

I followed them, thinking, *Be cool. Just act like this is normal.*

Hah! came a cruel answering voice. *This is as abnormal as it gets. Here you are, a poor kid with used clothing and a crap future, striding onto the property of a wealthy family. You're sweaty, skinny, and scared. The girl of your dreams awaits you in that tent, along with two other girls who'll probably laugh at you and your friends.*

A terrible thought occurred to me.

"Chris?" I whispered.

"What?" he whispered back.

"They know we're coming, right?"

Chris looked away.

"Hold *on*," Barley said, clutching Chris by the shoulder. "Please tell me they know we're coming. Please tell me we didn't just sneak out in the middle of the night and risk getting arrested for nothing."

Chris's non-answer was all the answer we needed.

Hell, I thought. I turned to Barley, who jabbed a finger at Chris in astonishment. "You brought us here on false pretenses!" Barley hissed. "They're gonna think we're stalkers! What if they have mace? Or pepper spray? You remember when I accidentally sprayed myself with that stuff? I couldn't see for *hours*, man."

But Chris had walked away. Blowing out nervous breath, I got moving too.

Barley clutched my arm. "You're not actually *following* him, are you? After this stunt? Those girls are gonna call the cops on us for sure."

"If that happens," I said. "Just pretend we're in a James Bond movie. Only we'll be getting away on a ten-speed rather than an Aston-Martin."

Barley's mouth worked for a moment, his hands flailing about in mute frustration. Then he said, "What if they get really mad at us? I hate it when people get mad at me."

"Then we leave."

I made to follow Chris, but Barley's fingers clenched my arm tighter. "*Will.* What if they tell their parents? I don't wanna spend the rest of my summer grounded, do you?"

I gave him a look. "My mom's too lazy to keep me locked up all summer."

For a moment he stared at me with something like pity, which was worse than any other emotion he could have exhibited. I yanked my arm free and followed Chris, who was already talking to the three girls. Her black hair curly and full, Kylie Ann Lubeck had on a tight pink tank top and a white tennis skirt, an ensemble that displayed her physical maturity to impressive effect. Rebecca Ralston's blond hair was swept off her face and cascaded over one shoulder, a look I suspected she'd affected for Chris's benefit. Rebecca was smiling, but Kylie Ann looked like she was about to summon lightning bolts from the heavens to smite us down.

As Barley and I neared, I took a moment to stare at Mia.

Though I'd seen her the night before, it was as though she'd aged three years since then. Her shortish black hair was gelled up in sharper spikes than usual. Her tanned, hard stomach showed between her black top and jean shorts, which were strategically ripped and tattered in several places. To me she looked like a less trashy version of a female rock star, and as I moved up next to Chris, she turned her vivid blue gaze on me.

Confidence, I reminded myself. *Be like Chris.*

"Hey, Will," she said.

"I'm fine," I answered.

She frowned.

I jolted. "I mean hey, Mia. How have you been?"

She giggled. "Good. You look like you've recovered from getting hit last night."

My ears burned, and it took me a gargantuan effort not to grin like an idiot. "I'm a pretty fast healer."

Rebecca said, "So what do you guys feel like doing? We can't be too loud or we'll wake my parents up."

Mia looked at me. "There's a creek a few blocks over. You guys wanna go swimming?"

I swallowed, almost mentioned I hadn't brought swimming trunks. Then my thoughts shifted to Mia, who didn't seem to be wearing a swim suit either.

The implications of this doused me like freezing water.

A little dizzy, I followed the others toward the road.

♦

I smelled the creek well before I spotted it, the scent like mud and crawdads and minnows. I inhaled deeply, the aroma cooling my nostrils. Mia was moving at the front of the group, she and Rebecca having taken the lead. Chris was next, followed by me and Barley and Kylie Ann, who sulked along a good ten feet behind the rest of us.

As I trailed Chris and the others through the forest, I experienced a powerful, half-buried memory from the second grade. Because my mom had to work a full-time job even back then, I'd been charged with getting myself to school on time, despite the fact that I was only seven. Mom had instructed me to leave the house by a quarter of eight, and since the school was only a short walk away, I usually arrived well before the eight AM bell.

The problem was our television. Or rather my secret habit of watching brainless TV before school. Oh, I still left by 7:45, but never before that, and on most days that wasn't a problem.

But on one particular October morning I had to lug my chemistry set to school for show-and-tell. And not just any chemistry set, but a *whopper* of a chemistry set, one whose box was almost as wide as my wingspan. I was proud of that set because I'd bought it with my own money, and I couldn't wait to show it off to my classmates. For once, I'd be the kid the other ones envied.

I left the house on time but quickly realized I'd underestimated how much the huge chemistry set would slow me down. I clutched the sides of the box in an awkward kind of hug, my backpack weighing me down from behind. At that age my legs weren't all that long either, so by the time I hobbled into the school parking lot, sweating and terrified of being tardy, the buses were already pulling away and the last stragglers were filing into the school. Still, I figured I'd make it into Mrs. Nicholson's classroom just before the bell rang. I was thinking this when my legs got tangled up and I sprawled face first onto my chemistry set, the miniature jars of powder and the test tubes within shattering in a heart stopping barrage of crunches and pops. Hot tears already stinging my eyes, I scrambled off the flattened box and peeled back the lid to assess the damage.

My chemistry set was destroyed.

Then the bell rang.

I sat there on my knees and stared down at the ruin of what had been the nicest toy I'd ever owned. I hated myself for crying, but I couldn't help it. There'd be no show-and-tell today, no triumphant reveal. My chest started hitching, and the tears flooded my burning cheeks.

I don't know how long I sat there like that in the now-silent parking lot, but at some point I became aware of someone standing next to me. I looked up, and though my vision was bleary, I knew right away who it was. The girl everybody made fun of because she'd gotten most of her black hair sheared off, the girl everybody teased and branded a little boy.

"I'll help you," Mia said.

I dragged the heel of my hand over my nose, looked away. "I don't need help."

When Mia didn't move, I said, my tone harsher, "Go inside. I don't want your help."

But rather than doing what I demanded, the little girl with the boyish black hair got down on all fours and started collecting the splinters of glass from within the box and whisking away the spills of powder.

Wordlessly, I joined her in the cleanup. With both of us on the job, it only took about five minutes. But she was late now too. And her hands, like mine, had been lacerated in several places by the shards of glass.

She saw me eyeing her bloody palms. "It's okay," she said. "They don't hurt."

She smiled, and my insides went queasy.

I wanted to ask her a dozen questions, to point out to her that she'd be in as much trouble as I was, but all I could manage was, "Why?"

She fixed me with her striking blue eyes, and I could tell she was surprised by the question. She gave a tiny little shrug and said, "I was watching you from Mrs. Nicholson's room, and I saw you fall."

As if that explained everything.

Together, we slunk into the school. Together, we got in trouble, but not nearly as much as I'd assumed. And we didn't say a whole lot more to each other for the rest of the school year.

But I was pretty sure it was the morning of the chemistry set debacle that I started to fall for Mia Samuels.

We emerged from the winding path and beheld a creek that was perhaps twenty feet across. It was really wooded there, and there was very little moonlight. But we could see well enough to get around, and from the look of the grassy banks, the water level was high. That wasn't too surprising since May might as well have been a monsoon season. We'd had six games postponed or canceled that month, and several more had been played in cold drizzle and mud puddles.

We were all kind of standing around staring at the water when Mia said, "Take off your shirt, Will."

I blinked at her, certain I'd heard wrong despite the fact that the only sounds were the whispering breeze and the placid gurgle of the creek.

She smiled good-humoredly. "Well?"

"You want me to take my shirt off?"

"Isn't that how guys swim?"

"I will," Chris said, and peeled off his red T-shirt. He had on cargo shorts and sandals, and I might as well admit now I envied his build. Chris had a washboard stomach and pectoral muscles that stuck out a little. This was in stark contrast to my own chest, which was slightly concave. But I did have a decent enough stomach, and I figured my scrawniness wouldn't scare Mia off completely. So I removed my shirt, kicked off my

50

sneakers, and followed Chris into the water. It was very cool, and I paused after a few feet of wading to avoid getting my privates wet. I always hated that. Girls didn't have to worry about their body parts shriveling up. At least I didn't think they had to worry about it. The truth was, I'd never seen a girl in the water in anything less than a swimsuit.

Which was why I was so shocked when Mia peeled off her shirt.

She was wearing a bra underneath, of course, and it wasn't the kind that revealed much of anything. But it was the *fact* of the bra that caught me so off-guard.

I turned and noticed Chris gawking at Mia and felt a pang of jealousy. *That's* my *girl*, I wanted to remind him, though that of course was complete rubbish. She wasn't *anyone's* girl, least of all mine.

What about Brad Ralston? a nasty voice reminded.

Oh yeah, I thought, my heart sinking. I'd forgotten all about Brad. *Shit.*

A crude voice spoke up: *Who cares about Brad? Mia's in her bra right in front of you! For God's sakes, enjoy it!*

That was immature, I knew. And more than a little disrespectful.

But I looked anyway. And almost fainted, the sight was so glorious.

"I'm not taking my top off," Kylie Ann said, her arms folded.

"Then don't," Mia answered as she waded into the creek.

I glanced at Rebecca, noticed she was her chewing her bottom lip.

Barley was standing a few feet from Rebecca and Kylie Ann. To Rebecca, he said, "You don't have to take your shirt off. I'm not going to."

I felt a wave of affection for my friend. Idiot though he was, he had a good heart.

Rebecca smiled at him. "Thanks." And she stepped into the water.

Under her breath, but loud enough for us to hear, Kylie Ann said, "Like we'd want Barley to take his shirt off anyway."

It was like someone had punched me in the gut. I looked at Barley in the desperate hope he hadn't heard, but his stricken expression said otherwise. Kylie Ann would have hurt him less by taking a baseball bat to his head. She was an even bigger bitch than I'd thought.

I made a secret wish that she'd get attacked by leeches.

"How deep is it?" Rebecca asked.

Chris was backpedaling slowly, his hands making lazy eddies in the water. "It's up to my chest, but I think that's as high as it'll get."

A moment later he disappeared.

I took a shocked step forward, but then he breached the surface, spluttering and laughing. We were chuckling too.

"Holy crap," he said, still spitting water. "I guess there's a drop-off."

"Better look out," a voice said behind me.

I turned in time to see Mia disappearing below the surface and jetting in my direction. Her dark legs were scarcely visible beneath the surface, but I could see well enough the way the water churned over her gliding body.

Something grabbed my ankle and yanked me off-balance. I fell sideways, the cold water not only swamping my nether regions, but my torso and head as well. Under the water I grappled with Mia, secretly exhilarated by the silky feel of her arms, the dizzying brush of her fingertips on my skin. We emerged a moment later, laughing and splashing each other. Chris and Rebecca were similarly engaged. Only Kylie Ann and Barley remained apart from the festivities.

Apparently sensing the awkwardness of just standing there knee-deep in the creek, Barley bent down, cupped some creek water, and flung it on Kylie Ann.

And splashed her right in the face.

She stood there, horrified, her hands held up like she was stopping traffic, for a good ten seconds. Then she turned and glared at Barley.

He ventured a smile. "At least the water won't feel so cold now, right?"

Her look was enough to wipe the smile from Barley's face.

I turned to Mia, who was arching an eyebrow at Kylie Ann's short temper.

My opinion of Mia rose higher.

Barley cleared his throat. "I was wondering, Kylie Ann...Have you ever heard of the Zodiac Killer?"

God. I turned away before my secondhand embarrassment became unbearable.

Mia and I picked up where we left off, Mia tickling me under water, me picking her up by the waist and hurling her backwards. My hand skimmed the flesh of her stomach and a powerful surge of heat rippled through my body. A couple of times the sodden cups of her bra yawned open, and though it was too dark to see much, the sight turned me on so much that my whole body trembled. Thankfully, the water concealed my erection.

The four of us continued to splash around in the creek, Chris and I hoisting Rebecca and Mia onto our shoulders, where they grappled like incredibly lovely gladiators until one or both of them would tumble off. After a time, Mia backstroked away from the group, moving upstream with an effortlessness I admired. I remembered that Mia had a reputation for being a great swimmer, in fact did it competitively. I swam after her and did my best to not look like a gangly eel.

"The water's not so bad now," I said, drawing closer to her.

She stopped backstroking and began to tread water. "The pool at the high school is usually freezing," she said.

I moved in a gradual loop around her. She rotated slowly, her striking blue eyes never leaving mine.

"I heard you do competitions," I said.

Her face broke into a smile. Her teeth were white and gleaming. "I love competing. I want to keep getting better."

"Are you going for the Olympics or something?"

She laughed. "My times aren't *that* good. You should come to a meet some time."

"Why are you dating Brad?"

I froze. What in the name of God was wrong with me?

I braced for Mia's inevitable anger and her demand for me to stay out of her personal life.

But she regarded me thoughtfully. "I wonder the same thing."

Again, I spoke without thinking. "You're too great a person to be with him."

Her eyebrows went up. "You think?"

"He's an asshole."

"Is that right?"

I nodded.

"And what about me?" she asked.

I attempted to keep the nerves out of my voice. "You're just right."

"You don't think I'm too forward?"

"Why? Because you're swimming in a..." I gestured vaguely.

"In a bra?"

"Yeah." I swallowed. "I think it's great."

She cocked an eyebrow.

"I mean, it's great if you want to—"

She fingered the shoulder straps. "Most bikini tops are more revealing than this," she said. "I hope I didn't make you uncomfortable."

"I'm not uncomfortable!" I said, my voice too loud and high. I cleared my throat. "I mean, I'm happy if you're happy."

She smiled at that. Then her expression clouded. "I didn't like the way Brad hit you last night."

"I didn't like it much either."

"Did it hurt?"

I considered lying. It seemed the manly thing to do.

But I said, "It hurt like hell. Check out this bruise."

I moved into shallower water, half-turned to reveal the baseball-sized weal on my ribs. I'd inspected it in the mirror that morning. You could even make out the stitching from the baseball.

Mia made a sympathetic face, caressed the bruise. Something about the way her full lips pooched out made my stomach do a somersault.

She ventured nearer. Beads of water glimmered on her dark skin. "Where did the other one hit you?"

"The ball?"

She cocked an eyebrow. "No, the meteor from outer space."

"Oh," I said. "In the hip."

Under the water, her hand closed over one of mine. "Show me," she said.

This close, I could see the tiny droplets of water in her hair, in her eyelashes. There was a languid look in her eyes I'd never seen there before.

"Show me," she repeated.

Feeling like I might puke all over the place but more aroused than I'd ever been in my life, I guided her hand to my left hip, which was still a little tender from the beaning Brad had given me. But Mia's touch was so gentle, it didn't hurt at all. The pads of her fingers slid over my bruised flesh, against the waistband of my cargo shorts, and somehow her face was hovering only a few inches from mine.

Kiss her! the voice in my head demanded. *You'll never get a better chance to kiss a beautiful girl!*

But my body wouldn't work. I was suddenly made of stone or steel or some other stupid, unyielding material. I stared at Mia's depthless blue eyes and told myself to kiss her before she swam away. Or disappeared. Nothing would have surprised me at that point. We were the same age, had gone to school together for as long as I could remember, but at that moment she seemed ageless. Like some mythical creature come to life. A sea sprite, maybe. Or some figure from ancient Greece, like the Goddess of Unbelievable Hotness. I made myself lean toward her. I formed my lips into a pucker.

Her eyes shifted to something beyond me, something in the direction of the woods. She gasped, and then her arms were around me. But it wasn't a passionate embrace.

It was terror.

"Mia, what—"

"*There's something in the woods*," she hissed.

Instinctively, I followed her gaze, and though I didn't see anything scary, I did notice the way the brush and low-hanging pine boughs were stirring.

Something had just vacated the edge of the woods.

Something big.

I said, "You don't think it was Brad and Kurt, do you?" and immediately regretted it. I was admitting how scared of them I was, how much I'd worried they'd come along and discover us here in the creek.

She shook her head. "I don't think so. It didn't..." She trailed off, and I realized with further alarm that she was trembling wildly. I pulled her closer, but though our bodies were pressed together in the water, I'm happy to report that my only thought was of calming her down.

Okay, *most* of my thoughts were on calming her down.

"What did you see?" I asked.

She shivered. "It was a face...I mean, it was shaped like a person's...but it *wasn't*. The eyes were as big as softballs. Only they were green. Almost like they were glowing."

I tried but failed to keep the dubious note from my voice. "You saw a creature with giant, glowing green eyes?"

She looked at me desperately. "I know how dumb it sounds, but I *saw* it. Him. Whatever it was. He had—" She gestured toward her face. "—this terrible leer. The teeth were long. Like knives, only curved. And the skin...it was completely white. Like something that lived underground."

Despite my desire to appear tough, Mia's words had an effect on me. I eyed the forest uneasily. "Maybe we should—"

"What's going on over there?" a voice called.

We turned and discovered Kylie Ann striding forward through the water.

She made a disgusted face. "You're not, like, kissing him are you?"

Almost, I wanted to say. *If I weren't a spineless loser.*

"*Mia,*" Kylie Ann said. "What about Brad?"

For the first time Mia looked worried about something other than pale creatures leering from the forest. "I..."

"She saw something, okay?" I said, my arms tightening around her. "Just take it easy."

Kylie Ann looked at me disdainfully. "Brad would totally kick your ass."

"Maybe you *want* us to break up," Mia said.

Whatever good spirits I had began to wither. Were Mia and Kylie Ann actually fighting over Brad Ralston? After what had happened between Mia and me?

"I could care less about you and Brad," Kylie Ann said, and she turned to wade back to shore. I watched after her sourly and considered correcting her grammar—it wasn't *could care less*, it was *couldn't care less*. It was an error that always irked me. But then Mia broke away from me and moved swiftly toward the bank.

Glumly, I followed.

When we rejoined the others, Mia was explaining to Rebecca and Chris what she'd seen.

They looked perplexed, but not particularly frightened.

It wasn't until we were making our way back to Rebecca's that I noticed the way Barley had paled.

"You feel all right, man?" I asked. "You're even whiter than usual."

"Uh-uh," Barley said. He looked like he was about to refund whatever he'd eaten for dinner.

"Was it what Mia said?" I asked. "The face in the woods?"

"Not now," Barley said, moving quickly ahead of me. "I don't want to talk about that now."

And with a last glance behind me, I hustled after him.

I didn't want to be alone with whatever Mia had seen.

◆

As we approached the Ralstons' house, Rebecca fell behind a little, her brow furrowed.

"What is it?" Chris asked. I noticed he touched her elbow as he said it. She didn't seem to mind.

"All the lights are on," she said.

I turned and realized she was right.

Mia was watching her friend, concerned. "I thought Brad was staying at Kurt's tonight."

Rebecca shook her head, began striding briskly down the road. "He was supposed to, but his truck's in the driveway."

Well, hell, I thought. *This isn't going to be pretty.*

Kylie Ann's tone was scathing. "Maybe they decided they couldn't trust you two."

"Shut up," Rebecca muttered.

When we neared the house, she started to jog.

"You want me to come with you?" Chris asked.

"I think that's a bad idea," Mia said.

Chris frowned at her, but then we both followed her gaze and spotted the shapes inside the kitchen window.

One of them belonged to Kurt.

Son of a bitch, I thought. It would be nice, I reflected, to go twenty-four hours without engaging in some sort of conflict with Kurt or Brad.

But if Kurt discovered us out here, I knew I wouldn't get my wish.

You think that's bad? the sarcastic voice in my head spoke up. *What happens when Kylie Ann tells Brad about your embrace with Mia?*

I was comforting her! I protested.

Not at first, the voice persisted. *At first you were putting her hand on your hip and gazing deeply into each other's eyes.*

I sighed, wishing I could relive that moment. What a coward. How could I have missed my chance to kiss her?

As we waited for Rebecca to return, Barley sidled up next to Kylie Ann. "Are you a gamer? Like first-person shooters or open world games?"

She looked at him like he'd vomited on her bare feet.

"I ask that," Barley said, his voice unsteady, "because you've got the hands for it."

She made a face. "You're telling me I have...gaming hands?"

Barley cleared his throat, gestured weakly. "Well, yeah. I mean...your fingers are long and spidery and—"

Kylie Ann grimaced. "Eww. Spidery?"

"Not furry or anything, not like a tarantula. More like a daddy long legs. Long and slender and sort of..."

Barley trailed off, looking like he was about to asphyxiate.

60

He was saved by the opening of the back door. Rebecca emerged, and before the door could wheeze shut, three more figures followed.

One was a nasty surprise: Eric Blades. The only facts I knew of him were these: He was going to be a senior. His dad was the superintendent of our school system. And he was rumored to be the biggest druggie in Shadeland High.

The other two were Brad Ralston and Kurt Fisher. Of course.

Eric Blades grinned his cocky grin. "Hey, Kylie Ann. I missed you, girl."

It was like Kylie Ann had transformed into a different person. She looked up at Eric Blades shyly, clasped her hands before her. "Hey, Eric."

"I thought we told you to stay away from our girlfriends," Brad said, his biceps popping. "I guess you guys don't value your health very much."

"You touch them," Rebecca said, "and I'll tell mom why the liquor cabinet keeps running low."

Brad glowered at his kid sister. "How about you shut the fuck up? You're already in enough trouble."

And looking at Brad and Rebecca standing there together, glaring at each other with palpable loathing, I recalled what had happened three years earlier, something so awful I guess I'd blocked it out.

The Ralstons were a lot like Chris's parents. Affluent. Superior. More into their country club friends than their kids. Which meant that Brad and Rebecca had often been charged with taking care of Emmylou, their young sister. Rebecca's dad was evidently a big country music fan, and the story went that since Rebecca's mom had gotten her way in naming Brad and Rebecca, Rebecca's dad got to choose their last child's name. To no one's surprise he'd named her after a country singer, someone named Emmylou Harris. I'd never heard of her before. Then again, I bet her songs weren't auto tuned, which had to count for something.

The Ralstons often made Brad and Rebecca babysit Emmylou back when Brad was in junior high and Rebecca still in grade school. Emmylou was three-years-old when it happened, but looking back, it's sort of amazing that it didn't happen earlier.

Because Brad was never into watching his baby sister.

He'd *tell* his folks he watched her, but that was because he wanted the babysitting money. Part of me wants to hate Brad for this, but to be fair to him, he was only thirteen when this happened. He was sort of a bully before the incident with the play set, but afterward he became a terror.

And Rebecca…her I blame even less. She was a fifth-grader at the time, just eleven. And she was the one who put the most effort into minding Emmylou, though she was a pretty uninterested sitter as well. She was more concerned with Skyping her friends and playing games on the computer than she was in making sure Emmylou wasn't in danger.

But of course Emmylou was. No one is sure how long Emmylou had been outside by herself that frigid March afternoon, her parents having gone to Indianapolis for a fancy dinner, Brad and Rebecca left as usual to babysit. But whatever the case, the last anyone saw her alive, she was messing around with a rope in the upper section of their play set. The game had something to do with hoisting a small tin bucket of sand from her sandbox to the second story of the play set and then watching the sand pour through the play set boards.

When Rebecca went to check on Emmylou, she found her baby sister dangling from the upper section of the play set, the girl having lost her balance and gotten tangled up in the rope. The rope had strangled her. Emmylou was unresponsive when the paramedics arrived.

I couldn't begin to imagine how horrible Rebecca felt then, and I could tell it still haunted her. Where before she was nice enough but mostly a typical kid, after the accident she'd become excessively kind to everyone, especially young children. Many afternoons found her at Purple Turtle, the local daycare center, playing with the kids and sometimes reading them stories. Rebecca never played any sports because she claimed they would interfere with her Purple Turtle time.

And I don't think it was simply an attempt to atone for her mistake, though there was certainly some of that in Rebecca's volunteering. No, I think it was the fragility of life that compelled Rebecca to volunteer, to get the little ones to understand that it wasn't worth it to take chances.

As you might expect, Rebecca also doted on Peach. And since so few people cherished my little sister the way I thought she deserved, I welcomed Rebecca's doting.

Brad, however...Brad's reaction to his baby sister's death had been decidedly unhealthy. Where before Brad was just sort of mean, he became incorrigible after Emmylou's death. Rather than simply threatening to hit other kids, he began to make good on his threats. On some level I knew that his bullying could be traced to the pain he felt over the accident, and when I remembered this, I actually felt sorry for him. It was on his shoulders that most of the blame was placed—by his mother, by his peers, maybe even by himself—and that sort of thing would be emotionally shattering for anyone. But it was almost like, in hurting others, Brad was lashing out at himself for ignoring Emmylou. Of course, I'm no psychiatrist, so I might be totally off base. But there's no denying that Brad became a different person after his baby sister died, and the person he became was a major downgrade from the mildly irritating kid he had been.

Then again, when Brad acted the way he was acting tonight, it was a lot harder to feel sorry for him.

I realized that Rebecca was close to tears.

Mia moved up next to her. "Becca? What's wrong?"

She wiped her eyes. "We better get inside."

Eric Blades stepped up between Brad and Kurt and grinned at us. "And you three pussies better get home."

Barley said, "I'm surprised you didn't offer to sell us drugs."

Eric's grin vanished. "What's your name?"

I admired the way Barley held his ground. "Dale Marley," he said, standing up a little straighter.

Blades stepped closer. I was surprised by how tall he was, about the same height as Brad. Blades's arms were bigger than I remembered too.

"You know who I am?" Blades asked Barley.

"I know you were gonna get sent to juvenile prison until your dad made a few phone calls."

Blades's dark eyes widened. "Who told you that?"

Barley hesitated. "My dad."

Kurt moved up beside Blades. "They own the gas station up on Washington Street. You know, the one nobody ever goes to?"

I winced. Though I hated to admit it, Kurt was right. People rarely did visit The Hilltop, the Marleys' store. I bought slushies from there sometimes just because I hated the thought of Barley's dad sitting on his stool all day in an empty store.

I said to Kurt, "Not everybody's dad can defend child molesters and rapists."

Everyone froze. What I'd said was true enough— Kurt Fisher's father, Kurt Senior—was a well-known defense attorney who'd made a name for himself defending clients of dubious morality. And getting them acquitted, no matter how guilty they were.

But to actually say that, to spit the ugly truth right into Kurt's smarmy face...I felt like I'd slathered myself in honey and run screaming into a bee farm.

"You're such a dick," Kylie Ann said to me.

Kurt's teeth shone in a feral grin. "It's okay, Kylie Ann. I like it when a pussy like Burgess tries to act tough."

"Actually," Kylie Ann said, "it's *not* okay." She turned to Mia and Rebecca. "Why don't you tell your boyfriends about what happened in the creek?"

Brad and Kurt looked at Mia and Rebecca. Then the boys looked at us. Blades was stepping toward Barley, who wore a look of abject terror. I couldn't blame him. Within moments all three of us were going to be reduced to a puddle of meaty pulp.

Rebecca clenched her fists, half-screamed, "Will you just stop it? For once?"

Everyone paused.

"Rebecca?" Chris said. "What's going on?"

Brad blurted out, "She's freaked out because Carl Padgett escaped."

I'm afraid my mouth fell open.

Eric Blades waggled his eyebrows in a way that struck me as wildly inappropriate, given the situation. "The Moonlight Killer is gonna strike again."

"Jesus," Chris muttered.

"That's why my parents are so mad at me," Rebecca explained. She shook her head, sniffling. "They said we put ourselves in danger by sneaking out. They've been so paranoid ever since..."

Mercifully, she didn't finish. We all knew why the Ralstons were so paranoid. Who wouldn't be after losing a child?

Barley stepped forward. "He's not coming here though, is he? Padgett's not coming to Shadeland?"

"Could be," Blades said, his voice dark with ghoulish glee. "They said he was heading south."

"I gotta go," I said, already moving toward my bike.

Kurt called after me, "Don't worry, Burgess. Your mom's too stoned to make much of a victim. There wouldn't be enough sport in it for Padgett."

Loud guffaws followed this, both Blades and Brad Ralston chortling as though my mom's addiction to prescription drugs was the funniest thing in the world. I heard Mia snapping at them to stop laughing, but her defense of me barely registered.

Because Peach might have heard the news. She would be terrified.

Or worse.

No, I told myself. Don't even think that. There's no way Padgett would randomly choose your house. There's no way something that awful could happen.

Yet I found myself pounding toward my bike. Brad, Kurt, and Eric taunted me, but I hardly heard them. The only thing I could hear was Peach begging me to stay with her, the way she always did when I tried to leave the house.

It was Peach's voice that trailed after me as I pedaled down the dark road toward home.

Chapter Four

Mom's Wrath and the Wendigo

Peach was indeed awake when I burst through
the front door, and she had indeed been crying. She
practically threw herself into my arms, and though this
would have ordinarily made me feel either flattered or
annoyed—Peach could be awfully clingy sometimes—in
this circumstance I experienced nothing but guilt.
Painful, deep, soul-scratching guilt.

She was whimpering something about me being
in trouble.

Despite myself, I smiled a little at the notion of
my little sister punishing me. "Okay," I said. "I'll serve
you breakfast in bed for a week."

She pulled away and craned her head up at me. A
yellowish string of snot drooped from her nose to the
front of my shirt.

"Not me, silly," she said. "Trouble with Mom."

I frowned, snatched some tissues from the box,
wiped off my shirt and then Peach's face. "What's wrong
with Mom?" I asked. In my frantic rush to get back to
the house, I'd forgotten all about my mother.

"She's really mad at you for sneaking out," Peach
explained. "She's been on the phone the whole time."

I know I should have felt more guilt about this,
but the only emotions Peach's words enkindled in me
were anger and resentment. Who the hell was my mom
to be furious with me over not being here? *I* was the one
who'd put Peach to bed. *I* was the one who'd made sure
she brushed her teeth and had her pajamas on right
side out and had a glass of water on her bedside table so

she wouldn't wake up and lie there thirsty in the middle of the night.

So I had snuck out once without telling anybody about it. So what? It was just bad luck that my duplicity happened to coincide with a serial killer's escape.

At thought of Carl Padgett, my mind returned to Peach. How much did she know? Surely my mom wouldn't have been dumb enough to tell her about that.

I had to tread carefully.

Walking her over to the couch and sitting beside her, I said, "What woke you up?"

She stared at me, eyes wide with the kind of solemn terror only a six-year-old can muster. "Mom was watching the news. I heard her scream."

Ordinarily, I would've taken this as an exaggeration, but the fact was, my mom was a habitual over-reactor. I could easily imagine her freaking out when she saw the news report about Padgett.

"What did you do then?" I asked Peach.

She lowered her eyes to where her hands were wrestling with each other. "I hid under the blankets."

"That was smart."

She glanced up at me, and I saw tears shimmering in her eyes. "I didn't even look over to check on you."

I realized with horror that she actually felt guilty about this. My sweet, innocent, six-year-old sister felt guilty that she hadn't tried to protect me.

A lump formed in my throat, which I only partially managed to choke back. "You did the right thing," I said. I took her by the shoulders. "You know how I tell you to never answer the door?"

She nodded.

"Well, that goes double now. In fact," I said, taking a deep breath, "from now on, I don't want you playing outside when I'm not with you."

She drew back. "Not even during the day?"

"Never," I said. "Unless I'm with you, you're to stay inside and keep the doors locked."

She searched my eyes. "Will...what scared Mommy?"

I paused, wondering how to proceed. Peach is an incredibly sharp kid, and I knew she'd ask the question eventually. But that didn't make it any easier to answer it once it was out. I considered lying to her, but a believable lie eluded me. "A bad man escaped from jail tonight," I said.

Peach's voice was very small. "Who?"

"You don't know him, but what matters now is—"

"*What's wrong with you?*" a voice hissed from the hallway. Peach and I both jumped at the sound.

Mom stared at us from the shadows.

I swallowed. "How long have you been standing there?"

She stalked forward. "Long enough to know how much you're scaring her. *Jesus*, Will."

My mouth went dry. I felt a nauseating mixture of anger and regret. Part of me was outraged with my mom's self-righteousness, but though it made me sick to admit it, she was probably right. I shouldn't have told Peach about the Moonlight Killer.

Mom strode nearer, her veiny forearms folded over her chest. "I've notified Dale's and Chris's parents too, so you three might as well tell us the truth about where you were tonight."

I stared at my mom and hated her then. I hated her frizzy brown hair, which she frequently spent money on to have dyed and styled. I hated her bloodshot eyes, her perforated earlobes, in which she often wore four or five pairs of earrings because she thought they made her look younger. I hated her stupid fuzzy pink bathrobe, the one she'd bought at Victoria's Secret for over a hundred dollars even though Peach and I rarely got new clothes.

But most of all I hated her accusing stare. Her assumed superiority. Her baseless belief that she could still treat me like a child, could still exercise power over me despite the fact that she no longer fulfilled any of the requirements of a parent. She cooked for us, what, once a week? At most? When was the last time my mom bathed Peach or did anything for her? Peach's teeth would've rotted out if not for me. Hell, her *skin* might have rotted off if not for me.

But it wouldn't do to say that now. Not in front of my sister.

I said, "I went swimming with some friends."

A look of mock delight spread over my mom's face. "Oh you *did*, did you? Swimming with friends! Isn't that just lovely? And am I to assume these were all *male* friends?"

I did my best to keep my voice steady. "There were girls and guys."

I didn't want to mention Mia or Rebecca yet. Not if I could help it.

Mom must have picked up on my apprehension. She smiled nastily. "And did these girls have names?"

I noted with misgiving that her eyes were clearer than they'd been in weeks. And her words weren't slurry at all.

She picked a hell of a night to be sober, I thought.

I knew it would make things worse, but I said it anyway. "I'm not telling you their names."

Her smile disappeared, her look cold and steely. "Yes you will. I'll call their parents and tell them where their precious daughters have been."

That did it. I thought of Mia, the way she'd touched me. There had been a powerful attraction between us, sure. And yes, we'd almost kissed. But that didn't begin to describe everything I'd felt in that moment—and what I hoped Mia had felt—and there was no way my mom would understand it, or for that matter even listen to my explanation. All my mom would see is a couple of teenagers getting cozy in the water, one of them shirtless and the other in her bra.

I'd die before I'd tell her.

So I got up and helped Peach to her feet. "Come on, kiddo. Let's get you back to bed."

I could feel my mom's disbelieving glare on the side of my face. Man, like a white-hot sun baking me through a car window. "You will tell me their names, and you'll tell me them *right now.*"

Peach was trembling. Mom and I didn't fight often, but when we did it was never pretty. This was shaping up to be a real hurricane of an argument, and Peach sensed it.

Unless I did something to head it off.

"Mom," I said, facing her with an effort. I was a good deal taller than she was, but at that moment it felt like her fury was towering over me. "I'm sorry about sneaking out. It was a rotten thing to do. But I'm really tired, and I need to get Peach to bed." I hefted my little sister up on my hip. She clung to me, but she was watching Mom closely for her reaction.

It wasn't good.

"Don't you walk away from me!" she snapped as I did exactly that. Trailing us down the hallway like a malevolent shadow, Mom said, "I asked you a question, and dammit, I want an answer. *Now*, Will Burgess!"

How dare you yell at me? I thought, gritting my teeth. The hallway was very dark back here by the only two bedrooms in the house, and I tried to concentrate on not tripping over one of Peach's toys and sending us both to the hospital with broken necks. But it was difficult to see, and it was even harder not to tell my mom to go to hell. To call her the lazy, worthless sack of garbage she was.

But if I did that, I'd only be making things harder on my sister.

Mom followed us into our bedroom. "Their *names*, Will."

"I don't remember," I said and lowered Peach onto her bed. There were about two-dozen stuffed animals in the way, so I had to raise her up for a moment to clear away the miniature zoo before laying her down again. I kissed her on the forehead and told her I'd be right back.

She watched me with huge eyes as I moved past Mom into the hallway.

Mom came with me, her voice rising. "You're lying!"

I closed the bedroom door, faced my mom. "Of course I'm lying. Can't you lay off for once?"

"For *once*?" She barked out a scornful laugh. "I hardly ever yell at you."

I felt my temple twitch. "You hardly ever talk to me either."

Her expression was appalled. "What are you—"

I stepped closer, my jaw clenched. "You hardly ever cook, you never clean. When's the last time you did laundry? We ran out of detergent weeks ago. Who do you think bought us a new bottle?"

Her voice was barely a whisper. "I've been busy with—"

"Swallowing pills," I said. "Ruining yourself. And *I'm* the one who looks after Peach. *I'm* the one who makes sure she's fed. A parent should never be too busy to look after her child."

"How dare you talk to me like that? I'm your *mother*, Will."

"You're *nothing*," I growled, my voice fraying at the edges. "You're a lazy burnout who stopped being a mother years ago, so stop acting like you care!"

I shouldered past her and left her gape-mouthed in the hallway. I barely made it out the back door before the tears came. I didn't want mom to see me breaking down, so I stumbled into the yard, made it to the back of the shed, where I sank to the grass and sobbed. The Hollow bordered our backyard, so I didn't have to worry about anybody seeing me. I didn't think I'd have to worry about my mom following me either. The words I'd spoken had cut her deeply, maybe deeper than she deserved. But I didn't regret them. The only thing I regretted was how alone my sister was in our bedroom. I told myself I had to get back there to help Peach fall asleep.

But I was selfish. I didn't want Mom to know I'd been crying, so I lingered outside for another hour until my cheeks were dry and all the lights in the house were off.

And when I came back into the bedroom, Peach was indeed asleep. She was clutching her Glo-worm doll. By the meager starlight filtering through the windows, I noticed her cheeks were still moist.

A flood of self-loathing washed over me as I slumped down on my bed.

You failed her, I told myself. *You're the only thing she has, and you failed her.*

I gazed at Peach's slumbering form in the dark and hated myself for not being a better brother. It was nearly dawn when I finally drifted into a fitful sleep.

♦

The next morning there was food on the table when Peach and I entered the kitchen. Mom was standing at the sink, washing dishes. She smiled briefly at Peach and nodded at the scrambled eggs on the table, but she didn't even glance in my direction.

Which was fine by me.

Peach and I ate in uneasy silence—eggs, bacon strips, and orange juice—until I could stand it no longer.

I said to Peach, "You wanna play with Juliet Wallace today?"

Peach's face, for the first time that morning, showed something other than nervous dread.

"It's Saturday," I explained. "So I'm sure her parents aren't at work."

I could tell Mom was listening to us from the sink, where she was pretending to dry dishes.

Peach glanced up at her. "Can I, Mom?"

I chewed my bacon and waited for Mom's scathing retort: *What, my opinion matters now? Since when did you care about my permission?*

But Mom remained on her best behavior. "I'll call the Wallaces in a few minutes, Honey. If it's okay with them, it's fine with me."

Genuine joy spread over Peach's face. She actually bounced in her seat. How long had it been, I wondered, since she'd looked that giddy?

Too damned long, I decided.

I stood and nodded toward the hall. "Come on, Peach. Let's get you ready."

"I can do that," Mom said.

I turned to look at her. She was still drying dishes, and her expression gave nothing away.

"It's okay, Will," Mom said, dropping the hand towel onto the counter and moving over to begin clearing the table. "I'll get her ready."

I hesitated awkwardly for another several seconds as the silence in the kitchen drew out. I'm not sure what I expected. Maybe a consequence for sneaking out last night. On some level I knew I deserved one, even though I was also sure I'd protest loudly if I received it. Or maybe I thought Mom would apologize for being such a lame-ass for so long.

Mom helped Peach to her feet and led her through the kitchen doorway.

Utterly bewildered, I went to my room to get dressed.

By the time I got my clothes on and brushed my teeth, Mom and Peach were in Mom's room preparing for Peach's play date. I decided to leave well enough alone and exited the house hastily. Ordinarily, I'd have called Chris or Barley from our house phone—none of the three of us had cell phones—but like I said, I was anxious to escape the bizarre atmosphere inside my house.

As I walked through our neighborhood, the feeling of wrongness intensified. It was just like *The Twilight Zone*. Most kids my age weren't aware of the show, but every New Year's Eve Chris, Barley, and I stayed up all night watching a *Twilight Zone* marathon on the Sci-Fi Network.

And just like a *Twilight Zone* episode, it felt like my neighborhood was completely deserted. My house was on the edge of town, but the first street I turned onto—Walnut Street—wasn't at all a lonesome place. Respectable two-story houses lined both sides of the road, the mature trees and meticulous landscaping making it all feel like an upscale park. Yet despite the fact that it was a sunny Saturday morning—the fifth day of June, I realized—there wasn't a single dad out mowing the lawn, not a mom pushing a stroller or taking a jog. No kids riding bikes. As I neared a white house with green shutters, I realized why.

People were glued to their TVs.

Feeling a bit weird, but too curious to do otherwise, I crept up the unfamiliar sidewalk so I could better hear the television playing in the house's front room:

"...and aren't sure where Padgett might have fled, though the stolen SUV was last spotted driving south on Highway 65," a male newscaster was saying. "So far, the names of the slain prison guards have not been released."

I remembered one of Barley's serial killer books and the grainy photograph of Carl Padgett it contained. Dark eyes. An arrogant smile that showed not a hint of remorse. A square jaw shadowed by black stubble.

The newscaster's jaunty voice returned. "...and at approximately eleven o'clock, a neighbor heard a scream from outside this local pharmacy."

A frantic man talking, the guy with a southern accent and a high, reedy voice: "I was walking out to my car, and at first I thought it was someone's radio. There were shouts, then what sounded like a man pleading about something. But then I heard some other sounds, and I knew it wasn't no radio."

"Could you describe the sounds?" a female reporter asked.

"Oh, man...I don't know how to...they was awful. Just awful. There was a loud grunt, then a bunch of thuds. And then I heard..."

A pause.

"What did you hear?" the reporter prompted.

"Chewing," the man said. He sounded like he was about to be sick.

I couldn't blame him.

The newscaster returned. "Police suspect that Padgett might have abandoned the Black Chevy Tahoe somewhere in Northwest Indiana, but they aren't sure when he..."

But I was already moving away from the house. I'd seen a shadow pass in front of the window and had no interest in being shot as a trespasser. Plus, I had a sudden desire to talk it all over with someone.

But who?

Chris would normally have been the obvious choice, but I was on foot rather than my bike. It would take forever to walk there.

I'd go to Barley's.

I turned from Walnut onto Monroe Street and spied Barley's house up ahead. I realized with some disquiet that I hadn't rehearsed what to say to the Marleys should Barley's mom or dad answer the door. They were both really nice, but they'd probably be pissed off at their son, and by extension, me, for the hijinks we'd pulled last night. I reached out, rang the doorbell.

While I stood there, a sparrow lit on the sidewalk below me, gave me a startled look, and fluttered away. I watched after it, thinking it was the first sign of wildlife I'd seen all day. As if even the animals were terrified of Carl Padgett

The lock snicked behind me. I turned, praying it would be Barley who answered the door.

It was. Thank God.

He was wearing a black CAMP CRYSTAL LAKE t-shirt, a reference to the *Friday the 13th* movies, which Barley adored. He said, "You're not grounded?"

I gave him a *you-can't-be-serious* look.

Barley glanced over his shoulder, as though one of his parents was about to attack him with a carving knife. "I am. They told me I can't go anywhere for a week."

"At least you're not Chris," I told him. "He's probably walking around with a handprint on his face."

Barley frowned, glanced down at his feet. "That's not funny."

He was right. It wasn't funny. At all.

What the hell was wrong with me?

"Who is it, Dale?" his mother called.

He went a miserable shade of green. "It's Will, Mom."

A long pause. So long, in fact, that I thought she might be going for her carving knife after all.

Footsteps approached, and then Barley's mom appeared. She was short and plump and ordinarily very cheerful.

She didn't appear very cheerful today.

"Dale isn't allowed to play this week," she said. Barley cringed, no doubt because of her use of the word *play*. I stifled a grin, knowing I'd use it to razz Barley the first chance I got.

I donned my most contrite expression. "I understand, Mrs. Marley. I'm really sorry about what we did. It was irresponsible."

She stared at me a moment longer, then sighed and pursed her lips. I had a feeling a compromise was about to be reached. Mrs. Marley was a secretary at the elementary school, and as such she had a heart for kids. I could tell she hated disciplining her son.

She said, "Well, Dale can't leave the house, but if you two would like to play in his room, I would allow that."

Barley looked slightly less green. "Sure, Mom. Thanks."

I thanked Mrs. Marley and followed Barley upstairs to his room. I hadn't been up here for a few weeks, and there were two new posters—one of them a retro movie poster for *The Day the Earth Stood Still*, the other a gigantic close-up of Hannibal Lecter.

"Awesome," I said, staring at Lecter's crazed eyes.

He eyed it morosely. "Doesn't seem as cool now that Carl Padgett is on the loose."

"I'm surprised your parents let you put it up."

"Mom doesn't like it much, but Dad told her it was harmless. Especially since he and I watched the movie last month."

I plopped down on a red beanbag. "Barley, we watched that movie in like the fourth grade."

He shrugged uneasily. "Yeah, but Mom and Dad don't know that. I just acted really surprised whenever something bad happened."

"I bet it was pretty uncomfortable, watching *The Silence of the Lambs* with your parents."

"You have no idea."

"What'd they do when Buffalo Bill tucked his private parts between his legs and started to—"

"Shut up, okay? *God.*"

I subsided, chuckling.

He shook his head and took the other beanbag, this one blue with a cracked vinyl cover. "I can't believe you didn't get grounded."

I arched an eyebrow. "You wanna trade parents?"

He chewed his bottom lip. "I guess not."

Before the mood could get too dreary, I said, "It's awfully nice of you to let me come over and play."

"Screw you."

I made an innocent face. "What? I love play dates."

"Damn it, Will," he grumbled. He grabbed a DVD case—a horror movie called *The Descent*—and chucked it at me. He missed, of course. "I can't help what my mom says."

"Relax," I said. "Your mom's really cool."

His eyes narrowed. "You making fun of her?"

"Simmer down, okay? I wouldn't make fun of your mom. She's nicer to me than my own mom is."

That seemed to satisfy him. "I'm glad you came over, actually."

"Yeah?"

He nodded. "I wanted to talk to you about something. I mean, I need to talk to you and Chris both, but since Chris is on house arrest, I'll settle for just you."

"I'm flattered."

"Remember that thing Mia saw in the woods last night?"

I smiled. "You mean the giant Gollum with green eyes and white skin?"

Barley's brows pinched together in what I realized was real fear. "Don't joke about it, man. This is really bad."

I sobered a little, but I failed to see what the big deal was. I said so.

Barley sat forward, his bare, sweaty calves squelching a little on the beanbag. Barley perspired more than anyone I knew. "Don't you remember the legends, Will?"

"Not that stuff again. You mean the wildebeest?"

"*Wendigo,*" he said, enunciating each syllable with the gravest respect.

"Why don't you refresh my memory?"

"You're so dense," he said, but I could tell he was warming to his topic. "It all started thousands of years ago, back when the only people in the area were the Algonquins and the Iroquois."

I settled into the beanbag. Barley was a dork, but he was a good storyteller.

He pushed his shaggy brown hair off his forehead. "My dad got most of this from Frank Red Elk—"

"You mean that weirdo who lives way out in the woods?"

"That *weirdo,*" Barley said, as if I'd just insulted the Pope, "happens to be the only full-blooded Native American left in the area."

"I thought he was a drunk who's always chasing women."

Barley waved that off. "So? He's still an impressive guy. Would you want to mess with him?"

Barley had a point there. Red Elk was about six-three, and he was built like a slab of granite. I hadn't seen him often, but when I did, I was always a little intimidated.

"Red Elk comes into the store a lot," Barley said. "You know, for gas and other things."

I nodded. "Like whiskey and condoms."

"Show some respect!"

"Sorry."

"Anyway, the store doesn't do a ton of business in the evenings, so when folks come in, they end up talking to Dad." Barley shrugged. "You know how easy Dad is to talk to."

I nodded. Mr. Marley was indeed easy to talk to. He wasn't exactly heroic-looking. Bespectacled. A fairly sizable belly. Only about five-foot-five. And older, for a man with two kids still in school. But Mr. Marley was also one of the nicest guys I knew. If I could choose a dad, he'd be the one.

"Some nights Red Elk comes by near closing time, and he—"

"Skip to the part about the Whack-a-Mole."

"*Wendigo*," he corrected. "Jeez you're an idiot sometimes. Anyway, Red Elk was all keyed up one night—this was a few months ago. He asked Dad how much propane it would take to blow up a house."

"I often wonder that myself. You have any propane lying around?"

"Dad asked him why he'd want to blow up a house. Red Elk said he'd been seeing things. Peculiar things. Pale figures darting through the trees. Weird clittering sounds right outside his window." Barley shivered. "White faces with green eyes watching him from the woods."

I suddenly didn't feel at all like laughing.

"Dad asked him what that had to do with propane. Red Elk said, 'Maybe I want to make sure I've got a last line of defense in case they come after me.'"

"They?'"

Barley shrugged. "They call them the Children. They live underground. Red Elk said they'd been in the area since way before the Algonquins and the Iroquois settled here. Said the Children were the reason the Native Americans left Peaceful Valley. That too many people were getting eaten alive by them. And dragged down into the caves."

"I'd move too," I said. "But why do they call them Children? Whose children are they?"

"The Wendigo," Barley explained. "The biggest beast of them all."

My heart began to thump. I knew there were caves in the Peaceful Valley area. They were a big reason why the land was being made into a state park, the Peaceful Valley Nature Preserve. Hell, there were caves in the Hollow near my house. But this stuff about the Children...that was a different matter entirely. Was it possible Red Elk really did know something the rest of the town didn't?

Mia would certainly believe him.

Barley's eyes shone. "Supposedly, the Children are huge. Legend says ten feet tall or more. They're the most fearsome cryptids on the planet."

"Cryptids?"

Barley rolled his eyes. "Don't you know anything? *Monsters.* They murder, devour, or change you into one of them. Legend has it they went on a rampage and killed everyone in the area. It wasn't until much later that the land was resettled." Barley nodded solemnly. "But the beasts were never defeated, were they? They just went underground."

I shivered a little. "Can we stop talking about cryptids?"

Barley didn't seem to hear me. "God, with the Children and the Moonlight Killer both on the loose, who knows how many people could die?"

"First of all, the Children are a fairy tale. They don't exist. And Padgett's on the run. He's not gonna go on a killing spree."

Barley looked at me meaningfully. "Have they caught him yet?"

I grudgingly admitted they hadn't.

"Still," he said. "The thing with Padgett scares me less than what Mia saw last night." He shook his head. "I truly hope the Children aren't real." He nodded at his new poster. "They make Hannibal Lecter look like a benevolent guy."

"What's so terrible about them?"

"They're twice as tall as human beings, and about three times as strong."

"So they're like LeBron James."

"LeBron James doesn't eat people," Barley said. "And he doesn't have an affinity for female victims."

I felt a chill. "Red Elk said that?"

"I hate to say this, Will, but I almost wish Mia had seen Carl Padgett last night rather than a creature with huge green eyes."

"Now there's a happy thought."

"I mean it," he said, his eyes big and earnest. "I'm scared of something happening, what with the storm coming and everything."

"What storm?"

He looked at me like I was a simpleton. "The one that's going to hit on Monday? You seriously haven't heard about it?"

I shifted uncomfortably. "I've been busy."

"It's supposed to be the biggest one in years. Like, tons of damage and enough rain to flood Mt. Everest. They're already talking about power losses and millions of dollars of damage."

I chuckled at the terror on his face. "You act like we're in danger, Barley. This is Indiana."

He shook his head solemnly. "I don't know, man. I'm picking up some seriously bad vibes here. I think it's gonna be a lot worse than anybody believes."

I rolled my eyes. "Nothing's going to happen, Barley. We're completely safe."

But it turned out, we weren't.
The first murder happened that night.

Chapter Five

The Heart-stopping Note, the Broken Church and the Moonlit Abduction

When I got home from Barley's, it was nearing four o'clock.

My house was empty, which meant Peach was probably still on her play date, and my mom...well, who knew where my mom was? Given the uneasiness of our recent truce, I was in no hurry for her to return home. It had been beyond weird being in the same room with her that morning, and if I could avoid a repeat of the same stilted interaction, I would.

I was so lost in thought that I almost didn't notice the note sticking out of the screen door. When I opened the door, the white piece of paper fluttered to the porch. My pulse suddenly racing, I picked it up and read the typed words...

Hi, Will. I heard you got in trouble last night. I'm sorry. I feel like it was my fault. And I'm sorry for freaking out on you in the creek. I can still see that face. Those eyes. That terrible grin.

It makes me shiver.

And so do you, to tell you the truth. Every time I think about you I feel like I've got the flu or something (only without the coughing and the sneezing). If it wasn't already obvious, I really like you. I have for a long time. But it's hard because Brad is my best friend's brother. I want to break up with him, but he's just so...possessive. But I want you to know how I feel. I really, really like you, Will. You're nice to me. You're

funny. You're a little shy sometimes, but that's actually
a welcome change from Brad. He's never been shy in his
life. In fact, he thinks everybody should bow down to
him like he's an emperor.

Anyway. I didn't write you to moan about Brad. I
wrote so you'd know how I feel. And I feel a lot. For you.
Does that sound stupid? It probably does, but oh well.
It's true.

So how about this...

Meet me and Rebecca and Kylie Ann tonight at
your treehouse (Bet you didn't think we knew where it
was, did you?). We'll be there at midnight. If you can't
come, I won't be mad at you.

But I hope you can come.

Love,
Mia

I reread the letter, then reread it one more time,
paying special attention to the words, "I really, really
like you, Will." I realized my palms were sweating, and
the paper was beginning to soak through around the
edges where I was clutching it. I wiped my hands on my
cargo shorts before I realized that those were just as
sweaty. I entered the house and went directly to my
bedroom, where I stashed the note inside the very back
of my top dresser drawer where I knew Peach couldn't
get to it. She could be nosy, and I didn't want her
discovering this particular treasure

It meant too much to me.

My stomach queasy but my steps light, I moved
into the bathroom and twisted on the shower.

While I waited for it to warm up—our water
heater was about a decade older than my mom—I
sprawled out on the floor and did as many pushups as I

could, which turned out to be twenty-one. That wasn't a lot, I knew, but it was better than sixteen, my previous high.

I stood up and looked at my chest in the mirror. Still concave.

I took a deep breath and flexed.

Hardly any difference.

Crestfallen, I leaned toward the mirror and inspected my chin and cheeks for signs of whiskers.

Nothing.

I sighed. *Stringbean*, I thought.

Would you relax? a voice answered. *Mia already saw you with your shirt off, and she still likes you, remember?*

Though that didn't reassure me much, it was something. Mia did like me. Or at least she *said* she liked me.

(*very, very much*)

The queasy feeling returned to my guts. What if she was just messing with me? What if her and Rebecca were merely teasing me and Chris as some kind of cruel entertainment?

They can't be, I thought. It was too terrible to consider.

An even ghastlier notion occurred to me. What if Brad and Kurt had put Mia and Rebecca up to it? It would explain a lot. After all, wasn't it too great a coincidence for Mia and Rebecca to invite us over to the Ralstons' house the night after we'd humiliated their boyfriends on the baseball diamond?

Oh my God, I thought. It all made sense.

Then I remembered Mia's fingers on my hip, the smooth feel of her skin. Her measureless blue eyes.

No way, I decided. The episode in the creek had not been faked. Mia really liked me. The note was sincere. It had to be.

Feeling better, I climbed into the shower, let the seething spray assault me, and thought of how exciting it would be to see Mia again tonight.

Then Barley's words came back to me: *...too many people were getting eaten alive by them. And dragged down into the caves.*

"Ridiculous," I said aloud, and lathered my hair with shampoo, the expensive stuff my mom bought for herself and that Peach and I were to under no circumstance use. I felt a childish, vengeful pleasure as I poured triple the necessary amount into my palm and used it to wash my arms and legs.

...an affinity for female victims, Barley's voice repeated in my mind.

My smile faded.

No, I thought. I needed to stop fretting about fairy tales. I wasn't going to miss tonight. Not for anything.

Compressing my lips, I squeezed more of mom's shampoo into my palm and began to scrub my feet with it.

◆

Barley couldn't get over the fact that the girls knew about the treehouse. "How the hell did they find out about it?" he demanded. "Do you guys realize the implications of this? What if they've been listening to us all this time? What if they've heard the stuff we say about girls?"

Chris and I, both of us dressed nicer than usual and smelling too strongly of cologne, merely leaned back on our respective lawn chairs. I'd toted them up the ladder earlier that evening so the girls would have better things to sit on than five-gallon buckets. Barley had actually combed his hair, though now it was parted too neatly, like a first grader getting prepped for picture day.

"I mean, what did they do," he ranted, "follow us to see where we were going? Or did they pay someone for information? Like Will's little sister?"

"Seriously?" I asked. "You think they bribed Peach?"

He shrugged. "It's possible. Girls can be ruthless. Some of the most violent crimes in American history have been perpetrated by women."

"Peach is six years old," I said. "She doesn't have any interest in money. Now if they paid her in Twizzlers and Nerds..."

"Hold on," Chris said. "Why are we sure they know where the treehouse is?"

Barley looked at Chris like he was an idiot. "Um, because they *said* so? Wasn't that sort of a giveaway?"

Something clicked in my mind. It was like I picked up on Chris's train of thought. That happened a lot to us, which was really weird. It was like we were on the same wavelength or something, like we'd been separated at birth.

Chris said, "We *did* tell them about the treehouse, remember? Last night on the way to the creek?"

Barley was nodding thoughtfully. "Yeah...you might be right. I was sort of nervous. I must've checked to make sure my fly wasn't open about sixty times."

"I don't blame you for being nervous," Chris said. "Being matched up with Kylie Ann had to be kind of scary."

Barley grunted. "We weren't *matched up*. Hell, she barely tolerated me. Unlike Casanova over here—" He flapped a hand at me. "—I still can't believe she stripped down to her bra."

"Shut up," I snapped.

Barley flinched. "Hey, take it easy. It's not like I talked about her boobs or anything."

"You just did," Chris pointed out.

Barley smiled sheepishly. "I guess I did. But they were really nice though, weren't they? Round and dark and—"

I was out of my chair, my hands shoving Barley hard. He went stumbling back, fell, and before I knew it I was standing over him, my fists clenched.

"Hey," he said, palms up, "take it easy, Will. Jesus, it's not like I said anything *that* offensive."

"It was offensive enough," I said. "Stop talking about her like that."

Chris watched me uneasily. "Calm down, man. You talk about tits all the time."

"It's different when you know the girl."

"But it shouldn't be," he answered.

And as it usually did, something in Chris's tone brought me back from whatever bloodred cloud I was in. In kindergarten the teacher had a conference with my mom because every time I got a question wrong I'd yank out my hair in clumps. Then they started making me see a child psychologist, which really sucked ass. Thankfully, the lady they were taking me to charged too much, and my mom's insurance wouldn't pay for it. So they left me—and my temper—alone.

Chris and Barley were watching me. The tension in the treehouse, which was only about twelve feet-by-twelve to begin with, made the space seem even smaller.

"I'm going down to meet the girls," I muttered.

"I'll come with you," Chris said.

Barley scrambled to his feet. "What, and leave me here? No freaking way."

"You stay here," I said to Chris. "I need a few minutes alone."

Chris looked disappointed, but he saw that I meant it. Sometimes only time could calm me down. Time and solitude. Going in search of the girls would provide both.

I made it to the bottom of the ladder and began walking a narrow squiggle of dirt that wasn't even a trail. It was merely a slender strip, no wider than a foot, carved through the tall weeds in a meandering pattern that made it difficult to stay on it without stumbling into the poison ivy and nettles. We kept it that way for a reason. We didn't want other people, especially jerkoffs like Brad and Kurt and Eric, to learn the treehouse's location. It was *our* place, the one spot on the planet where we could go and not have to worry about parents or teachers or bullies.

And the more I pondered it, the more I realized there was no conceivable way the girls could know where it was. At least, not precisely. They might know the general *direction* of the treehouse, but they'd never find the place without a guide. In fact, the girls might even now be lost in the forest.

My protectiveness of Mia kicked in, and I doubled the pace of my footsteps.

Then I froze.

A shape had flitted across the trail in front of me.

Memories of the newscast flooded over me:

There were shouts, then what sounded like a man pleading about something. But then I heard some other sounds, and I knew it wasn't no radio.

I was in one of the darkest parts of the forest, a dense thicket of spruce trees, tall, stout, tenebrous ones that swallowed up whatever moonlight might happen to filter through the clouds.

Could you describe the sounds?

Oh, man...I don't know how to...they was awful. Just awful. There was a loud grunt, then a bunch of thuds. And then I heard...

My body felt submerged in ice water.

Chewing, the guy on TV had said.

And with a rush of terror, I realized *I* heard something too. It was coming from the spruce trees ahead. The sound was unmistakable. Laughter, high and soft and malevolent. I took a step backward, my body quaking. It was Carl Padgett. The Moonlight Killer. I took another backwards step, but I knew it was futile. I was about to be butchered and eaten.

Arms enfolded me from behind.

I gasped and tried to break away, but my captor came with me, and I realized he was laughing, laughing that same high laugh, almost a feminine laugh...it was almost like...

I stopped struggling. "Mia?"

"If I let you go," whispered the voice at my ear, "will you promise not to hit me?"

I exhaled, my whole body going limp. The arms loosened their grasp. I turned and looked into Mia's eyes.

She was biting her lower lip and trying her best not to laugh at me, but she couldn't hold it in.

"You're gonna get it," I said.

She backed away, giggling now. A shimmering silver swath of moonlight caught her face. She looked more radiant than ever.

I darted my hand under her guard, tickled her. Laughing, she stumbled back. Her teeth were gleaming white, her skin a deep brown. She must have spent the day in the sun, I decided, because she was even tanner than she'd been the night before. I reached for her, but she retreated nimbly away. I could tell how much she was enjoying this, how happy she was she'd been able to sneak up on me. I moved after her, laughing a little myself. She wore blue jeans, despite the heat of the night, and a white tank top that was just tight enough to set my imagination racing.

"Are you two gonna flirt all night?" a voice asked from behind me. "Or do we get to see this famous treehouse?"

I turned and beheld Rebecca Ralston standing in the pool of moonlight. I noticed she was wearing the peridot necklace Chris had evidently given her. With her blond hair and her bright smile, she looked almost as pretty as Mia did.

Almost.

I tried to conceal my disappointment at the interruption.

Maybe Rebecca picked up on it. She said, "Or if you want, you can just tell me the way, and you and Mia can come when you're ready."

Before I could answer, Mia said, "Sure."

I turned to her, surprised.

"If it's okay with you," she added with an impish smile.

Of course it's okay with me! I want to marry you! I almost screamed.

"Okay," I said, doing my best to look cool. I indicated the direction. "It's that way about fifty yards. Just follow the trail."

Rebecca clicked on a flashlight I hadn't noticed. "Got it," she said and stifled a yawn.

"What's wrong?" I said. "Am I that boring?"

She chuckled. "Long day. Purple Turtle was a madhouse."

I thought of asking her if she'd been to a therapist lately. I couldn't imagine volunteering at a daycare center. The screaming and the singing and the poop. I'd be insane within an hour.

She started past us, but paused. "Is your mom home with Peach?"

"Of course. Why wouldn't she be?"

She gazed at me a long moment, looked like she was about to say something, then shook her head. "No reason," she said. She moved past us. Leaving Mia and I alone.

Mia said, "Rebecca's a little paranoid."

"I noticed."

"I'd be paranoid too if I'd been through what she has."

I fell silent, realizing I would be too. I had a sudden urge to go home and check on Peach. I got frustrated with her sometimes, but if anything ever happened to her, I wouldn't want to go on living.

Maybe I relied on her as much as she relied on me.

"I take it you got my note?" Mia said.

"Yeah," I answered. Then, knowing I should say more, I added, "Thanks."

Smooth, my inner critic muttered. *Real smooth.*

"I was thinking about your poem this morning," she said.

"My poem," I repeated stupidly.

"Yeah," she said, smiling. "The one you read in Mrs. Herbert's class?"

"You remember that?" I could hardly believe it. Hell, I could barely remember it myself. At the time I'd been mortified at being made to read my poetry in front of my peers, but Mrs. Herbert was a hard ass, and if you didn't read your work aloud, you got an *F*. I'd been tempted to take the *F*, but Chris had talked me into reading it.

Mia closed her eyes.

"The sooty walls enclose my heart
A room full dark and glazed with frost.
I wander without eyes through the darkness
And remain a child apart."

I could only gape.

She opened one eye and looked at me shyly. "Was that right?"

I nodded. "How did you..."

"I liked it so much I wrote parts of it down. Rebecca and I still talk about it. Yours was the best in the class."

"I got a *C* because I didn't use iambic pentameter."

"That's because Mrs. Herbert wouldn't know good poetry if it bit her in the crotch."

We both laughed.

"'The Broken Church,'" Mia said, repeating the title of my poem. "What made you call it that?"

I shrugged. "I don't know. It just seemed to fit."

It felt unspeakably weird talking about my poetry. I'd been convinced that it sucked. I said so.

Mia shook her head. "You're too hard on yourself. I could tell that about you right away. Even when we were little, you got mad at yourself for everything."

I must've scowled at her. "You act like you know me so well...you've hardly ever talked to me."

"That's because I've always been dumb." She kicked the trail, scuffing the dirt with the toe of her white shoe. "Maybe it's because Brad is Rebecca's older brother. It's shallow, but I sort of worshipped him." She rolled her eyes, mocking herself. "You know...the big, handsome older man?"

She looked hopefully at me, but I couldn't help but be annoyed. That word, *worshipped*, had wedged in my brain like a splinter under a fingernail. Brad didn't deserve to be worshipped. He deserved to be beaten with a hammer.

"I don't blame you for being mad at me," she went on. "You're right. I mean, I've never been *mean* to you, but I haven't exactly been attentive either."

"You've treated me like a leper."

She gave me a wry smile. "Are you being cruel to pay me back?"

"Maybe."

She punched me lightly on the shoulder. "Jerk."

"We can't all be as studly as Brad."

She laughed incredulously. "Hey!"

"Okay," I said, backing away. "I'm sorry."

"No you're not."

"You're right. I'm not."

Her eyes flashed delightedly, and she punched me on the shoulder again, harder this time.

"Hey, that's gonna leave a bruise."

"You deserve worse."

I rubbed my shoulder, grimacing a little.

"Is the broken church supposed to represent your home?" Mia asked.

I stopped rubbing my shoulder. "Huh?"

"The poem is about losing trust," she explained. "I know you and your mom don't get along. Your dad was never in the picture. You have to take care of your little sister all the time. That has to be difficult for you."

I stiffened. "How about we leave Peach out of it?"

"If you want."

I didn't answer. There was a sour feeling in my belly.

"What's her real name?" Mia asked.

"Audrey," I muttered.

"Why don't you call her Audrey?"

I sighed, glanced up at the black strip of sky threading its way through the spruce boughs. "I don't know. Maybe because it's the name my mom gave her?"

"You two fight a lot?" Mia asked. "You and your mom?"

"That's sort of personal."

"Don't you trust me?"

I considered lying to her. Then, I decided to tell the truth. "I don't know. Not yet, I guess."

She nodded. "I can respect that. If I'd been through what you've been through, I'd have a hard time trusting people too."

A heat began to build at the back of my neck. "I don't think who I trust is any of your business."

Mia nodded, looking like the world's youngest shrink. "I'd expect you to do that. Put up walls. I bet you push everybody away."

"Would you please stop psychoanalyzing me?"

"Sure. When you stop acting like I'm playing a practical joke on you."

I was speechless.

"Don't tell me it hasn't crossed your mind," she said. "I'm Brad's girlfriend, and Brad and Kurt don't like you."

"'Don't like' isn't strong enough," I grumbled. "Those guys despise us."

"They do," she agreed. "I suspect it's because you're smarter than they are. And you and Chris are better athletes too."

I couldn't help thawing a little. "You think so?"

She nodded. "Rebecca's dad started Brad a year late in school so he'd be more physically mature than his classmates." She frowned. "Too bad he's not more emotionally mature too."

I studied Mia's face. There was more darkness there than I was accustomed to. More anger. "So why do you date him?"

She wouldn't meet my eyes. "Habit, I suppose."

"That's a shitty reason."

She glanced at me, and her look was defiant. "I did like him. Last year, at least." She sighed. "What do you want me to say? That I've been superficial? That I liked being the girlfriend of a popular upperclassman? That it made me feel older, more mature? That I enjoyed going with a boy who had his own car?"

Maybe that should have made me feel better, but it didn't. "If those are the only reasons, why are you still with him?"

She shook her head, her expression stormy. "I hate myself for it, okay? I never should've dated him. I was just…dumb. Materialistic."

The image of Mia riding in Brad's car flitted through my mind. I scowled at her. "Yet you're still together."

"I won't be for long. It's just…it's hard to know how to break it off. And when. I've never been in this situation before."

"Are you scared of him?"

"Are you?"

"No," I lied.

She gave me a strange look then. "Brad said today he and his friends are going to kill you and Chris."

I tried not to show how frightened her words made me. "They wouldn't actually *kill* anybody."

She chewed her bottom lip, appeared to think something over. "Do you know the real reason Brad has that scar on his wrist?"

Before I could answer, a voice from the trees said, "I could kill *you* for dragging me out here."

Kylie Ann Lubeck emerged from the spruce trees.

"Wait," I said. "Has she been listening the entire time?"

"Don't worry," Kylie Ann said sourly, "I couldn't hear most of it. Just your voices. Believe me, that was more than enough."

I looked at Mia.

"Kylie Ann has performance anxiety," Mia explained. "She had to pee, but apparently she couldn't because we were talking too loud."

Kylie Ann looked around with distaste. "It wasn't just your voices—it was all the bugs and the weeds and the—" She shuddered. "Can we just go back to your house?"

"*You* can," Mia said lightly. "I'm going with Will."

"Well isn't that sweet?" Kylie Ann said. "Makes me want to puke."

She pushed past us in the direction Rebecca had taken a few minutes earlier. Her curly black hair cascaded over her toned shoulders, and the rest of her body was just about perfect too. But though some girls had personalities that enhanced their looks, Kylie Ann was the opposite. I wanted to give her the benefit of the doubt, but man, it was difficult.

I looked at Mia, who wore a wry grin.

"She's like a ray of sunshine," I said.

Mia chuckled. "Come on. Take me to your secret fortress."

And taking my hand, she led me down the trail.

◆

We made it to the clearing and pulled up next to Kylie Ann.

Who was staring up at the treehouse in disbelief. "I am *not* going up there."

Mia looked over at her. "Afraid to break a nail?"

"First of all," Kylie Ann said, "it's really freaking high. Secondly, it doesn't look safe. And if these morons built it, I'm *positive* it's not safe."

"You're a really warm person, Kylie Ann," I said. "I can feel the love coming out of you in waves."

"Not to mention," she went on, "there's not even a real ladder. Those boards look like they're full of splinters, and who knows if they're even bolted to the tree properly. I could get to the top and have one come off in my hands, and then I'd be in the hospital with a fractured neck."

"That wouldn't be a big loss," I muttered.

Mia elbowed me in the side.

"Come on up!" a voice called from the treehouse. Craning our necks, we saw Rebecca poking her face through the window opening. A moment later, another face appeared. Chris.

Barley appeared in the trapdoor opening, an eager smile on his face. "Hi, Kylie Ann. Have you ever been in a treehouse before? We can tell ghost stories!"

I felt a wave of affection for my friend.

Kylie Ann rolled her eyes. "Goody."

Mia said to them, "I don't think Kylie Ann's going to join us."

"Big surprise," Chris said. "Kylie Ann won't go anywhere unless there's someone playing the violin and handing out mints."

"Hey!" Kylie Ann shouted.

"Well, it's true," Chris said. "You need to stop being such a stuck-up princess."

I looked away so Kylie Ann wouldn't see me smiling.

She looked like she was about to murder someone. "That's it," she said, "I'm going home. And this time I *am* telling Kurt and Brad where you two are."

Mia shook her head. "Why are you like this?"

Kylie Ann rounded on her. "Why do you cheat on your boyfriend with this loser?"

Mia's gaze went stony. "He's not a loser."

But Kylie Ann was too worked up to stop now. She motioned toward me. "Look at him. Old clothes. One of his shoes has a hole in it. For Christ's sakes, why don't you just go to the homeless shelter and hook up with one of the bums?"

Mia stepped closer to her, her expression seething. "You're an ass."

Kylie Ann recoiled with a breathless little laugh. She put up a hand to show she was done with the argument. "You deserve anything Brad does to you."

And with that, she moved away.

"Come on," I said, feeling sick to my stomach. "Let's go up."

Mia allowed herself to be led toward the ladder.

But Kylie Ann evidently wanted to have the last word. She stopped on the far edge of the clearing and shouted, "You're a bitch, Mia!"

Mia opened her mouth to say something, but that's when a large, pale hand shot out of the shadows and closed over Kylie Ann's mouth. She was lifted off her feet, and then she disappeared into the forest.

For an endless moment, Mia and I could only stare. We looked at each other.

"Will?" she said, her voice small and terrified.

We heard a strangled cry, the sound of someone being dragged away through the forest.

"What was that?" Barley called from above us.

"We have to go after her," I said.

Mia clutched my arm. "Do you think it was…"

She let the rest go unspoken.

"Stay here," I said.

I took off into the forest.

I'm not sure why I sprinted after Kylie Ann. After all, she'd just called me a loser and made fun of my clothes. Part of me hated her. She represented everything I'd come to loathe. People who believed themselves better than others. Selfish people.

I was pretty sure I hated Kylie Ann Lubeck.

But that didn't mean she deserved to die.

I lunged into the forest at a point about twenty feet to the left of the trail, where I thought I'd seen the brush moving after Kylie Ann had been dragged into the darkness. Immediately I was beset by nettles, vines, by slender branches that whacked me in the chin as I tried to give chase. Thorns tore at my clothes, my skin. Behind me I could hear Mia shouting. I heard Chris, Barley, and Rebecca too, all of them calling my name. But I knew time was short. Whoever had taken Kylie Ann had done so with the intent of bearing her off to a secluded place. I don't know how I knew this, but on a gut level I did. Who had taken her didn't matter at that point, though later it would become the primary question on all our minds. But at that moment, the only thing that mattered was finding her before she disappeared entirely.

My shoe snagged on a root, and I damn near landed on my face. But somehow I pinwheeled my arms, got control of my body, and regained my balance.

I listened.

Silence for a moment. Then a rush of movement to my left.

I wheeled in that direction, closing my eyes as I slammed into the intersection of two pine trees. Their furry branches scraped over me, reminding me of a large car being run through a narrow carwash. Then I burst out of the trees and found myself in a small clearing. My eyes darted around the shadowy space, scanning for any sign of Kylie Ann or her abductor.

Straight ahead, the slender trunk of a sapling tremored. As if someone had just rushed past.

I darted toward it, and as I did I distinguished a small gap in the next thicket of pine trees. Whoever it was had likely taken Kylie Ann in there. Or *through* there. Either way, I was gaining on them. The abductor was encumbered with a tall, well-built young woman. I only had to worry about myself. Feeling a surge of confidence, I bolted into the clearing and had taken three long strides when something cracked me on the bridge of the nose. My feet flew out from under me, and I struck the ground on my back. I thought for a moment I'd run straight into a sturdy branch, but then, through my grogginess, I glimpsed something that froze my blood.

Kylie Ann's panic-stricken face.

Or her eyes rather, which were vast moons.

Her mouth was covered with a huge, veined hand.

My vision blurred, doubled, but I could still make out the large figure hefting her over its shoulder and disappearing into the darkness. The hand removed from her mouth, Kylie Ann let loose with a strident wail. My teeth gritted, I made to rise, but I hadn't gotten halfway to my feet before the world tilted wildly, and I landed on my side. I had to get to Kylie Ann, had to save her. But my knees buckled again, my strength failing. Something wet pattered onto my hand, and looking down, I realized my nose was bleeding.

Holy shit, I thought. Not bleeding. *Gushing*.

I'd never had a nosebleed before, and the sight of all that blood made me woozy. The taste of it was hot and coppery. Whoever it was had really nailed me.

I tried to gain my feet again, but I fared even worse this time.

"Will!" a voice yelled. "Jesus, man, what happened to you?"

It was Chris, I realized. Chris and the others.

A hand touched my back. "Dude, you're bleeding all over the place."

"No kidding," I grunted.

Chris helped me to a sitting position. Then he took his shirt off and held it to my spraying nose.

"Does it hurt?" Barley asked.

I moaned.

A face appeared in my blurred vision, and it took me several moments to recognize who it was.

"Did he hurt you anywhere else?" Mia asked. "He didn't stab you or anything, did he?"

I realized with faint amusement that she was patting down my torso, my back, scouring my body for wounds.

I shook my head. "Just the nose."

"Take it easy, man," Chris said. "Take it easy. You're safe now."

"What about Kylie Ann?" Rebecca asked.

"Gone," I whispered.

There was a moment of heavy silence.

"She's gone," I said.

PART TWO

MONSTERS

Chapter Six

Badgered by the Cops and Attacked by a Black Mustang

Everybody was so freaked out about Kylie Ann's abduction that we got in very little trouble for sneaking out of the house.

At least at first.

At first the only thing we had to deal with was the police, an experience that was the exact opposite of what I expected it to be. I suspect this was because my only knowledge of police procedure came from movies and TV. I expected them to separate us into stark interrogation rooms with two-way mirrors and a lot of cigarette smoke. In movies the smoke was so thick you could barely see the angry faces glowering at you from across the table. But in Shadeland they apparently did things differently.

I sat in front of Bryce Cavanaugh's desk studying the chief's face. His hair wasn't gray exactly, but had rather gone that bluish black non-color that guys in their forties sometimes had. His eyes, I noticed, were a curious brown, very light and larger than average. Cavanaugh resembled an aging meerkat, only without the cuteness factor.

Mia waited about ten feet away, right across from one of Cavanaugh's deputies, a simpleton named Terry Schwarber. Terry was only twenty-six or twenty-seven, and was known to have been quite a hellraiser until a year ago when he joined the force. Now he was striving to act professional, but this new persona just didn't fit him. Schwarber had grown a mustache in order to appear older, but it looked fake, like something he'd glued on before leaving the house.

Of course, I couldn't be too critical of Schwarber's appearance. With the twin wads of cotton crammed up my nostrils, I looked pretty absurd myself.

Police Chief Cavanaugh hadn't started with me yet—he'd talked to Chris and Rebecca first, probably because their parents were anxious to get them home. Rebecca was frantic with terror, and though she never spoke the name aloud, I could tell the incident was dredging up all sorts of feelings about her baby sister. Kylie Ann's abduction wasn't like losing Emmylou again, but I suspect some of the old guilt Rebecca felt was resurfacing.

Barley came next. Cavanaugh's tone this time wasn't as polite, but it never crossed over into all-out hostility either. After talking to Barley, Cavanaugh had escorted him out, and I could see through the window the chief talking to Barley's dad. Probably angling for a good price on honey ham.

I heard Schwarber say to Mia, "How come you ladies were in the woods in the first place? Your mom said you were grounded."

I turned and listened.

"My mom didn't say that," Mia answered. "You must be thinking of Kylie Ann."

Schwarber frowned.

"The girl who was kidnapped?" Mia prompted.

Schwarber started. "Oh, I know that, I know that. What I meant was," and here he jerked a thumb at me, "didn't these tools get you in trouble once already?"

Mia's expression was dignified. To me she looked and sounded like a person twice her age. Certainly someone more mature than Terry Schwarber. "My mom and dad weren't happy about the way we left Rebecca's without asking, but it wasn't like we were out vandalizing people's houses. Or spray painting their windows."

Schwarber coughed loudly, his face reddening. As a teenager, he had been notorious for decorating his neighbors' windows with red spray paint.

I swallowed my lips to avoid smiling.

Schwarber cleared his throat. "Well anyway, I'd think you would've avoided bad influences."

"Nobody influenced me," Mia said. "I wanted to see Will, so I did. And he's not bad." She looked at me. "He's the opposite of bad."

It was my turn to blush. I resisted the urge to do cartwheels around the office.

Schwarber gave me a sour glance. "Believe me, the guys you're interested in now won't be the same guys you're interested in later on."

Mia said, "I don't think who I'm interested in is any of your business, Deputy Schwarber." She gestured toward her face. "And my eyes are up here."

Schwarber went a deeper shade of crimson.

At that point Police Chief Cavanaugh sauntered through the door. As he moved past Mia, he placed his hand on her bare shoulder in a way I didn't like. I know it sounds like I'm being possessive, but I was pretty sure I wasn't imagining it. More than once as I waited my turn to talk to the cops, I noticed Cavanaugh and Schwarber casting glances at Mia that lingered for much longer than I thought was appropriate. It had something to do, I suspected, with the air of maturity that attended her like a visible aura. Rebecca was pretty too, but it was the kind of pretty you'd expect from a fifteen-year-old. Mia, on the other hand, possessed an exotic quality that got men's attention whether they were her age or old enough to be her father. It made me want to protect her, of course, but more than that it made me want to kick someone's ass.

That wasn't the healthiest way for me to feel, given my current situation.

Cavanaugh eased down into his black swiveling chair across the desk from me. He arranged his nameplate, which was a block of wood with a burnished gold insert. POLICE CHIEF BRYCE P. CAVANAUGH, it read. I wondered what the P. stood for. Pedophile, maybe.

He adjusted his big calendar blotter, then he interlaced his fingers and favored me with a smile that didn't touch his eyes. "So you're the big hero."

I shrugged. "My name is Will Burgess."

"I know who you are. Your little sister's in the same class as my Annabelle."

I realized with a sinking feeling that I'd heard of Annabelle. Peach had never told me the girl's last name, but for several months she'd been complaining about an Annabelle who'd been making fun of her clothes, her pigtails, the way she talked. It had gotten so bad that Peach didn't want to go to school anymore, and I'm sorry, but that shouldn't happen to any kid, especially a freaking kindergartner. I'd told my mom about it dozens of times, but she'd always had the same answer: "Things like these have a way of working themselves out."

Which meant Peach was going to get bullied and no one was going to stick up for her.

Something must've shown in my face because Cavanaugh's grin widened. "Annabelle tells us that Audra doesn't get on well with other kids."

"It's Audr*ey*," I said, "and she prefers to go by Peach."

He made a pained face. "Never a good idea to name a kid after a piece of fruit."

112

"Furthermore," I said, my voice tightening, "Peach gets on fine with other kids. The ones who aren't nasty."

I expected a rise out of the chief then, but he only made a vague gesture. "Well, kids tend to weed each other out that way. What's it called? Self-selection?"

"I call it bad parenting."

Cavanaugh's grin evaporated. He glanced askance, and following his gaze, I realized that Schwarber and Mia were both watching us. Mia looked delighted.

Perhaps sensing he'd been shown up by a kid, Cavanaugh laughed what I assumed was meant to be a nonchalant laugh. "Are you comfortable, Miss?" he asked Mia.

Mia glanced at me, her eyes twinkling a little. "As long as Will's here."

Cavanaugh looked at Schwarber. "Then I assume you're ready to continue your discussion with her?"

Schwarber frowned at the chief, his already low IQ dropping about twenty points.

I said, "He means he wants you to stop eavesdropping."

Schwarber gave another of those pitiful little jolts and pretended to arrange the objects on his desk. "Yeah, well...where were we?"

I looked at the chief, who was anything but amused.

"Did you get a good look at him?" he asked.

I sobered, remembering why I was here: Kylie Ann.

"I didn't see him," I said. "Well, I saw a shape, but it was sort of blurry. And it was dark."

"So it could have been anybody."

"Well, it—"

"Or nobody."

I'm afraid my face went blank. "Excuse me?"

"Well, if you didn't see who it was, how do you know she was kidnapped?"

"I saw her dragged off the trail."

"By who?"

"I told you, I don't—"

"Or maybe you were being a little too forward and the Lubeck girl was trying to get away from you."

I felt like he'd kicked me in the gut.

Mia's voice was aghast. "Will was with *me*, he wasn't anywhere near—"

"Deputy Schwarber," Cavanaugh interrupted, "why don't you escort Miss Samuels to the waiting area. I'm sure her folks are eager to have her back."

Mia stalked toward the chief, her expression livid. "I want to know what you're implying."

Cavanaugh ignored her. "Terry?"

Like a trained monkey, Schwarber leapt to his feet and hurried over to Mia. He started to take her by the arm, but she ripped her arm away with a force that shocked me. "*Don't touch me!*" she snarled. She rounded on Cavanaugh. "You can't ignore what happened tonight, and you're damn well not going to blame Will just because he doesn't have anyone here to stick up for him."

It's hard to explain my feelings at these words. On one hand, I was a little moved by the way she was defending me. I couldn't remember anyone other than Chris caring enough to take my side in anything. But at the same time I felt a deep and burning shame, like I was some charity case.

Cavanaugh wore a patient smile as he rose and ushered Mia toward the door.

114

But to my astonishment, Mia was not to be put off. "Don't you touch me either!"

I spotted Mia's parents in the waiting area, which was little more than a glassed-in foyer. Her mom, from whom she obviously got her stunning looks, was wringing her hands in worry. Mia's dad, who was short and bald and obviously a lot older than Mia's mom, looked just as scared.

I reached out and took Mia's hand. Her head jerked toward me, and for a moment, I glimpsed the ferocity she'd been directing toward Cavanaugh and his deputy. Then her expression softened.

"It's okay," I said. "They know I didn't do anything to Kylie Ann. Isn't that right, Chief Cavanaugh?"

He looked like he'd swallowed something bitter. I could tell he wanted to argue, but he also knew if he did, he'd have Mia on his hands, which was roughly akin to wrestling a surly mountain lion. He said, "Miss Samuels, we merely want to talk to Mr. Burgess. There's nothing for you to fret about."

That wasn't exactly reassuring, I reflected, but it seemed to placate Mia somewhat. She made to leave with her parents, but before she did she said, "Don't let them take advantage of you, Will."

I smiled, thinking I'd marry her right then if I could. "Don't worry. I can handle them."

Schwarber gave me a freezing look, but the chief proceeded with the Samuels family out the door. For nearly a minute, Schwarber and I sat in uncomfortable silence. I considered asking him how he got his mustache so perfectly straight, but figured he wouldn't feel like sharing his grooming secrets. Finally, Cavanaugh reentered and resumed his position across from me.

"Now," he said, "how about we cut the bullshit, and you tell me exactly what happened in those woods?"

◆

As I had when they first picked us up, I went through the entire story from beginning to end, leaving nothing out. I even included a few details about my interactions with Mia, though they were none of Cavanaugh's business. Schwarber slouched a few feet away from the chief, a superior look on the deputy's face. He was a lot cockier with Cavanaugh's authority to back him up, though his questions weren't any more intelligent.

Schwarber said, "I'm not sure I'm understanding your explanation."

I looked at him. "Where are you getting lost?"

He spread his hands as if it were obvious. "Why didn't you stop the guy?"

"Are you really this stupid?"

He sat forward, "Look, you little piss ant, I don't need your—"

"What Terry means," Cavanaugh said, "is your story doesn't add up. If you saw where the kidnapper took the Lubeck girl, why didn't you do anything to stop him?"

"I *did* do something. Didn't Chris and the others tell you?"

"They told us the same crap you're telling us. That doesn't make it true."

"So we're all lying?"

He shrugged. "You guys get together, come up with some B.S. story..."

"Kids do it all the time," Schwarber said.

I nodded. "You'd know, of course."

Schwarber scowled at me.

"Okay," the chief said, enumerating his points on his fingers. "You witnessed her being taken, you gave chase. You lost sight of them, then you followed them into a thicket. But before you could save Miss Lubeck, something struck you in the face."

"That's right."

He made a clucking sound. "Pretty far-fetched."

I gestured to the ridiculous white cotton balls crammed up my nose. "You think I punched myself?"

"Why'd you give up then? Cavanaugh asked.

"I told you, I was dizzy. I had blood gushing out—"

"*I know what you told us,*" Cavanaugh snarled. "What I want to know is why you didn't get off your ass and save that girl from this so-called attacker?"

I narrowed my eyes. "Why do you keep saying 'so-called'?"

"Because we haven't found one sign of this supposed perpetrator."

"What about the state police?"

"The state police have got nothin' to do with this," Schwarber interjected. "This is a local matter."

Flabbergasted, I looked from one cop to the other. "You haven't told anybody? What about an amber alert?"

Cavanaugh said, "My men are on it as we speak. Bill Stuckey and his crew have been combing the area for the past two hours, and they've not found a trace of evidence to support your story."

"It isn't just *my* story," I said. "Four other people verified it. What the hell?"

"Watch your tongue, boy," Cavanaugh said, his eyes deadly cold.

But my wrath had come unbottled, and there was no way to stopper it again. "'*Boy*?" I said. "I thought they only talked like that in shitty movies."

"You need to show some respect for this office."

"This *office*?" I said, looking around. "Cheap wooden paneling and green paint straight out of the 1950s? This place is a joke, just like you." I nodded at Schwarber. "And you. Listen, that's the ugliest mustache I've ever seen. It looks like you glued a black pipe cleaner to your lip."

Schwarber looked furious enough to slug me then. He might have, if the front door hadn't opened. My stomach sank.

Bill Stuckey trudged toward us, his huge gut and barrel chest reminding me of an immense ocean barge. His craggy face was huge too, like some college mascot's. Like Cavanaugh, Stuckey was in his forties, but unlike Cavanaugh, Stuckey had never been to college. In fact, I'd be surprised if Stuckey had graduated from high school. From all the stories I'd heard, the guy made Terry Schwarber look like a neurosurgeon.

"Any luck, Bill?" Cavanaugh asked.

Rather than answering, Stuckey halted beside me, his crotch about an inch from my face. He smelled like mushrooms and old sweat. "The kid change his story yet?" Stuckey drawled.

"Still lying to us," Schwarber answered.

"Look," I said, shifting to avoid Stuckey's crotch and his withering mushroom stench. "Don't I get a phone call or something?"

Stuckey belly-laughed, a sound that reminded me of a horse whinny. "Phone call? You hear that, Chief?"

"I heard it," Cavanaugh said.

"Phone call," Schwarber said, giggling like an idiot.

I glanced from cop to cop, waiting for them to let me in on the joke.

"Am I...like, not even allowed to call my mom? This is still America, right?"

Cavanaugh looked at me blandly. "Your mom was notified you were here as soon as you arrived."

"And?"

"She didn't seem too concerned."

Thanks for caring, Mom, I thought. I sat forward, doing my best not to show how hurt I was by my mom's apathy. "So you're saying I'm free to go?"

"You're not a prisoner, Mr. Burgess. You can leave at any time."

I looked at the phone on the chief's desk. "I can call my mom?"

Schwarber grinned an ugly grin. "You that dense, kid? Your mom's conked out on the couch. Stuckey's the one who talked to her. Tell him, Bill."

Stuckey stifled a burp. "Terry speaks the truth. Your mama could barely keep her eyes open when I was there. She didn't really care what was happening as long as I let her sleep."

I felt like I'd been slapped. "What about Peach?"

"That the little girl?" Stuckey asked. "I barely saw her. She peeked around the corner now and then, but she looked too scared to come out of her room."

"Told you she didn't get on well with other people," Cavanaugh said.

I resisted an urge to leap across the desk and throttle the bastard.

Restraining myself with an effort, I got to my feet. "Can I have a ride home?"

Cavanaugh chuckled. "From one of *us*? Kid, we've got work to do. I've got to deal with the Lubecks, who're

beside themselves with worry. And if your story actually
is true, I'll have to contact the state authorities."

I stared at him, the implications of his words
sinking in. "How am I supposed to get home? It's the
middle of the night."

Stuckey said, "Hell, kid, it ain't that far. A few
miles at most, if you cut through the Hollow.

Oh man, I thought. *The Hollow.*

"Thanks for your help," I mumbled on my way to
the door.

"Don't mention it, kid," Cavanaugh said. "And
good luck getting back to that palace of yours."

The sounds of the deputies' laughter chased me
out of the station.

◆

After Kylie Ann's abduction and the crap I went
through with the police, I was sure my night couldn't get
any worse.

Then I beheld the black Mustang motoring down
Masonic Road, and I realized things were about to get
much worse.

Though my house was located near the end of
Masonic, it was a road I seldom traveled. When I was
coming home from a baseball game or the main part of
town, I either took River Road to the graveyard or cut
straight through the Hollow.

Tonight, I would have rather chopped off my
pinkie toe with a meat cleaver than cut through the
Hollow. I kept seeing that large, veiny hand clamping
over Kylie Ann's mouth.

Was the kidnapper still lurking nearby?

Masonic Road bordered the cemetery, and that
was enough to make me jumpy to begin with. Added to

that the fear of Kylie Ann's kidnapper, and I was downright terrified. So when I heard the thump of the car stereo, I assumed it was someone unfriendly. After all, how many people blasted rap music at three in the morning?

I turned and saw it was Eric Blades and his black Mustang.

Part of me wished it was the kidnapper instead.

My first instinct was to scream for help. I know how that sounds, and frankly, I don't care. I'd had enough trauma for one night, and I didn't want to deal with anything else. If my mom weren't such a loser, I would have been at home like my friends were. But I wasn't. I was by myself on a dark road on the edge of town with only a few scattered houses and a whole lot of dead people.

I bolted toward the dead people.

This might sound boneheaded, but it was actually strategic. Most people tend to avoid graveyards. I mean, they'll visit one when they want to remember their loved ones, but very few actually seek cemeteries out for recreation.

Chris, Barley, and I, however, hung out in the cemetery the way drunks hang around bars. Other than the treehouse, it was where we spent the most time. So I figured I'd have a major advantage if I cut through it. I had an intimate knowledge of the graveyard. I couldn't exactly navigate it with my eyes closed, but with the moonlight I figured I could make it through safely.

But when the driver gunned it and the Mustang rocketed down the road, I realized just how much danger I was in. I had been pretty sure it was Blades to begin with, but seeing the way he sped toward my house with the intention of cutting me off, I *knew* it was Blades. Now the only question was who was with him.

And whether they would beat me to my back door.

I chugged ahead, moving rapidly through the silent field of headstones. Unlike the woods, the graveyard was relatively flat. No roots to trip me up, no stinging rods of nettles to savage me as I barreled past.

I was thinking this as my foot caught on something and I face-planted in the dirt.

Dirt? I asked myself, my heart slamming in my chest. *There shouldn't be fresh dirt here, there should be grass.* But looking over my shoulder I glimpsed the newly tilled mound of earth, realized that with hundreds—maybe thousands of graves to choose from—I'd beelined for the recently excavated one.

I pushed up on my hands and knees, watched the Mustang nearing my house.

I wasn't going to make it.

No! I thought, real fury taking hold of me. I was sick and tired of getting the worst breaks. *I* was the one the cops had ganged up on. *I* was the one whose mom was such a stoner she wouldn't even crawl out of bed to pick me up. Now I was the one these goons had targeted during the small hours of the morning.

I blundered to my feet and pelted toward my yard.

The Mustang cut its lights. As it knifed down Masonic Road it reminded me of some vicious sea predator. A killer whale maybe. Only this thing was *all* black. The paint job, the rims, even the *fenders.*

I was forty yards from the house and closing. The Mustang was closer than that, but it had to turn, park, and the jerks had to get out before they could catch me.

I still had a chance.

I put my head down and pounded through the last row of graves. Then I was in my side yard, the sounds of car doors slamming to my right. I shot a look that way and saw Blades had parked in the driveway, which was more politeness than I'd expected from him. I wouldn't have been surprised to see him careening through the yard to sideswipe me.

I heard shouting voices. *Drunken* voices, I realized. Several of them.

I was ten yards from the back porch.

A sudden, horrible thought crashed down on me: What if Mom had locked the door?

No way, I thought as I mounted the steps. No way my luck could be *that* awful. Peach would never let her lock me out.

I gripped the knob, turned it. A dark figure swung around the edge of the house. Holding my breath, I pushed against the door.

It swung inward.

Gasping, I launched myself forward and felt something paw at my shirttail. Someone was shouting at me, laughing, all of this somehow sport to my pursuer. I cleared the door and made to slam it shut, but just before I could ram it home, some obstruction blocked it.

A voice howled in agony.

I bared my teeth in a grin, realizing I'd crushed someone's fingers in the door. There were three shapes at the base of the porch, another right in front of me howling and clutching his fingers. I braced myself on the doorframe, reared back, and kicked the howler in the chest. He went flailing backward and took out two of his companions. The one assailant still standing lunged forward, but I was too quick for him. I slammed the door in his face, and twisted the lock.

The assailant rattled the knob, pounded on the door, the blows heavy and determined. They might even wake up my mom, which was fine with me. Let her share in my misery for once.

I backed away from the door, recognizing the face in the windowpane.

Brad Ralston.

I'd never seen someone look so angry.

Or huge.

Other faces joined him in the windowpanes, reminding me of vampires in a blood frenzy. One belonged to Kurt Fisher. And a dark, scraggly face I didn't at first recognize.

Then I had it. Pete Blades, Eric's older brother.

Which meant Eric was the one whose fingers I'd crushed.

A new fear rose in me. What if my attackers wouldn't be content with scaring me? What if they shattered the windows and climbed into the house? What if they wanted to really injure me?

What if they hurt Peach?

It was this thought that galvanized me, sent me rushing over to the phone. I knew Cavanaugh and his men wouldn't help me, but the four assholes outside my house wouldn't know that. If they had any fear of the police at all, they'd scatter once they saw me calling for them.

Someone grabbed me from behind.

Hissing, I dropped the phone and whirled to face my new nemesis.

Peach stared up at me with huge eyes. She was grasping her blanket and one of her stuffed bears.

"Why did you sneak up on me like that?" I demanded, my heart thundering.

"I didn't sneak up," she said. "I heard people yelling and then the door slammed. I thought it was the monster."

I decided to disregard that last bit. Peach was always talking about monsters. "It was just a bunch of guys from school," I said, trying to make my voice as steady as possible. I glanced out the window and saw them heading back to the Mustang.

"See?" I said. "They were just messing around."

As usual, Peach saw through me. She always did.

"It didn't *sound* like they were messing around."

"Well, it's over now," I said, turning her toward the doorway. "And you should have been asleep hours ago."

"I couldn't," she said. "I told you, the monster kept me awake. And you weren't here."

"There are no monsters, Peach," I said, doing my best to choke down the guilt. We moved together down the hallway, my hands on her slender shoulders.

"But it was *real* this time."

We passed into our bedroom. I was unspeakably weary, but I knew it sometimes helped her to talk things out. "Okay, Peach. What did the monster look like?"

She sat down on the edge of her bed but made no move to get under the covers. I crouched before her and donned what I hoped was a patient expression.

She bit her lip, unwilling to make eye contact with me. I reached up, brushed a lock of hair off her forehead and said, "Tell me about it."

"It had a scary face. It was white. The eyes were big and green."

My heart threatened to stop in my chest.

She leaned toward me. "The eyes *glowed*, Will."

Holy God, I thought. *Holy God.*

Her words tumbled out, releasing now in a terrified flood. "I closed my eyes and hoped it was a nightmare, but when I opened them, it was right there, and it was *smiling* at me!" She pointed toward the window over my shoulder. I spun, certain I would see it too, the hideous green-eyed face.

But the only thing in the window was a ghostly scrim of clouds.

Chapter Seven

House Arrest, Basement, Hand

Mom woke up before we did. Of course, Peach and I slept in until almost noon, so it's not like this was a major accomplishment.

For the second time in as many days she had breakfast on the table. Waffles, syrup, and milk. Granted, this wasn't a gourmet meal—the waffles were straight out of a box—but the fact that Mom had cooked two days in a row was nothing short of remarkable. The sweet taste of syrup was soothing in my mouth, and the milk tasted cold and fresh. I realized with new amazement that she'd been to the store already today, and since it was Sunday, Barley's parents' store was closed until noon. That meant she'd driven all the way across town to Payless, the biggest grocery store in town. For most moms this would have been routine, but for mine it was tantamount to completing a transatlantic flight with a hang glider.

"I've been thinking," she said as she bustled from the table to the refrigerator to refill my milk, "that I should start going to my group again."

I stopped in mid-chew. Mom's group was like a more clandestine version of Alcoholics Anonymous, only this one was conducted in the basement of the Lutheran church and was meant for addicts of all kinds. At the behest of Child Protective Services she'd started going a couple years ago and had attended a grand total of two meetings. "Those junkies are nothing like me," she'd grumbled, proving exactly why she needed to go.

But now she sounded intent on returning.

I knew I needed to choose my words carefully. "Sure, Mom. Any time. You know I'll watch Peach."

She didn't meet my eyes, but I could see her face tremble on the edge of some powerful emotion. Guilt? Frustration? Gratitude?

Who knew? When it came to my mother, the normal rules of humankind didn't matter. She was a species unto herself.

"I know you will, Honey," she said, refilling my milk. "And I want you to know I appreciate all you do for your sister."

I could scarcely believe my ears.

I tried to play it off. "I don't mind hanging out with her," I said, reaching across the table and ruffling Peach's hair. "She's nuts, but I'll keep her around."

Mom smiled, and for a moment I glimpsed a flicker of the woman I'd known back when I was little. Before the car accident and the back injury that had started Mom on the prescription drugs and the cycle of self-destruction that still held our family hostage.

"Thank you, Will," Mom said, and then, unaccountably, she leaned over and kissed me on the forehead. When she straightened, wincing a little at the pain in her back, I saw Peach staring at me in shock. I stared back, my expression every bit as bewildered as hers. Then, we both began to smile.

For the first time in several days, I felt good.

Mom moved to the fridge and returned the milk to its shelf. She closed the fridge door, wincing again, and I realized she hadn't taken her pills this morning. That was why she was in so much discomfort, but it was also why she was so lucid. I know this sounds heartless, but I rather liked the trade-off. At least our family felt normal for once.

She ambled over to the sink and poured herself a glass of water. She said, "Will, I want to apologize for last night. I should have driven to the station to get you."

A sick heat began to build in the pit of my throat. I knew she was right to apologize, but for some reason the prospect of discussing last night's events appalled me. Mom's statement meant she remembered Bill Stuckey coming by. It meant she knew how negligent she'd been. She probably even realized I'd had to walk home in the middle of the night with a kidnapper on the loose in the immediate area. I knew I deserved her apology and a hell of a lot more, but I still didn't want to hear it. Not then. Things had been going too smoothly. I didn't want anything to disturb that feeling of normalcy.

But Mom was going on. "I failed you last night." She paused, stared down at her feet. "And while I can't go back and make it up to you, I can do better from now on." Her face crumpled, and she looked at me with tear-filled eyes. "I'm so sorry, Honey."

Overwhelmed, I couldn't speak. Peach was watching me closely, her brown eyes bigger than ever, but I was no longer able to return her stare. I couldn't even chew my waffles. The syrup had congealed in my throat.

"And that means," Mom went on, "that I can't let you leave the house today."

I frowned at her.

"It's not a punishment, Will," she rushed on. "Please believe that. It's to keep you safe. All signs point to that...escaped *killer* being the one who took Kylie Ann Lubeck, and that means no child is safe. Not until he's apprehended."

"Mom, I..."

I trailed off, seeing the look in her face. Her lips quivered. Her cheeks started to dimple. Then she was cupping her mouth. Her shoulders spasmed. Fat tears spilled over her bottom lids.

I felt like throwing up. I didn't know whether to leave the room, to comfort her somehow, or to simply look away.

I looked away.

My sister asked, "Are you okay, Mommy?"

Mom coughed out a sob. "Mommy's fine, Sweetie. And so are you two, thank God. No thanks to me. But now we'll set up some ground rules to make sure you *stay* safe."

I didn't like the sound of that, but then again, the whole atmosphere in the kitchen was off to me—Mom's weeping, my own confused emotions, even the lighting was peculiar, the sky outside having gone a sickly shade of yellow. Distantly, I remembered Barley's comment about the impending storm, how cataclysmic it was supposed to be.

"I don't want either of you leaving the house," Mom said. "Not without me."

"We can't even go outside?" Peach whined.

"You can go outside if Will is with you, but under no circumstance are you to leave the yard. And neither one of you should leave the other's sight."

"And where will you be? Sleeping?" I asked before I could stop myself.

Mom cringed a little, but she didn't get mad. "I deserve that. I'd be angry at me too. I'll do better from now on."

I watched her dubiously.

"I promise, Will," she said, wiping her eyes. "I'm going to change. I just...I just need your help, okay?"

I had absolutely no faith in her but decided it was pointless to argue. If her resolution lasted a day or two, that would at least be a change in our pitiful routine. Up until that point, I'd assumed my mom would be a drugged-out zombie for the rest of her life. Having her back was kind of a novelty.

But I refused to indulge in false hope. I'd been burned too many times.

"From now on," Mom continued, "we check in with each other every hour. If I have to go somewhere—today's Sunday, so I should be around most of the day—but if I do go somewhere, I'll tell you."

"You go back to work tomorrow," I pointed out.

"Which makes it all the more important that you and Peach stick together."

"Yay!" Peach said, bouncing in her seat.

I eyed her good-humoredly, some of the weirdness in the kitchen dissipating. I didn't particularly like my mom suddenly playing the role of house overlord, but maybe, I decided, this was part of it, part of her rehabilitation. I still only gave it about a two percent chance of sticking—she'd vowed to get straight before—but if telling us what to do made her feel more in control of her life, then I'd go along with it. The yellow haze in the sky foretold bad weather anyway. I was sure my friends would be housebound as well, so what else was I going to do? Roam the streets of Shadeland and hope that Eric Blades and his evil-looking Mustang didn't veer around a corner and turn me into road kill?

"Can you swing me on the goon-goon?" Peach asked.

I chuckled. "Sure."

The goon-goon was Peach's name for the rope swing I'd rigged on a big sycamore branch in the back yard. It was only about twenty feet from the woods, and right next to the graveyard, but it would be broad daylight, and we'd be together. I acted like I was only humoring Peach, but deep down I was looking forward to it. It was kind of fun spinning her on the swing and watching her hair whip around like a pinwheel. She made this high-pitched, delighted squeal too, which was sort of entertaining.

Mom was smiling at us from the sink. She was grasping a coffee mug, the steam rising around her face.

It was a good moment, the kind we'd had too little of as a family.

It was a moment I'd look back on later after everything good in my life was destroyed.

◆

"Higher," Peach demanded.

I realized I'd been drifting, my eyes on the graveyard and my mind on last night's mad dash to the porch. Despite how long Peach and I had slept in, I was severely sleep-deprived, and when I felt that way, my whole personality was altered. I was quieter, first of all, in a mood Mrs. Herbert would have deemed *taciturn*. I was also more emotional, which really bothered me. I hated crying, but the truth was, I cried a lot more than the average guy. Chris and Barley knew that about me, and they never mocked me for it, but it still annoyed the hell out of me when it happened. Like I was defective or something. I couldn't help wonder if I'd cry as much if I'd had a father in the house growing up. People who had fathers took them for granted, but I felt that absence nearly every day.

I wasn't close to tears now, however. Quite the opposite. As I pushed Peach harder and then backpedaled out of the way so she wouldn't kick me in the face, I thought of Kylie Ann, of the hand that had shot out of the darkness last night and closed over her mouth.

I didn't like Kylie Ann much. Okay, I didn't like her at *all*, but that didn't mean I wanted her to get kidnapped. Part of me had been tempted to turn on the TV to see if it was on the news, but I'd refrained, maybe because I knew I'd feel responsible for her abduction. I knew I'd done my best—I had pursued them after all, and gotten punched in the nose for my troubles—but that didn't lessen the sting of failing. And now she was...

I shuddered, mentally retreating from the horrid possibilities.

I looked up and saw Peach's face, which was crimped in a look of pain. "What's wrong?" I asked.

She swept by me on the goon-goon, her body twirling. "Tummy ache," she moaned. "I think I have to go to the bathroom."

"Ah."

When she swung toward me again I snagged the rope, steadied her as quickly as I could without hurling her off the swing, and helped her off the goon-goon. Clutching her belly, she hurried toward the back door.

I found myself alone in the yard. I remembered Mom's directive—*Don't let each other out of your sight*—and drifted toward the house. I knew I was in no real danger; whoever had taken Kylie Ann—even if it had been Carl Padgett—wasn't going to strike in the middle of the day. Padgett was The *Moonlight* Killer, after all. And no other criminal would have the guts to go after a kid like me who was already in high school. Not in broad daylight.

I hoped.

My eyes glided toward the alcove between the porch and mom's bedroom window. It was just a small space in which we stored the wheelbarrow and some of our old toys. I headed in that direction, moving aimlessly and with nothing much on my mind except the hope that Peach had made it to the toilet before her bowels uncorked. I was the one who cleaned up messes.

I reached the alcove, studied the rusty tricycle, a cracked whiffle ball bat.

To the right of those things, the mossy stairwell to the basement.

I hadn't ventured down those steps in maybe a year, and then it had only been to relight the pilot light on our ancient water heater. But today something felt different. Maybe it was all I'd gone through in the past forty-eight hours. Being threatened by Brad and his buddies. Seeing Kylie Ann abducted. Or being cracked in the face by her kidnapper.

It occurred to me that no one had ever asked me if I was okay. You got hit in the head in baseball or any other sport and they performed a dozen tests to make sure you didn't have a concussion. Yet they didn't check you if you got your bell rung by a dangerous criminal? Where was the logic in that?

For whatever reason though, the gloomy basement stairwell didn't look as menacing this morning as it usually did, and I found myself striding down the steep steps, my nostrils already picking up the dank odor wafting up from the nearly lightless dungeon.

I opened the door and was assaulted with the vile aromas of stagnant water, unwholesome grime, and a vague tinge of sewage. I also glimpsed one of my least favorite things, the rainwater cistern meant to prevent the basement from flooding. A circular black hole in the concrete, I'd always imagined a demon, or maybe Satan himself emerging from its depths.

I went inside anyway, figuring Peach would be on the toilet for at least ten more minutes. She took her time doing her business anyway, and when she had a stomachache she could kill a whole hour in there with no problem. This wouldn't have been an issue if we'd had more than one bathroom, but if someone was in there, you either had to hold it or go in the woods.

Many times I'd ended up going in the woods.

But today I didn't have to go at all. In fact, despite all I'd been through, I felt strangely content. Mom's decree to stay in the house was, in a bizarre way, kind of liberating. I could laze around here without feeling like I was missing out on something elsewhere.

But I was feeling more than that.

I've read about these things called dowsing rods, this phenomenon involving branches that help people find water underground. I felt a little like a dowsing rod at that moment. There was a tingling in my bones, like I was catching the residual electricity from a nearby power transformer. Whether this was a premonition or not, I don't know. All I know is when I spotted the old boxes piled on a rotting wooden shelf on the far wall of the basement, that mental dowsing rod jerked down and told me I'd found what I was looking for. Moving with the surety of some primitive instinct, I cut through the scattered debris Mom had abandoned down here—my Thomas the Train push-along car, Peach's first crib, a microwave that had ceased working long ago—and knelt before the shelf.

The boxes were stacked two high. Flanking them were dented paint cans I was sure had long since dried up. I selected one of the boxes. It was damp. About six inches high and a couple feet wide. I made to lift it, but it was pretty heavy, and I had an idea it might come apart in my hands if I tried to lug it upstairs. I dragged the box toward me instead and eased it down on the clammy concrete. I brushed away a membrane of cobwebs and wrinkled my nose at all the desiccated flies and ladybugs collected in the gob of webs. I opened the box gingerly, suspicious of brown recluse spiders and other unpleasant surprises. But other than the musty stench, the only things I discovered within were my old school projects, a few of them dating back to kindergarten. There was a misshapen clay bowl painted green and black. That one, I was pretty sure, had been a Mother's Day gift back in first grade. I found a whole folder full of graded assignments, most of them spelling tests and quizzes on addition and subtraction, and a few early writings mixed in too. One was a report I'd done on tsunamis back in third grade. Another I remembered fondly from the same year: a stapled book I'd created about wolves that featured original artwork, pictures I'd snipped from magazines, and a few scientific facts I'd copied from the encyclopedia. Nobody cared if you plagiarized in the third grade.

All of it would have been really cool and nostalgic if not for the fact that it was beginning to rot or crumble because of the conditions down here. It pissed me off that Mom didn't care enough to preserve these items in a closet upstairs. Disgustedly, I shoved the contents back inside the box and plopped it on the shelf. If my childhood memories didn't matter to Mom, I reasoned, why should they matter to me?

A distant part of me said that was dumb logic, but at the moment I didn't care. It hurt my feelings. It seemed Mom was always hurting my feelings. Or maybe I was just too emotional, and I needed to be tougher.

I was preparing to leave when the dowsing rod dipped again.

By their own volition, my hands reached out and grasped another box, this one on the bottom shelf. This box was bigger, heavier, and when I tried to handle it the same way I had the last one, a huge flap disintegrated in my grip. I squatted closer to the box, moved it with greater caution, and soon it was sitting before me on the concrete.

Every molecule of my body thrumming, I spread the moist flaps of lid and wrinkled my nose at the reek that puffed out of the box. Rather than old math assignments and science reports, this box appeared to be crammed with newspaper clippings. The first one showed my mom as a 4-H fair queen.

Or first runner-up, I amended. The clipping was damp, but it revealed a completely different woman than the one I knew. This version of Michelle Burgess was smiling, attractive, and—I admit that this weirded me out a little—well, *curvy*. There were four or five pictures like it from the local newspapers, but though I could still read the captions beneath the pictures, the moisture down here had begun to fade the words. At least my mom was an equal-opportunity neglector; she didn't care enough about herself to preserve these either.

Beneath the fair queen articles I found several items that perplexed me. There was a photo of Barley's family's store, its grand-opening from more than twenty years ago. There was an article about some real estate agent starting his own office. I'd never heard of him.

I dug deeper into the pile, noticing that there were several clippings that featured the real estate agent. His name was Ted Dexter. He looked like an actor from some eighties sitcom. He had feathered hair and a big smile. Many of the clippings were just advertisements for Ted Dexter Realty.

Below, I found other familiar faces. My baseball coach. The superintendent of our schools, Jim Blades, who back then was an industrial tech teacher. There was an article about a teenage girl who disappeared sixteen years ago. A really old shot of a younger and thinner Bryce Cavanaugh, who was shooting a jump shot for the Shadeland High School basketball team.

Then I came to a picture that made my skin gather into goose flesh.

Carl Padgett.

The date at the top of the page was from seventeen years ago.

The sight of the Moonlight Killer as he was back then was more than a little chilling. From outward appearances he seemed like a normal guy. What was more, I realized with dawning amazement, he *had* been a normal guy back then. Or at least everyone had believed him to be normal. The three clippings in which he was featured showed him at various groundbreakings: a local restaurant that had since gone out of business. A Baptist church and a gas station. Padgett looked normal in every respect, from his button-down shirts to his bushy sideburns and jovial grin.

He looked nothing like the man who murdered nine children.

Wait a minute, I thought. The articles were all local, which meant, at the very least, that Carl Padgett had spent time in Shadeland. Not only that, I thought as I shuffled the pictures, but he'd shared at least a passing acquaintance with many of the same people I knew.

Had Padgett once lived in my town?

"*What are you doing?*" a voice yelled.

I shrieked in terror and tossed about a dozen clippings into the air.

"Will Burgess," my mom said, her voice fast approaching, "you promised me you'd watch your sister!"

I scrambled to shove the clippings back inside the box, but I could hear her footsteps right behind me, and there were still half a dozen scraps of paper lying about.

"What are you—" she began to ask, then I heard a sharp intake of breath. *"You have no right to look at those!"*

I was so stunned by the force of her anger that I found myself cowering before her. Never mind that I was a good deal taller than she was—at that moment I might as well have been Peach's size.

She elbowed past me, began stuffing the remaining clips into the box. Then, without regard to the fragile state of the moist cardboard, she hoisted the whole thing back onto the shelf and slammed down the lid with pointed fury.

She brandished an index finger. "Don't you *ever* come down here again. These things are none of your business."

Ordinarily I would have been enraged by being spoken to like that, but this was no ordinary moment. I had the feeling that if I attempted to question her about the contents of the box, she might well lose it completely.

My belly churning, I made for the basement door.

"Chris is on the phone," she muttered.

I turned and blinked at her in the semidarkness. "Huh?"

She gave me a mordant look. "Chris Watkins? Your best friend? He's on the phone. It's why I came looking for you. You left the door open. Otherwise I never would've known you failed to watch your sister."

139

This was too much. "I didn't *fail* Peach. I do more for her than you do every damn day, and you know it."

My voice sounded frail and croaky, but despite mom's anger with me, she seemed to realize she'd gone too far.

She blew out a long, frustrated breath. "I know you didn't mean...look, Will, just don't go snooping again, okay?"

I said nothing.

She searched my face. "How much did you...oh, never mind. You better talk to Chris."

Alarms went off in my head. "Is something wrong?"

She hesitated. "I think it has to do with the Lubeck girl."

◆

"Chris?" I asked. "You there, man?"

His voice was subdued. "Hey, Will."

With a sinking feeling, I realized Mom had probably been right. I didn't want to ask the question, but I did anyway.

"Any news on Kylie Ann?"

"You haven't heard?"

"Uh-uh," I said. "Is it bad?"

He didn't answer for so long I feared we'd been disconnected. Then, I heard him sigh. "Yeah. It is."

With a new tug of misgiving I realized he was struggling to keep his voice under control.

"Come on, man, what's going on?"

For the billionth time I rued my family's lack of technology. How many kids in the western hemisphere didn't have access to the Internet or a cell phone? I was the last person to find out everything. Like I was some pioneer who'd time-traveled to the twenty-first century.

"It isn't good, Will. They don't know for sure, but if it's true, it's really..."

"*What* isn't good? Would you just spit it—"

"They found something."

My body turned to stone. I sat there staring at the kitchen wall and repeated the words in my head: *They found something. They found something. They...*

"Chris," I said slowly, "are you telling me they found evidence of the kidnapping?"

He said, "You know how Dad always has his scanner on?"

I did. Since Chris's dad was a lawyer, he made it his business to know anything that happened in Shadeland as quickly as possible. As a result, he often kept the police scanner on for long periods of time. I assumed that Chris, having nothing else to do today, had staked out a spot near the scanner in the hopes of hearing some news about Kylie Ann.

"Anyway," Chris went on, "it was Deputy Schwarber who found it. Dumb luck, I guess. They were searching down by the creek, just a few hundred yards from where Kylie Ann was...you know."

"Taken," I said.

"Uh-huh."

I swallowed. "You said Schwarber found *it*, but you haven't told me what he found. That's kind of an important—"

"Her hand, Will. They found her left hand."

Chapter Eight

Dark House and a Ghastly Memory

If Mom's attendance at work had been better, she
could have stayed home with us the next day. Problem
was, her attendance over the past several years, like her
parenting, had sucked ass. Which meant she was about
a half step from being fired.

She explained to us through tears of humiliation
that she'd arranged all-day play dates for us that
Monday. Peach was to spend the day with Juliet
Wallace; I was to hang out with Chris. But today, the
notion of spending the day at Chris's made me sick in
the pit of my stomach.

Because I didn't want to be separated from Peach.

The Wallace's were good people. Mrs. Wallace
was a stay-at-home mom, and she adored my little
sister. Several times she'd pulled me aside to tell me
how thankful she was for me and the way I cared for
Peach.

But I wouldn't be caring for her today. Today
she'd be several miles out of town. And as mom dropped
her off at the Wallaces, I couldn't shake the feeling that
I was making a grave mistake.

After Chris's bombshell about Kylie Ann
yesterday, I hadn't let my little sister leave my sight.
When Mom put her to bed at around 8:30, I turned on
the TV and got the full story on the abduction.

Carl Padgett, it turned out, had been spotted and
positively identified on the south side of Indianapolis,
which was ninety minutes from Shadeland, on Sunday
morning. That meant that if Padgett had been the one

to kidnap Kylie Ann, he'd either killed her and left her in Shadeland, taken her with him to Indianapolis, or freed her somewhere in between.

On the way over to Chris's, I ran through it in my head. Every time I did, the same scenario played out: Padgett grabbed Kylie Ann, knocked me over the head, and then carried her deeper into the Hollow, where he'd lopped off her hand and then...what? How did you get inside the mind of someone so twisted? Why would Padgett sever a girl's hand and then take her somewhere else?

The only answers were too awful to stomach.

The more I thought about it, the sicker I felt. Kylie Ann had been a beautiful girl. Icy, yes. Stuck-up for sure. But beautiful. And just the type to enflame the perverted mind of someone like Carl Padgett.

Back before he'd been apprehended, he'd murdered nine children between the ages of five and fifteen. Most were girls, but there were a couple boys too. In every case he'd left a piece of their bodies behind. A foot. A hand. A finger.

It had to be Padgett who'd taken Kylie Ann.

"You okay, kiddo?" Mom asked.

I was leaning against the passenger's window, watching the houses get nicer and nicer as we drove through Chris's neighborhood.

"I'm sorry I can't be home today," Mom said, "but you know Ron."

I grunted sourly. Yes, I knew Ron. Even though my mother's looks had begun to deteriorate over the past few years, her boss still looked at her like a juicy cut of prime rib. He always called me "Champ" and mussed my hair, a habit that suggested that the sum of his experience with children had come from watching crappy movies.

I wished Ron would have an aneurism.

"I'll pick you guys up by five," Mom said. "Okay?"

In my periphery I could see her hopeful stare. I knew it was petty, but I was mad at her for her prior bad attendance, for backing herself into this corner. Because now that we needed her, she couldn't be here.

Stop it, I told myself. *Remember that she's trying. She can't undo everything at once. You've got to be patient with her, especially now.*

I knew all that was true, but the best I could muster was a "Fine."

She watched me a moment longer, then smiled sadly.

Soon I was ringing Chris's doorbell. His mom answered.

I turned and waved at Mom. She waved back, beeped, then made a slow U-turn out of the Watkins's huge driveway.

"Hello, Will," Mrs. Watkins said. Her expression was polite, but little more than that.

Feeling awkward, I stuffed my hands in my pockets, said, "Thanks for letting me come over today. I know it's a bad time."

Some of her reserve seemed to go away, and her smile became less forced. "It'll be good for both of you. I know Chris needs to take his mind off of..." She let the thought fade to nothing.

Once inside the house, Chris led me up the curving staircase.

"Aren't we going to the basement?" I asked.

He spoke over his shoulder as he neared the top of the stairs. "Foosball can wait. I've got a surprise for you."

"You learned to pee standing up?"

In answer, he saluted me with a middle finger.

144

We entered his room and I noticed the computer was on. What was more, the tiny green light at the top of the monitor was glowing, signifying he'd been Skyping someone when I'd shown up. But whoever he'd been talking to was gone, and the only thing showing on the monitor was an empty chair and an unfamiliar kitchen.

"That's not Barley's house," I said.

Chris only grinned, leaned toward the monitor. "You still there?" he asked.

"Hold on," a muffled voice replied, and I felt my belly do a little tap dance. *No way*, I thought. *It can't be.*

Mia appeared on the monitor, looking flushed and incredibly full of life.

"Hey, Will," she said.

I realized I was standing behind the chair and only my midsection was showing. How she knew it was me, I had no idea. Were my clothes that identifiable? My stomach and hips?

I remembered how she'd touched my hip.

"Sit down, dipshit," Chris said in a harsh whisper.

I sat down. And looked at Mia.

Her smile broadened. "It's great to see you!"

She bit her lip and gave a nervous shrug. "I should probably be a little less enthusiastic, huh? Given the circumstances."

Chris said, "Anything new on Kylie Ann?"

Mia shook her head. "Nothing. Did you hear Padgett was spotted in Indy?"

"Yeah," I said. "That's good news, isn't it?"

She looked troubled. "I don't know. It's only good news if they find Kylie Ann, right?"

There was a long, painful silence.

She hugged herself, shivered. "Let's talk about something else. Where's your sister today?"

I told her.

She smiled. "I like how you call her Peach."

I like how you breathe, I wanted to say.

"So...how are you gonna spend your day?" I asked.

Mia appeared to search the room behind me. "Is Chris still there?"

"Not at the moment," I said. Which was true enough. He'd apparently gone downstairs for a snack or something. Or perhaps he was in the bathroom dropping the kids off at the pool.

"Good," she said. "I want to show you something."

I had an ungentlemanly thought, then felt a rush of guilt. "Go ahead," I said in a hoarse voice.

"Hold on," she said. She got up and disappeared. I felt an irrational sense of loss. I knew she'd be back, but having her in front of me—even on a computer—had filled a void I wasn't aware had existed. I knew what I was feeling was what most would describe as a crush, or more nauseatingly, puppy love, but deep down I knew it was more than that. I'd known Mia Samuels since the second grade, and though we'd never dated, I'd always looked at her differently than other girls. There was something genuinely good about her, something real. Not to mention the fact that she was the prettiest girl I knew.

I was remembering Mia in her black bra when she reappeared.

I blushed, hoping what I'd been thinking didn't show in my face.

"Here it is," she said. She was clutching a multi-colored notebook with stickers and tassels and all sorts of wild shapes adorning its cover. "I wanted you to see I wasn't lying."

"Lying about what?"

Rather than answering, she started to read, "'He's lost in his thoughts most of the time, so it's a good thing he looks so cute when he goes to that remote mental place. He reads a lot, I can tell. When he talks, he sounds like someone twice our age. His eyes are the nicest shade of blue, and though he never combs it, I love his dark hair.'"

I realized with a combination of elation and disbelief that she was talking about me.

She grinned at my reaction and went on. "'He thinks I don't notice him, but I do. Sometimes I catch him looking at me. He always looks away before I can smile at him. But that's probably a good thing. Brad can't stand him, and if Brad knew how I felt about Will, he'd probably try to kill him."

You don't know how true that is, I thought.

She continued, "'He always leaves English before me, which I like. Rebecca and I walk behind him and Chris so we can watch them. Sometimes Rebecca and I argue about which one has a nicer butt. I'm right, of course, but Rebecca thinks—"

She cut off, looking anxious. "I thought I heard something."

"Is there more?" I asked, dry-mouthed.

"Maybe," she said, looking mischievous. "Do you want to hear it?"

"Uh-huh," I croaked.

She smiled her dazzling smile, turned the page. She scanned it until she settled on a passage and read, "'Whenever I break up with Brad, I hope Will doesn't have a girlfriend. I'd love to...'"

I sat forward. "Love to what?"

She looked at me primly. "It's a little bit personal, if you must know."

"I don't mind personal."

"I'm sure you don't," she said. Her look sent lightning bolts through my stomach.

She read, "'I'd love to know what his kisses are like. I bet he's gentler than Brad. Of course, a Shop-Vac would be gentler than Brad.'"

We both laughed.

Mia composed herself and went on. "'When I imagine kissing Will, I think...'" She broke off, frowning. "I can't read this part out loud. It makes me feel like I'm a prostitute."

My heart was thudding. "I don't think that about you. Really, I'd like to hear more."

"*Will*," she said.

"Please?"

"It's *embarrassing*."

I knew I should let her off the hook, but my pulse was racing too fast, my excitement over her too great. I'd never really had a girlfriend before, and though Mia wasn't my girlfriend—not yet, at least—I was beginning to understand how nice it might be. "Look," I said, "just pretend you're not the one who wrote it."

"But I did write it."

"I know, but tell yourself you didn't. Pretend you're reading a novel."

She arched an eyebrow. "A romance novel?"

"Or an action-adventure book."

She snorted laughter.

"And Will," I went on, "isn't me. It's this strapping hero the main character has a crush on."

She tilted her head. "Is that what you think, Will? That I have a crush on you?"

Hell, I thought. "It isn't you, remember? It's the main character."

"Who happens to be named Mia."

"It's a fabulous name," I said. "You two just happen to share it."

She smiled at me. Embarrassed, I could tell, but enjoying herself too. She straightened in her chair, crossed her legs, and read, "'When I imagine kissing Will, I think of the water. The lake, maybe, warm and smooth. He has his shirt off and—" She broke off, glancing up at the ceiling with maddening coyness.

"Go on," I said, trying to keep the pleading note out of my voice.

She sighed. "'—and so do I.'"

My body turned to rubber.

She looked up at me in a way that did not make her look like a teenager at all. I tried not to fall out of my chair.

"'His skin is warm. His arms are around me, and even though they're thin, they're strong. Will kisses me tentatively at first, but then he relaxes, and we kiss more passionately. And...and...'" She shut the notebook with a pop. "I'm sorry, but I'm *not* reading the next part. There's no way I can pretend some action-adventure author wrote that." She stared at me. "Well?"

Not knowing what else to say, I murmured, "When did you write that?"

The ghost of a smile played at her lips. "Two months ago."

◆

The conversation went wonderfully, but toward the end of it I started to think about how unfair it was that I could only use a computer when I was at Chris's or Barley's house. I tried not to show it, but the thought stuck in my brain like a pesky burr. And as sometimes happened, I found myself feeling resentful toward Chris even though he'd done nothing wrong.

"Must be nice to have a new Mac," I said when my Skype session ended.

Chris glanced at his new computer uneasily. "It's okay."

I knew it was nasty, but I said it anyway. "I guess I wouldn't be excited either if I got everything I wanted."

"Come on," he said, "you know that's not—"

"The hell it isn't," I barked. "You try being the poor kid everybody makes fun of. The one the cops are mean to. The one who got his nose bloodied by some psychopath in the woods."

Chris scowled at me. "Don't you think I'd rather that have been me?"

And the way he said it, I knew he was telling the truth. It reminded me of something that had happened in the first grade. Three of us boys were in the bathroom. Me, Chris, and a kid named George Gates. We'd finished lunch, and the kindergartners were getting ready to eat. But before they did, a few of them needed to use the restroom.

George got the bright idea to hold the doors shut so the younger kids couldn't get inside. Before I knew it, I was blocking the doors and laughing along with George. Chris was in a stall going number two and didn't even know what we were doing. And as the pounding on the other side of the bathroom doors grew more frantic, part of me realized how stupidly we were behaving. But it wasn't until one of the kids outside wet his pants and told a teacher what we'd done that I realized how horrible my behavior was.

Ten minutes later we were all three outside the principal's office. George went in first and got paddled so hard that *my* butt began to ache. Moments later,

George stumbled out, sobbing, and Chris was called in to talk to Mr. Carroll, our gargantuan, paddle-wielding principal. I was sure Chris would tell him the truth, that he'd been in the stall the whole time and that he'd had nothing to do with the kindergartner wetting his pants. But the concussive sound of the wooden paddle connecting with Chris's rear end told me otherwise.

Several smacks later, Chris exited the office with tears in his eyes. Mr. Carroll followed. The hulking man looked down at me and said, "You can go back to class now, Will."

And that was it.

When I finally got up the nerve to ask Chris why he'd confessed to something he hadn't done, he gave me a funny look, like I'd insulted him by asking the question.

"One of us had to get paddled, right?" he said.

And now, sitting on Chris's bed, having just treated my best friend like crap for no reason at all, I realized that yes, Chris truly did wish he had been the one who'd come face-to-face with Kylie Ann's abductor. Not so he could be a hero, but so I wouldn't have had to suffer.

He was a better friend than I could ever hope to be. A better person.

I exhaled shuddering breath, disgusted with myself. "I guess Kylie Ann's in worse shape than I am, huh?"

Chris didn't say anything to that. The silence drew out.

My shoulders slumped. "Sorry for being such a dick."

He shrugged one shoulder. "You can't help it. You were just born that way."

I raised my middle finger at him, and we both chuckled softly.

It went a little way toward defusing the tension I'd created, but not nearly enough. Maybe to break up the morose mood we were in, we decided to play catch in Chris's huge back yard. As we moved through the kitchen, we spotted Chris's mom watching the TV that folded out from beneath a cabinet.

Chris said, "Have they found any sign of Kylie Ann?"

Chris's mom didn't remove her eyes from the screen. "They've combed the woods, but they can't find anything. It rained in the morning, so the dogs are having trouble picking up her scent."

"What about Padgett?" Chris asked.

"I think he's long gone," she replied. "He's too smart for them."

"Oh you think that, do you?" a voice half-shouted from behind us. We all turned in surprise and saw Chris's dad stalking forward, his fingers white on the coffee mug he grasped.

Chris's mom paled. "I was only saying that if they haven't found him yet, they might not—"

"He's a real *hero*, isn't he?" Mr. Watkins snapped. "Chopped off that girl's hand and left it in the woods. What do you think he did to her before he killed her?"

Chris's mom flinched and glanced at Chris, who was watching his dad with wide-eyed dread. "I think the boys are scared enough without—"

"You're the one complimenting the son of a bitch, Caroline," Mr. Watkins said, his mouth splitting in a nasty grin. "So don't go telling me what I can and can't say in my own house."

I looked up at Mr. Watkins, for the first time noticing just how large he was. He had a big gut on him, and I was pretty sure he was on the verge of a heart attack. But he was also nearly six-and-a-half feet tall and imposing as hell. Looming over his wife, he reminded me of a grizzly bear about to maul a defenseless camper.

Looking like she was going to puke, Mrs. Watkins put a hand on each of our backs and led us away. "You two better go outside," she murmured.

I nodded, eager to go, but Chris's look of dread changed to one of outright terror. "We can wait, Mom. You don't need to stand there and let him yell at you."

"And you can shut your goddamned mouth!" Mr. Watkins snapped, his face going a livid red. "You've already caused enough trouble."

Chris looked at his dad, stricken. But I managed to get him outside. As the door wheezed shut, I heard Mr. Watkins growl, "Why the hell is that Burgess kid over here? You think that deadbeat is doing our son any good?"

My cheeks burned as I moved down the porch steps, but Chris was standing on the second step gazing through the screen door.

"Come on, man," I said. "Let's throw each other pop flies."

Chris didn't answer. I could see his chest heaving.

His father's raised voice echoed through the door, reminding me of distant thunder. Chris's mom said something in response, her tone suggesting an apology, though what she had to apologize for I had no clue.

We heard a flat, meaty smack. Chris's shoulders hunched, his expression one of physical pain.

Oh God, I thought. I went toward Chris, reached up to touch his elbow, but dropped my hand when I realized I had nothing to say. What could I say? Sorry your dad's abusing your mom?

The dull smacking sound came again. Chris whimpered.

What's wrong with people? I thought weakly. *What kind of a man would do that to a woman? And why does Chris have to live with him?*

I put a hand on Chris's shoulder. "We'll figure this out."

"It never ends," he whispered. I could see his bottom limp trembling.

"It will," I said, knowing how lame that sounded. I squeezed his shoulder. "It's not your fault, but we'll make sure—"

"Yes it is!" he growled. "It *is* my fault."

My eyes began to sting. I gripped his shoulders, squared up to him, and said in a low firm voice, "You didn't make this happen—your dad did. We'll tell somebody, find a way to put a stop to it."

"I'll put a stop to it right now," he said.

Pushing away from me, Chris gripped the door handle and started to twist it. I have no idea what Chris would have done had he confronted his dad the way he apparently intended to, but the sound of the doorbell prevented the confrontation from occurring.

Chris's dad grumbled something. I followed Chris inside, and we discovered Chris's mom weeping in the kitchen, her bottom lip split and bleeding. Chris made to put his arms around her, but she pulled away, her eyes fierce. *"Don't touch me."*

"Mom," Chris said, his voice unsteady. "You have to—"

"Don't tell me what I have to do," she said distractedly. "That's your father's job, remember?"

She stormed out, leaving her son staring after her with tears on his cheeks.

I wanted to comfort Chris but the right words eluded me. The painful silence was interrupted by the sounds of conversation emanating from the foyer. Without making eye contact with each other, Chris and I followed the voices.

And were met with a pair of policemen, state troopers from the looks of them. They stood across from Mr. Watkins in the foyer, looking like the antithesis of the Shadeland police force. Instead of the stubborn malice of Bryce Cavanaugh or the moronic self-importance of Terry Schwarber, these two policemen looked competent and professional. One was short, stocky, and had a salt-and-pepper crew cut. The other was tall and lean and black, and he looked a little younger. The short, white cop was scribbling on a pad of paper. The tall, lean one had his hands folded before him. We approached as the two cops conversed with Mr. Watkins.

"...them everything he knew last night," Chris's dad was saying, his voice curt and borderline hostile. "I don't see the need to repeat it."

"Mr. Watkins," the lean cop said. "I can appreciate your desire to protect your son—"

"If you appreciated it, you wouldn't be here," Mr. Watkins said.

The lean black cop glanced at the stocky white one, who was eyeing Chris and me. The white cop smiled. "Hey, fellas."

I nodded at him, but Chris didn't.

Chris was watching his dad.

I realized Mr. Watkins was pretending nothing had happened. He'd just belted his wife at least twice—one of the blows violent enough to draw blood—and here he was acting like the concerned father and irate taxpayer.

He's a great actor, I thought wonderingly. *And a complete son of a bitch.*

"I didn't give you permission to talk to my son," Mr. Watkins said, his tone cold enough to freeze lava.

The black cop grunted good-naturedly. "He was just saying hello."

"I don't care what he was saying," Mr. Watkins said. "I should never have invited you in. Now," he said, ushering them toward the door, "if you two would—"

A new voice spoke up. "Have you found her yet?"

We turned and saw Chris's mom. She looked a little wan, but other than the extra lipstick she'd applied, she looked fairly normal.

Just another perfect day at the Watkins mansion, I thought.

The tall black cop smiled apologetically. "We haven't, ma'am. That's why we'd hoped to talk to your boys."

Mr. Watkins was growing red-faced. "I've already told them they can't speak to Chris. Now I'd like you both to—"

"I'll talk to you," I said.

All heads swiveled toward me.

Chris nodded. "I will too. If it helps Kylie Ann."

"It *won't* help Kylie Ann," Mr. Watkins said with finality. "The Shadeland police chief interrogated my son last night for the better part of an hour, and Chris is not going to tell you anything new today."

"Mr. Watkins," the stocky cop said, "we feel that, in the interest of being thorough, it makes more sense to..."

"Go through it again," the taller cop said.

"But what purpose—" Mr. Watkins began.

"Cavanaugh doesn't know what he's doing," I said.

156

Again every face swiveled toward me. I noticed the state policemen trying to stifle grins.

"Well if you're such an expert," Mr. Watkins said with a nasty smile, "why don't you go with them?"

I forgot for a moment how gigantic Mr. Watkins was. "Why are you in such a hurry to get these guys out of the house?"

Mr. Watkins's face tightened. I believed in that moment he would have strangled me if there hadn't been witnesses. "They're out of line," he said in a controlled voice.

"Hah!" I said, glancing around. "You say that with a straight face? Why don't you tell them why your wife keeps covering her mouth?"

The atmosphere in the foyer changed instantaneously. Chris's dad looked like he was about to explode from mortification or fury or both. Chris looked scared enough to pass out. The stocky cop was watching me uncertainly, but the tall black cop was staring at Mr. Watkins as if seeing him for the first time. And what he saw there, he didn't like.

"There something you need to tell us, Mr. Watkins?" the tall cop asked.

Mr. Watkins's mouth opened and shut, reminding me of a little kid attempting to blow bubbles. At last he managed, "We had an argument, yes, but that was it. I think Will's imagination is working overtime."

I knew I should shut up, but it was like my mouth was on autopilot and I was simply hanging on for the ride. "Was it my imagination she was bleeding a minute ago?"

The tall cop looked ready to wring Mr. Watkins's neck, but Mrs. Watkins surprised us all by saying, "Maybe you should go with them, Will."

I felt like *I'd* been slapped. "Mrs. Watkins, he shouldn't—"

"I appreciate your concern," she overrode me, "but I think you better go."

I opened my mouth to protest, but she added, "*Please*, Will."

I glanced at Chris and was stunned to see how sickly a hue he'd gone. I knew how traumatized he was, and though I wanted to help him, a part of me figured it would be better if I did leave with the cops. I know that sounds cowardly, but it really wasn't.

Because somehow I knew a great many things about the Watkinses I'd never known before. I knew despite their money, their house was an unhappy one. I knew Chris's dad had struck Chris's mom before, and I knew it had been covered up. And somehow, I was sure that Mr. Watkins would hurt his wife again.

As I followed the cops outside, I understood that this was a cycle for the Watkinses. And when I got into the back of the car, a terrible new possibility occurred to me.

Did Mr. Watkins abuse Chris too?

It would certainly explain a lot. It had crossed my mind before, mainly because of how quiet Chris got when someone mentioned his dad, how the light would go out of his eyes, to be replaced by a brooding expression that made him seem far older than his fifteen years.

"So," the white cop said as he steered us out of Chris's driveway, "my name's Jim Flynn. This is Detective Wood."

The tall black cop turned in the passenger seat and gave me an embarrassed grin. "David is fine."

I thought I'd have a difficult time calling either man something other than Officer or Sir, but I nodded and kept quiet.

Officer Flynn eyed me in the overhead mirror. "You were right about Cavanaugh, by the way. I'm good friends with the county sheriff. Larry Robertson? Off the record, he can't stand the chief. Or his deputies, for that matter."

"They've botched this investigation, haven't they?" I said.

Detective Wood glanced at me. "That's like saying Carl Padgett is a mildly dangerous jaywalker. This investigation has been a disaster."

"That's not going far enough," Flynn said. "They haven't just made the wrong decisions. They've made the worst possible decisions at every turn."

"And that began with not contacting us the moment Kylie Ann Lubeck went missing."

Flynn glared out the windshield, thin-lipped. "We'd have her back by now."

Wood shook his head. "Precious hours were wasted while those dolts stumbled around the woods." Detective Wood glanced at me. "They give you a hard time, did they?"

"They didn't beat me or anything," I said, "but they treated me like I was a criminal. Oh, and they made me walk home at three in the morning."

Wood's mouth fell open. Flynn slowed the car to a halt. He was staring grimly ahead.

"Come again?" Detective Wood asked.

I told them about how Cavanaugh and his deputies had made a joke of it. As I talked, the two men exchanged glances, their expressions rapidly changing from astonishment to outrage.

Detective Wood moved in his seat to face me. He spoke slowly and with a gravity that made me a little nervous "Will, you seem like a sincere person. But you need to know this: You better not mislead us in any way because that could get you in a lot of trouble. You understand?"

"Of course," I said with a touch of heat.

"Then son," Officer Flynn said, "you better tell us the whole thing, from beginning to end. Please don't leave anything out, particularly as it pertains to the missing girl."

"Or the Shadeland police force," Wood added.

"*Especially* the Shadeland police force," Flynn said.

And as we made our way back to Masonic Road, I told them the entire tale.

♦

By the time I finished, we'd been sitting in my driveway for ten minutes.

"...and then Brad and the rest of the guys got in Blades's Mustang and drove away," I said.

Detective Wood studied me. "Anything else?"

I mulled it over. "I'm pretty sure that's all." I considered telling them about what Peach had seen in the window—the pale, grisly face with the glowing emerald eyes—but something, probably protectiveness of my sister and a desire to keep her from being thought a silly little kid, prevented me.

Flynn turned to Wood. "What do you make of it?"

Wood scowled out the passenger window. "Will's account dovetails with the facts Cavanaugh supplied pretty nicely."

Flynn eyed my house. "Doesn't look like anyone's home."

"Mom doesn't get off work for several more hours."

"You've got a little sister, don't you?"

"She's at a friend's."

Wood gave me a probing glance. "You spend a lot of time on your own?"

"I'm fine," I said, and made to get out. But the door wouldn't budge.

"Hold on," Wood said. "I've got to open it for you."

As Wood let me out into the sweltering day, I was again surprised by how tall he was.

"You sure you want to stay here alone?" he asked.

I shrugged and tried to look tough. "Padgett's already left town, hasn't he?"

"We're not assuming anything," he answered. "We don't even know that Padgett is the one who abducted Kylie Ann."

"So you don't know anything," I said.

I thought that might piss off Detective Wood, but he actually smiled a little. "Imagine working a cash register at Wal-Mart. You come on at six PM, and you're taking over a register somebody else worked all day. The cash, change, everything is totally inaccurate because the other guy couldn't add or subtract, much less handle large bills or credit cards. But you're the one whose butt is on the line if the register doesn't add up at the end of the night."

I nodded. "I get it. It must suck cleaning up after Chief Cavanaugh."

"'Suck' isn't a strong enough word. If you were a trifle older, I'd use the real word, but for now, yeah, I'll tell you that it sucks."

He clapped me on the shoulder and got back into the cruiser. "Take care."

I thought the state troopers would drive away then, but Detective Wood leaned toward me, a hesitant look on his face. "Can I ask you something?"

I waited.

"Mind you," he went on, "I don't expect an answer."

"Okay," I said, but I already knew what the question would be. Worse, I had no idea how to answer it.

"You said something back at your friend's house that was pretty interesting."

I shifted uneasily.

Officer Flynn leaned toward me from the driver's seat. "Something about Mr. and Mrs. Watkins."

I licked my lips. "Oh. That."

Detective Wood asked, "Did he hit her?"

I hesitated. "What happens if I say yes?"

"Tell you the truth," Wood said, "that all depends on how we decide to handle it. Mr. Watkins is a well-known man and someone who'll fight any charge that comes his way."

I grunted. "I'm sure."

Flynn looked like he'd just detected a bad smell. "Watkins isn't very popular with those of us on the force."

I wanted to smile then, show them I was on their side, but all I could think of was Chris. What would happen if the cops went over to arrest Chris's dad? How would that affect my friend? And what would that do to Mrs. Watkins? Would her husband abuse her twice as violently?

Apparently, my internal struggle showed on my face, because Wood said, "Look, Will. We're not here to put you in a bad spot. If you want some time to think about it, how about this..." He plucked something from his shirt pocket and offered it to me. A business card. "Take this and think it over. I think you know what the right thing is. Guys like Watkins never change. He'll keep doing this until someone stops him." He eyed me steadily. "Someone who'll stand up to him."

I held his gaze a long beat, then pretended to study the card.

"Talk to you soon, Will," Wood said. Flynn also said his goodbye, and then they were backing out of the driveway.

I watched them go with a vague sense of regret. They were the first two adults I'd encountered in a while that I felt I could trust. Oh, the Marleys were good people, but Flynn and Wood were different; they seemed to know Shadeland's business, but they came with none of the biases or entanglements that the other adults in my life possessed.

But now Flynn and Wood were gone. Which meant I was stuck here with nothing to do.

Man, it was hot. I was perspiring freely now, my shirt sticking to my back. The air was so humid it felt tropical. The storm would hit soon.

My muscles tensed. *Yes*, I decided. I knew how I could spend the next several hours. Mom wouldn't be home until late afternoon. She didn't want me to go to the basement again, but she'd never know if she wasn't here to catch me.

Excited, I hustled around the side of the house and swerved around the corner.

And ran right into Eric Blades.

He jarred slightly, but he'd evidently been prepared for the collision. I, on the other hand, landed right on my ass.

"That was rude," Kurt Fisher said. "I want an apology."

Eric grinned, the guy's complexion darker than I remembered. He wore a black tank top, and his arms were heavily veined. Kurt looked the way he always did. Fairly short, but arrogant and muscular, his black crew cut lent him a militaristic aura. Definitely not the kind of guy whose bad side you wanted to be on. Of course, I'd been on Kurt's bad side for as long as I could remember, as if I'd offended him with my birth or something.

Sitting there on my rear end, I turned and discovered Pete Blades, Eric's older brother. Pete had a heavy shadow of beard, and though I knew he worked at the pharmacy, he didn't look clean-cut now. He'd traded in his striped button-down shirt and his nametag for a burgundy T-shirt and a pair of black shorts. He was heavier than Eric and a good deal older. I thought he was twenty-four or twenty-five, which made this situation even more surreal. What kind of guy that age hung around with high school kids? Even worse, what kind of guy participated in the beating up of a fifteen-year-old, which was where I was pretty sure this was going?

I got up, dusted myself off, and gave Pete Blades my most caustic look. "I bet your bosses would be really proud to see you now."

Pete smiled, unabashed. "It's funny you mention that, Burgess. See, working at the pharmacy, you find out a lot about people. Which ones can barely afford their meds. Which ones go to extreme lengths to make sure they get them." He gave me a penetrating look. "Which ones falsify their prescriptions because they ran out over a year ago."

"I don't know what you're talking about," I said in a thin voice.

"You know exactly what I'm talking about," Pete said. "And you know that if I turn in your junkie of a mom, the first people that'll show up will be Child Protective Services. You and your little sister will be taken away and put in different homes, and your mom'll be lucky to stay out of jail."

I could only stare.

"And that's why," Eric Blades said with a wicked grin, "you're going into the Hollow with us. Kylie Ann and I were just getting to know each other, and I'm not going to let Carl Padgett or some other freak hurt her."

For once I was at a complete loss for words. Eric turned and cut across my backyard in the direction of the Hollow. I followed him, drifting along like a wraith. Kurt and Pete were talking and chuckling behind me, but I couldn't make out their words. There was a lot of profanity, and I could tell most of it was about me and my family, but at that point I was too stunned to care. I mean, I knew my mom was addicted to her prescriptions, but I still believed they were sanctioned by a doctor. That she'd been forging the doctor's signature shouldn't have been surprising to me, but it was. Whatever good will my mom had built up with her recently improved behavior was burned away in a flash of contempt so powerful it left me feeling desolate and hopeless.

We stepped onto the path single file and entered Savage Hollow.

The forest closed around us, the day so humid that a patina of sweat formed on my arms and back. Early-season mosquitoes began to feast on me, and hordes of gnats buzzed at my ears. We'd walked for several minutes through the deepening forest before an unpleasant thought occurred to me.

"Where's Brad?"

It was Kurt who answered. "His girlfriend's," he said with a sneer.

"I spoke to her an hour ago," I said.

Eric stopped and turned, and the trail was so narrow I had no choice but to stop too to keep from slamming into him.

"It's time you let go of this delusion, Burgess. You have any idea what kind of girl Mia is? How experienced?"

"You're lying," I said.

His grin widened. "What do you think she and Brad are doing right now? While her parents are gone? He's fucking her *brains* out."

My hands balled into fists. "Shut up."

"That make you mad, does it?" Kurt asked at my ear. "That make you mad, you puny little bastard?" He chuckled. "Hell, I guess you really *are* a bastard, aren't you, Burgess?"

A black rage swept over me, but before I could act, Kurt shoved me into Eric.

"Get the hell off me," Eric said gruffly and spun me around.

Straight into Kurt's fist.

The punch, which caught me flush on the mouth, was so unexpected and violent that my head snapped back and I stumbled sideways into the weeds. Thorns tore at my bare arms and legs. Sizzling rods of nettles seared my calves. I started to push myself out of the snarl, but then there was a blur of movement to my left and a foot whooshed up and thumped me in the belly. I flopped down on my side and curled into the fetal position, my midsection throbbing and my breathing reed-thin.

"Get up," Kurt growled.

"You don't have to do this," I said.

166

"Get *up*," he demanded.

"You don't have to be like your dad."

Evidently, that was the wrong thing to say. When he grasped me by the shirt and jerked me to a standing position, his expression was absolutely homicidal.

His fist, which felt as hard as marble, crunched against my rib cage, and before I could recover from the vicious jab to the side, he uncorked another blow, this one a looping left fist to the jaw.

I collapsed against Eric, who shoved me forward again. Kurt seized me by the shirt and brought his face up to mine.

"What did she do with him?" Kurt shouted.

How should I know? I wondered.

"Tell him!" Pete demanded.

"Did they kiss?" Kurt asked.

I wobbled on my feet, but I managed to put on a confused look.

"You were with them," he barked. "You were there both nights!"

Pete moved up and studied me over Kurt's shoulder. "Or maybe him and Mia were too busy making out for him to notice."

Everything was moving too fast. I felt like I was on some out-of-control carnival ride stuck in a continuous spin.

"If you don't tell me the truth in five seconds," Kurt said, "I'm going to turn your face into hamburger. Even your stoner mom won't recognize you. Five..."

I tried to say something but couldn't.

"...four..."

My mouth felt like it was crammed with cotton balls, but I still managed to say, "You're talking about Chris and Rebecca?"

He ignored me. "...three..."

"Hold on," I said, putting a hand up. "Just let me..."

"...two..."

"They didn't...do anything," I managed.

Kurt shook me, his nose about a centimeter from mine. "You lying to me?"

"Promise," I said. "I wasn't with them...the whole time." I sucked in a ragged breath. "But I would know if they kissed. Chris would've told me."

Kurt turned his face this way and that, studying my battered face the way one would a priceless work of art. "And what about you and Mia? You try to put the moves on her? Or did the slut put the moves on you?"

"Go to hell," I said.

Kurt's fist crashed into my gut. I crumpled to the trail, doubled over and gasping for air.

"Enough," Eric said. He loomed over me. "Where did that guy grab Kylie Ann?"

I armed moisture off my lips, and when I looked down I saw it was blood. My vision doubled, tripled, and a wave of nausea plowed through me. "Hold on," I panted. "Just give me a second."

"You think Padgett's going to give Kylie Ann extra time?" Eric demanded. For the first time, the possibility that he cared about Kylie Ann occurred to me. I peered up at him through a veil of wooziness. His expression was unreadable.

It took a major effort, but I managed to get to my feet. The pain in my bruised stomach still prohibited me from standing upright.

"Start talking," Eric demanded.

I looked around and saw the treehouse in the distance.

Eric must've seen the surprise on my face. "Of course we know about it. We've even used it from time to time."

I stared at him, not wanting to believe it.

"Look at that!" Kurt said. "Poor Burgess is mad that we know about his secret fort!"

Eric nodded at his big brother. "Pete here's taken at least three girls up there, haven't you, Pete?"

"More than that," Pete said with a satisfied grin.

I toiled to hide it, but the truth was, I was furious with them. Ever since we were little we'd regarded the treehouse as our private hangout, the one place where we could hide out from the world and not have to worry about adult intrusion. Or the interference of jerks like these guys.

And now all that was shattered. It had been an illusion to begin with, but it was an illusion I would have rather clung to.

"Tell us about Kylie Ann," Eric said, seizing the nape of my neck. "Now."

In Mrs. Herbert's class we'd studied the myth of Sisyphus, the guy who was consigned to an eternity of pushing a boulder up a hill, only to have it roll down again so he could start all over. That's how I felt about recounting last night's awful episode with Kylie Ann and whoever had taken her. I'd told it to Chris, Rebecca, and Barley, to Cavanaugh and his goons at the station, to Flynn and Wood in their cruiser, and now to these pricks. I was sick of it, wished it had never happened, but as I took them through the story, something peculiar occurred. Some formless memory began to squirm in the recesses of my mind. Something that might be important. Something that could maybe lead us to Kylie Ann. But it wasn't here in the forest. It was...it was...

"Wait a minute," Kurt said.

I'd gotten to the part where the kidnapper punched me in the face, and I fell silent with little regret. Talking about my failure to save Kylie Ann was my least favorite part of the story, so being allowed to delay it was fine by me. And anyway, it gave me a chance to contemplate that other thing, that inchoate memory that refused to clarify but also refused to go away.

"Wait for what?" Pete asked.

"I thought I heard something," Kurt said.

"You're full of it," Pete said.

"No, he's right," Eric said. "I heard something too." He nodded into the dense thicket beyond the treehouse. I thought of the legends Barley had talked about. The creature Mia and Peach claimed to have seen.

The Wendigo.

"Come on," Pete said. "Let's get on with it."

"Shut up for a minute," Eric said, all his arrogance gone. "You guys feel that?"

"Feel *what?*" Pete Blades answered. But now he sounded uncertain too.

I slowly swam back to full awareness, and as I did I noticed the way all three of my attackers were glancing about the Hollow, their foreheads creased and their breathing heavy. On some level it did my heart good to see them scared out of their minds, but on a deeper, atavistic level, I'd begun to share in their trepidation.

There was definitely something wrong here. Something alien to the Hollow.

Something hostile.

Not only had we stopped talking, the entire forest had fallen silent. No birdsong, no rustling in the underbrush.

The fine hair on my arms stood on end; my throat gone dry and dusty.

"We'll deal with Burgess later," Eric muttered and amazed me by moving back in the direction we'd come.

Pete stared at his little brother unbelievingly. "What, we're just going to let him go?"

"He's not telling on us," Kurt said. "He knows he'll be separated from his darling little sister if he breathes one word about this. Don't you, Burgess?"

I couldn't meet Kurt's gloating face. The truth was, he was right. I hadn't had the chance to sort it all out in my mind yet, but Pete's claims held a sort of twisted logic. I knew he had access to the prescriptions, and though I doubted he was some sort of handwriting specialist, I also doubted he had the intelligence to make something like that up. Maybe one of his coworkers at the pharmacy had mentioned it, the suspicion that my mom was procuring her pills illegally. Whatever the case, I had no doubt at all what would happen if she was busted. I was only fifteen, Peach not even half that. In a perfect world they'd let us stay in our house with me assuming the role of parent. Or, they'd send us to the same foster home. But really, what family wanted a fifteen-year-old boy to feed? To help put through college? I even had my doubts about Peach's viability as an adoption candidate. Didn't most families want newborns?

I realized with a start that I'd been left behind.

That feeling of wrongness was stronger than ever. The sensation of being watched.

It took all the self-control I had to not bolt down the trail after Kurt and the Blades Brothers. But there were other ways back to my house. I didn't like taking them—I'd almost certainly end up with burs on my clothes and a serious case of poison ivy—but they'd be preferable to following my tormentors. It was entirely possible they'd decide there really was no danger and double back to beat me up some more.

Grimly, moving as fast as I could without tripping over a rock and busting my neck, I started through the forest.

Chapter Nine

Nurse Peach, the Grave, the Child

Peach and Mom were home early. I was shocked,
but I was also extremely happy to see them.

Mom's face twisted with concern when she saw
me enter the living room, where she and Peach had been
playing UNO, Peach's favorite game. "What happened to
you?" Mom dropped her cards and sprang from the floor
to cup my face in her hands. "*Who did this?*" she hissed.

I was a little taken aback by her intensity. First
of all, I'd been so happy to get out of the Hollow in one
piece and so weary after having hiked through the
brambles and the heat that I'd forgotten all about my
face. Secondly, Mom rarely showed much concern about
my wellbeing. I know how horrible that sounds, but it's
the truth. Maybe, I mused, her decision to sober up and
be a proper mother really was permanent.

"I'm fine, Mom," I said.

"You're not *fine*, Will, you've been *assaulted*." She
sucked in breath, covered her mouth in horror. "Was it
the same person who took the Lubeck girl?"

I considered pointing out to her that if it had been
the same person, I'd probably be dead. Or missing one of
my hands. But good taste prevailed, and I said, "Just
some kids from school. I handled them okay."

"Looks like they handled you," Peach said from
the floor.

I gave her an annoyed glare, but regretted it
when I saw how distressed she looked.

Mom was not to be put off. "I want *names*, William. We're not going to ignore this." She scooped the phone off its cradle.

Under other circumstances, I would have appreciated her indignation. But the chances of my telling her who did this were roughly equivalent to the chances of my being drafted by the Cubs this summer.

I'd have to be careful how I played this. There was no way I was going give her names, but I also didn't want to start an argument. She was acting the way a mom was supposed to act, and I needed to encourage that. It sounds weird, but in a way I was proud of her.

"I'm not ignoring it, Mom, but this isn't one of those things where you call somebody's parents and talk it out. They're not the kind of—"

"I'm not talking about calling their *parents*, Will, I'm calling the police. Have you seen your face? It looks like you've been trampled by a herd of buffalo."

I laid my hands over hers. "The police aren't going to help, Mom. Remember how they made me walk home last night?"

She blanched at the memory. I hated to see the newfound spark in her eyes dim a little, but she needed to give up the notion of settling this for me.

As gently as I could, I guided her hands together and placed the phone back into its cradle. "Even if Cavanaugh weren't a total jerk," I added, "he's too busy to worry about something as small as a scuffle between kids."

"What's a scuffle?" Peach asked.

"This wasn't a *scuffle*, Will," Mom said. "This was a *beating*." Her expression went hard. "It was the Fisher boy, wasn't it. Kurt Fisher and Brad Ralston?"

"I haven't seen them since our last game," I lied. "Trust me, Mom, it's no big deal." I offered a hand to Peach. "Come on. I need help getting cleaned up."

"Can I be the nurse?" Peach asked, hopping to her feet.

"As long as you don't kill me," I said.

Mom watched after us, crestfallen. I couldn't tell if it was my refusal to tell her the truth or my selection of Peach as my nurse that hurt her worse. I gave her what I hoped was a reassuring smile, but she only gazed at me with that same somber expression.

Sorry, Mom, I thought, moving with Peach down the hallway. *You can't be absent from my life for years and then just expect to play hero again.* Maybe that was cruel, but it was how I felt. Besides, Peach actually was a good nurse. Her favorite show was called *Doc McStuffins*, which was about a little girl who healed her stuffed animals. Peach loved to be the one to give me a Band-Aid when I needed it.

Entering the bathroom, I caught a glimpse of myself in the mirror.

Holy shit, I thought.

I looked awful.

My left eye was swollen almost completely shut, the lid so stretched and purpled that I feared it would simply burst and spew blood and pus all over the mirror. My lips were lacerated and crusted with blood. None of my teeth felt loose, which was something, but the ache in my nose was bad enough I thought it might be broken. One side of my jaw was so puffy it looked like I had a tumor there, and there were various other weals and cuts on my cheeks and forehead.

No wonder Mom had been so freaked out.

I eased down on the toilet lid and leaned back. "Close the door," I whispered to Peach. In front of Mom

I'd tried to hold it in, but now, in the presence of my little sister, I could let my guard down and express some of the massive pain I was feeling.

"It was Brad and Kurt, wasn't it?" Peach muttered.

"Kurt was there," I said. "Brad wasn't."

"He beat you up by himself?"

I glanced at her with the eye that wasn't swollen shut. "You think he could?"

She gave me a little shrug. "I don't know."

I held her wide-eyed gaze with my good eye and tried to see myself as she was seeing me. Her big brother, her hero, sitting here battered like some vanquished warrior. I was her protector, and if I could be defeated, who would save her from the monsters?

I mustered a crooked grin. "Kurt had two friends with him. They ganged up on me."

Peach smiled, reassured. I almost cracked a joke at how delighted she looked but decided to let it go. As far as she was concerned, the world had been put back on its axis. Her big brother was still invincible.

"The medicine basket's in the cabinet," I said. "You'll need a washcloth, gauze pads...whatever you can find in there."

"I know where the basket is," she said loftily, but she followed my directions. I watched her fondly as she slid the basket off the shelf. It looked almost as big as she was. It was a pretty crappy system—all the medical stuff heaped in a big pile—but at least it was all in one place. She set the basket on the sink and selected a bottle of Tylenol.

"Aren't you gonna wash these cuts first?" I asked.

"We have to deal with the pain," she said as though I were the little kid and she the older sibling. "Then we'll clean you up."

"Okay, Doc," I said.

She fiddled with the bottle for a few instants, her tongue poking from the side of her mouth. She sighed. "I can't get the top off," she grumbled.

"Here," I said. I twisted the lid off for her and shook out three pills.

"Not too many," she cautioned.

"Right. Could you get me some water?"

"Wait here," she said. She opened the door and scampered out of the room. She was back a moment later with the glass from her nightstand. "You need fresh water," she explained and dumped out last night's supply. Refilling the cup, she handed it to me and watched me down the pills. "Why did they hit you?" she asked.

"It's complicated."

She reached into the cabinet, produced a fresh washcloth, and soaked it under the tap. "Was it about a girl?"

"It's always about a girl."

She dabbed at my bloody lips. "Why are boys so dumb?"

"That's not a nice word, Peach."

"Stupid?"

"That's worse."

"Well? Why are they so dumb?"

I chuckled, but it hurt to laugh. My ribs felt like a rug that had been beaten for too long. "Boys are insecure."

"What's inse—"

"It means you don't think you're good enough, so you're afraid the girl you like is going to find someone better. It makes you act mean."

In a small voice, Peach said, "That's how Annabelle makes me feel. Like I'm not good enough."

I blinked at her for a few moments before realizing she was talking about Chief Cavanaugh's daughter. I remembered the things Cavanaugh had said about Peach last night.

Something deep in my soul ached.

Why, God, I wondered, did sweet little people like Peach have to feel such terrible things? Why did such a good-hearted, loving girl get treated like dirt?

I swallowed the thickness in my throat. "You're better than Annabelle is, Peach. You're better than anyone. Don't ever doubt that."

She wetted another corner of the white washcloth, which was already stained red in several places. "You're just saying that because you're my brother."

"It's true." I hesitated. "You're a great kid. Most sisters wouldn't help their brothers like this. You've got a really caring heart."

She pulled away and frowned. "Are you making fun of me?"

I shook my head, held her gaze for a long moment.

The storm clouds left her face, and she began cleaning my cuts again. "Thanks."

I felt better than I had for hours. Peach always had a calming effect on me.

"Why is there dirt on your face too?" she asked.

"I doubt they bothered to wash their fists before using them on me."

She reached into the basket, came out with Neosporin. "This will stop you from getting…" She frowned, searching for the word.

"Infected?" I asked.

"Uh huh," she said. "Infected."

She began to daub the first aid cream on my cuts, but my thoughts had veered in another direction. Something about that simple word—*dirt*—had revived the tickle in the back of my mind. Now why did I keep getting stuck on that word? Why did it keep reminding me of last night? Not of Kylie Ann Lubeck or Chris or Mia or even Cavanaugh and his deputies. No, something about the black Mustang...about being chased by Eric Blades and the others...something about the graveyard...

I sucked in breath, my whole body tensing.

"Did I hurt you?" Peach asked, jerking the tube of Neosporin away.

I swallowed, shook my head distractedly. "Peach...when was the last time there was a funeral in the cemetery?"

"What's a furenal?"

"*Fu·ne·ral*," I corrected. "Where they bury the body."

A look of recognition shone on her face. "A few weeks ago? You were at baseball practice."

I felt like I'd been slugged in the gut.

Her brown eyes searched my face. "Will? What's wrong?"

"I have to call Flynn and Wood."

"Are those people?" she asked.

I pushed past her, exited the bathroom, hurried into the hall on legs I couldn't feel, and dialed the number Wood had given me.

"What's happening?" Peach called, hurrying after me.

I waved her quiet, concentrated on the phone.

"Hello?" Wood's voice answered.

"This is Will," I said. "Burgess."

A pause. "You sound like something's wrong, Will."

"It is."

Peach buzzed about me like a gnat.

"Do you need us to come over there?" Wood asked.

I nodded, then remembered Wood couldn't see me through the phone. "Yes. As soon as you can. Bring shovels."

"Shovels?"

"Uh-huh. I think I know where to find the rest of Kylie Ann."

◆

"What's going on?" Mom asked, coming in from the kitchen.

"I think I know—"

I cut off, remembering my little sister. I'd been about to share my suspicion with Mom, but I realized I'd already said too much in front of Peach.

"Can you go to the bedroom for a minute?" I asked her.

"Is Kylie Ann the one they can't find?" Peach asked.

Mom looked at me, thin-lipped. "*Will.*"

I cleared my throat. "Peach, can I talk to Mom alone for—"

"She's staying over at the Wallaces tonight," Mom said.

"We're having a sleepover!" Peach said, hopping up and down.

I frowned. On one hand, this was good news. If my hunch was correct, the last thing I needed was having Peach wandering into the cemetery and seeing something that would haunt her for the rest of her life. But the idea of her spending the night somewhere else?

I didn't like it.

"Isn't six a little young for a sleepover?" I asked.

"She's done it before," Mom said, a trifle frostily. "I think I know what's appropriate for my daughter."

I glanced at Peach. "When are you leaving?"

"We were going to leave ten minutes ago," Mom said. "Then you came home looking like you'd been mugged."

I bent down and gazed at Peach. "Will you promise to be safe?"

She nodded.

I put my hands on her shoulders. "And not to go *anywhere* with *anybody*, no matter what they say to you?"

Peach nodded.

Mom said, "You're scaring her, Will."

Good, I thought. A little fear wasn't such a bad thing.

"Come on, Honey," Mom said, and after favoring me with a long, appraising look, she led Peach out to the car.

Flynn and Wood showed up soon after. They had another guy with them, this one a little younger.

They all three carried shovels. They also grilled me for several minutes about who had rearranged my face, but after it became apparent I wasn't going to tell them, they laid off and followed me through my yard.

Detective Wood nodded at the younger guy, who looked like a college football player. "This is Dane Hubbard. He's new to the force."

Hubbard nodded at me. He had a neck like an oak tree and shoulder muscles that looked like balloons someone had inflated under his shirt.

Flynn stopped a few feet from where I stood in the yard. "You said you have an idea of where Kylie Ann might be?"

"I don't know for sure, but—"

"Show us."

I nodded and led them into the cemetery. I didn't want my hunch to be right. I didn't want to find *anything* in the graveyard. In fact, a goodly chunk of my brain was telling me I'd imagined the freshly turned dirt, that the emotional turmoil had played tricks with my perceptions and that what I'd tripped over hadn't been a pile of graveyard soil at all, but rather my own feet.

Then I spotted it. A raggedly dug plot of dirt.

It wasn't rectangular, the way graves were supposed to be. It was more like a misshapen oval, with clumps of soil tossed haphazardly about. From the woods the buzz of cicadas rang out like a warning.

"This the place?" Flynn asked. His voice was low and tight.

I glanced at him and saw him eyeing the pile warily. Detective Wood and Officer Hubbard wore similar expressions. It made me like them more, trust them more. These were real human beings, despite the barrier of authority that existed between us. I was terrified of what we'd find under all that dirt, but I was glad these men were with me.

Wood hunkered down before the mound. He scooped up a handful of the soil and let it sift through his long dark fingers. "Will's right. It's freshly turned."

That seemed pretty obvious to me, but I kept my mouth shut.

"That the Mustang that chased you last night?" Wood asked without taking his eyes off the mound.

"Huh?" I asked.

He nodded to his right. I turned in that direction and saw, at the far end of the cemetery lane, almost entirely concealed by a copse of trees, Eric Blades's black Mustang.

Wood watched me, waiting.

I nodded. "Yeah, that's the one. You think Eric's around somewhere?"

Flynn hefted a black-handled shovel. "Unless Blades has a car that steers itself, I'd wager he's in the woods looking for the Lubeck girl."

Hubbard eyed the mound of dirt. "He should've looked over here."

"We don't know that yet," Flynn said. He raised the blade of the shovel and stabbed the earth. A black spider scuttle over the shovel blade, but Flynn didn't seem to notice. "Could just be the Shadeland Cemetery staff isn't as good at bookkeeping as it should be."

"That possible, David?" Hubbard asked.

Wood slammed his own shovel into the dirt opposite Flynn's. "Don't know. Seems like a pretty big oversight to me. How many people this place bury per year?"

"Not enough to forget about one of them," I said.

Wood nodded. "Will, you've been very helpful, but I think it might be better if you headed back to your house for the time being. If we do find something..." He trailed off, letting that hang in the air.

"I'd rather stay," I said.

Wood gave Flynn a dubious look. Flynn kept digging, but he said, "I'm afraid we'll have to pull rank on you here. Something like this could stick with you the rest of your life. And not in a good way."

"He's right, kid," Hubbard agreed, the muscular guy taking a spot beside Wood and shoveling a big spadeful of dirt. "You don't wanna be around for this. I remember some of the stuff I saw during training. It messed with my head in a serious way, and I was prepared for it. You...you're a lot younger."

"And you knew Kylie Ann," Flynn added.

Wood paused and leaned on his shovel. "Let's not get ahead of ourselves, fellas. We don't know there's anything buried under here but a perfectly normal casket. That guy we talked to from the cemetery...he sounded a little out of touch."

Flynn chuckled. "Acted like he belonged in a group home."

"Be nice, Jim," Wood said, though he was smiling too.

The three of them continued to shovel. Hubbard lifted his shirt to mop sweat off his forehead, and I caught a glimpse of abdominal muscles so protuberant that I was reminded of Barley's comic books. This guy was built like Superman or Wolverine, which was yet another reason for me to stick around here. If Kurt or Eric decided to get violent again, I had the feeling they'd back down pretty quickly once they caught sight of Hubbard.

The young cop studied me. "You don't plan on going back to the house, do you."

I stood my ground.

He grinned. "You're as stubborn as I used to be."

Flynn snorted. "'Used to be?' You're one of the most pig-headed guys I know."

Hubbard muttered a curse, but he was grinning.

"Flynn's right," Wood said, shoveling the dirt aside steadily. "You make Will here seem downright sensible."

Hubbard straightened. "Now hold up. When have I ever—"

184

But something made us all freeze. It had been the sound of Flynn's shovel hitting something other than soil. Flynn and Wood exchanged a solemn glance, then Wood was moving around to where Flynn stood, the shovel held loosely in his grip.

"Keep it where it is," Wood murmured to Flynn, who didn't move the shovel at all.

Wood knelt and began the job of brushing dirt away from the shovel tip, his eyes narrowed in concentration.

Something in my belly tightened. I kept my eyes on Wood's face and studiously avoided looking at his fingers. Because if they did reveal something...

I shivered.

"Anything?" Hubbard whispered.

I didn't know why the muscular cop had lowered his voice, but it somehow seemed appropriate. Wood's hands moved briskly for a time, then with more finesse and care. His expression went from quizzical to grim.

"You got something?" Hubbard asked.

But I already knew the answer. Flynn did too, apparently. Perhaps from his vantage point he could glimpse what Wood had found, but I doubted it. He probably knew his partner well enough to read his face. Or his cop's sixth sense was so finely tuned that he'd known what they'd find even before his shovel bumped against it.

I took a step backward, the reality of the situation beginning to take hold of me.

"It's her, isn't it?" Hubbard asked.

"You want me to call it in?" Flynn asked in a low, respectful voice.

"In a minute," Wood said. He turned and gazed up at me, and his face looked about twenty years older. "I want you to turn around now, Will. I won't make you go back to the house, but I don't want you to see this. Okay?"

I nodded and did as he asked, not only because I agreed with his advice but because I didn't want him or the other policemen to see the horror in my expression. A couple days ago this had been a living girl. More than that, it had been a girl I knew, a girl with whom I'd gone swimming, a girl who'd hung out with Mia and Rebecca.

And now...

"Let me help with that," I heard Flynn say. I could hear him and Wood pushing away dirt and occasionally grunting with the effort of uncovering the body, but other than that the graveyard was eerily quiet. I focused on the side of my house, which was about sixty yards away. I tried to breathe through my mouth, though on some level I knew that was sort of silly. Kylie Ann hadn't been buried for long and she likely hadn't begun to rot yet.

Ugh. I trembled, aghast at the run of my own thoughts. I'd made a mistake staying with the cops, I realized that now. I should have gone back, should have heeded their—

"That what I think it is?" Hubbard said, his voice thick with dread.

"It's her arm," Wood confirmed. "It's where her hand used to be."

God. I felt myself teetering a little. I wished I were home in bed. Or *under* the bed. Anything to escape this macabre scene.

Wood's voice was strained. "Jim, could you..."

"Hold on," Flynn said. I heard scraping sounds, as if Flynn were whisking away dirt.

I made the mistake of turning then. What I saw nearly made me faint.

Kylie Ann's curly head was poking out of the ground. Her eyes were open. They weren't staring at me, but they didn't need to be. Just seeing that dead gaze was enough to make me shudder uncontrollably.

Then I saw her forearm. The pale stub of bone jutting from the meaty wrist.

Oh my God, I thought. *Oh my holy God.*

I was about to puke.

"Guys," I started to say, but I never finished my sentence. Because at that moment a warbling scream erupted from the woods.

As impossible as this sounds, we all forgot about Kylie Ann's staring corpse for a moment. Flynn and Wood were gaping toward the Hollow. Hubbard looked like he wanted his mommy. I did my best not to pee myself.

Wood was the first to react. He stood, dusted himself off, and moved away from the grave. Flynn strode up beside him, both men honing in on the source of the scream. It sounded like someone was being flayed alive.

Flynn started across the graveyard.

"Wait a minute," I said to Flynn's receding back. "Don't you guys have to like, call for backup or something?"

"No time," Wood answered. I noticed he'd already drawn his weapon, what looked to me like a sleek silver handgun. I had no idea what kind it was. Barley might, but that's only because he spent so much time playing games where you shoot anything that moves. I trailed after Wood and Flynn, but a moment later a huge object shot past me—Officer Hubbard, I realized. The guy was enormous, but once he got up a head of steam he moved like a freight train.

All three cops were sprinting toward the forest.

Toward the screaming.

I knew if I delayed any longer, I'd lose them completely. I could wait here, but that seemed foolhardy and maybe even dangerous. No one had mentioned Carl Padgett's name, but if he had been the one to murder Kylie Ann, he might still be prowling nearby. Didn't they say serial killers always returned to the scene of the crime? They wanted to hear people whispering about them, wanted to revel in the cops' inability to catch them.

It suddenly seemed very unlikely that Padgett was heading south after all. What if he was right here in this graveyard, lurking behind a headstone?

The policemen had nearly disappeared into the forest.

I bolted after them.

◆

The cops slackened considerably when they reached the trail leading from the graveyard to the woods. The same trail, I realized, Eric Blades would have taken if he really had decided to search for Kylie Ann in the forest.

Was it Eric's scream we'd heard?

I had no idea. But I kept as close as I could to the trio of cops without getting in their way. I had no desire to get shot on accident. We'd only been in the forest for a minute or so when we first became aware of it.

The smell.

At first I figured it was a dead animal stinking up the Hollow, a bloated raccoon carcass or a flyblown possum. But as we ventured deeper and deeper into the trees, I realized the stench was more complex than a mere decomposing animal. Oh, there was rot in the smell, but there was age in it too...and vitality. I know how weird that sounds, but it's as close as I can come to capturing the quality of the stench. The stink of raw meat, of dripping pink juice...that was the vitality I was scenting. The undercurrent of wormy soil...that was the age. And the whole odor was shot through with rot. My mind conjured squirming maggots and hot sewage. For the second time in the last five minutes I found myself on the verge of puking.

Then we heard it again.

The screaming.

It came from our immediate left. My skin prickling with goose bumps, I followed the three cops toward the sound. I realized as we drew closer that it *was* Eric Blades we heard. I'd never heard a human being make a noise like that, but he had a pretty recognizable voice, and I was almost certain it was Eric.

Whatever was happening to him wasn't good.

Flynn had both hands on his gun, which was shiny and silver like Wood's, and he had it pointed toward the forest floor. "You stay here with the kid," he said to Hubbard, who nodded quickly, perhaps eager to let Flynn and Wood handle the situation. Hubbard pulled me closer, but not before drawing his own handgun, this one the antithesis of the kind Flynn and Wood carried. It looked like something out of a Clint Eastwood movie, and though I suppose the sheer size of it should have reassured me, the twitchy way the big cop was acting was scaring the shit out of me. The gun looked like it could blow a hole through cinderblock.

"Should we go back?" I asked Hubbard and immediately regretted it. It sounded even more cowardly than it had in my head. Hubbard hardly seemed to notice. He was peering into the woods, toward a place that was much darker than what surrounded it.

"Hold the phone," Hubbard said. Seemingly forgetting me, he crept toward the shadowy place. There were gigantic uprooted trees bookending the tenebrous glade, and a great many leafy boughs hanging protectively over it. I couldn't shake the sensation that what I was looking at was an entrance of some kind. I hadn't explored this part of the Hollow in months, and when I had, I didn't remember it looking like this. But now the trees, the branches, the rocks, and the dirt...it all looked somehow...

Arranged.

Yes, it looked like it had been arranged this way. I realized with another ripple of disquiet that Hubbard had halved the distance between us and the dark place, but something prohibited me from calling to him.

"Help us!" a voice behind us shouted. We whirled and discovered Flynn and Wood hustling over a rise. They supported something between them, something that flopped bonelessly.

It was Eric Blades.

But instead of the cool, cocky jerk he'd been earlier today, he now looked like some shell-shocked soldier being dragged to the infirmary. Eric was no longer shrieking in that insane high-pitched voice, but he didn't seem to be conscious of his surroundings either.

Gently, they laid Eric down on a bed of dead leaves and began examining him.

Hubbard was watching them, a look of bafflement on his face. "Why did you move him?"

Wood and Flynn exchanged a glance.

"You wanna tell him?" Wood asked.

"Not particularly," Flynn answered.

Wood was peeling back one of Eric's eyelids.

Flynn clutched Eric's wrist, felt for a pulse. To me, Eric

looked like he'd overdosed on drugs, which wouldn't have surprised me. Other than a sizable rip in the center of his black tank top, he didn't appear to be injured.

I thought Hubbard would ask his question again, but I realized something else was gnawing at him. He'd half-turned and was again peering into the sunless glade on the eastern side of the clearing.

"Hey, guys, I don't know..." Hubbard said under his breath.

"What do you make of this?" Flynn asked.

I stepped closer and saw what he and Wood were looking at. After first glimpsing the rip in Eric's shirt, I'd assumed he'd gotten spooked by something, taken off running, and been raked by an outreaching branch. But upon further inspection I realized it was something worse than that.

The slit in his torso was at least an inch deep. I could see the pinkish white muscle tissue peeking out from the bubbling pool of blood. The gouge was long and gruesome, but somehow it seemed too...well, *precise.* The word that kept recurring in my head was *incision,* as crazy as that sounds.

It didn't occur to me at that point to wonder what had made the incision. That wouldn't happen for another thirty seconds.

At least I think it was thirty seconds. So much took place afterward that it's hard for me to measure the way time passed then. I remember Hubbard remaining in the same place instead of joining Flynn and Wood. Almost like the younger cop was standing a post. I remember Eric moaning, his head thrashing weakly on the moist bed of humus, as well as the way Flynn tried to quiet him. I remember Wood frowning over the foot-long gash in Eric's chest, remember him taking out his cell phone and cursing his lack of a signal.

Most of all I remember the feeling of being watched.

Just as I'd felt earlier that day, when Kurt and the others were terrorizing me, I now experienced the most uncanny sensation of being observed by some alien intelligence, something hostile and—I couldn't escape the word—*hungry*.

"Detective Wood?" I said.

Wood pocketed his cell phone in disgust. "What, kid?"

"I think we need to get out of the forest."

He didn't look up from Eric Blades. "We're going to. In just a minute."

"No, I mean now. We need to leave *now*."

Wood looked up at Flynn. "The kid feels it too."

Flynn gave me a strange, sidelong grin. "It's like there's someone else with us, right?"

"That's why we got out of there," Wood told me. "We found this kid laid out in an open place. Almost like he'd been put there as bait."

"It felt like something was going to pounce on us," Flynn agreed.

I glanced about the forest. The drone of the cicadas, which had been well nigh deafening a few minutes ago, had dwindled to almost nothing. The forest had grown preternaturally silent, as if it was holding its breath in anticipation of some dire event.

Wood had his fingers around Eric's gash, apparently examining the extent of the damage.

"Can't we go?" I said.

Wood and Flynn exchanged another of their glances. Flynn said, "Maybe he's got a point, huh?"

"Uh-huh," Wood said quietly.

"What say you, Hubbard?" Flynn asked, rising. "You ready to...hey, Hubbard, what are you *doing?*"

I turned in time to see Hubbard step into the shadowy enclave. Looking at it this time, I couldn't shake the feeling it had been arranged in just that way to lure people in. I didn't want to think about who or what had arranged it, but even as Hubbard stepped closer, the shadows overtaking him, I heard Barley's words recur in my mind.

They call them the Children. They live underground.

Could the overhang toward which Hubbard was creeping be an entrance to some subterranean network?

The Children are huge. Legend says ten feet tall or more. They're the most fearsome cryptids on the planet.

Hubbard bent closer to the cavelike enclosure. My entire body thrummed with nervous tension.

"Hey, Dane?" Flynn called. "You think you might wanna exercise a little caution over there?"

"I hear something," Hubbard said, but his voice was distracted, faraway.

They murder, devour, Barley had said, *or change you into one of them.*

"Hey really, Hubbard. You don't need to prove your valor to us," Wood said, taking a step in that direction. "Let's just get Blades out of here, and then we can sort out what's really..."

But he trailed off into thunderstruck silence when the figure emerged from the darkness.

It was Pete Blades.

But something was terribly wrong with him. He was staggering like the world's worst drunk, and what was worse, he was as white as sun-bleached sand.

Hubbard backpedaled.

Flynn and Wood had their weapons out.

"What's wrong with him?" Flynn asked.

"The hell should I know?" Wood barked. For the first time since I'd met him, Detective Wood looked seriously frightened.

"That your brother?" Flynn asked over his shoulder. I turned and looked at Eric Blades, expecting some sort of answer, but he was lying there with a hideous grin on his face. His eyes were glassy, his gaze upturned to the drab gray sky. As I stared down at him, thunder rattled the whole forest, making all of us jump. Cold raindrops began to pelt us.

Pete Blades took a couple more shambling steps, then stood there teetering on his feet.

Wood's voice was steady again. Or *steadier*, at least. "I'm gonna come over there and make sure you're all right. Just stay where you are and—*Hubbard, what the hell's wrong with you?*" Wood shouted.

Because when Pete Blades had stepped past Hubbard, the brawny cop moving out of his way, Hubbard had seen something that had made him yelp like a kicked dog and clap a hand over his mouth in terror. Hubbard was mumbling something into his palm, but it was so fast and garbled that it could have been anything. Clearly, he was spooked beyond all reason, but we could see Pete too, and from our vantage point there was nothing disturbing enough to cause that kind of a reaction.

Then Pete described a slow, awkward turn, and we realized why Hubbard had lost it.

Pete's back was shredded.

No, *shredded* isn't a strong enough word. One of my favorite foods used to be pulled pork sandwiches. I ate them every August at the town fair. By the time you gobbled down half a sandwich, the meat juice and barbecue sauce always soaked into the bread and made it all squish together in a pink-and-white goulash.

Pete's back looked like that now.

I'd never eat pulled pork again.

"Mother of God," Flynn said. Around the clearing, the rain let loose in a freezing torrent. Thunder rumbled through the forest, and somewhere to the northeast lightning bleached the sky.

Flynn lowered his gun and bit one of his knuckles in horror.

But Wood's instincts took over. He strode over to Pete as the big guy sank to his knees, and did his best to keep him from toppling over. At the same moment Hubbard began a blundering sideways retreat toward the trail. "I'll radio in, fellas," he muttered. "They'll have the paramedics here in no—"

But he never finished.

Because at that moment we saw it emerge from the darkness.

I realized everything Barley had said was true.

The creature rose up as it stalked out of the darkness, its sleek white legs moving with a slithery fluidity. This was the *thing*, I knew, that Mia and Peach had glimpsed the other night. The leering face. The lambent green eyes. The dripping scimitar teeth.

Only this creature was even worse than they had described.

It rose to its full height, which was at least nine feet, maybe ten. Its slender white arms hung down to its knees, the hands and feet long and bony. The creature had some sparse black strands stringing down from its alabaster pate, but other than that it appeared hairless.

There was blood smeared all over the creature's grinning mouth.

For the first time I connected the beast standing before us with what had happened to Pete. The exposed shoulder blades, the gristly strings of muscle and glistening purple of his organs. This creature had done that to Pete, had reduced his entire back to ground chuck.

And now it was stalking toward us.

Hubbard noticed our expressions, and maybe on some primitive level he knew what kind of danger he was in even before he turned and beheld the creature towering over him. Whatever the case, he followed our shocked stares and craned his head up to see the hulking figure, and when he did, I saw his big arms suddenly droop, as if all the life had drained out of him. He squared up to the beast, but it wasn't to confront it— it was so he could back away, straight toward us.

One of the creature's long arms shot out. Fingers like white, flexible flutes encircled Hubbard's neck. Then Hubbard was rising off the ground, the creature's insidious face twisting in delight. Hubbard must've weighed two-fifty or more, but he rose higher and higher until his head was actually at a level two or three feet above the creature's. Without Hubbard's bulk blocking my sight line, I could see the creature's entire hideous body. It was humanoid in shape, but it was cadaverously thin. Yet despite this apparent scrawniness, the beast possessed unspeakable strength. Lightning flashed again, illuminating the creature's corded muscles, its sinews and tendons. Yes, I thought sickly, this beast might look like some sort of upright salamander, but its body was a powder keg of brute power.

It was also, emphatically, male.

Thunder shook the forest, a fierce wind now rocketing through the clearing. The rain assaulted us with sadistic abandon.

Wood and Flynn had been transfixed by the sight of the beast. It was Wood, though, who reacted first.

"Now just...just put him down," Wood said, bringing his gun up toward the creature.

"You might hit Hubbard," Flynn said from the corner of his mouth.

"And if I don't shoot it," Wood replied, "there isn't gonna *be* a Hubbard."

I was inclined to agree with Wood.

As the two men had spoken, the drumming of Hubbard's feet had gone from intermittent attempts to kick his captor to a frenetic flailing. I realized with dawning dread that the creature was squeezing Hubbard's throat.

"I said put him down!" Wood demanded.

The creature brought up a hand, cocked it.

"Wait a minute," Wood said.

"Oh no," Flynn muttered.

The creature grinned. It wasn't until that moment that I understood what true evil looked like.

"Please listen to us," Wood said.

"If you let him go—" Flynn began.

He never finished because the creature's open hand swept toward Hubbard's face. Even above the ungodly rumble of the thunder and the full-throated roar of the rain, I heard the concussion of the creature's taloned fingers on the muscular man's face.

Hubbard's head didn't come completely off.

But it was close.

What did happen was the front and left side of Hubbard's throat split open at the blow, and his head sort of unhinged backward. Blood geysered from the ragged throat hole and painted the beast's satanic features a lurid red.

Wood cursed and Flynn let loose with a yodeling cry of horror. I thought Wood would open up on the creature then, but the creature anticipated him, thrust Hubbard's limp, dangling body down as a shield between him and Wood's outstretched gun. Wood fired three times, but Hubbard's body absorbed two of the slugs. The beast gasped as one shot opened a hole in its side. Its green eyes flashing, the beast stepped toward us, at the same moment giving Hubbard a shake so violent that the cop's dead body flopped like a rag doll in its grip.

"Help me with him," Flynn said, and it took me several seconds to realize he was talking to me. Flynn was getting Eric Blades to his feet, and he wanted me to help him.

Now that's ironic, I reflected. *Blades was attacking me a couple hours ago, and now I'm supposed to risk my life for him?*

To hell with that.

I began to move toward the trail.

"Will!" Flynn called.

I stopped and looked at him, and in his face I saw more than I wanted to, his expression more eloquent than any words could have been. *You're better than this, Will. Don't let this kid die just because he made some mistakes. Everyone deserves a chance.*

Shit, I thought. He was right.

Wood had set his feet far apart, his face full of resolve now. His arm extended straight out, he fired on the creature again but only hit Hubbard's broad frame.

Leering, the creature took another step.

"You leave us alone," Wood said, his voice rising, "or so help me I'll—"

The creature reached up and ripped Hubbard's head off his body.

Wood's mouth formed a shocked O.

Like a big league pitcher, the creature reared back and hurled the severed head at Wood.

◆

Several things happened at once.

The severed head crashed into Wood's chest.

Wood fired his gun.

A maroon hole opened in the creature's shoulder

The creature snarled as the slug spun its spidery body sideways.

One more thing must've happened at about that moment, though I'm only speculating about it now. One second, Eric was supported between me and Officer Flynn. The next he was gone. I don't know how it happened, but he was just...gone.

But Eric was the last thing on my mind. I only wanted to survive.

"Let's drop the motherfucker!" Wood shouted and fired again.

At the second blast of Wood's gun, Flynn's trance seemed to break. He brought up his own firearm, squeezed the trigger. The creature's walkingstick body jolted and jagged with the slugs, but it merely lowered to a knee, as if gathering itself.

"*Joe?*" Wood said in a tight voice.

"Son of a—" Flynn started to say, then the creature was exploding off the ground, the lightning strobing over the forest, enameling the leaping body with flashes of ghastly silverlight. I thought at first it would continue to rise higher and higher until it simply disappeared into the sky, but the creature was bound by natural laws after all. It came down behind Officer Flynn.

To his credit, Flynn reacted quickly.

It still didn't save him.

When the creature had leapt into the air, Jim Flynn had tracked it with his handgun, had even fired two rounds as it arced over his head to land, impossibly, on its feet right behind him. Flynn had begun his spin, meaning to blast the creature in the face, but before he could whirl all the way around, the creature's razor-sharp talons flashed out, and then Flynn's gun—with his hand still gripping it—tumbled into the brush.

My stomach performed a massive lurch. *Please don't kill Flynn*, I thought, knowing how fruitless the wish was.

His eyes as large as tea saucers, Flynn gaped at the spouting stump of his forearm. The flaps of dangling skin reminded me of a blood-soaked mop.

The creature pounced on Flynn, opened its bear-trap jaws.

"*No!*" Wood bellowed. He'd started forward to intervene when I seized him around the waist and shouted for him to *Stop, Stop!*

He ground to a halt maybe fifteen feet from where Flynn lay pinned under the creature. "But we can't...," he started to say, but he trailed off when he saw what I'd already seen.

The creature's head was buried in Flynn's chest. The cop's eyes already stared sightlessly in death as the creature fed.

"We have to go," I told Wood, pulling him away.

"Can't," he muttered, but he was moving backward with me, in the direction of the trail.

"He's gone," I said. "Flynn's gone. We have to run."

Wood's face was ashen, his expression one of benumbed disbelief. But he was a smart man, and he understood very well what was happening. Had we lingered in that clearing a moment longer, the creature would have ripped us to shreds just as he had Pete Blades, Dane Hubbard, and Jim Flynn.

But at that moment, it looked as if the beast was too absorbed in devouring Flynn's body to pay us any mind. We rushed out of the clearing and broke into a sprint. We quickly put some distance between us and the creature. Within a couple minutes we neared my back yard.

I was badly shaken, but I was also elated to be alive. We had evaded the creature, or at least it seemed we had. Every step we took down that path brought us closer to our salvation. Once in my house, we could barricade ourselves inside, summon the entire Indiana State Police force.

Still, the closer we got to the edge of the forest, the more restless I became. The beast wouldn't be content with its kill. It would be coming for us.

Detective Wood insisted I stay ahead of him. This might not sound like a big deal, but to me it was. It was an adult putting my own wellbeing ahead of his own, a grown man acting like a grown man.

"Careful now," he said as we pelted toward a bend in the trail, a gradual decline that threaded its way through a thicket of pine trees. I felt a hand on my shoulder, firm but not rough. I was amazed he'd not only been able to keep up with me—I'd been sprinting with the fuel of mind-shattering terror—but by the fact that he didn't seem winded at all. The trail was narrow, but as we slowed, he was able to brush past me with little effort. "Better let me lead. That thing might try to head us off," he explained.

The rain was still spitting uncontrollably, but the thunder sounded a little more distant. "You have kids?" I asked him.

"Three," he whispered. "Now shut up and let me concentrate so I can live to see them again."

He waded into the murk, the gun strafing the woods. Every few seconds he'd shoot a glance behind us, his eyes constantly scouring the rain swept forest for the beast. It would be wrong to say I felt safe at that moment, but Wood's stalwart presence did give me hope.

He took a couple more steps, then halted, his eyes widening. He whispered, "You hear something?"

I shook my head, shivered. I wished he'd keep moving. The pine boughs surrounding us were shifting and bouncing with the wind and rain, and I considered it the perfect place for the creature to ambush us. If it stole through the grove of pines, we wouldn't see it until it was upon us.

"Okay," Wood said and licked his lips. "When I say go, you go. I'll take the rear again." He threw a nod ahead. "This'll take us to your house, right?"

I nodded. "It's not far."

"Good." He squinted down the trail. Rain dripped from his nose. "This looks like it opens up after the pines. That correct?"

I nodded again.

He frowned. "That means we'll be exposed once we're out of these trees. I want you to take off running and promise not to stop for anything. If that son of a bitch gets me, it gets me. You keep going, all right? You call 911, tell them what happened, and have them contact Jack Shaeffer from the state police post. He'll know what to do. Don't even bother with those local assholes."

I managed a smile. Of all the things Wood had to worry about, my enlisting Bryce Cavanaugh and his deputies for help was the least likely of them.

"Okay," Wood said. "You ready?"

I nodded, not feeling ready at all.

"Run," he commanded.

I ran.

I ran so fast and hard that I nearly face-planted in the middle of the trail. I almost overbalanced, got control, and pelted on. Several times I nearly went down. The earth was slick and muddy from all the rain, and I wasn't exactly behaving rationally. This sounds terrible, I know, but I was fully committed to Wood's plan of not stopping for anything. I liked the guy and all, but I wanted to live, and scampering like a terrified rabbit seemed the best means of achieving that end.

It took me almost no time to reach my backyard.

I didn't spare a backward glance until I was halfway across my yard, and when I did I was heartened to see Wood emerging from the forest. He was throwing glances over his shoulder, perhaps feeling, as I did, that our escape was too good to be true.

I spotted Mom's car in the driveway, which meant she'd returned from dropping off Peach at the Wallaces.

Good luck explaining all this to her, I thought. She'd never believe our story about the beast. Or, I thought with a clenching of the gut, the gory murders.

I climbed the back porch, opened the screen door, and waited for Wood. Moving swiftly, he approached the porch, mounted it, and shepherded me inside. No sooner was the screen door groaning shut than he was whipping the wooden door closed behind it and twisting the lock. I didn't think the lock would keep that creature out, but I didn't say anything.

"Where's your phone?" he asked.

"Right through here," I said, rushing into the living room.

"Need to get ahold of Jack first," Wood murmured to himself. "Then we'll notify the...oh my God."

Across the room from us, a man pressed a gun to my mom's temple.

I'd seen his face a hundred times on TV, online...

...old newspaper clippings in my basement.

The Moonlight Killer grinned at us.

"Put down the gun," Carl Padgett said.

For a long moment, no one moved. I couldn't even breathe.

Then Detective Wood obliged, placed the gun on the carpet at his feet. "Now just calm down," he said. "No one needs to get hurt."

"Except you," Padgett said and turned the gun on Wood. Padgett squeezed the trigger three times, the gunshots impossibly loud in the small room. Wood's body jarred, tottered, then tumbled backward and thumped lifelessly to the floor.

I choked back a scream, unable to process what I'd just seen. *No*, I thought, the horror of the moment digging in. *No.* I gaped at Wood's hemorrhaging chest, the trickle of blood seeping from between his open lips. He didn't deserve this, was too good a man to die this way. I thought of his kids, felt a sob rising in my throat.

"Don't look so surprised, boy," Padgett said. His voice was an obscene mixture of merriment and malice. "These pricks who become cops, they deserve anything they get. This here—" he said with a nod at Wood "—this is just a black piece of garbage."

My lips trembled, but I fought back the tears. I couldn't let Padgett see me cry. He turned the gun on me. "Maybe you want to see how it feels too?" he said. "Huh, boy? Wanna feel the cool kiss of death?"

"Don't hurt him," Mom said, but her voice was small, frail.

"'*Don't hurt him*,'" Padgett whined in a tremulous falsetto. "Maybe I should do you instead, huh?"

He aimed the gun at my mom.

"Let her go!" I shouted. I took a step toward them, acutely aware of the dead cop spread-eagled on the floor beside me. Wood deserved better. He deserved a medal, not a bloody death.

The gun darted toward me. "That's close enough, Will."

I frowned. "How do you know my name?"

Padgett's expression morphed into something even uglier, something ancient and vile and dripping with venom. "Why dontcha tell him?" Padgett said. "Why dontcha tell him the truth?"

"Please don't," my mom whispered.

I looked from Mom to Padgett and back to Mom. "What's he talking about?"

She shook her head. "Nothing, Will. He's just—"

"I'm *talking*," Padgett interrupted, "about the fact that your mother had your name changed when you were a baby."

Mom squirmed in Padgett's grip, but he squeezed her arm hard enough to make her whimper.

"Don't hurt her!" I yelled.

Padgett looked at me, delighted. "Ahhh," he said, nodding. "So the kid does have some balls. And here I thought you were some faggoty mama's boy."

I clenched my fists. "Shut up."

"That's more like it, kiddo."

"Don't make him mad, Will," my mom said.

"I'm not afraid of him," I lied.

"You don't see it yet, do you?" Padgett said.

I paused, my heart squeezing painfully in my chest. But my mind was racing. "See what?" I asked. But I wasn't sure I wanted the answer.

Mom's voice teetered on the edge of panic. "Carl, please don't—"

I was growing panicked too, my breath coming in thin sips. "What's he talking about, Mom?"

"I'm talking," he said, "about your real name. William Marcus Padgett?"

My mouth fell open.

His black eyes glittered. "Be happy, kiddo. Your daddy's one of the most famous criminals in American history."

PART THREE

THE MOONLIGHT KILLER

Chapter Ten

The Cistern, the Drive, and the Gruesome Discovery

"I don't believe you," I said.

Padgett chuckled, the gun waggling a trifle too much in his big hand.

Swaying too close to my mom's head.

Don't hurt her, I thought. If ever I'd doubted my feelings for my mom, those doubts were erased as I watched the gun waver toward her head, hover, then swing away. Each time the barrel swept past her eyes, her pale cheeks, my mind leapt with terror. The man clutching my mother was a monster, a butcher and defiler of children.

And adults, I amended. How stupid I'd been to think he only preyed on kids. He'd slaughtered those prison guards and the owner of the SUV in which he'd made his getaway, then he'd killed Kylie Ann Lubeck. And then...and then...

With an effort, I forced myself to gaze down at Detective Wood.

Who lay sprawled in a lake of his own blood.

The carpet beneath him had formerly been a cheerless beige, but now Wood was surrounded by a wine-colored penumbra. Staring at his moveless body, I could almost believe this good, brave man was only resting. But when my eyes happened on the ragged splotches on his chest, the places where Padgett's bullets had punctured Wood's blue shirt, I knew he wasn't resting.

I knew he'd never see his three children again.

I bit down on a sob. Outside, the rain and wind buffeted the house.

"Ah, don't take it too hard, kiddo," Padgett said. "Pigs like him, they can be replaced easily. There's always some other pig ready to take his place."

"Shut up," I whispered.

"Guys like our state cop here, they figure they're right, and that belief will protect them from guys like me." Padgett smiled a flinty smile. "But guys like me are the real enforcers. We're the *doers*. We're the ones who come out on top, the guys who get to live." His smile broadened. "The guys who get the girl."

My hands bunched into fists. "Shut your mouth!" I hated the sound of my voice, which had risen hysterically, but I couldn't help it. Because I knew what he was talking about, knew it and refused to face it. The horrible, disgusting truth.

As if he could read my thoughts, Padgett nodded. "I don't blame your mama for keeping it secret, Will. I don't have the greatest reputation."

"You're a pedophile and a child killer," I said.

I thought that would infuriate him, but he only watched me evenly. "That's between me and my darlings. What I want to know is how it feels to have a famous daddy."

"Stop," Mom pleaded. "Just—"

But the rest of it died the moment he shoved the gun against her head. I took an involuntary step forward, but Padgett didn't notice.

"*Don't tell me what to do, woman,*" he snarled. "*Don't ever tell me what to do.*"

She closed her eyes, tears streaming from beneath her lids.

Padgett said, "Why don't you tell our son here how we met? That'd be a nice way to pass the time before I throw your ass in the basement."

Her eyes shot wide.

I moved forward, extended an arm. "You can't—"

The gun swung toward me, the barrel pointing straight between my eyes. I was sure at that moment I was dead. Padgett would shoot me and he'd shoot Mom, and then he'd bury us with Detective Wood in the graveyard.

I had to distract him. I said the first thing that popped into my head. "I thought you were in Indianapolis."

Padgett tossed back his head and crowed laughter. His laugh reminded me of a possessed donkey, a loud, strident braying that set my teeth on edge.

I felt a flush of anger. "What the hell's so funny?"

He wiped a tear from his eye, slowly got control of himself. "You know, it's the damnedest thing. Sometimes luck is on your side, you know? I got to Shadeland on the night I escaped, and I've been here ever since. But people are so skittish, and communication's so fast these days…all it takes is one frightened grandma, and you've got reports of Carl Padgett sightings all the way from here to Texas. And the whole time I was holed up in the Hollow."

A chill took hold of me. He'd been here the whole time? In the woods behind my house?

"That's right, kiddo," he said, studying me. "I saw those fellas beat up on you."

I gaped at him. "You were there?"

He nodded. "And I watched you stand there and take it."

Before I could answer, Mom said, "Will, there's something you need to know about Peach."

Padgett's face went hard, his eyes and nostrils doubling in size, and he shoved the point of the gun against her ear.

I started forward, but Padgett growled, "Sit your ass on the couch unless you want me to paint this room with your mama's brains."

I complied.

"So after I got to Shadeland," he went on conversationally, "I cased the town and found it pretty much the way I'd left it."

I stared at him incredulously. "What do you mean, 'left it'?" You're not from here, you're from Bedford."

"Ah," he said. "That." He brought his lips revoltingly close to Mom's ear and said, "Maybe you should tell him that part, honey."

My stomach roiled at the word *honey*, but I forced myself to ask, "What's he talking about?"

"*He...*," Mom said, her voice tremulous and so brittle it sounded like it would shatter. "*He...*"

"Well, hell," Padgett said. "Since your mama here's lost her tongue, I might as well tell it. I used to do a lot of work here. I probably built half the buildings in this town. And I got to know several of the local ladies."

"You're lying," I said.

Padgett smiled, unabashed. "See, to you I'm a monster. The boogeyman. You can't imagine your mom falling for me." He tipped me a lewd wink. "But she did, Son. They *all* did. For a while I had my run of the place. More pussy than I could handle. Whether they were single or married, they were linin' up to get serviced by Mr. Carl Padgett."

I couldn't take it. "No woman could stand you. I can smell you from here."

"You know it's true, boy. I can see it in your eyes. And speaking of your eyes, they're mine. Or haven't you noticed?"

My legs tingled. My bowels churned. It was as if my entire body was revolting at the idea of carrying Carl Padgett's genes.

"Yep," Padgett said, eyeing me steadily, "you favor me more'n your mom. Got my eyes, my chin. Hell, the same wiry build. But if you develop your physique, kiddo, you'll be the strongest guy around. Just like your daddy."

"Stop saying that!" I shouted.

"It's the truth," he said. "Anyway, I had so many good times in Shadeland, this place felt more like home than anywhere else."

"If you spent so much time here," I said, "why doesn't anyone ever talk about you?"

"You know how people are, Will. If I was some rock star or sports hero, they'd gladly claim me. Probably name a street after old Carl Padgett. But a *murderer*? Hell, they probably don't even admit to *themselves* I ever spent time here." He pitched a deep sigh. "But Will, I can't tell you how good it felt to come back. To see your mama's cute little ass again."

Before I could answer, he stood up, dragged my mom to her feet, and nodded toward the kitchen doorway. "Now, how 'bout we all head to the basement. There's something down there I need to show you."

◆

When I glimpsed the heap of newspaper clippings, I felt a tug of foreboding. I don't know why, but I was mad at myself and mad at Mom for not stuffing them back into the box. It was just like us, I reflected, to leave a loose end like that. Mom made a habit of being lazy, and apparently I was adopting that trait as well.

But why, I wondered, should I care if Carl Padgett discovered the newspaper articles? What possible ill could come of it?

Just as I knew he would, Padgett spotted the spill of papers on the far side of the basement. Turning his back to us, he strode over, bent, and retrieved some clippings.

His face spread into a look of real joy. "Why *Michelle*! I didn't think you cared enough to save these."

I glanced at my mom. She looked like she'd swallowed a rotten oyster.

He shuffled through the articles, examining each in turn. "Jeeee-zusss," he said, shaking his head. "This is just like taking a time machine back to the years I spent here. There's me at the Baptist church dedication. There's me at the—" Padgett's expression changed, his voice going stony. "Wait a second."

He turned to Mom and held up a clipping for her to see. "Ted Dexter? You've got the nerve to have this little worm's picture in your house?"

The moment was so surreal I felt like I was watching a movie. Here was Carl Padgett, a warped, depraved psycho, berating my mother for keeping an article about a man she'd known years ago.

Mom's chest hitched, a pitiful little sob escaping her lips. "He was...Audrey's dad."

I could only stare at her. I'd always wondered who our fathers were. I just never imagined Peach's dad would be an insurance salesman.

Or mine a child-killing cannibal.

Padgett's face went livid with rage. "You're a sad, pitiful excuse for a woman, Michelle. You spread your legs for that loser? I'm surprised Will still calls you his mama."

I couldn't take it anymore. I strode forward and swung at Padgett.

Who feinted to the left like he'd known what was coming. My fist whooshed harmlessly by his face, and then he unloaded with a hard-fisted blow to my stomach that lifted me a foot off the ground and left me lying on the concrete gasping for air.

For a time, all I was aware of was the sound of Padgett doing something to my mom. He wasn't hurting her—at least it didn't sound like it—but she was asking him hushed questions, which meant he was doing something that scared her.

As I lay there, I noticed a bunch of old tools on the bottom shelf of our workbench. Pliers, a hammer, a mallet made of crumbling rubber.

And on the floor under that, an axe.

I swallowed. If I could get to that...

Padgett seized me by the hair and hauled me to my feet. It felt like he was removing my scalp.

When I looked at Mom again, I realized what he'd been doing to her.

Her wrists were bound behind her back by wire.

"It ain't much sport cuffing a pup like you," he said. "You're young, sure, but you don't have to be so clumsy. Fight like you've got a brain, Son."

"Quit calling me that."

He thrust a forearm under my throat, placed something cold and hard against my temple. My mom screamed.

"Or what?" he growled. "What're you gonna do to old Carl?"

The headlock was choking off my airway, but even if I could've spoken, I wouldn't have known what to say.

To my mom, he said, "Get in."

She looked at him, uncomprehending.

"The *cistern*," he snapped, "the cistern! Get your skinny butt in there."

She shook her head, her face pale. "I don't want to."

The barrel of the gun burrowed into my temple. "You want our son to live?"

Her gaze was heartbroken, helpless. I tried to shake my head to tell her *No, don't do it*, but after a moment her shoulders slumped and she shuffled over to the circular hole in the floor.

I stared down at it in dread. The black water lapped lazily against the muck-slimed rim. Mom watched that black circle of water with a look of such doom that I redoubled my efforts to break free of Padgett's grip. But the viselike forearm under my chin tightened, and for many moments I couldn't draw breath.

"Stop it!" my mom shouted. "Just stop it, Carl. I'll get in."

The forearm loosened on my neck, and though I was able to breathe again, the sight of my mom lowering to her side, then letting her legs dangle into the murky water made my throat tighten all over again.

"Don't make her get in there," I pleaded. "Don't make her—"

Mom's body splashed into the hole.

Her lower body disappeared, then her torso. Her chin dipped under the water, and just when I thought her eyes would too, her body jarred, and she came up spluttering and gasping.

When the water stopped sloshing in the cistern, I could see it rose to the level of her chin. There were about six inches between the top of her head and the rim of the cistern.

Padgett sounded disappointed. "Hell, I reckoned it was deeper than that."

"It is," Mom said, her voice echoing a little. "I found a foothold."

"Good luck stayin' above water," he said. "'Specially when it rises and this whole basement floods."

My mom's face was shadowed by the sable water, but I could see well enough the terror on her face as the reality of her situation took hold.

I gnashed my teeth in mute frustration. I had to help her.

"Come on, kid," Padgett said. He began dragging me toward the door.

"No!" I said, but he clamped down on me again, and this time it was the exquisite pain that affected me more than the lack of air. It felt like my larynx was being set ablaze. But still, I struggled against him.

"Listen," Padgett growled into my ear. "You do what I tell you, and your mama will live. We gotta get rid of that police cruiser, and I need a new ride. We do all that quickly enough, and your mama will be just fine."

He kicked open the door and shoved me toward the stairs.

I threw out my arms, caught myself, and whirled. I was about to leap onto Padgett when he raised the gun, pointed it straight at my forehead.

"Think about it, kid. You die, who's gonna save your mama? If you get away from me, you really think I'm gonna leave her down here alive?"

He let those words sink in.

Nodding, he said, "The only way to do this is my way. You come along while I conduct my business. You behave, and your mama lives. But we gotta be quick. You hear the storm out there? The water's rising fast in that cistern."

"Why should I trust you?" I asked.

He grinned. "A father would never lie to his boy."

◆

We'd ridden in silence for a few minutes when Padgett turned to me. "Why'd you let those sissies beat up on you?"

"Like I had any choice," I said.

"You've always got a choice, boy."

"When there are three of them and one of you?" I asked. "Not to mention they're all older—one of them ten *years* older?"

Padgett sighed. "I hate to break this to you, kiddo, but I can tell you've been raised by your mama. A dad worth anything would never let you get away with the kind of shit your peddlin'. Three guys? So what? You go after the toughest one, make him pay for tryin' to punk you, the other two'll piss their pants and run away."

I shook my head, glared out the side window. "You don't know Eric Blades."

Padgett eyed me, interested. "Blades the one with the Mustang?"

I didn't answer.

Padgett turned the windshield wipers on full blast. The rain was picking up, the sky darkening. "I know the type. Lean. A little reckless. Bet he's into the drug scene, isn't he?"

I tried not to show my surprise at the accuracy of his guesses.

Padgett nodded meditatively. "I can see how a kid like that might seem harder than most, but deep down he's still just a kid. He'd scare just like anybody else."

"I think you're the coward."

I waited for a backhand to the mouth—I even steeled myself for it—but Padgett merely settled into his seat, a wistful grin on his whiskered face. "Let me tell you a story. One that'll illustrate my point."

I glared out the windshield. As he talked, the reek of Padgett's musky body odor and foul, sour-milk breath began to envelope me.

"The moment that bastard judge sentenced me, I knew how it was gonna be. My lawyer warned me what happened to guys like me in stir. My lawyer says, 'The inmates will kill you within a week, Carl. Our only hope is to impress upon the warden how much danger you're in. Then, maybe, they'll keep you away from all the mad dogs.'"

Padgett chuckled. "You believe that, Will? My lawyer, he calls the other inmates mad dogs. Like *I'm* the one who ought to be afraid." He chuckled, drew a hand over his mouth. "Mad dogs."

Padgett flipped on his signal and hooked a right toward the country. Was he planning on taking me to some deserted spot and executing me there?

I glanced down, wondered if I could hit the door lock, thrust open the door, and tumble out without dying or getting run over.

"But I knew there was no chance of that," Padgett went on. "No judge—and certainly no warden—was going to mitigate my sentence in any way. See, kid, they *want* certain convicts killed. The sex offenders, the child killers…they say you're sentenced to ten years or

218

whatever, but what they're really saying is, you're gonna die in stir. They stick you in a cell with one of their most violent *mad dogs*, and they look the other way while their guy guts you. Most pedophiles, they don't last a month in prison. Hell, they often pay a prisoner to do the job. You believe that? They pay a guy to kill another guy? And they say *I'm* the monster? Hell."

My fingers edged toward the door button. I'd have to be quick, wait until Padgett was making a left turn. Then I'd run no risk of being crushed. The only peril I'd have to contend with was landing and rolling without rupturing bones. If I could do that, I believed I could outrun Carl Padgett.

"So they put me with their number one badass, a guy by the name of Henry Carlisle." Padgett looked at me. "Ain't that a cool name? Henry Carlisle? Sounds like a president or something. Or maybe some dead British philosopher. But the hilarious part is, Carlisle was nothing but a petty thief who, upon being released from prison the first time, killed the partner who informed on him."

My index finger settled on the door button, but we were going way too fast to attempt my escape. Forty-five at least. At that speed I'd probably have my skin torn off by all the gravel on the shoulder of the road, and then Padgett would simply double back to finish the job as I lay there bleeding and begging for my life.

No, I had to wait.

Padgett nodded. "Yeah, Carlisle was a real hoss. About twice my size, with arms on him like Samson. And tattoos? Jesus, you never seen so many tattoos. Guy looked like a walking work of art. I mean, it was *bad* art, of course. All his tats were faded and butt ugly to begin with. But still..." He shook his head, screwed up his eyes to peer through the rain. "Really pissin' out here, isn't it?"

I kept quiet, deliberating. If he took a left at the T-road ahead, I might be able to leap out. He'd have to slow to almost a stop to make the turn in this severe downpour. But if Padgett took a right, the back wheel might crunch over my leg, and then I'd be worse off than I was now.

"Anyway," Padgett said, "long story short, they pair me up with big ole Henry Carlisle, and the first night he comes after me just like I knew he would. Carlisle wasn't gonna wait for the perfect chance, kinda like you're doing now, waitin' for the perfect moment to jump out of this here car."

I froze.

"Kind of moron you think I am, boy? Of *course*, you're gonna try to escape. You figure, hey, this Padgett fella's gonna kill me anyway and leave my mom down in that hole. Why not make a break for it?" He turned to me. "Am I right?"

I felt like someone had taken a baseball bat to my knees. I let my hands rest in my lap.

"So Carlisle comes after me. He's got a knife—an honest-to-goodness *knife*. Looked like something you'd gut a catfish with." He smiled bitterly. "In prison movies it's always somebody shankin' this guy or shankin' that guy. But why sharpen a scrap of metal when the guards simply hand you a giant fucking fillet knife?

"So about ten minutes after lights-out, Carlisle comes for me. He's got his big gleaming knife, and I've got my bare hands and nothin' else."

Padgett fell silent. Waiting, I could tell, for me to ask him to go on with his story. I didn't want to give Padgett any kind of encouragement—I hated the son of a bitch. But I had to admit I was curious. So grudgingly, I said, "What happened?"

Padgett nodded, clearly relishing his narrative. We crunched to a stop at the T-road, and Padgett resumed his story. "One thing they don't talk about is how strong I am. I mean, you caught a glimpse of it when I knocked you on your ass in that basement, but you've never actually seen me in action. You know I was in construction, but I was never just a designer, Will, I was a *builder.* I loved to get my hands dirty, to lift things over my head and watch the other guys shit themselves in shock at how strong I was."

Padgett turned right.

"So Carlisle, he's used to guys quailing before him, beggin' him for mercy. I suspect he'd killed a good many guys, and he sees me as nothin' more than another toe tag. He comes at me, the knife glinting, and I barely have time to roll away. The blade punctures my mattress, buries itself there, and that's all the time I need. Carlisle, bless his tattooed brain, he leaves the knife stickin' in the mattress and goes for me with his bare hands. I give him a crack on the bridge of the nose, quicklike, and he stumbles back, dazed. I grab that knife of his and yank it out. Then, I go after him. I work him around the cell, jabbing at him, and corner him by the bunk beds. I fake with the knife at his face, and of course he throws his hands up—no one, no matter how crazy, wants to be disfigured, right?—and when those tattooed arms go up, that blade goes in. Right here." Padgett raised his right arm and tapped the place under his armpit. "But I don't kill him right away, because that wouldn't have the right effect." He turned to me. "You know what I mean?"

When he saw the look on my face, some of his mirth died away. "Naw, I don't suppose you would.

221

Little sissy like you. So I'll spell it out for you, kiddo. What I did to Carlisle, it had nothin' to do with him."

I arched an eyebrow. "You took his life. How can you say it had nothing to do with—"

"The other *inmates*," Padgett blurted. "It was all about the other inmates. I knew it might be awhile before I could escape." Something terrible flitted across his features. "More than a decade, as it turned out. And if I was gonna be in stir for any length of time, I knew I had to make a statement. Henry Carlisle might have been their prized killer, but I knew there'd be others. I didn't want a bunch of other Henry Carlisles coming after me every time I turned my back. This road look familiar, Will?"

I realized with a sick jolt we were about to turn right again. This would take us along the western edge of Peaceful Valley, but far worse than that, it would take us in the direction of a neighborhood I knew.

Where the Wallaces lived.

Where Peach was staying.

But Padgett didn't know that. Did he?

We drove on, the cruiser picking up speed as it headed into the tree-lined part of the road, the beginnings of the Peaceful Valley Forest. "People who've never killed before, everything they've learned about the human body has come from TV and movies. Oh, and high school biology class. But here's somethin' I bet you didn't know. Bones are really hard. Sure, they're spongy inside, but a bone's not an easy thing to break. So as I shoved my hand inside that cut I'd made under Henry Carlisle's armpit, I had to pull down hard to break his ribs. Oh, I didn't need to break all of them—just two. Still, it took some effort."

Ahead, on the left, I saw the first couple houses. Most of the homes out here were two stories, all of them built on two or three acres. A quiet neighborhood and—at least I'd always thought—a safe place for Peach to visit.

Out of the corner of my eye I tried to study Padgett's face. Did he know? Or was it merely a coincidence he chose this place to stash the cruiser? I knew there were plenty of ponds and marshes out here—Peaceful Valley was full of them. In fact, I remembered there being a large, swampy area at the end of this road. The perfect place to sink a car. So it was entirely possible Padgett had chosen this route strategically.

Still, I held my breath when the Wallaces' tidy brick home came into view, about six lots away now. I dug my fingers into the seat to keep them from tapping.

Padgett's voice was conversational, as if he were commenting on the rain. "I reached into Henry's wound, and I made sure he was looking at me. Those big doe eyes of his." Padgett chuckled. "Once I'd snapped those ribs it was fairly easy working my hand into Henry's guts. I dug into his lung, knowing once I did he'd be beyond making any noise. It didn't take long for me to find what I was hunting for."

The Wallaces' house was only three properties away. It was raining hard now. I prayed that would keep Peach and her friend Juliet inside.

Two properties away and no sign of the girls.

"You starin' at something in particular?" Padgett asked.

With a rush of terror, I snapped my eyes forward, did my best to remove the guilty look from my face.

Please keep driving, I urged. *Please don't stop.*

We rolled past the Wallaces.

I kept my eyes straight ahead, cursing myself for being so careless. How ironic would it be if Padgett didn't know where Peach was until I gave her whereabouts away?

Some protector I was.

Padgett was talking again. "…and when I finally had it, I walked over and left it outside the cell. Then I went to work on ol' Henry." He glanced at me. "You know about my calling card?"

"Of course I do," I muttered, my stomach roiling. "You write a message in your victim's blood, usually to taunt the police. You got the idea from Jack the Ripper."

"Not bad, kiddo. But Jack the Ripper could only manage five kills. I'm still going."

God, I thought. Padgett was actually gloating about his crimes. It shouldn't have surprised me at that point, not after all I'd seen. But it still made me queasy.

We were a couple houses beyond the Wallaces', and Padgett showed no sign of slowing.

A question occurred to me. "Why did you kill Kylie Ann?"

"Why do you think?" he asked, grinning.

My mouth went dry.

He rolled down the windows, and we were immediately assaulted by stinging rain.

The last house in the subdivision came and went. Woods swallowed the road, and after about twenty yards, pavement gave way to gravel. Soon I glimpsed the scum-covered swamp peeking through the trees ahead. Padgett maneuvered the cruiser off the dead end road, through a narrow gap in the trees, and halted about fifteen yards from the edge of the black tarn.

"Come on, kid," he said, climbing out. "Unless you wanna sink with this here car."

I got out and surveyed the woods around us.

"And if you try to run," Padgett said, "I'll drown your mom without blinking. You doubt me?"

I sighed. "No."

He crept around the woods, frowning at the ground. I had a brief recollection of the beast. Of Officer Hubbard's decapitation. Were the creatures out here too? And would they go for me first or Padgett?

Padgett surveyed the ground a few moments longer, then he seized on something, ambled over to it, and bent over. I saw as he straightened that it was a large rock. Not quite as big as a volleyball, but not far off. Padgett hoisted it to waist level, staggered over to the open door, and dropped it on the floor with a deep thud. A moment later, the engine gunned, the accelerator pressed flat, but the cruiser still in park.

"Stand back, Son. Unless you wanna end up a hood ornament."

Without waiting for an answer, he thrust the car into gear. The cruiser peeled out for a moment, its back end sluing toward me. Then it hurtled toward the swamp. The cruiser's front end dipped down, plunging under the water's surface, but the car kept going. The sludgy water rapidly devoured the car. Lapping over its white hood. Swallowing its roof. Soon even the tailgate disappeared into the black swamp's gullet.

I could hardly bear the smug look on Padgett's face.

"Now what?" I asked. "We're stuck out here."

He grunted noncommittally, began walking back the way we'd come. "Guess we'll have to commandeer a new one."

Acid boiled in my throat. There were about twenty houses along the road. The chances of Padgett choosing the Wallaces' wasn't great. But I still felt like shrieking in terror.

Be cool, dammit! a voice in my head commanded. *He won't know if you don't tell him. So for the love of all that's holy, be cool!*

Okay, I thought. *Okay.*

I said, "You never told me what you wrote on the walls."

Padgett chuckled. "Ah, that."

"Well?"

He smirked at me. "It read 'HENRY CRIED LIKE A BABY.'"

I could feel him eyeing me, but I refused to look up, to let him see how disturbed I was.

He watched me. "Well, kid, aren't you gonna ask?"

"Ask what?" I muttered.

"Ask what I put outside the cell?"

"Let me guess," I said. "His still-beating heart?"

Padgett waited until I looked up at him. When I did, his look was cold enough to chill my marrow.

"It had stopped beating by then," he said.

◆

There were, I saw with a quick count, four houses before the Wallaces. The Wallaces' garage door was closed, and their house didn't look any more inviting than the others.

Padgett passed the first house without a look.

"What are we doing?" I asked, doing my best to keep the tightness out of my voice.

"You know what we're doing," Padgett answered.

I halted in the road and gestured toward the first house, an older one with dark wood siding and a yard half-eaten by the forest. "You need a car, right?"

"That's the size of it."

"Then let's check this house."

"Don't like it."

My breathing was growing labored, and it wasn't from the exertion of hiking down the lane. "What's wrong with it?"

"Keep moving, kid."

I did as he instructed. There were still three more houses before the Wallaces, and fifteen more beyond that. The chances of Padgett—

"What about that brick one down yonder a ways?" he asked.

The Wallaces.

Oh God, I thought. *He knows!*

Impossible, I thought. But what other explanation could there be?

I opened my mouth to talk him out of it, but what could I say that wouldn't arouse suspicion? Padgett possessed a razor-sharp ability to read people, some ancient, reptilian trait that allowed him to scythe through lies, penetrate through any sort of deception. No matter what I said, he'd know I was trying to keep him away from the house. So how could I stop him?

You can't, the cynical voice replied. *Because he knows, Will. He picked out the Wallaces' when he was still four houses away. He knows, and he's just wringing every last ounce of terror from you before revealing the truth.*

No! I wanted to scream.

Padgett was only a couple homes away now. I trailed along like a mute puppy. Desperately, I studied the last couple houses before the Wallace place.

The one next door had its garage door open! And what was more, there was a car inside.

"Over here!" I called. "It's a Mercedes!"

"Nah," he answered. "Too conspicuous."

I hustled up beside him. "But it's perfect. One stall is empty, and the other one's got a nice sports car inside. That means the owners are probably gone, and they left this one for the taking."

"Or it means someone's still home and will see us entering his garage."

He cut across the Mercedes people's yard and headed straight for the Wallaces' front door.

"Listen to me," I said, my voice cracking. I pointed at the Wallace house. "Those people are probably home. Living out here they'll own a gun. The moment you step through that door, they'll blast you."

"Nice try, Son."

My legs felt leaden, but I moved with him toward the front porch. I was fairly sure he'd done all this on purpose—the odds were just too remote for such a thing to be a coincidence—but a small part of me still clung to the hope that I could put him off.

Padgett mounted the porch, and without pause he opened the front door and walked inside. I moved through the doorway after him.

The entryway was very dim. It was also really slick from our shoes. The door behind me hung open, but very little daylight filtered in. Directly in front of me, I could make out a stairway leading up. It had been awhile since I'd been inside the Wallaces' house, but I was pretty sure the kitchen was to the right and the living room to my left. I went right.

I had no idea where Padgett had gone.

My skin was cold all over, my clothes plastered to my body. It didn't help that the house was deathly silent. My sneakers squelched on the hardwood floors, and with every step I took I felt I was disturbing some sacred ceremony. Halfway to the kitchen, I froze, realizing my mistake. If Peach and Juliet were here, they wouldn't be in the kitchen or the living room. I'd have heard them by now. If the pair of them weren't watching a show, they were squealing and laughing so boisterously that it made your ears bleed.

I glanced back at the stairway. Would they be up there, in Juliet's room?

Either there or the basement.

I made for the upstairs.

I took the steps two at a time, but I still tried to be as quiet as I could. Padgett was lurking somewhere, and maybe if I was fast enough, I could get Peach and Juliet out of the house before he grabbed us. That would still leave Mrs. Wallace vulnerable and maybe her husband too, but though it sounds horrible, I didn't care as much about them as I did the girls.

Especially Peach.

Please let her be in Juliet's room, I thought.

I padded down the hallway, noticing as I did there were no wet footprints. So Padgett hadn't come this way. Not yet.

I lunged through Juliet's door and was greeted with a dark room. Everything in here was pink and green and stuffed animals.

But no kids.

"Peach?" I whispered. "Juliet? You two in here?"

I eyed the closet, the pooled darkness under the bed. It was possible they were hiding from me, but I doubted it.

Time's wasting! a voice in my head screamed. *They're down in the basement, and Padgett might have found them already!*

I dashed down the hall and clambered down the stairs, trying but failing to conceal the sounds of my footfalls. I felt clumsy, stupid. One step behind Carl Padgett. Or several.

The thought arose in my mind: *Kill him.*

The idea filled me with dread, but there was logic in it. I didn't give myself time to think, but instead made straight for the kitchen. I caught sight of the knife rack next to Mrs. Wallace's stainless steel stove. I crossed to the rack, selected the biggest knife, a wicked-looking thing with a long, wide surface, and an extremely sharp blade.

Get him before he gets you.

I made for the basement doorway and remembered to check for wet footprints. There were none that I could see. So if Peach was down there, Padgett hadn't gotten to her yet.

I rushed down the steps, listening for the sounds of the girls playing, for the music from one of their shows. *My Little Pony* or something with Barbie and a fleet of mermaids. But the basement was as silent as the rest of the house.

As silent as a graveyard.

Don't even think that, I told myself. *Just make sure they're not down here. Then...then...*

Then what?

I bounced on my heels, the terror swarming over me like an army of voracious red ants.

Think for a minute, Will. Just think.

I stood there, doing my best to make my mind function despite my galloping terror.

Why, the voice asked, *would Padgett enter the house without knocking?*

Because he knew the door was unlocked.

Okay. So he's been here already.

My whole body clenched. *No!*

Yes, and you know it. He's been here already, so he went inside. And he didn't bother watching you while he did it. He left you standing on the front lawn. Why?

I have no idea!

Yes you do, Will. Why would a serial killer allow the only person who can get him captured to roam free?

Because it's a game to him?

Yes, but there's something more. Something you're forgetting.

I ground my jaws, agonized by the incompleteness of my thoughts.

Think, Will! If he's been here before, he not only knew the door would be open, he knew where everyone in the house would be.

No, I thought. *No no no no no—*

Yes. And he knows you won't leave here without Peach.

I thrashed my head wildly, as if to escape the voice.

But he *knows where Peach is.*

I remembered my mom's words then:

Will, there's something you need to know about Peach.

"*No*," I whimpered.

If she was dead, my life would be over.

Then save her!

Yes, I thought, my head clearing. I would do everything I could, including killing Padgett.

I looked around the silent basement. There was no one down here. I turned and charged up the basement stairs, my panic pursuing me, unshakeable as a shadow. If Peach was still here, there was only one part of the house in which she could be. I reached the main floor, turned, and made for the rooms I hadn't checked.

I'd just entered the family room when I saw it.

And vomited.

I staggered over to the couch, leaned on it for support. My mind refused to function, refused to process what I was seeing.

But I knew I had to.

My whole body weak with dread, I examined the remains.

Mr. and Mrs. Wallace had been home when Padgett had come earlier. I didn't know exactly how it had all transpired, but the aftermath was plain enough.

Juliet's parents had been hacked to pieces.

Body parts were strewn everywhere. On the floor. On tables and chairs. On the end of the couch on which I was leaning sat Mr. Wallace's severed head. His eyes were open in a permanent look of surprise.

I scoured the room for signs of Juliet. Or…or…

I couldn't even *think* the name. If something had happened to my sister, I didn't want to live. Or I only wanted to live long enough to kill Carl Padgett.

The wood floor was greasy with blood, the formerly white rug gone dark. I made out scraps of clothes, clumps of skin and hair. Even a woman's shoe that still contained a foot.

But none of it looked like a child's.

"You'll get used to it," a voice said.

I jumped and discovered Padgett watching me from the far side of the room. He must have been there all along, but I'd been too horrified to notice.

"You can't escape who you are," he said. His tone was bereft of emotion, as dead as the Wallaces were.

"Where is she?" I asked in a choked voice.

"Don't you mean 'they'?" he answered. "Or don't you care about the other girl?"

I felt white-hot flames licking my neck. I welcomed the anger. Anything was better than the horror consuming me.

I turned to face him, my shoulders heaving with rage. "You'll burn in hell."

His eyes flicked down, and I saw with surprise that I still held the big cleaver.

He nodded, licked his lips. "Why don't you try it, kid? Or are you too much of a mama's boy?"

I darted at him. As distraught as I was, I remembered my mistake earlier, my failed attempt to punch him in my basement. I'd come in too high, and he'd easily dodged me. I needed to be sure this time.

I swung the cleaver at his side. Surprise registered on his face for a split second, but just before the cleaver embedded in his ribs, he hopped backward. He avoided the worst of the blow, but the blade still slashed a line through his chest.

"I *knew* you were my boy!" he crowed.

"I'm not your boy, you son of a bitch!" I snarled. Planting my feet, I raised the cleaver again.

His fist shot out, cracked me in the mouth.

My head snapped back, my feet slipping in the Wallaces' blood. I went down, and before I could recover, he gripped my wrist, slammed it on the floor two, three, four times, until I relinquished the cleaver. Then he reared back and punched me in the mouth. Pain bloomed in my mouth. The world went a dismal brownish gray.

Padgett shook me, slapped my face to bring me back to full consciousness.

"Look at me, boy."

"Where's..." I tried to say, but my voice came out a raspy whisper. "Where's Peach?"

"Hidden," Padgett said. He gripped my cheeks, swiveled my head up to face him.

I stared into his dark brown eyes and saw nothing but madness there, noxious eddies swirling in stygian depths.

"Where is she?" I croaked.

"In a worse place than your mama," he said. "If you cooperate, you'll see your sister soon enough. If you don't, I'll eat her heart for supper tonight."

Chapter Eleven

Padgett's Past and a New Nightmare

I woke up in the Wallaces' black Toyota Highlander.

Of course I didn't know that right away. At first all I could tell was that I was in some sort of moving vehicle, and that my throat hurt so badly it felt like someone was frying it with a blowtorch.

We moved toward town, the rain ebbing a little, but the clouds behind us blacker and more ominous-looking than ever. Padgett glanced at me, said, "Sleeping Beauty's awake."

"Go to hell," I muttered.

Padgett angled the Highlander onto the grassy shoulder. The banging of raindrops on metal was deafening. My head felt like it was being vised apart from within.

Padgett studied me from the driver's seat. He seemed even larger now, even more unbeatable. I felt like I was Peach's size, not someone nearly old enough to drive.

"Will, I know you're curious about your daddy—"

"You're not my dad."

"—but you're too prideful to ask me about my past."

"I don't care about that," I said, perilously close to tears. I couldn't rid my mind of the Wallaces' mutilated bodies. Through gritted teeth, I said, "I don't care about you."

"I understand, Son. I've been out of your life a long time."

"You were never *in* my life."

"Son, long as you draw breath, I'm a part of you, whether you admit it or not."

I clenched my jaw, my vision blurring. I couldn't remember a time when I'd been too angry to speak, but that's exactly what I was now.

"You just simmer down," he said, his tone easy. "Let Daddy tell you a story."

"I hate you," I said. I looked out the passenger's side window so he wouldn't see my face. I wanted to make a break for it, but we were in the middle of nowhere. If I ran now, I couldn't get help soon enough. Padgett would have all the time he needed to motor back to town, to kill my sister and Juliet. To make sure my mom never made it out of that cistern.

No, I had to let him get whatever it was off his chest so we could get back to Shadeland as rapidly as possible. Then, if the opportunity arose, I'd get away from him and get help.

"It wasn't too far away from here we were renovating an old farmhouse," Padgett said, looking around. All I could see were amorphous blurs and a hell of a lot of rain. "Me and my guys, we mostly did commercial work—you know, businesses, churches, an occasional bridge repair. But between big jobs we'd take on smaller ones. Residential stuff. The farmhouse I'm talking about, they wanted everything updated—the farmer who'd owned it had died, and his daughter and her husband wanted it to look and feel like a new place rather than the one she grew up in."

I let him ramble, every muscle in my body tensed. *Just get to the end*, I urged. *Just finish so we can get back to Shadeland.*

"Well," Padgett said, "me and two of my guys— Greene and Kitchell—we kept having issues with the basement. The foundation down there was cracked, and water kept getting in, which proved a major pain in the ass. We couldn't run the ductwork the way we wanted to because we were always ankle deep in rainwater. Situation like that, you don't dare attempt anything electrical. Not unless you want to barbecue yourself on a bare wire.

"So the owner, she told us to do whatever it took to shore up the foundation and eliminate the flooding. She'd gotten a small fortune from her daddy the farmer, so budget was no concern. I had no problem taking her money, so me and my guys, we ripped out a whole section of that concrete floor We figured we'd install some tiling, make the drainage a whole lot more efficient."

I drummed my fingers on my knees, willing him to bring the story to a close. It was positively spitting rain now. Was my mom gasping for breath and spluttering even as Padgett spoke? I imagined her standing on tiptoes, and I had to suppress an urge to scream.

"Why don't you tell me the rest of this on the way to town?" I suggested.

Padgett reached down, produced his gun, and placed it on the dashboard in front of him, the barrel staring me right in the eyes. "Why don't you show your father some respect?"

I felt my bowels do a slow somersault.

"So as I was saying," Padgett went on, "we removed that section of basement floor expecting to find crumbling clay pipes. What we found instead was a tunnel."

I looked at him. He could tell he'd gotten me, and though I longed to lunge for the gun and remove that smug expression from his face with a well-placed gunshot, I remained quiet, wondering where his tale would go.

He resumed. "Being young and excitable, we went inside right away. The owners weren't there, so we had nothing to stop us from exploring all we wanted. It was muddy in the tunnel, but the passage was wide enough and tall enough we didn't worry about a cave-in. My buddy Kitchell—we called him Kitch for short—he was damn near six-foot-eight, but he only had to hunch over a little." Padgett shook his head, a wistful expression on his face. "You shoulda seen us, Will. We were like little kids again, explorin' a brand-new place. I'm sure you can relate."

I could, but I sure as hell wasn't going to admit that to Padgett.

"We'd gone about fifty or sixty feet in when we noticed something that made us pause. We only had flashlights, and I suppose we could've gone into town to buy some lanterns too, give us more light. But like I said, we were just like kids finding a buried treasure, and we weren't going to leave without exploring some more."

Padgett hesitated. "Going back through it in my head, I'm not sure of the order. Whether we saw the way the ceiling was sagging first...or the thing with the green eyes."

My body turned to stone.

He saw the look on my face, smiled. "So you've seen 'em too, huh? I thought there was more you weren't telling me. You and that bastard cop—"

"Wood wasn't a bastard," I interrupted. "He was a better man than you'll—"

"—you guys acted like you'd seen a ghost. But what you really saw was one of *them*. Am I right?"

238

The blood pounded in my ears, my headache so bad now it was like a giant drill boring into my brain.

"I thought so," he said. "Well, I don't blame you, kiddo. Seeing the Children for the first time is a hell of a thing. None of us knew what to do either. Maybe that's why Kitch got killed so quickly."

I listened, the dread like a slowly constricting noose. It was growing harder and harder to breathe.

"That skinny white son of a bitch, it took Kitch down like he was a baby instead of the hoss he was. All Greene and I saw was a flash of green eyes, a blur of white limbs, and then that thing was taking our buddy down and burying its ugly face in the side of his neck."

Padgett shook his head, whistled softly. "*Jee-sus.* You think you've seen it all, and then you see somethin' like that. The blood spouting everywhere like red streamers, the sound of gurgling and screaming. And the smell of that beast. Holy Mary Mother of God, that smell is somethin' I'll never forget. Like a backed-up toilet. And a poorly-maintained zoo. Just ranker than you can imagine."

But I didn't have to imagine it. I'd smelled it earlier that day.

"If Greene and I had fled right away, we might've gotten out of there in time, and nothing would have changed. I mean, Kitch would've still been dead, but I could always find more workers. I paid well enough."

"You didn't try to help him," I said.

"Wasn't time to do *anything,*" Padgett said. A little defensively, I thought. "That thing was done with Kitch in a matter of seconds, and just as Greene and I took off running, that ugly son of a bitch followed us. I've never been so scared. Greene was terrified too, and that's saying something. Dude was a former Marine, not the kind of guy who'd scare easy. But we were both shittin' ourselves with terror."

Padgett paused, thinking. "Something hit me in the shoulder, and I screamed like a little girl, thinking it was the beast. Greene yelped too, and about then I realized it was the ceiling falling down in big, muddy clumps. Not the beast." His voice went lower. "Not yet, at least."

"What do you—"

"We ran like crazy. I was faster, but Greene had a head start on me. Cuz of that, when the beast lunged for us, it hit us both at about the same time."

"It killed Greene too?"

"Just shut up and listen, would you? Jesus. Your attention span always this short? It's like you got A.B.D. or somethin'."

I didn't bother correcting him.

Padgett heaved a huge sigh, went on. "When it struck us, my blue jeans must've slowed down those talons some. I got scratched, but it was shallow. Barely noticeable, in fact. The kind of thing you don't even need a Band-Aid for."

I tilted my head. "But Greene..."

"Greene got slashed to the bone. The thing's claws sank into his calf muscle like ice picks. It would've killed him for sure had the ceiling not fallen in."

"It fell on both of them?"

"Almost. A whole section caved in behind us and buried the beast up to the shoulders. Greene and I scrambled away and were climbing back into the basement when the rest of the tunnel collapsed. We were damned lucky to get out of there alive."

"I wish you hadn't."

Padgett crowed laughter. "That's my boy! Love seein' that mean streak in you."

"Can we get back to town now?"

He placed a hand on the gun, fingered it idly, but I got the message: *Keep interrupting and you'll get shot.* My bowels did another one of those sickening somersaults.

"Greene and I knew people'd never believe us about the beast. And it was easy enough to blame it on the cave-in. We said Greene's injury was a result of climbing back inside the basement in a hurry, that he scratched it on a sharp piece of concrete."

Padgett stared down at his lap, something new seeping into his angular features. "We thought we'd heard the end of it. But it turns out that Greene and I didn't get away from that thing after all. Not all the way."

I waited, the rain roaring incessantly, my headache so bad now I thought I might vomit. Even worse was my frustration at just sitting there while my mom and my sister languished in mortal danger. I eyed the gun, wondered if I could grab it before Padgett could react.

"You're not fast enough," he said.

I gaped at him.

He nodded, clearly relishing my shock. "The telepathy is part of it," he said. "It's how I stayed alive in prison, how I knew when someone was coming for me in the yard. Once, a guard was about to pistol whip me for no reason at all, but before he did I just looked at him and said, 'You touch me with that Smith & Wesson, I'll eat your kids when I get out of here.'"

I shook my head slowly. "What are you trying to tell me?"

"That I *got* something from the beast in that tunnel." He waved that off. "Correction, I got a *great many* things from the beast in that tunnel."

To my supreme relief, he snatched the gun from the dash and pocketed it. "Before I was marked by the beast, I was an ornery as hell. I liked messin' around with married women. I drank like a fish. Hell, I even fudged my business numbers so I hardly paid any taxes." He shook his head. "But I never killed. Thought about it some…thought about it a *lot*, in fact. But I never did it. Never acted on those urges."

"I don't believe you."

"Doesn't matter what you believe, Son. What matters is the truth. That once I got infected, I was liberated from all those fears that'd held me back." He made a fist, tapped it on the wheel. "I got the *courage* to act on my desires."

"That's not courage. That's—"

"But Greene?" Padgett interrupted, staring at me sidelong. "He got even more than that. In the hours between our escape from the tunnel and nightfall, he started to transform."

I held his gaze, not comprehending.

Padgett gave me a *You're-too-stupid-to-live* look. "He became one of them."

"You're lying," I said.

"Wish I was. We were living in trailers outside of town, so there was no one within a half mile of us. I went next door to check on him, and when I did, I heard this terrible screaming inside his trailer. My first thought upon going in was that he'd gotten killed by the beast I saw on the floor. Then I realized—"

"—he *was* the beast," I finished.

Padgett nodded. "He wasn't all the way changed yet, but he was most of the way there. Glowing green eyes, fish-white skin. He'd grown a good foot-and-a-half, so now he was even taller than Kitch had been, though a good deal scrawnier. But when he latched onto my

242

wrist, asking me to save him, I realized he wasn't weak at all. Was stronger than any man had a right to be. And what was even more peculiar, when he'd begged me to help him, he hadn't said the words aloud. He'd spoken them *in my head*."

I was holding my breath, but barely conscious I was doing so. "What did you do?"

"I killed him, of course," he said, as though the act were as pedestrian as flushing the toilet or taking out the trash. "I could see what he was becoming, and I saw what was in his mind."

"And that was?"

"Murder," he said. "The same thing that was in my head."

He turned in his seat, his eyes alight with a childlike enthusiasm. "What happened to me in that tunnel was a revelation, Will. It took away all the fear in me and replaced it with steel...with *conviction*."

He licked his lips. "When I bashed Greene's head in with that hammer, it was like all that pent-up anger that'd been in me my whole life was released. I'd never felt more peaceful."

I stared at him. "When you were bashing your friend's head in."

"He wasn't my friend anymore, Will. He'd gone over. I'm not exactly sure how it works...the biology of it. But I guess I just got a smaller dose. Had I waited any longer, I've no doubt he would've broken into my trailer and eaten me alive."

"So you killed him," I said. "And you got away with it."

Again with that shrewd look, like he and I were conspirators together. It turned my stomach. "That was my first kill, and you know what they say: You never forget your first. But for me it was just a...a what do you call it? An appetizer." He nodded. "I got rid of his body, and though the cops hassled me a little, they believed it in the end. That he'd gone away because of the guilt he felt over leaving Kitch behind during that cave-in."

I didn't want to hear what was next, but short of trying to kill Padgett myself, there was no way to stop his story.

He said, "I held out for about a month after that—you know, no reason to attract attention so soon after Kitch and Greene died—but then the hunger became too much for me."

I closed my eyes. "I know the rest of it. I don't need to hear about how you killed and ate little kids."

He patted the steering wheel, laughing a little. "I gotta tell you, Will, I'm mighty disappointed in you. All the things you're not asking me."

"I'm a little distracted by the fact that my mom might be drowning as we speak. Can we please *go*?"

He didn't acknowledge that. "Don't you want to know why I broke out when I did? I mean, why now instead of five years ago?"

"I don't give a shit."

"You're a poor liar, Son. And I'll tell you anyway: I escaped because the creatures are stirring again."

That word—*creatures*—sent a frigid breeze up and down my arms. "How could you—"

"*Because I'm one of them, Will,*" he said, his black eyes glittering. "Don't you see that? I didn't change over all the way, but the strength, the lust for blood. The thoughts that you'd call evil, and the desire to act on them...I'm part beast."

I looked at him, marveling. "You actually *want* to make contact with those things?"

He grunted. "Wouldn't you? Before, I was just a regular guy. Strong, smart, good-lookin'. But otherwise normal. But when I got outa that tunnel?" he said, eyebrows raised. "Carl Padgett 2.0."

"You were depraved to begin with."

He didn't look annoyed. "I had thoughts in that direction, sure. Curiosities, I suppose you'd say. I might've messed around with girls who were younger than me, but nothin' so horrible I would've gone to jail for." He winked. "Not for long, at least."

"You're a sick bastard."

"From where you're sittin', sure. But if you could live in this body, Will, you'd see what benefits there are to it." He studied the rain-battered windshield. "The change."

"Or maybe you're just using it as an excuse to do what you wanted to all along."

He stroked his chin analytically. "I've thought about that. But it don't add up. You can explain away the acts, but what you can't account for is the *style*. The execution." He chuckled, a horrible, spine-tingling sound. "'Execution.' That's funny as hell."

"I don't believe a word of it," I muttered, even though I did. The tale was too awful to be anything but true.

"That's all right," he said. "I suspect we'll be seeing the Children again soon." He jerked the Highlander into gear and grinned at me. "It's about time I was around my own kind."

My skin misted in goose pimples, but I was thinking hard now. "Are you trying to tell me you're the reason the Children have started to go aboveground? That you're somehow summoning them?"

"Try the other way around, kiddo. I'm a hell of a man, but I'm not that special. No, I've been hearing them in my head, telling me the time is coming when they'll rise again, when they'll rule the land the way they used to."

"You're completely insane," I said, but I'm afraid my voice shook.

"You're right to be afraid, Will. It's real. What woke them was that damned state park they're gonna be opening. The preliminary digging they've done, that's roused them from their sleep." He looked at me shrewdly. "Very soon this whole area's gonna be a bloodbath." He smiled a ghastly smile. "And I aim to be in on it."

♦

We'd driven in silence for a minute or so when Padgett said, "Since you don't seem to be much of a detective, how about I fill you in on the timeline?"

"Where's Peach?" I asked.

"The irony of it is," he went on, "you'd get some clues if you'd just listen. You ever hear of that concept? Listening?"

I glanced at him sourly, but said nothing. I wanted to snap back at him, but somewhere in my mind, in that realm where logic still resided, I knew he was right. Wasn't that always the problem with villains? Wasn't arrogance their weakness?

So let Padgett talk, I told myself. *Maybe you really will learn something useful.*

"I'm listening," I said.

Padgett drew in a luxuriant breath, shivered. "*Jee-sus*, Will. Can't tell you how good it feels to breath clean air again, to see something other than dirt and rust."

"The jail was that dirty?"

He scowled at me. "Never you mind what the jail was like."

I fell silent and stared out the window.

"So here's how it shook out," he said with a self-satisfied grin. "You went into the woods with those fake tough guys, and I watched you let them roll right over you."

It was becoming increasingly difficult to stay quiet. But I did. For Peach.

"When you got back, it wasn't long before your mom and little sister headed out."

"I know that," I muttered.

"You didn't know I was hiding in the car."

I stared at him, gapemouthed.

He slapped the steering wheel as if he'd just heard a hilarious joke. "I tell ya, it's a damned good thing your mama drives a station wagon. It was the easiest thing in the world to lay down in the back seat and wait. I considered surprising them while we were still in your driveway, but then I got curious. Where was your mama going? To your sister's friend's house, it turned out. They were all inside the Wallaces' when I came waltzing in. You shoulda seen everyone's faces! It was beautiful. I told your mama it was nice to see her again. She looked at me like I was a phantom. Hah!" He pounded the wheel in glee. "Then all I had to do was lock your mama and the girls in a safe place while I dealt with Mr. and Mrs. Wallace."

A terrible notion occurred to me. "Did Peach and Juliet see what you did to Juliet's parents?"

He gave me a hurt look. "Now, come on, Will. Give me a little credit. I don't want to spoil a kid's innocence before I have to. They were locked in a closet. And when I was done, we just went out the front door, lickety-split."

I couldn't bear his teasing grin. Staring out my window, I said, "Then you went to my house?"

"You know better than that, Will. I had to hide the girls somewhere, didn't I? Oh, they cried a good deal and your mama screamed a lot, but by that time it was stormin' so loudly there was no way anyone was gonna hear them."

I considered the timing of it all. The storm had let loose just when the police and I had discovered Eric Blades in the woods. The next ten or fifteen minutes had been a riot of lightning and thunder. That meant Padgett had been hiding Peach and Juliet at right about that time. I calculated the distances, held them up against the time frame. It didn't tell me enough, but it did tell me they had to be fairly close to my house.

Padgett nodded. "We'd just gotten inside your house when you and that pig showed up. I wasn't surprised by that—his cruiser being in your driveway and all—but I do have to say when your mama and I first pulled up, I reckoned my time as a free man had come to an end."

I slouched against the window, a fist supporting my chin. "There were three of them."

"The state cops?" Padgett said, his voice sharp.

I didn't say anything. From the corner of my eyes, I saw him watching me, interested now. "What happened to the other two?" he asked.

I considered telling him about the creature in the woods. Pete Blades and his gore-streaked back. The decapitation of Officer Hubbard. Flynn's death.

But what was the point? I could see no advantage in telling him the truth.

And maybe, my mind whispered, *Padgett not knowing about the creature might end up helping you a great deal.*

248

Keeping my voice as natural as possible, I said, "The other two policemen went on searching for Kylie Ann."

Padgett rolled his eyes. "Hell, kid. How dumb you think I am?"

"They'll be wondering where their car is, don't you think? When they find it gone, they'll call for reinforcements."

"We both know there was only one cop," he said. "Otherwise, you would've mentioned the other ones earlier."

I felt a rush of frustration.

At least we'd reentered Shadeland. We were moving past the baseball field and heading downtown.

"Where are we going?" I asked.

"To settle another score."

"You're going to kill again?"

He didn't respond.

"Because if you are," I said, "you're digging your own grave."

"Shit, kid, who's gonna catch me? No one even knows I'm here. I'm a ghost."

I nodded toward the window beyond him. "That cop might pull you over."

When he turned his head I pushed the lock button and threw open the door. Padgett gasped, made a grab for me, but I was already tumbling out of the Highlander, the crumbling macadam along the road's edge biting into my shoulders as I tucked into a clumsy roll. The Highlander was screeching sideways, Padgett having stomped on the brakes, but I was up then, my knees and elbows hurting but my body pretty much intact. The police station was about six blocks away, but before that there were gas stations, the liquor store. I was underage, but I figured the owner of Bill's Fine

Spirits wouldn't blame me for barging in, given the circumstances.

I charged up the hill, past tall, historic homes, the liquor store and a gas station coming into view over the rise. The rain had slackened a little, but it still gave everything a gauzy, indistinct quality that made me feel more than ever that this was some bizarre nightmare.

The roar of a revving engine shattered the illusion.

Behind me, the Highlander was reversing, peeling out in a shower of dusty gravel. Then it leaped up the hill after me like a voracious deep-sea fish.

I pelted up the hill, acutely aware that there were no sidewalks on which to take refuge. I could dash into someone's yard, take a chance on ducking between houses or hiding under some shrubs, but the prospect of being overtaken by Padgett here among the looming Victorian houses terrified me.

I had to make it to the business district. I had to go where there were other people.

I chugged up the hill, nearly to the top. My feet slipped on the wet road, stealing what little momentum I'd built up. Behind me, the Highlander swallowed up my paltry lead.

I made it to the top of the hill and charged across Vine Street without checking for traffic. If a driver ran me down, at least that would bring an ambulance. At least someone would see me being attacked by Padgett.

But there were no cars. I veered into a yard, threw a glance over my shoulder, and was stunned to find the Highlander decelerating. I assumed it was some sort of ruse and pumped my legs even harder, but then I saw why Padgett had slowed down. I was nearing the liquor store parking lot.

Where a police car was parked.

Padgett knew he couldn't kill me with a cop less than a block away.

Slowly, the Highlander turned left onto Vine Street. I knew where it was going.

Back to the forest.

Back to Peach.

No!

I gained the liquor store parking lot just as Chief Cavanaugh exited the building. I was too breathless to shout at him, but it didn't matter. He had spotted me, had stopped by his car door.

I slowed to a jog about twenty feet from the car. Cavanaugh eyed me over the roof of his cruiser. His gaunt form and pale eyes never looked so reassuring.

But I hadn't the first clue what to say. Where the hell was I supposed to start? With my mom, who might be drowning? With the serial killer who had butchered Juliet Wallace's parents?

But when I reached Cavanaugh's car, the words tumbled out without thought or volition. "Carl Padgett's back. He's got my sister somewhere in the woods. He's going to kill her and her friend. Plus, my mom's in serious trouble too."

Cavanaugh barely reacted. "Will, there's a lot happening right now."

"Help me, Chief Cavanaugh," I said, scarcely able to suppress my panic.

Cavanaugh gave me an appraising look. "Okay. But I'm gonna need your help with a situation."

Alarm bells went off in my head. I glanced back toward Vine Street, wondered how close Padgett already was to Savage Hollow. "What kind of situation?"

Rain thunked on the car roof between us. The chief scratched the back of his neck. "It's pretty involved, Will. There are a lot of worried people. Did you know Mia Samuels and Rebecca Ralston are missing?"

My stomach plummeted. Had Padgett somehow snatched them too?

Cavanaugh nodded. "Like I said, I need your assistance. Will you come with me?"

I chewed my lip, not wanting to go with Cavanaugh but not having any good reason not to. I didn't think Padgett had gotten to Mia or Rebecca, but I was really worried about them. And Cavanaugh was likely my only chance at saving Peach.

A sudden vision of the tall, pale creature strobed through my mind. Chills raced down my back. "Okay," I said. "But only if you take me to my house so we can save my mom."

He nodded. "Deal."

Cavanaugh moved around the cruiser, opened the back door and helped me in. The dry back seat was a welcome change from the rain-swept day, though I refused to allow myself to get comfortable. Cavanaugh climbed in behind the wheel and started the car. He glanced back at me, his eyes emotionless.

"Thanks for coming willingly, you little prick. Now I won't have to chase you down and arrest you for assaulting Eric Blades."

◆

I gaped at Cavanaugh in the overhead mirror. "What?"

He leaned forward, peered through the rain. "You heard me."

"Are you that stupid? Take me to my damned house!"

Cavanaugh's eyes swung up to the mirror. "You'll want to watch your mouth, Burgess. You're already on my bad side."

I sat forward. "My mom is about to drown, and my little sister and her friend have been kidnapped. Can't you *hear*?"

"The only thing I hate more than a smart-aleck kid," Cavanaugh said, "is a liar."

Cavanaugh backed out jerkily and drove swiftly away from the liquor store, the kind of cop who sped just because he could. The laws didn't apply to him, but he had no problem busting others.

I hated him.

"Listen for once in your life," I said, my voice growing thin. "Carl Padgett is back in Shadeland. I was just with him."

We were nearing the police station, but I could tell I'd gotten Cavanaugh's attention. He was eyeing me in the mirror, no doubt trying to figure out why I would tell such a lie.

"Tell me what you're after, Burgess," the chief said.

I gritted my teeth, shook with rage and frustration. "I need you to save my mom and my sister!"

He blew out disgusted air, shook his head. "You and those idiot friends of yours have been watching too many scary movies."

It was too much. I made a fist, hammered it on the Plexiglas divider. "Let me out *right now*, goddammit! If you're too stupid to help me, I'll find someone who will!"

The cruiser stopped. We'd reached the station.

Cavanaugh sighed, cut the engine. "If you cause me any more trouble, I'll throw your mom in jail for forging those prescriptions."

I gaped at him.

"That's right," he said, turning in his seat and smiling a little. "I know all about her ugly little habit."

I shook my head. "She's going to die if you don't get over there."

"Bullshit," he said, like that was that.

He climbed out, opened my door. I was preparing to lunge at him when I noticed how he'd taken a step back, a hand perched on the butt of his holstered gun.

His pale blue eyes were utterly emotionless.

I swallowed. Silently, I followed the chief inside. When I came through the door I beheld five people. Seated to the left with his chair tipped back and his feet crossed on a desk was Terry Schwarber. He was staring at his cell phone and sipping coffee from a mug that said TED NUGENT FOR PRESIDENT. About twenty feet or so away from Terry sat the monolithic Bill Stuckey, who was squinting over a newspaper. Since I'd always assumed Stuckey was illiterate, this came as a mild surprise. Or maybe he was just looking at the pictures.

In the jail cell to the left, Barley watched me with a miserable look on his face, like he'd failed me or something. From the cell to my right, Chris watched me with an expression I couldn't quite decipher.

Why had Cavanaugh arrested them?

The chief saw me staring at my best friend, said, "Eric here told us how you three ganged up on him earlier."

Barley hung his head, and Chris muttered something that might have been "Asshole."

Eric Blades sat with his back to us in the center of the room.

The sight of him unnerved me, not only because he was so upright in his chair or because he didn't appear to be moving at all, but because I'd assumed he'd gone to the hospital. Judging from the size of the gash in his stomach, I was surprised he was still conscious.

Schwarber looked up from his phone. "Well, that was quick."

Cavanaugh nodded. "Burgess has been hallucinating."

I ignored that. "What exactly did Blades tell you?"

"Keep your trap shut," Stuckey growled. He tossed the newspaper aside and rose to his full height. It was like watching a monstrous breaker growing out of a peaceful surf. "You wanna run your mouth after the crap you pulled today, I can crack your head for you."

"Into the cell," Cavanaugh said.

I'd noticed the cells the last time I'd been here, but I hadn't really studied them. Now I took in their cramped spaces, their dingy cinderblock walls. It was as though Cavanaugh kept them ugly to make people's stay here as awful as possible.

Chris gaped at the chief. "You're locking Will up too?"

"Don't worry," Stuckey said with a mean grin. "At least you two can kiss each other through the bars."

Barley said, "Don't we get a phone call? That's like, in the Constitution."

"Phone lines are all down," Cavanaugh said. "Anyway, I'm going over to your parents' house. That's better than a phone call."

I stared incredulously up at the chief. "Why drive to Barley's? My mom and sister—"

"I hear another word about your mom and sister, I'm gonna crack someone's skull."

Stuckey lumbered toward me, as though eager to crack my skull.

"Don't touch me," I said, backpedaling. "Don't—"

Stuckey seized me by the back of my neck, hurled me bodily into the open cell. Before I could gain my feet, the cell door rammed shut. Then Stuckey locked it, just like I'd seen cops do in the movies. Only this was real.

"Come on, Bill," Cavanaugh said. "Let's head over to the Marleys', see what we can find. Terry, you stay here and watch these idiots."

"Says the king idiot," Chris muttered.

If Cavanaugh heard that, he gave no sign. He'd made it nearly to the door when he paused and frowned down at Eric Blades, who hadn't said a word since we'd arrived, and who was sitting with his eyes closed and his hands stuffed in his jeans pockets.

"You okay, Eric?" Cavanaugh asked.

The chief's kind-hearted tone caught me off guard. Then I realized why he was being so deferential. Eric Blades was the son of the school superintendent. He was considered an important person, at least in the chief's eyes.

Blades didn't answer.

Cavanaugh studied the back of Blades's head a moment longer, then he nodded. "Deputy Schwarber here's gonna stay with you. These jerks give you any trouble, just let him know, and he'll bust some heads for you. All right?"

Again, no answer.

Cavanaugh went out. A moment later, Bill Stuckey lumbered after him.

Leaving us with Terry Schwarber and Eric Blades. For a long moment the police station was almost silent. The only sounds were the low hum of the air conditioner and an occasional squawking noise from Schwarber's phone.

I glanced at Blades. "How'd you get away from the creature?"

"Huh?" Chris said.

"What creature?" Barley said at the same time.

How could I explain to them all that had happened since I'd been in the forest with the state police? Pete Blades. The monster. The dead cops. Carl Padgett shooting Detective Wood through the heart. My mom, maybe already drowned in that hole in our basement.

And the Wallaces. God, the way their body parts had been strewn all over their living room. The bloody writing on the walls. Peach and Juliet, trapped somewhere with a cannibalistic serial killer. A man who was maybe not a man after all, but part monster.

"Will?" Chris said. "What are you talking about?"

Barley's voice shook. "Seriously, man. You're starting to scare me."

Join the club, I thought. I'd been in a state of perpetual terror for several hours now. If my nerves got wound up any tighter my whole body might explode from the pressure.

I looked at Chris. "Where were you when Cavanaugh picked you up?"

Chris looked down, his face reddening. "My house. When my dad hits my mom..." He grimaced, got control of himself. "...Mom always goes over to Barley's house. Mrs. Marley helps her...I don't know. Clean up, I guess. And Barley comes to stay with me."

I tried to suppress the surge of betrayal I felt. "Why didn't you ever tell me?"

Chris wouldn't look at me. "I guess I didn't want you to worry."

My throat went tight. I suddenly wished there weren't bars between us because I'd never wanted so badly to hug my best friend as I did then.

The silence drew out.

Something made me look at Eric Blades. He was sitting there with his head down and his eyes apparently closed. Like he was an elderly man dozing in a nursing home rather than a drug-dealing delinquent.

"Why didn't the creature kill you?" I persisted. "He killed your brother. He killed the cops. Why did he spare you?"

Without looking up from his phone, Schwarber said, "The hell are you talking about? Quit stirring things up, Burgess. You've already caused enough trouble."

"Tell him, Eric," I said. "Tell the deputy about your brother's death. Tell him about Hubbard and Flynn."

Eric did not answer.

I willed him to open his hateful brown eyes, to return my stare.

Then Eric did open his eyes.

My legs liquefied beneath me. I grasped the bars to keep from melting to the floor. Because Eric's eyes were no longer brown.

They were green.

And much larger than they'd been before.

♦

"Uh, what the hell is wrong with his eyes?" Barley asked.

I thought of Padgett's story, of his friend Greene. The one who'd transformed.

"Dude," Chris said. He backed away from the bars. "There's something seriously messed up here..."

He wasn't all the way changed yet, Padgett had said, *but he was most of the way there. Glowing green eyes, fish-white skin.*

Barley smiled uneasily. "That's some kind of trick, right? Like, contact lenses or something?"

But I knew they weren't. The similarity was too great to ignore. The eyes leering out of Eric Blades's sockets were uncannily like those of the monster. And wasn't his skin a good deal paler than it had been? I thought so.

(*You* know *so. You know what's happening, you mewling little coward.*)

I shook my head. Blades continued to watch me with those huge, unblinking green eyes.

(*You're not worried about your family. It's not about your mom, it's not about Peach—*)

"Shut up," I said.

(*—it's about you, you sniveling little worm, it's always about you*)

"Shut up!" I shouted.

"Hey, Will?" Barley said. "You're really freaking me out."

Chris asked, "You know something we don't?"

(*Tell them! Tell them about the slit on my stomach! Tell them about how the glorious beast fed on my brother, the way he feasted on those pitiful policemen!*)

Oh my God, I thought. The voice was in my head. Eric Blades—or whatever Eric Blades was becoming—could read my thoughts.

(*I can do more than that. I can pry your ribcage open and devour your entrails. And I will, boy. I will right after I dine on this deputy.*)

I shot a look at Terry Schwarber, who was still gazing serenely at his iPhone. *You moron!* I thought. *You're in danger, and you don't even realize it!*

"Deputy Schwarber," I said. "There's something you need to know."

Without looking up, Schwarber said, "Shut your pie hole, Burgess. I got things to do."

Barley was watching Schwarber. Barley's eyes narrowed. "Hold on a minute. Is that...is that Angry Birds?"

I realized with dull anger that it was indeed Angry Birds.

"I told you to shut it," Schwarber growled.

Chris came forward, clutched the bars. "Put down the damned phone and look at Blades!"

Blades's eyes seemed to grow larger, his leer becoming increasingly hideous. A chill coursed through my body.

"Deputy Schwarber!" Barley shouted.

"Dammit," Schwarber said, "you broke my concentration. I was almost to the end of the level." He slapped his thigh in disgust.

But he didn't look up.

Blades, however, continued to watch us.

"What did that thing to do you?" I whispered.

In answer, Blades reached down, grasped the bottom of his T-shirt, and drew it up.

The gash in his stomach had almost entirely healed.

But it wasn't his stomach that shocked me the most. It was his hands, the hands he'd been hiding in his pockets. They were long, spidery, and very pale. The fingers, I estimated, had almost doubled in length.

My God, I thought. *He really is turning into one of them.*

The thing that had once been Eric Blades began to nod.

"Please let us out of these cells," Barley said.

Schwarber made a scoffing sound and continued to play Angry Birds.

Enunciating as clearly as I could, I said, "Put the phone down, Terry, and look at Blades."

The use of his first name did it. Schwarber finally tore his eyeballs off his game and glanced at Blades.

"What am I supposed to see?" he asked.

With a sinking feeling, I realized he was far enough behind Blades that he didn't have a good view of the boy's eyes. Nor could he see the freakish hands now, for Blades had interlaced them in his lap. To conceal them from the deputy, I was sure.

"Okay, I looked," Schwarber said. "Now leave me alone."

Blades grinned at me.

(*I know where your mom is. Why don't you tell me where your sister is?*)

Goosebumps misted down my arms. It wasn't just the fact that the Eric-thing could communicate telepathically, it was the quality of its voice. Raspy and buzzing, the way I'd imagine a green bottle fly would sound if it could form human speech.

(*When I leave here, I'll find her. I'll eat her. Then I'll drag your mom out of that hole and feast on her too*)

"Leave them out of this!" I shouted.

I tried to clear my mind, but the images came, unbidden, of all the people I cared about. Peach. My mom. Chris and Barley. Mia.

(*Ahhh, your sweet Mia. She's already there, Will. I sent her to the forest*)

"You didn't," I said.

(*Oh yes. I sent all four of them—Mia, Rebecca, Brad, and Kurt—to the Hollow. Just before I came to the station. I told them I knew where Kylie Ann was. Lucky the phones were still working, huh?*)

I shook my head. "But why?"

The Eric-thing smiled.

(*Fresh meat*)

"NO!" I screamed.

Schwarber stood up, his face hard. "What the hell's your problem, Burgess? I know you got a screw loose, but now you're startin' to make me mad."

My fingers tightened on the bars. "Would you *look* at Blades, for Christ's sakes? *Please?*"

Schwarber tossed up his hands, moved toward me. "I already did that, you little shit. What do you want me to do it again…" He trailed off as he caught sight of the thing leering at him from the chair. "Holy Mother of God."

The Eric-thing rose. And rose. And rose.

It was at least seven-and-a-half feet tall.

Terry Schwarber gaped up at it.

For the first time, I actually pitied the deputy.

The Eric-thing's leer spread wider, its face becoming vulpine, hideous. It strode toward the deputy, who backpedaled

"Hey," Schwarber murmured. "Hey, I didn't mean anything by…"

Schwarber sank to his knees. The posture reminded me of a whipped puppy cowering in terror from its abusive owner.

"Shoot it!" Chris shouted.

With a start, I realized that Schwarber was indeed armed. Of course he was—he was a cop.

"Now!" I chimed in. "Shoot it in the face!"

Our words must've broken through because Schwarber did reach for his gun, but his hands trembled so wildly that he couldn't dislodge it from his holster.

"*Please,*" Barley whispered. It occurred to me Barley used the same voice when rooting for a movie character in extreme danger.

The creature's long-fingered hands stretched toward the deputy.

"I...I..." Schwarber moaned, his hands still fondling the gun as though they'd never operated one before.

The creature's hands drifted closer. Its smile grew. I realized it was reveling in Schwarber's terror. It loomed over the deputy, taking its time.

"Hurry!" I shouted.

"*For God's sake*," Chris said.

Schwarber finally extricated his gun. He raised it toward the Eric-thing.

But he was too late. He'd just gotten the gun trained on the Eric-thing's face when it swatted the gun aside like an oversized gnat. The blow didn't rip off Schwarber's hands or anything, but it did knock him off balance. The gun went skittering across the room.

Schwarber clambered away, moving on all fours like an overgrown toddler. He bumped into a table, knocked over a clock. He switched course and promptly headbutted the desk on which he'd just been resting his feet, this time upsetting his own coffee mug. It rolled to the edge, hung suspended for a moment, then the TED NUGENT FOR PRESIDENT mug shattered into a dozen pieces.

The Eric-thing stalked after the deputy.

"Get the gun!" Chris yelled. "It's right by the door!"

Schwarber looked stupidly up at Chris, like his words had been spoken in Portuguese.

"The gun!" Chris growled. "The *gun!*"

Schwarber followed Chris's pointing finger to where the gun lay, then he nodded and set off after it, still on hands and knees.

The Eric-thing snagged the deputy by the
waistband of his trousers. Schwarber continued to
crawl, but the creature's hold on him was implacable.
Schwarber crawled doggedly on, his butt crack
beginning to show as his belt strained against his body.

The Eric-thing lifted him off the floor.

Schwarber dangled horizontally five feet off the
ground, reminding me of a plastic animal rotating on
some baby's crib mobile. For the first time I noticed how
much Blades's frame had changed, the way the
vertebrae stood out beneath the tank top, how knobby
the shoulders had become. It raised its free hand, the
mottled talons wickedly sharp. Schwarber's limbs swam
in the air, a sight that would have struck me as
hilarious were the poor bastard not about to die. The
creature brought a forefinger up to Schwarber's throat;
it became clear to me what its intentions were—to
puncture the deputy's jugular and to drench its face
with his blood. Schwarber writhed away from its
fingernail, so it rolled him over in its arms and cradled
him like an infant. Schwarber moaned. The creature
opened its jaws.

"You're weak, Eric!" I yelled.

The thing's teeth paused an inch from the
deputy's throat. Schwarber's face was a mask of
surprise and desperate hope.

The Eric-thing just looked mildly amused.

"You get away with being a druggie because of
your dad," I raced on. I had no idea what I was saying,
but if I could distract the thing, I might buy Schwarber
enough time to survive this ordeal. Maybe Cavanaugh
and Stuckey would return. Maybe the state police would
show up. "You think Kylie Ann liked you? She was just
humoring you to get you off her back."

The green eyes narrowed a little, the creature thinking.

"Don't make it mad," Barley said.

"I'm trying to—"

"Barley's right," Chris hissed. "It'll kill Schwarber for sure."

I glanced at Chris, saw his imploring look, and realized he was probably right. But what else could I do? If I just let it happen, I'd never forgive myself. No one deserved to die this way, not even a dolt like Terry Schwarber.

Then I experienced one of the strangest feelings of my life.

It was like rough, malicious hands were rummaging through my brain for something, sorting through the facts and discarding whatever they didn't need. It wasn't painful exactly, but the sensation was somehow worse than pain. It was a *violation*, a feeling of nakedness, of shame and embarrassment.

I realized the Eric-thing was reading my thoughts.

Its face changed, the eyes shooting wide.

"She's dead," it croaked.

With a thrill of dread I understood it had found what it was looking for, the gruesome discovery the state troopers and I had uncovered in the graveyard.

"That's right," I said. "Kylie Ann's dead. The Moonlight Killer got her. Padgett is here, somewhere in Shadeland. *He's* the reason why you and your brother were in the forest, remember?"

The Eric-thing was staring at me, but not really seeing me. It was looking *through* me, and with a sickening lurch in my gut I understood it was reconciling my words with my memories, scouring my story for lies. But this time I was telling the truth.

265

"Go get him," Chris said, picking up on my attempt to get rid of the Eric-thing. Some distant part of my brain recoiled at the possibility of the Eric-thing on the loose—especially when Peach and Mia were probably somewhere in the forest—but at least it would buy us some time. Maybe Schwarber would release us if we managed to save his life.

The deputy was weeping quietly, his silly mustache bobbing like an over-caffeinated caterpillar. He was still trying to escape the creature, but his attempts were feeble, half-hearted. It was as though Schwarber knew he was at the mercy of the beast, and no amount of resistance would make the slightest difference.

"Come on, Eric," I said. "Please put the deputy down."

The Eric-thing's face spread in a leer of sinister cunning. "*Your sister is out there. And her friend.*"

My throat constricted. I tried to shake my head no, to persuade the Eric-thing to put Peach out of its head, but it was nodding now, a grotesque chortle sounding from the depths of its throat.

"*Young flesh,*" it rasped. "*I'll get her before Padgett does.*"

"Hey," Schwarber said in a high, tinny voice. "You can let me go now, okay? You can just—"

The creature buried its teeth in Schwarber's throat.

I looked away, but I'd already seen too much. The teeth piercing skin. The blood burbling over elongated fangs. The deputy's arms and legs whirring in a paroxysm of agony.

Barley was screaming. As far as I could tell, Chris wasn't making any sound at all. I wished he would though. Maybe it would help drown out the smacking sounds coming from the middle of the room.

As the Eric-thing fed on Schwarber, I moved to the back of my cell. It didn't do any good though. The sounds remained crystal clear. I glanced askance at Barley, and though my eyes were bleary, I could see well enough how he was frozen in place, his hands gripping the bars in panic, his mouth open in that neverending shriek.

After what seemed a lifetime, the station fell silent. I took a deep breath and turned to see what was happening.

The Eric-thing was striding toward me.

Oh hell, I thought.

Its face and the front of its body were stippled with blood. Here and there scraps of the deputy's tissue were stuck to its black tank top or oozing slowly down its blood-slicked limbs. I would have puked if I hadn't been so terrified. It reached out, apparently meaning to rip the cell bars apart.

It can't do it, I thought. *It can't.*

Then, *Please don't let it find the keys!*

The Eric-thing's eyes shot wide. My breath clotted in my throat.

Damn it, I thought. I'd given it the idea!

The creature chortled, turned, and began scanning the station for the keys.

I clamped down on my thoughts, determined to not help it anymore. Could it read everyone's thoughts, or just mine?

The creature's hands balled into fists. It couldn't locate the keys.

With a snarl, it vaulted toward my cell, its body knifing through the air with breathtaking agility. It landed with a meaty thump, its walkingstick fingers cinched over the bars, its toes actually poking through the confines of Eric's sneakers and grasping the bars like a primate on exhibit at the zoo.

You're safe, I told myself. *There's no way it can—*

The bars began to bend.

"Leave him alone!" Chris shouted.

Yes, I urged, *leave me alone*. I didn't want the Eric-thing attacking Chris or Barley, but I certainly didn't want it attacking me either.

The bars hadn't bent much, but they had given enough for me to spot subtle curves in their centers. The gaps weren't wide enough for the creature to climb through, but if it kept at it long enough...

"I'll kill you if you hurt him!" Chris bellowed. His hands were gripping the bars, his teeth bared in fury. "I'll kill you, you ugly motherfucker!"

The creature's muscles flexed, the bars slowly bending.

Another noise sounded beneath the groaning steel and the screaming. I turned and saw what it was.

The outer station door.

There were figures racing through the foyer. When they reached the double doors and pushed through, I saw who they were.

Barley's parents. Chris's mom. Cavanaugh and Bill Stuckey.

They entered the room in a tight cluster.

And saw the mutilated remains of Terry Schwarber.

Barley's dad clapped a hand over his mouth. Chris's mom reeled toward the door. Barley's mom wore an expression of blank surprise. Cavanaugh tilted his head like he couldn't believe what he was seeing. Bill Stuckey uttered a weird, keening moan.

They looked up from the corpse and spotted the creature clinging to the outside of my cell.

And the creature turned and saw them.

Chapter Twelve

The Eric-Thing and the Electrical Terror

As much as I detested the man, I had to give Police Chief Bryce Cavanaugh credit for one thing.

He could draw his weapon quickly.

Too bad his aim was even poorer than his intellect.

Cavanaugh's first shot went wide by ten feet. I'm not sure how he could miss that badly, not at a distance of only twenty-five feet. But he did. In fact, the slug went so far wide that he almost hit Barley, who stood there, mouth agape and likely wondering how his parents had become part of this nightmare.

Barley's mom, God bless her, actually took a couple steps toward her son, as if she could somehow save him from the Eric-thing. As if Barley, who was relatively safe behind the framework of steel, was in more peril than she was. The creature had started toward Barley's mom when two things happened simultaneously. One, Barley's dad snagged the back of her shirt and hauled her into his arms. Secondly, the chief fired off his second shot, this one only marginally more accurate than the first.

The slug shattered one of the overhead fluorescent lights.

Everyone stared at the monster.

Chris was the first to speak. "Get out of here, Mom!"

"Kill it!" I yelled to Cavanaugh.

Cavanaugh's expression hardened a little as he took aim. The creature took a couple long strides at him, which should have increased his chances of nailing it, but again he missed, this shot passing very close to the creature, which would have been a good thing had I not been in a direct line behind it. The slug ricocheted off the cinderblock behind me and sent up a cloud of dust and concrete shrapnel that bit the back of my neck.

The sounds of the shots were explosive, but I could still hear the Eric-thing growling beneath the ringing in my ears.

"Mom!" Chris yelled. "Mom, get out of—" Chris turned and glanced at someone. "Hey, you've got a gun too! Use the damned thing!"

I followed Chris's gaze and realized he'd been addressing Bill Stuckey, who despite his mountainous girth and his bluster, had evidently lost the ability to move. Stuckey stood there like the world's ugliest wax figure as the Eric-thing approached.

Cavanaugh fired again.

Again.

And missed both times.

The creature was nearly upon the group.

Chris's mom slapped Bill Stuckey on the shoulder hard enough to make him flinch. Stuckey gave her a pathetic, wounded look.

"Use your gun," she urged and nodded toward the creature. "Shoot it!"

Cavanaugh fired again. This time his aim was true. Or tru*er*.

The slug caught the Eric-thing in the side. It froze, squalling, its long fingers clutching its wound, and though nothing should have surprised me at that point, the sight of the black liquid sluicing over its fingers made me gasp in shock.

"Shoot it again!" Barley's mom demanded.

Cavanaugh did. His aim from fifteen feet was apparently much better than his aim from twenty-five. He shot the creature in the belly this time. The creature bellowed in pain.

Cavanaugh shot it again, the slug slamming the Eric-thing in the chest.

I was sure it would go down then, that this danger, at least, would be past us. But it glanced down at its bleeding body for a long moment, as if to confirm it had been shot. Then it bent toward Cavanaugh and roared.

The sound set my teeth chattering. Cavanaugh's face twisted in fear. Evidently out of ammunition, the police chief reared back and hurled the gun at the Eric-thing.

Unsurprisingly, he missed.

The creature leapt forward, swung, and Cavanaugh went flying backward through the double doors.

"Oh, for God's sake," Chris's mom muttered. She grabbed for Bill Stuckey's gun.

For the first time, Stuckey showed signs of consciousness. "Hey!" he protested, pushing away Mrs. Watkins's hands. "What are you—"

While they tussled for the gun, the creature turned its attention to them.

"Mom!" Chris yelled.

But he was too late. The thing groped for Stuckey with one hand and Mrs. Watkins with the other. I was sure then that Stuckey would finally live up to his tough guy image, but rather than drawing his gun and shooting the creature, he uttered a shrill yelp and bolted for the far corner of the station. The creature lifted Chris's mom into the air.

Outside, thunder rumbled hard enough to shake our cell bars.

Mrs. Watkins was windmilling her arms as if the sheer force of air resistance would propel her away from the Eric-thing's leering maw.

But it did no good. The creature lifted her nearer its jaws.

Chris screamed at it to *Let her go, let her go.* I stood there in a gray fog of horror. I have no idea what Barley was doing. Maybe he'd fainted dead away.

But Chris's mom was about to be eaten just like Schwarber had been.

Then the beast threw back its head and howled.

The sound was earsplitting and utterly alien. But the pain on its contorted features was unmistakable. I'd been so fixated on the Eric-thing and Chris's mom that I hadn't noticed Mr. Marley sneaking up on it, hadn't noticed the Swiss army knife in Mr. Marley's hand. So when he sank it into the creature's back all the way to the hilt, everyone in the room was stunned. Judging from the look on his face, no one was as surprised as Mr. Marley.

The creature dropped Mrs. Watkins and turned its blood-slicked face toward Barley's dad. Mr. Marley's face went slack with dismay. The creature stepped toward him, its look plainly advertising that Mr. Marley would pay for stabbing it.

A blur of motion from my right, and then Mrs. Marley was smashing the creature in the face with a wooden chair.

Barley's mom was the sweetest woman I'd ever known. No matter what she was doing—tending house, cooking dinner, helping kids at the elementary school— she displayed an inexhaustible patience and a warmth that made you want to be hugged by her.

But now, holding the jagged remains of the splintered chair, she looked like a savage.

The creature was stunned by the blow, but only for an instant. Then it wrested the mangled chair from her grip and roared at her.

The sound made me want to crawl under the shabby cell bed.

The creature raised the fractured remains of the chair with the apparent intention of braining Mrs. Marley with it.

Then Mr. Marley went crazy.

Barley's dad had always been the male version of Mrs. Marley. Kind, laid-back, easy to talk to. I couldn't imagine Mr. Marley hurting anyone. I certainly wouldn't have imagined him standing up to a more than seven-foot-tall monster who bent steel and feasted on human flesh.

But Mr. Marley did.

It started with him picking up a slender shard of wood from the broken chair. It was maybe as long as my forearm, with a tip that was dagger-sharp. Just before the Eric-thing attacked Mrs. Marley, Mr. Marley plunged that wicked shard right into the monster's belly.

This time its reaction was even more intense. It doubled over, shrieking, but rather than standing and marveling at what he'd done to it, Mr. Marley jerked the long shard out, raised it above his head, and jammed it into the back of the thing's neck, just to the left of its spine. The beast dropped to its knees and batted at the wooden spike embedded in its neck. This time Mr. Marley relinquished the weapon. He swept his wife behind him in a protective gesture, then sidled along awkwardly with her until they had reached the spot where Stuckey was hiding.

274

"Gun," Mr. Marley said.

After a moment, Bill Stuckey's hand appeared from under the desk. It clutched the gun.

Wordlessly, Mr. Marley accepted it and strode over to the creature, which had just dislodged the shard of wood from its neck. Barley's dad squeezed the trigger.

Nothing happened. The Eric-thing tossed the piece of wood aside and stalked toward the Marleys.

Mr. Marley leaned toward Stuckey without taking his eyes off the approaching creature. "What's wrong with it?"

"S-Safety," Stuckey muttered.

Mr. Marley stared hard at the gun. "Where is it?"

"Trigger," Stuckey replied.

"What do you mean, 'trigger'? How do you—oh hell."

The creature had reached them.

As the Eric-thing reached for the gun, Mr. Marley fiddled with the trigger. Then the gun erupted and the creature's fingers disintegrated. It flailed backward, its hands jetting black spume into the air. Mr. Marley followed, evidently having mastered the safety mechanism. He shot the thing in the stomach, the chest. It sagged sideways on a desk, but Mr. Marley was taking no chances. He shoved the gun against its temple and squeezed the trigger again.

I was reminded of a coffee pot being dropped from a ten-story building.

The black ichor splattered all over the desk, the blotter and papers instantly soaked with the liquid. A horrid stench filled the office, the mingled odors of fecal matter, hot iron, blood, and something that reminded me of the zoo.

The Eric-thing slumped backwards onto the floor and lay without moving.

The double doors swung inward, making us all gasp.

Cavanaugh stood there, hands on knees, panting like he'd just run a four-minute mile. "You...you get him?"

We all stared down at the creature. It hardly resembled Eric Blades anymore, especially painted as it was with gore.

"I think it's dead," Mrs. Marley said.

Cavanaugh glanced over his shoulder. "You can come out from under that desk now, Bill."

Sheepishly, Stuckey scooted out from his hiding place and made his way over to us.

"How did you..." Cavanaugh began, wiped a hand over his mouth. "How did you finally kill it?"

Mr. Marley glared at the chief. "I'm not saying one more word until you let my boys out of those cells, you vindictive son of a bitch."

♦

Cavanaugh let us out.

As we emerged, we took special care to avoid the corpses of Terry Schwarber and the Eric-thing. The police station smelled like a slaughterhouse.

An especially unsanitary slaughterhouse.

"Now tell me how you did that," Cavanaugh said and nodded at the Eric-thing. I edged farther away from it, on some level afraid it would spring to its feet again and rend me apart.

Too many horror movies, I guess.

Mr. Marley said, "It's obviously something...unnatural, I guess. But it can be killed." He glanced at Cavanaugh. "I shot it in the head."

"Why does it matter?" Mrs. Watkins asked. "It's dead now."

"It matters," Cavanaugh said, "because there might be more of them."

Stuckey's face wrinkled in disbelief. "Come on. *Them?* That thing was just a kid who had some, I don't know, some really severe medical condition."

Chris arched an eyebrow at Stuckey. "You mean like turning into a monster?"

Stuckey blanched.

Mr. Marley shook his head. "Look, Cavanaugh, I know the legends you're alluding to, but there aren't anymore of these…things out there. It's simply not possible."

"Yes there are," I said.

Everyone turned to stare at me.

I swallowed, hating to disagree with Barley's dad. Especially after he'd been so heroic in slaying the Eric-thing. "I saw one earlier. It killed three people."

The silence in the room was oppressive. I was acutely aware of how everyone was looking at me. Most of the adults—particularly Mrs. Watkins—wore dubious expressions. Like I was just some over-imaginative kid trying to get attention. But Chris and Barley seemed to be listening. And strangely enough, Cavanaugh wasn't mocking me either.

Cavanaugh said, "Who'd the thing kill?"

"Pete Blades," I said. "And two state troopers."

Cavanaugh and Stuckey exchanged a look.

Cavanaugh moved closer to me, but now his bearing wasn't hostile. "You said *two* state troopers, Will?"

"Carl Padgett killed the other one," I explained. "Detective Wood. Now will you take me to my house? I've gotta get my mom out of the basement."

"You were telling the truth," he muttered, more to himself than to the group.

The outer door swung open, and someone barged inside.

Mr. Watkins.

He glanced at Chris and his mother, looking relieved. "There you two are. I've been looking all over—"

"Stay away from us," Chris said.

Mr. Watkins smiled, glanced around. "What's wrong with everyone?"

Mrs. Marley's face went hard. "You abusive coward."

Mr. Watkins frowned, looked like he was about to snap back at her. Then he noticed the carnage strewn all over the floor and said, "What happened?"

Cavanaugh ignored that, asked me, "Where do you think Padgett is now?"

My voice was trembling with suppressed anxiety, but I managed to say, "He has my sister and Juliet hidden in the Hollow. I bet he's there."

Cavanaugh's frown deepened. "Juliet...that the Wallace girl?"

I nodded, doing my best to conceal my exasperation. If only he'd listened to me earlier! "We've got to get moving. I don't even know if my mom's still alive. Peach and Juliet...Padgett's with them now."

"Jesus," Cavanaugh said.

"There's more," I said.

"How much more could there be?" Bill Stuckey moaned.

"Mia and Rebecca," I said. "They're in the forest."

The muscles in Chris's neck tightened. "How do you know that?"

"Brad and Kurt," I said. "They're there too."

Barley moved up next to me. "Will...you're guessing. There's no way they'd—"

"Eric Blades sent them there. After he started to...turn."

Barley glanced from me to Chris. "But he never said that. He hardly said anything."

"He *thought* it," I said. "I know how crazy it sounds, but he was talking to me inside my head."

I could see Chris trying hard to believe it, to convince himself I didn't belong in a strait jacket. "Like telepathy?"

I looked at him. "You didn't hear it?"

He shook his head.

I glanced at Barley, who shook his head too.

"Damn," I said.

"Listen, kid," Cavanaugh said brusquely. "I'm prepared to act on what you're tellin' me, but I've got to know, and there can be no playing around with this. Are you telling me the truth?"

I met his stare. "I have to go to the Hollow."

"Me too," Chris said.

Mrs. Watkins shook her head. "Uh·uh. There's no way you boys are going to the forest. Not with Padgett on the loose, and certainly not with those..." She shuddered. "...those *things* running around."

"You can't stop us," I said.

Cavanaugh straightened, hiked up his belt. "You kids aren't going to the forest, and that's final."

"You're calling the state and county police, aren't you, Chief Cavanaugh?" Mrs. Marley asked.

"On what?" Cavanaugh demanded. "The storm's wrecked everything. Phone and power lines are down. The towers aren't working."

"And even if you do get ahold of them," Chris said, "they'll take how long to get here?"

"Look," I said, squaring up to Cavanaugh. "We've talked long enough. I'm going to get my sister."

"I am too," Chris said. "Rebecca and Mia need our help."

Barley glanced at his mom and dad, who both shook their heads. He gestured toward us. "If Will and Chris are going, I have to go too."

"No, you're not," Mr. Marley said.

Barley's voice was plaintive. "I can't just leave my friends. Not now. They're up against—"

"They're right, Barley," I said. "You go somewhere safe."

He looked at me like I'd torn up his favorite comic book.

Chris went over, placed his hands on Barley's shoulders. "Your parents are right. You need to stay safe."

Looking miserable and abandoned, Barley slunk over to where his parents stood.

Chris's dad moved closer, his gaze on his son unwavering.

"And who says you're going anywhere?" Mr. Watkins said.

Chris eyed him balefully. "Who says you have any say?"

Mrs. Watkins cleared her throat. "Chris, please don't talk to your father—"

"*He's not a father,*" Chris snapped. He glared at his dad. "And he's sure as hell not a husband."

"Enough," I said, making for the door. "I'm getting Peach."

"What about your mom?" Cavanaugh asked.

I glanced back at him. "Send Stuckey to get her out of that hole. Unless he's dumb enough to screw that up too."

♦

Cavanaugh drove, and Mr. Watkins rode shotgun. Chris and I sat in the back of the cruiser, speaking in low tones. I told him the whole story, but I had to repeat myself a couple times because of how much the storm had picked up. The rain was punishing the windshield so relentlessly that Cavanaugh's wipers couldn't keep up. Wind rocketed straight at us, causing the cruiser to shudder on the wet asphalt.

Stuckey had taken Chris's mom with him to my house. The rain was coming down in sheets, and I didn't hold out much hope my mom would still be alive in that hole. But maybe...if she was able to stand on her tiptoes...

"Where first, kid?" Cavanaugh said.

"Go up River Road, then I'll tell you when to pull over."

"How do you know where you're going?" Mr. Watkins asked.

"I think I know where Padgett hid them. Where he's been hiding since he escaped."

Mr. Watkins turned in his seat. "And that is...?"

"I expect Will here thinks Padgett's hiding out in the caves," Cavanaugh said.

Chris frowned. "Which ones, though? There are caves all over the forest. In the Hollow, in Peaceful Valley..."

"He's right," Mr. Watkins said. "They honeycomb the entire area."

Cavanaugh eyed me in the overhead mirror. "Go on, Will."

I thought hard. "Padgett had to be able to stake out my house. He watched the Blades brothers and Kurt attack me, and he knew when my mom was home and when she was out."

"I thought Padgett was the one who rearranged your face," Chris said.

I smiled wanly. "It's been a busy day."

"So you figure," Cavanaugh said slowly, "that the caves Padgett's been hiding in are the ones in the heart of Savage Hollow." His eyes flicked up to the mirror. "That about right?"

I nodded.

Cavanaugh eyed me steadily. "You think you know which one it is?"

I swallowed. "I think so."

God, I hoped I was right.

Mr. Watkins shook his head. "I still don't see why we don't go to the county with this."

"Normally we would," Cavanaugh said. "But we happen to be in a once-in-a-decade thunderstorm, and unless you've got some means of communicating I'm not aware of, you better just accept it and focus on helping us get those little girls."

Mr. Watkins shook his head. "But what if Padgett is too much for us?"

"I told you," Cavanaugh said. "Once Stuckey gets Will's mother to safety, he's going to the state police post on Highway 43 to get reinforcements."

The cruiser slowed. Ahead, I made out two or three cars stopped on the road.

Cavanaugh leaned forward in his seat. "Now what do we have here?"

"Flashing lights?" Mr. Watkins asked.

Chris and I crowded the seats in front of us so we could better see through the windshield. We could barely make out, through the wildly thrashing wipers and the freshets of rain assaulting the glass, an orangish-yellow light flashing just around a curve. It was a utility vehicle. With all the telephone lines down, it made sense. Still, the delay couldn't have come at a worse time. The clock was ticking.

"Hold on," Cavanaugh said. He parked the cruiser but left it running. He climbed out and moved into the maelstrom.

Chris said, "You think they've gotten your mom yet? Or are they…"

He let that hang, but I knew what he was thinking. The storm was too violent to see whether or not one of the cars stopped ahead of us belonged to Bill Stuckey. If Stuckey and Mrs. Watkins were delayed, my mom's chances of survival would diminish.

I eyed my door in mute frustration. The cruiser's back doors only opened from the outside.

"Let me out," I said to Chris's dad.

"Why should I?"

I ground my teeth, flailing for a lie. "Because I'm about to piss my pants."

Sighing, he got out, came around, and opened my door.

I pushed out of the cruiser. The rain crashed down on me like a tidal wave.

My hair was plastered to my head, the rain considerably colder now than it had been earlier on. I swept a hand across my forehead so my hair wouldn't drip into my eyes, and as my vision penetrated the shimmering sheets of rain, I distinguished a man in a white helmet talking to—or rather arguing with—Chief Cavanaugh. I hustled toward them, scanning the stopped cars as I did in the hope that none of them was Stuckey's cruiser.

I distinguished three cars but recognized none of them.

I finally reached Cavanaugh and a burly utility worker. I saw from the decal on the door of the white truck that he was from TIPMONT, the local power company. A second later I spotted the problem: an entire set of power lines lay sprawled across the road. Since the lines had fallen at a diagonal, they didn't reach all the way across. Whether or not it was safe to pass seemed to be the crux of the argument. Cavanaugh was motioning toward the forest, and the utility worker was spreading his hairy arms in a helpless but stubborn gesture.

"What's the problem here?" a deep male voice asked.

I turned and saw a tall man in an expensive gray suit glowering at Cavanaugh and the electrical worker. The man looked about fifty, with salt-and-pepper hair that had no doubt been neatly styled before but was now becoming soggy and matted. Behind the tall man, a white Audi's door hung open.

"That's what I've been trying to explain," the beefy worker said with an irritated nod at Cavanaugh. "This road is closed for the foreseeable future. You all shouldn't even be this close to the downed lines. One of those things starts to spark, it'll be just like a rattlesnake."

"I understand all that," Cavanaugh said, an impatient edge to his voice. But there's enough room right there to pass—" He indicated the space between the concrete retaining wall and the severed power lines. "—and this is a life-or-death situation."

"And I," the tall man in the suit added, "need to get to Lafayette for a meeting."

The utility worker put his hands on his hips, squinted. "I know you?"

"I'm Jeff Perlman, from Perlman, Fisher & Myers, and I'm not wasting any more time with you."

Great, I thought. *Yet another lawyer.*

Cavanaugh regarded Perlman coldly. "You will listen to this worker and turn around right now."

Perlman grunted mirthless laughter. "And I suppose you're going to pass?"

Cavanaugh nodded. "What I do is none of your business, but yes, my authority supersedes a downed power line."

The burly worker scratched the curly hair at the base of his neck. "Technically, Chief, it doesn't. The public's safety comes first, and it's just not safe—"

"My *sister*," I broke in, "is not safe. She's in those caves up there, and we need to get through. Right now!"

The utility worker blinked at me a moment. Cavanaugh gave me a disapproving look, but he didn't contradict me.

"You'll let us *all* through," Perlman said, "or there'll be hell to pay."

A voice spoke up from the other side of the white truck. "You can take that bullshit and shove it."

We turned and saw a short, tough-looking Hispanic guy coming toward us. He addressed Perlman. "You, Mr. High and Mighty, need to get your ass back in your car and let us do our jobs." The worker's nametag said JUAN.

"What's happening up there?" a woman's voice called.

We turned and spotted a man and woman standing in the road about twenty feet behind Jeff Perlman. They looked familiar, but with the wind and rain pelting them they were difficult to identify.

"Will Burgess?" the woman said.

I nodded, seeing Chris coming up behind them.

"Have you seen Rebecca or Brad?" the woman asked.

And then it clicked. Of course. The people were the Ralstons, parents of Rebecca and Brad.

But then something happened that obliterated every other thought in my head.

Chris had gotten about halfway between the Ralstons and where I stood. But he stopped there, a look of awe overtaking his face.

"Umm...what is that?"

He was looking up to where the TIPMONT truck was parked. A third worker stood in a raised bucket, apparently examining the pole and the lines grafted to it. But it wasn't the guy in the bucket at which Chris was staring.

It was the creature in a nearby tree.

The guy in the bucket, he didn't see the creature at all. He was so immersed in examining the pole that he didn't notice the beast climbing closer. I was appalled at how nimble its movements were, how lithe its body.

It was ten feet away from the guy in the bucket.

"Uh, Larry?" the burly worker said.

Larry didn't turn.

"Oh shit," Juan muttered. He licked his lips, shouted, "Larry! Get out of there!"

The storm was so loud that I'm sure Larry couldn't make out his co-worker's words, but the urgency of Juan's tone must have broken through because Larry turned and squinted through the leaden day. He cupped a hand to his ear, shouted, "What?"

"Move the truck," the burly man muttered to Juan.

"Can't," Juan answered. "The braces are down."

I looked and saw this was true. White arms protruded from the sides of the truck to make sure it didn't overturn once the bucket was extended.

The creature was five feet away from Larry.

"Oh man," Chris said.

Chris was staring with open-mouthed terror at something to my right. My eyes moved that way, and I discovered two more creatures standing at the edge of the forest.

Watching us.

I understood how a steak must feel right before it's eaten. Or a lobster awaiting death in some murky supermarket water tank.

"What are those things?" Dr. Ralston asked. It was the first thing he had said.

"The Children," I said.

"Let's get to the car," Chris said in a shaky voice.

I began to nod, but that was when a shouted expletive made us all turn toward the worker in the bucket. Larry had finally noticed the creature in the tree. But perhaps that was because it was no longer in the tree.

It was standing in the bucket with him.

♦

The bucket couldn't have been more than four-feet-by-four. Just enough for a man to be able to move around in comfortably.

But with two bodies inside it, the bucket looked very crowded.

The creature in the bucket was even taller than the one who'd caused such mayhem with the state police. I could see that by the way it towered over poor Larry. I don't think he would have had a chance no matter what piece of equipment he'd been holding, but the fact that he was only gripping a plastic flashlight certainly didn't help him much.

Neither did the other two creatures approaching him.

Both of these were new to the scene, one of them monkeying through the branches the way the first one had, the second perched atop the cab of the utility truck, reminding me of an emaciated general marshaling his forces. We all stood there staring up in dread—the two utility workers, Chief Cavanaugh, Chris, me, Jeff Perlman, the Ralstons, Mr. Watkins, and one more onlooker, an old man with his pants rucked up to his nipples.

Ten people.

Five monsters.

No, I realized, that was wrong. There was a sixth creature emerging from the forest. It was angling toward the utility truck, but was still a good thirty yards away. The pair of creatures at the edge of the forest still hadn't moved. Had I not been so terrified of them, I would've offered them some popcorn so they could enjoy the show.

The show started when the beast on the cab of the truck sprang straight into the air and landed on the side of the crane bucket.

On impact, the whole truck rocked, its steel braces groaning with the extra load. I assumed it was constructed to bear the weight of one man, maybe two. But now there were three figures on or in the bucket, and though the creatures were wiry, they were immensely powerful. And muscle, I remembered from my eighth grade health class, weighed more than fat.

I reckoned there was at least seven hundred pounds weighing down the bucket.

Larry looked like he was about to make a jump for it, but before he could, the beast in the bucket seized him by both shoulders. Larry brought the flashlight up and cracked the creature in the chin.

The creature lifted Larry into the air.

"Make it stop," Chris said. I'd never heard Chris sound so scared or helpless, not even in the cell when the Eric-thing was attacking. I could relate. Watching poor Larry being manhandled like that was like watching a doomed skydiver plummet to the earth, his defective parachute still tucked uselessly inside its pack.

At first I was sure the beast would simply take a chomp out of Larry's face. But it didn't do that. Evidently incensed at being smacked with the flashlight, it gave Larry a single, violent shake, and the dull crunching sound told the rest of the story.

Larry dangled in the beast's arms, his neck broken.

The creature who'd leapt onto the bucket was now clawing its way inside. The creature who'd killed Larry snarled at his fellow beast, evidently wanting the meat for himself. The creature climbing into the bucket lashed out, tore away a swath of Larry's back.

The two beasts set upon Larry's carcass, their movements causing the entire truck to rock drunkenly on its braces. The third creature climbed through the trees, then lunged forward, no doubt intending to join in the fun. But it jumped too far and only avoided missing the bucket entirely by snagging the side of it.

The truck began to tilt.

"The car," Chris said. "We need to get back to the car."

I nodded.

The old man began to hobble toward his car, an older yellow Cadillac.

Jonathan Janz

The tallest creature I'd seen so far made a move toward the old man.

Cavanaugh fired.

The chief's aim had apparently improved. The slug caught the creature in the shoulder. It stumbled back, roaring, and took refuge behind the cruiser. The other two creatures on the ground began to stalk toward Cavanaugh.

"Hey!" I shouted. "Over here!"

One creature turned toward me. The other darted toward the old man.

"I'm right here!" I yelled. "Come after me, you ugly white cocksucker!"

What the hell are you doing? a voice in my head shrieked.

The truth was, I had no clue. I just couldn't bear to see that defenseless old man turned into Children food.

And I didn't want to see Cavanaugh get eaten either. He was a better person than I'd assumed. Or at least he was *capable* of being better. I still hated him for the way he'd treated me and especially for the way he'd talked about Peach, but I'd come to feel a grudging respect for him over the past hour.

Cavanaugh fired at the immense creature menacing the old man. The creature tumbled forward and pawed at its back.

The old man finally made it to his Cadillac and climbed in.

"Look out, Will!" Chris shouted.

I looked up and saw a creature headed straight for us. I did the only thing I could think to do. I ran.

Chris was right beside me.

We'd made it maybe twenty feet before we heard Cavanaugh shout, "Get down!"

290

I spun around in time to see the monster bearing down on us. Chris swung an arm over me and drove me to the asphalt. A shot sounded.

The creature skidded on its knees, squalling in pain.

A groaning sound ripped through the muffling veil of storm. I whipped my head around and saw the utility truck rocking again, but this time I could see it was toppling over. It leaned on the braces for a long moment; then it yawed deliriously toward the forest. The bucket had been thrust against the wooden pole, and now it steamrolled the pole, dragging a trio of power lines with it. The lines twanged and cracked as they tore off branches, scraped over boughs. The truck lurched farther, one line tearing loose of the pole before snapping completely. The ends of the split power line spat orange sparks and undulated like enraged serpents. The crane bucket jarred, and the three creatures were disgorged from the bucket, the remains of the ill-fated Larry spilling out around them like pig slop.

Something snagged my ankle.

I looked down and saw the beast Cavanaugh had shot. It was still grasping its back with one hand, but the other one was towing me closer. Pure malice shone in its slitted green eyes. It rose to a crouch and drew me nearer. I kicked at it with my free leg, but it only opened its mouth, its saber-like teeth right above me.

Something darted toward it.

Chris.

My best friend tackled the beast, its fingers instantly releasing my ankle. They both went tumbling to the ground. Chris scrambled to his feet as the beast reached for him. I looked for whatever I could find, but there was nothing. Just useless bits of gravel on the roadside. Chris stared up at the creature, his blue eyes wide with terror.

A shot cracked. The creature spun sideways.

Cavanaugh was striding toward us, his gun extended.

The beast snarled at him. Cavanaugh took aim.

And was slammed to the ground by another creature.

It was, I realized with a sinking sensation, the one he'd shot before it could kill the old man. But now Cavanaugh was batting at the thing, his gun lying several feet away. The creature knocked Cavanaugh's arms aside with one hand, and with the other it tore down at the chief, its deadly nails digging bloody trenches in the side of Cavanaugh's face. The chief's head whipped sideways with the blow, and for a fraction of a second I was sure his eyes battened onto mine. Then the creature dove forward and buried its face in Cavanaugh's throat.

I looked away, sickened.

The creature that had grabbed my ankle moments earlier loomed over me. It grinned, the face like some hideous white jack-o-lantern.

Chris leaped on its back.

Or its lower back, rather. The thing was so tall that Chris would have needed a pole vault to reach its shoulders.

Beyond Chris, I saw a flash of fish-white skin, then heard the sharp crunch of broken glass. The creature who'd taken refuge behind the cars was on the offensive again. It was tugging Mrs. Ralston out of the passenger window. Her husband was trying to fend the thing off, but I figured her odds of survival were pretty low.

The sound of Chris yelping in pain brought me back to the battle right in front of me.

Chris was still clinging to the creature's back with all his might, but the thing's arms were long, its hands unbelievably powerful. It kept swiping at Chris with awkwardly aimed blows. If I didn't save him soon, one of the creature's blows would connect, and it would only take one brush with those razor-sharp talons to end my best friend's life.

Or turn him into one of *them.*

I looked around frantically. Something bolted toward me.

I spun sideways expecting an attack, but it was Juan, the stocky utility worker. He carried two objects, slender steel rods I recognized through the pounding rain as crowbars.

"Here!" Juan shouted and tossed a crowbar to me. I caught it with my left hand, then brought it up with my right, my movements precisely as they'd be if I were turning a double-play. Spinning back to Chris, I realized the thing had just about pried him off its back.

I aimed a home run swing at one of its knees.

The turned end of the crowbar bashed the side of the beast's knee with such force that I heard the splintering of bone. The creature's strident wail told me the damage was severe. The creature completely abandoned its attack on Chris and toppled over, its fingers clamped around its wrecked knee.

Something dark and red inside me reveled in its agony.

Chris had fallen onto the grassy shoulder but was still within reaching distance of the creature. I was thinking this as the beast's hand flared out, gripped Chris's wrist, and jerked him toward it. Chris screamed. I stepped forward and brought the crowbar down again, this time smashing the creature in the wrist. There was a juicy snap, and then its head was thrashing from side to side, a buzzing screech issuing from its fanged maw.

Its good leg swept out and knocked my feet out from under me. I hit the ground on my side and gave my elbow an awful knock. Bone-deep tingles rippled up my arm, the pain vibrating in my teeth. I scrambled up, shuffled around to the beast's head, and swung again. I clobbered it in the temple this time, but impossibly, the creature seemed like it was recovering. It clambered to its hands and knees and glared up at me in green fury.

"*The other end,*" Chris shouted through the rain.

I glanced at the creature's nude buttocks.

"Not its ass!" Chris yelled. "Stab the thing with the chisel end!"

I rolled my eyes at my own denseness. The creature groped for me. I flipped the crowbar around so the sharp chisel would point down. Without pause I jammed it at the beast's face. The chisel punched through its nose and kept going another several inches, where it lodged against bone and cartilage. The creature's limbs began jagging in what I hoped were its death throes, and a moment later, it flopped onto its back, the crowbar still buried in the middle of its face. It reminded me of a narwhal.

"Look!" Chris said.

I whirled and saw Juan battering at the creature that had hold of Mrs. Ralston. She was half-in, half-out of her car, but she didn't look mortally wounded. Not yet.

Within the vehicle, Dr. Ralston had climbed over his wife's body to fight off the creature. Why the beast was so fixated on Mrs. Ralston I didn't have to guess. Its long, erect phallus made its intentions clear.

294

I heard an engine revving. A moment later, the burly construction worker went dashing past us, seemingly ready to join the effort to save Mrs. Ralston. At the same moment, Jeff Perlman's white Audi swung into the other lane in an attempted U-turn.

Perlman's timing couldn't have been worse.

Granted, it was difficult to see with the storm blowing around us, and yes, Perlman was in a state of panic. But I still couldn't believe his stupidity in smashing into the burly utility worker with his car.

In movies, the guy who gets hit always bounces up on the windshield and either tumbles back down or somersaults over the roof. In this case, however, the white Audi's front fender smashed into the worker's thighs and sent him zooming into the concrete retaining wall. The worker, ironically, had shed his white helmet before joining the fray. Whether that would've helped him or not, I'm not sure, but when he ricocheted off the Audi and slammed into the concrete headfirst, I knew he'd never get up again. The poor guy lay without moving, his face turned away from us. It was an ignominious death, but at least it was quick.

Unlike Jeff Perlman's.

Perlman tried to keep moving after mowing down the utility worker, but the Audi was hydroplaning on a flooded section of road. Its back end slued wildly toward the Ralstons' car, then overcorrected, swung around, and crashed into the retaining wall. The engine stalled.

"We gotta help Rebecca's mom," Chris said.

I nodded, but as we hustled over to the Ralstons' car I couldn't take my eyes off Perlman in his Audi.

He hadn't noticed the creature striding toward him.

It was the one who'd killed Cavanaugh, the biggest beast of all. I realized with bleak astonishment that, despite our superior numbers, we'd only killed one of the six monsters. While two of the utility workers and Chief Cavanaugh had been murdered.

The giant creature ripped open Perlman's door. The lawyer gaped up at it in awe.

I looked away as Perlman's wails began.

◆

I still had hope for Mrs. Ralston. For one thing, there were four of us fighting to save her and only one beast to fend off. The biggest creature was leisurely dining on Perlman—whose wails were only growing louder. The other three beasts were still immersed in vivisecting the ill-fated Larry. I had hoped the severed power lines might do us a favor and electrocute one of the bastards, but though the lines hopped and spat amber gouts of fire, the creatures remained safely enshrouded by the veil of forest.

How long, I wondered, until the trio tired of dining on Larry? How long until other Children showed up for the feast?

Children.

Oh my God, I thought. Peach. Her friend Juliet.

I had to get to the caves!

But Mrs. Ralston was in big trouble. I owed it to Rebecca to save her mom if I could. I ran toward Mrs. Ralston, then I bared my teeth, my sneakers skidding on the wet road.

I'd forgotten the crowbar. It was still lodged in the creature's face.

"Where are you going?" Chris yelled as I sprinted away.

I didn't answer, but I assumed Chris had gone on to help Dr. Ralston and Juan. After what seemed like forever, I reached the beast's carcass, positioned a sneaker on the thing's forehead, reared back, and wrenched loose the crowbar. I backpedaled away, amazed it hadn't attacked. I smiled, thinking my luck had begun to turn.

Then I saw the creatures emerging around the overturned utility truck. The trio had evidently finished gorging on Larry. Their naked bodies were slathered with blood.

They were stalking toward me.

I heard shouting behind me. I whirled and discovered that the situation with the Ralstons had changed. Mrs. Ralston was safe, at least for the time being. But somehow her husband and Juan had ended up on the grassy shoulder doing battle with the beast. Juan was swinging the crowbar at the creature to keep it at arm's length, and Dr. Ralston was circling it gamely, but from the thing's expression I could see this was merely sport for it. Whenever it wanted, it would slaughter these two men and return its attentions to Mrs. Ralston.

A large rock sailed out of nowhere and collided with the beast's forehead.

We all turned and saw Chris coming out of his pitching motion. Unable to help myself, I grinned at the intense look in his eyes. He could throw a hell of a fastball.

The thing teetered for several seconds, looking like it might lose consciousness. But then its vision seemed to clear, and it turned and roared at Chris.

The sound chilled my blood.

A car engine revved. I thought it was the old man's car, but no, his yellow Cadillac was still idling.

Then I realized whose car it was.

Mrs. Ralston was escaping.

Had I not seen the black car pulling a U-turn I wouldn't have believed it. But it was, and within seconds she'd be motoring toward town while the people who'd fought valiantly to save her would probably be creature food. As her car swung lazily into the other lane, the colossal beast who'd killed both Cavanaugh and Perlman pushed away from Perlman's car and strode toward Mrs. Ralston's. Her car began to accelerate, but the creature leapt through the open passenger's window. The car veered toward Perlman's Audi, rear-ended it. After a brief tussle, the creature managed to haul Mrs. Ralston out of the car. She screamed and screamed. Her husband, apparently not bothered by the fact that his wife had just attempted to abandon him, began sprinting over to intervene.

He needn't have bothered.

Evidently annoyed by Mrs. Ralston's shrill screams, the giant beast picked her up by an ankle, lifted her above its head, and whip-cracked her to the asphalt. If a broken neck didn't kill her, the trauma to her head did. The creature hoisted her over its shoulder and lugged her toward the forest.

Dr. Ralston gave chase.

"She's dead!" I yelled. "Don't get yourself—"

The creature spun and punched a hand through Dr. Ralston's chest.

I moaned. *Poor Rebecca*, I thought. She'd lost her little sister a few years ago, and now both her parents were dead too.

Juan hollered something, drawing my attention. The creature Chris had plunked with the rock was looming over Juan. Juan was still waving the crowbar back and forth to ward it off, but I could see he was tiring. Soon the thing would simply snatch it from his grip and impale him with it.

Chris moved to the creature's right, hefted another rock. The creature abandoned Juan and faced Chris, who shot me a meaningful look.

The monster's back was to me.

I jolted, realizing that Chris was creating a diversion.

As stealthily as possible, I hustled up behind the beast, praying it wouldn't turn and see me. I closed the distance to fifteen feet. To ten.

Five feet away, I brought the crowbar up, the chisel end facing the beast.

Baring my teeth, I plunged the iron blade into the creature's back, right where I believed the heart would be.

My momentum carried me into it. We fell together, and for a revolting moment I lay atop the beast, its foul stench enveloping me and its black blood spraying over my hands and wrists. With a gagging cry, I scrambled away. The thing rolled over. Chris took my place, the big rock still in his hand. He slammed the rock down with all his might, the thing's forehead imploding. Chris smashed its face again and again, obviously taking no chances. Black ichor spurted all over Chris's chest and throat, but Chris kept hammering at it.

"I think it's dead," a voice said.

We turned and saw Juan smiling crookedly at us.

He nodded at me. "You sure got him good, didn't you?"

I began to smile. Then I saw three figures materialize behind him. The ones who'd overturned the truck and feasted on Larry.

Juan's smile slid off his face; he turned toward the creatures.

One of them leaped forward like a white panther and slammed him into a mud puddle. Chris and I would've saved him if we could have, but the beast's hellish claws were already a blur of motion, scraps of the man's shirt and flesh flying into the air like bloodstained confetti.

The other two creatures stalked toward me and Chris.

"Should we run?" Chris muttered.

"Run where?" I demanded.

There truly was nowhere to go. The road ahead was blocked by the constantly spitting electrical wires. If we took refuge in the forest, the creatures would chase us down within seconds.

The monsters were closing in.

Chris seized my arm, damn near making me piss myself in surprise.

"What?" I demanded, my heart slamming.

"Cavanaugh's gun," he said.

I glanced toward where he was pointing and saw it lying on the puddled asphalt. Maybe it was too wet to still work, but it was the only chance we had.

I nodded. "I'll draw them. You grab the gun."

"Huh?"

"I'm faster than you," I said.

"You're not faster than *them*," he answered.

They drew closer.

"Will..." he said, "...don't..."

But I was already off, darting toward the retaining wall, thinking I could get past them and make them turn their backs to Chris. But I'd underestimated how long the creatures' arms were, how crisp their reflexes. The beast on my left nearly snatched me off the ground with its long reach. The one on the right went for me too, but this beast was cleverer. The thing

300

immediately headed me off, forcing me back toward its partner. As they bore down on me, I was sure I was a goner. Whether Chris retrieved the gun no longer mattered. All that mattered was that two monsters were closing in on me, and I was rapidly running out of space.

The nearest creature groped for me. I dove straight for the gap between its legs, remembering how mad Coach Aldrich got at me whenever I attempted a headfirst slide. It was dangerous, Coach always claimed, and maybe he was right.

But breaking a wrist was a hell of a lot less dangerous than being eaten alive by monsters.

The wet asphalt actually saved me. I hit the road and slid smoothly over the moist black surface for a good seven feet, which proved just far enough to elude the beast's swiping talons. I leaped to my feet and pounded toward the overturned utility truck. Maybe, I reasoned, the wildly coiling wires could save me from the beasts. If the creatures valued self-preservation—and if they understood the risks of the severed electrical lines— they wouldn't follow me. But that was too many *if*s for me, especially when our lives depended on it.

One of the beasts grabbed me, slammed me to the ground.

The force was more than enough to knock my wind out, but it hadn't been a killing maneuver.

The beasts wanted me alive.

They loomed over me, their mandibles dripping with slaver, their lantern eyes alight with lunatic hunger.

They reached for me.

A shot rang out.

It didn't hit either of them. I could see that easily enough from their expressions. But the gunshot made them turn. I lifted my aching head and discovered two things at once:

Chris, waving his arms at me.

And the yellow Cadillac.

It was about to run me and the creatures over.

"Roll!" Chris was bellowing.

At the last second, I understood. I rolled to my right.

And found myself between two writhing electrical wires.

I looked up as the yellow car lurched forward, the old man hunched behind the wheel like the world's oldest NASCAR driver.

Both creatures leapt into the air. I thought for sure they'd clear the Cadillac. One creature did clear it, rising higher and higher into the air, moving like no living thing should move.

But the other one's feet didn't quite clear the windshield before the car slammed into them. The beast swung wildly over in a graceless flip, and when it struck the wet road behind the Cadillac, I heard something snap.

A moment later, the creature who'd avoided the car landed near his maimed partner.

Another gunshot sounded.

The creature on its feet described an awkward pirouette and grasped its shoulder. Chris strode forward, closing one eye to aim. The injured creature made it to all fours, but collapsed again, both its legs seemingly broken.

Chris shot the healthier one again, this time nailing it in the belly. Its body jackknifed, the black liquid spilling out of its stomach like crude oil.

Chris moved closer, squeezed the trigger.

Nothing.

The creature looked up at Chris and grinned.

Chris's eyes widened. Then he dove toward me.

The yellow Cadillac slammed into both creatures in reverse, the big car steamrolling them in a hail of squeals and snapped bones.

Beside each other on the ground, Chris and I stared at the yellow car in shock.

The old man rolled down his window.

"You boys get in," he said. His voice was kindly, but his eyes were fierce.

I shook my head. "Thanks, but my sister's in the Hollow."

A dark crease formed between the man's eyebrows, as if he couldn't believe my stupidity. He turned to Chris. "And you?"

Chris shrugged and nodded at me. "I'm with him."

I figured the old man would chew us out then, or at least protest and call us fools. But instead he smiled sadly and said, "You two have big balls. I hope they don't get you killed."

And he drove away.

Chris and I watched after him.

"Where'd your dad go?" I asked him.

He shrugged. "Probably dead."

"Or he ran."

"Wouldn't put it past him. The asshole."

I frowned at him a moment, said, "Let's get my sister."

"If they don't get us first," Chris answered.

I followed his gaze toward the road.

Where one of the creatures who'd been run down was already stirring.

"Let's go," I said.

Together, we clambered over the retaining wall and began chugging up the slope into Savage Hollow.

PART FOUR

SAVAGE HOLLOW

Chapter Thirteen

The Caves and the Worst Moment of My Life

Chris and I scrambled up the steep, muddy incline for several minutes. Then we heard voices. I thought it was Mr. Watkins at first, but these voices were too youthful to be his.

We crested the ridge, bulled through a tangle of shrubs, and beheld four figures arguing in a clearing.

Mia, Rebecca, Brad, and Kurt.

My first emotion was relief that Mia was alive. Ever since the Eric-thing had told us he'd sent these four into the forest, I'd been fretting about her. She had her back to me, but I could see she was safe and healthy, though she was obviously worked up about something.

Chris looked at me, wide-eyed. I stared back at him uncomprehendingly for a moment, then discerned the meaning of his look.

Rebecca's parents—Brad's parents—had been murdered by the creatures.

And they had no idea.

Just how on earth did you break that kind of news to someone?

"...can't go back until we find Kylie Ann," Mia was saying.

"You didn't even like her," Brad said.

"I said she could be difficult," Mia answered, "but she was still my friend."

Chris came forward. "Kylie Ann is dead."

They all turned and saw us. I moved out of the shadows and took my place at Chris's side.

Rebecca was clutching her throat. "How do you know that?"

I shook my head. "There's too much to say...we don't have time."

"Time for what?" Mia asked.

"Time for them to steal our girlfriends," Brad said. He came forward, a wintry gleam in his eyes.

I ignored that. "Carl Padgett has my sister."

Mia's mouth opened, her eyes bright with fear.

"I have to go," I said, and made to move past her.

"I'm coming too," she said.

"So am I," Rebecca said.

"The hell you are," Kurt said and grabbed Rebecca by the arm.

Chris moved toward them. "Let her go."

"Fuck you," Kurt said.

I expected Brad to go after me then, but he said, "Let's go with them."

I started to move past.

He shot out an arm to bar my way. "Right after you tell us what you're really doing here."

I considered telling him then, informing him of how the creature snapped his mother's neck by whipping her like a wet towel, how the beast had punched through his father's chest like it was soggy cardboard. But I couldn't do that to Rebecca.

"Brad," I said, taking care to keep my voice under control, "I know you don't believe me. But if you come with me you'll understand everything soon enough. Either way, I need to get to the caves."

His brow furrowed. "Caves? What do the caves have to do with anything?"

"My sister is in one of them," I said. "So is her friend."

"What if I don't believe you?"

"I never would have believed most of the things that happened today. But I've *lived* them. And I'm telling the truth."

Without another word, I pushed past him. I didn't look back, but I heard Chris and the others scurrying to catch up. I began to jog through the forest. Then to run. I took a wide trail for half a minute, then branched off onto a narrower trail. Several times I heard voices calling out behind me—usually Brad or Kurt. When the trail would curve I'd catch glimpses of the girls trailing behind.

But my mind was absorbed by Peach. By Carl Padgett.

By the Children.

What if the creatures we'd fought on River Road had been part of a larger group? What if a whole battalion of them were marauding through the forest, ripping and eating anything that moved or breathed? Carl Padgett was a sick, abhorrent individual, but even if he hadn't harmed the girls, who was to say that the Children hadn't found where they'd been hidden? What if the cave where Padgett had taken them had actually been part of the creatures' subterranean network?

What if Padgett had already given my sister to the beasts?

I raced on, the feeling of dread tightening around my throat like a barbed wire noose.

A horrible truth occurred to me. Even if we all survived this, what then? I was still the son of a monster, the spawn of a cannibalistic serial killer, and what kind of life would I have when people found out? I could imagine explaining myself before a father-son basketball game.

Hey, my dad won't be able to attend. He's busy serving consecutive life sentences for eating children.

Or what about applying for a job?

I know genetics aren't on my side, but I promise to do my best to avoid dissecting our clients and scrawling horrific messages on the wall with their blood.

"Will!"

I sucked in a surprised breath and skidded to a halt.

I turned and glared at Chris, who was jogging up to where I stood. "What?" I snapped.

"The caves," he said, between big, heaving breaths. "They're right over that rise, aren't they?"

He was right. Of course, there were more than a few caves in the Hollow, but the largest one—the one I was banking on to be Padgett's lair—was less than thirty yards away.

I heard Padgett's raspy voice echo in my brain: *Can't tell you how good it feels to breath clean air again, to see something other than dirt and rust.*

At the time, I'd thought Padgett was talking about his jail cell, but what if he'd been talking about his short time hiding out in Savage Hollow? And those words, *dirt and rust...*where would he be likely to see those things?

Dirt?

In a big clearing.

Rust?

The abandoned Studebaker.

It made sense. I only hoped my hunch was right.

Peach's and Juliet's lives depended on it.

Together, Chris and I mounted the small incline and hunkered down next to a squat gray boulder.

Together, we surveyed the circular dale laid out before us.

In the center of it lay the rusted-out remains of the baby blue Studebaker. I remembered sitting in the passenger's seat last summer while Chris pretended to drive.

Ranged around the Studebaker were numerous cave entrances.

Very few of the caves in the hollow were the kinds you saw in movies—huge, gaping holes that resembled the massive mouths of giants. Most of them were overgrown with weeds and brush, and were only visible if you stood straight across from them. Even then, the majority of the cave entrances were little more than slanted holes in the ground, the caves themselves narrow throats of rock slimed with mud and moss and suitable only for small animals or snakes.

But the caves in this clearing were large enough for a man to stand up in. Padgett would have chosen a cave like that, I reasoned. Someone with as much pride as he had.

But more important than the size of these holes was their proximity to civilization. These caves were only minutes from the treehouse, and less than a ten-minute hike to my back door.

Yes. This was where Padgett would have taken my sister and Juliet.

But which one were they in? How far inside were they hidden? And how could we save them once we found them?

If they're still alive.

No, I thought, smashing away the idea. I refused to entertain the notion that Peach could be…I couldn't even *think* the word.

No...this was about finding her and saving her. End of story.

And killing Padgett

My chest tightened. I frowned, the notion digging into my brain with the insidiousness of a deadly germ. I realized I *did* want to kill Carl Padgett, and not just to save my sister. If I could take out Padgett, no one would know he was my dad.

Rebecca asked, "Is that where you think he took her?"

Chris looked at me. "You're positive, Will?"

I took some time to think about it. "I'm sure."

"Sure of what?" Brad said in a voice about ten times too loud.

"*Shut up*," Rebecca hissed. "What if Padgett hears you?"

Brad snorted. "You mean the killer that was spotted in Indianapolis? What a fucking joke."

I suppressed a groan, considered explaining how Padgett himself had delighted in the mistaken sighting, but what was the point?

The clock was ticking on my sister's life.

I moved forward.

Mia snagged the tail of my shirt. "Where are you going?"

"Hah!" Brad said before I could answer.

Chris looked at him sullenly. "What's so funny?"

"I get it now," he said. "You get it too, don't you, Kurt?"

Kurt nodded, but it was obvious from his expression that he had no idea what his best friend was talking about. Brad was not only taller than Kurt, he was smarter too. Not that that was saying much.

Brad smirked at me. "You make up this serial killer story, and Mia thinks you're a big, brave guy."

"He's not lying," Mia said.

Brad ignored her. "Tell me something, Burgess. What happens when you come out of the cave with nothing? You gonna keep this charade up, or are you finally gonna admit you're full of shit?"

Mia's nostrils flared. "He's not—"

"*Shut your mouth*," Brad snapped.

"The *hell* I will," Mia shouted. "You don't own me, you son of a bitch!"

"Look at you trying to be tough," Brad said, grinning. "You think I'm afraid of you?"

The sick, angry feeling in my gut intensified.

"You should be," she said, her blue eyes fierce.

"Tell you what," Brad said, rising. "I'll go in there with Burgess. That way, when he comes out, I'll be able to deny whatever wild stories he tries to tell."

I opened my mouth to tell Brad this was an opportunity to save two young lives, to maybe lay to rest whatever guilt he still felt about Emmylou's death. But there was no way to talk about it without making things worse, and certainly not in front of Rebecca.

Chris said, "Let's go then."

"You're not going," I said to him.

Chris looked at me like I'd slapped him. "Huh?"

"You heard me. You're staying out here."

His eyes glinted. "The hell I am. If you think I'm gonna let you face Padgett alone, you're nuts."

"The girls are going to be out here by themselves," I said. "I need you with them."

"I'll be with them," Kurt said.

I ignored Kurt. "Like I said, the girls will be out here alone."

"Umm...seriously?" Rebecca said. "What is this, medieval Europe? We're perfectly capable of defending ourselves."

I clenched my fists to keep from yelling at her. "Listen, it's not about chivalry or women's rights or whatever. It's about..." I sighed. I hadn't wanted to tell them about this, but I couldn't see any way around it. "There are other things in the woods."

Mia cocked an eyebrow at me. "Other *things?*"

"Remember what you saw that night near the creek?"

A shadow flitted across her face. "What about it?"

"It's real."

There was a long silence.

Kurt interrupted it. "Okay, I have no clue what the hell you guys are talking about. Can somebody fill me in?"

"Put it this way," Chris said. "You'll want to keep a low profile out here."

I glanced at Chris. "You stay hidden too."

He gave me a pained look, but he didn't argue. That was a good sign. He'd seen what the Children could do.

I started forward with Brad in tow.

But Mia moved after us. "I'm going too."

I rounded on her. "Think about it. When we find Peach and Juliet, we'll need to haul ass out of there, right?" I nodded toward the entrances. "Those caves are gonna be narrow. It'll be tough enough navigating them with me and Brad. Add my sister and Juliet to the equation, and it gets even harder. If you go in there with us..." I shrugged, hoping she'd see my point.

"Come on, Burgess," Brad said. "Let's go see this big bad serial killer."

I ignored him, set off through the clearing until I reached the largest cave, the one I suspected Padgett would have chosen. It *had* to be this one, I told myself. He was crafty, but he was also arrogant. He wouldn't select one of the muddy ones he'd have to wriggle into like a worm.

I stepped toward the cave entrance then stopped, a stark realization crashing down on me. I didn't have a flashlight. I glanced at Brad.

"What?" he said. "Lose your nerve already?"

"It's not that, it's—"

"Here you go," a voice said.

I turned and saw Rebecca coming toward me, a small but brightly gleaming blue Maglite in her hand.

I gaped. "How did you—"

"I figured we might have to search the caves for Kylie," she explained. "It made sense to bring a flashlight."

I gave her an admiring glance.

As Brad and I entered the cave, I could still see that smile of Rebecca's, that mixture of sarcasm and good humor. I could see why Chris liked her so much. She was maybe the only girl I would approve of for my best friend.

And I would have told her that if I'd known she'd be dead in twenty minutes.

◆

"Give me the flashlight," Brad said.

I kept moving, the ceiling of the cave just high enough for me to walk without hunching over. "Your sister gave it to me."

"And it belongs to my dad, dickhead. So fork it over. Now."

I could hear the strain in Brad's voice. Unlike me, he did have to bend over to avoid knocking his head on the ceiling.

"*Hey*," he barked, "are you hard of hearing?"

"Lower your voice," I whispered. "I don't want Padgett to know we're coming."

He chuckled. "Still keeping that up, huh? We've been walking for, what, ten minutes now?"

In truth we'd only been in the cave for two or three minutes, but it did seem like longer. Most of the way had been level, but a couple times we'd moved downhill. So far we hadn't encountered any places where the tunnel split, which was something. I didn't relish the idea of getting lost down here.

Rough hands shoved me forward. I stumbled and nearly went down.

I spun and glowered at Brad, who was grinning at me through the murk. "That was stupid," I said. "What if the flashlight breaks?"

"You scared?"

"Don't push me again," I said, and continued on.

Trailing me, Brad said, "You're not so good with the threats, are you?"

Before I knew what I was saying, the words were out of my mouth. "You know, nobody blames you for Emmylou's death."

Behind me, I sensed Brad growing very still.

I hurried on, doing my best to keep my tone level. "You didn't mean for her to—" I licked my lips, struggling for the right words, "—for her to get hurt. It was just a senseless accident."

"Senseless?" he repeated in a low, hoarse voice.

"Yeah," I said. "You were only what? Fourteen? You didn't know she'd die that way."

Brad didn't speak. I kept my back to him, knowing if I looked him in the eyes—even in the dark of the cave—that I'd be unable to say what I wanted to say. "That scar on your wrist," I went on. "I know how you got it. You didn't punch any window."

Brad's voice was barely a whisper. "Tell me how I did it then."

I swallowed. "I think you tried to kill yourself. I think you felt so guilty over your sister's death that the only—"

His fist smashed me in the back of the head. I stumbled forward, Brad scrambling up beside me. He pistoned a knee into my ribs, doubling me up, then brought down an elbow right between my shoulder blades. With a breathless grunt, I slumped forward on the moist cave floor. I shot out a hand, meaning to snag his foot and trip him up, but he danced away, came at me again, and stomped on my lower back. I gasped, the pain was so exquisite. I rolled over, trying to gather my strength, but Brad wasn't taking any chances. He kicked me in the side. Bright pain bloomed in my ribs. I tried to roll away, but he followed, his shoe drilling me in the left buttock. I gained my knees, but Brad tore down at me with a savage fist and clocked me in the side of the face.

I went down, panting. The flashlight had tumbled to the cave floor. I glanced up at Brad, tried to clear my carouseling vision, but it was no use. The blow to the head had really scrambled my eyesight.

Brad was laughing. "You're such a pussy, Burgess."

My vision clarified a little. Brad had circled me, was standing farther down the tunnel. The Maglite shone in his direction, front-lighting his big frame.

"Please don't do this," I panted. "I mean it, Brad. I'm sorry for what happened to your sister."

"*Shut up!*" he thundered. His big foot thumped me in the ribs.

He loomed over me. "Here's what's gonna happen," he said. "You're gonna tell Mia you're a liar, and you're gonna admit how easily I whupped your ass."

Something sounded from deeper in the tunnel.

Brad gave no sign of hearing. "Then I'm going to kick the living hell out of your buddy and make sure my sister sees what a loser he is too."

The sound came again, but Brad was too busy talking to notice it.

"And then, after my sister realizes how stupid she was to stray from Kurt, we're gonna kick the shit out of you two again."

I realized what the sound was now. Furtive footfalls. Coming nearer.

"*Brad,*" I grunted.

His eyebrows went up. "Oh, you got something to say?" Another kick, my ribs too numb to feel it.

"*Brad,*" I repeated. "*Please listen.*"

"Get your sorry ass up," he said, beckoning me forward. "I'm gonna enjoy this."

A figure materialized out of the darkness behind him. At first I thought it was one of the Children.

Then I saw the machete.

Carl Padgett raised the blade high above his head.

"*No!*" I shouted.

Brad noticed where I was looking. He spun and started to raise his arms.

The machete whooshed down.

Brad's head snapped back, his entire body rocked by the jolt. He landed on his back, the machete buried in his face.

"Man, that felt good," Padgett said, wiping his brow. He leered at me. "Now, Will. It's time to come to Daddy."

◆

As Padgett moved forward, I got shakily to my feet. I could hear Brad's blood gushing out onto the slimy cave floor, could smell something foul wafting out of Brad's body, the boy having apparently voided his bowels when he'd been murdered.

There was a lump in my throat. Yes, Brad Ralston was a bad person. But he'd been through something terrible.

He didn't deserve to die.

Padgett evidently read something in my expression. "Feel bad for him, Will? I heard the things he was saying to you. Don't you have any goddamned pride?"

I choked back a sob. "Where's Peach?"

"Where do you think?"

"Tell me," I growled.

He smiled. "Or what?"

"Or I'll kill you."

His grin widened. "It's about time! I'd started to worry you weren't really mine after all. But seeing that look in your eyes—"

"Shut your fucking mouth," I said. "Where's my sister?"

He nodded. "Good, Will. Good. The less you feel, the better. Once you stop caring altogether, that's when you're finally free."

I shook my head. "I'm nothing like you, Padgett."

"Keep tellin' yourself that, Son."

I gritted my teeth. "Don't call me Son."

He licked his lips, grinning broadly. "Uh-huh. I like it. Why don't you show your daddy how tough you are? Show me what a big man—"

I launched myself at him. Padgett evaded my first punch, but I pivoted, caught him with a left-handed jab in the belly. He didn't cry out, but the blow was a solid one. *Take that you son of a bitch!* I followed with an uppercut to the jaw. Padgett's teeth clicked together, and moaning, he reeled backward. I moved with him, showering him with hard jabs to the body. Padgett swung at me, but it was an awkward swing, and it missed me by a mile. I moved in, pounding his midsection with hard right jabs. *Yes*, I thought. *Feel this one, you murdering bastard!* I could tell he was growing winded. He made to cover up, but I instinctively crouched and hammered him in the mouth. Padgett flailed backward.

I'm doing it! I thought.

Then he was gone.

I realized with a flood of terror that Padgett hadn't been in trouble at all; he'd been luring me backward into the gloom. I had a memory of the gun he'd used on Detective Wood, steeled myself for a blinding flash of light and a bullet to the chest.

Nothing.

I squinted my eyes into the gloom. Padgett could be anywhere.

Turning, I saw the flashlight was about fifteen feet behind me. I spun to retrieve it, and at that moment Padgett hurtled out of the dark and rode me down like a lion taking down a baby gazelle. Then Padgett was the one raining blows, only his were more ruthless, more effective. I was face down, with Padgett straddling my midsection. His sharp fists crashed against my back, my ribs, the impacts almost metronomic in their regularity. I couldn't breathe. The pain was ghastly, continuous. I writhed beneath him, tried to buck him off, but he was relentless. It occurred to me I'd die this way, be simply beaten to death, and in desperation I reached behind me and grabbed at the only thing I could—his genitals. I squeezed with what little strength I had left, but it was enough to elicit a surprised cry from Padgett. He flopped off, holding his privates, and I scrambled forward, at first moving in the direction of the downed flashlight.

Then I saw Brad Ralston's corpse.

And the machete.

I lunged ahead, the machete only five or six feet away. I pushed forward, extended my arm—

—and gasped as Padgett seized my leg.

"You miserable…little…*cockroach*," he growled. I glanced back at him and felt my blood freeze.

His eyes glowed a dull green.

No! I thought. *He can't really be one of them!*

He seized hold of my waistband, dragged me backward, and I knew in moments I'd be under him again. Only this time I wouldn't escape. This time he'd beat me until I looked worse than Brad and was just as dead. I spun around, facing Padgett. I saw him grinning down at me, his face satanic-looking in the meager glow of the flashlight. The hollows of his eyes were gaping black ovals, the whiskery grin broader and more diabolical than it had ever been. He cocked his right fist, ready to knock me into oblivion. But it wasn't his right hand I was thinking about.

He'd brought his left hand up to the middle of my chest to hold me in place. I waited until the last possible moment to make my move. Then, with both hands, I grasped his left wrist, jerked his fingers toward my mouth.

And bit down.

His eyes bugged in his head and he squealed like no human I'd ever heard before. Hot blood, thick and coppery, flooded my mouth. Padgett's scream rose higher and higher. My front teeth had cleaved nearly all the way through his fingers, and I ground my incisors to finish the job. Padgett slapped my face with his free hand, then jammed a thumb into one of my eyes. This finally broke my lockjaw hold on his fingers, but I'd effectively incapacitated him. He rolled off, still squealing, and in the scant illumination I saw more than I cared to. His middle finger was almost severed at the top knuckle. The ring finger was even worse, the tip of it flapping around like the lid of a water bottle. Blood spurted from the wounds, Padgett screaming and cursing as he crawled away from me.

I knew I couldn't show mercy. Peach's life and the life of her friend depended on my remorselessness.

My vision bleary, I rose and stepped over to where Brad lay. It took me a moment, but I was able to wrench the machete loose from his skull. Padgett was cursing steadily now, as angry as he was in pain. He pushed to his feet, turned to face me.

I pumped the machete straight into his belly.

There was an endless moment where neither of us moved.

Then I slid the long blade out, stepped away from Padgett's swaying form.

The Moonlight Killer toppled forward, grasping his perforated guts.

I considered skewering him again. Or even beheading him, vampire-style. But I had to know if my sister was alive.

As I hurried down the tunnel, the machete in one hand and the Maglite in the other, a sense of unreality washed over me. I'd just killed Carl Padgett, the most notorious child killer the Midwest had ever seen, The Bedford Cannibal. Padgett the Blade.

Dead.

By my hand.

I ventured deeper into the cave, the pale wash of luminescence fluttering on the walls because my hand was so unsteady. Around the corner, the tunnel opened up.

The wavering flashlight beam picked out crudely drawn figures, cave art I would have assumed was ancient had it not looked so fresh. My skin crawled at sight of the Children feasting on innocent people, the slender white figures all eyes and teeth, their victims' mouths opened wide in voiceless wails.

Padgett had created a shrine to the Children.

Farther on I made out new shapes, unfamiliar to me but just as disconcerting. There were black creatures with vast wings and luminous red eyes. And a huge black-winged creature, perhaps meant to represent the mother or father of the other ones. I crept deeper into the cave, my ears straining to detect the slightest sound. Another drawing appeared, this one another Child, but roughly five times taller and stronger.

Did a creature like that exist?

My eyes lowered to the cave floor. I distinguished a few bread crusts, an empty beef jerky wrapper. I braced myself, expecting to see little arms and legs strewn about the cave like broken doll parts. *No,* I thought. *Not Peach. Please let her be okay.* I crept around the corner, shone the flashlight at the far wall.

The beam picked out a pair of small pink sneakers with fluorescent yellow Nike swooshes. Next to those were a cheaper pair of shoes, these pink also, but faded, with no discernible name brand.

There were still feet inside the shoes. Bare ankles. Calves. Knees.

I tilted the Maglite higher.

Two small faces squinted at me.

"Go away!" Peach yelled.

She's alive, I thought, my whole body turning to jelly. I realized she couldn't see me, could only make out a male figure gripping a flashlight.

"Oh my God, Peach," I breathed, and lurched forward.

I heard her suck in breath. "Will?"

I dropped to my knees and threw my arms around her. Juliet was sniffling loudly, clearly toiling to hold back tears of terror.

Peach was weeping, but her body was as stiff as plywood, her voice frantic. "*Will, he's coming! You have to get out of*—"

"He's dead," I tried to say, but I was sobbing too hard to make my words clear.

She pushed against me. "Will, *no*. He'll come back, he'll kill you!"

I moved back from Peach, shined the light on her. "Aren't your wrists tied or something? How did he keep you here?"

Her wet eyes were simultaneously beaten and imploring. "He told us he'd kill us if we tried to leave."

I bit back a cry of rage. Had Padgett hurt Peach and Juliet?

"Listen," I said. "We need to get out of here."

"But he'll—"

"He's *dead*, Peach!" I snapped. I hated myself for the way she shrank from me, but I had to make her understand, had to get them out of the cave. The Children were still lurking. "He's back there," I explained. "I killed him with a machete."

"What's a ma—"

"A big knife," I said impatiently and held it up so she could see.

"Is that blood?" she asked, her eyes huge.

"Yes," I said." "Padgett's. Now get up, before the Children come."

"Children?" she asked.

God, I thought. *Was this what it was like to be a parent?*

Somehow I got her and Juliet to their feet. Juliet was sobbing uncontrollably and breathing so hard I thought her chest might explode. But I finally managed to get them moving.

"Both of you grab hold of my hip pockets," I said. It was what I always did with Peach when we crossed the street and I had my hands full.

"Why?" Peach asked.

"I have to hold the flashlight."

"Can I hold it?" Peach asked.

"*Grab my pockets*," I repeated.

We neared the place where Padgett's body would be. I had to be careful. It was necessary for me to probe the tunnel for the corpse's location; if I failed to do that, we might trip right over him and end up in a puddle of blood. If Peach and Juliet weren't already scarred for life, landing on a corpse would sure as hell do the trick.

Then again, if I illuminated the body in too much detail, I'd probably send the girls shrieking in the other direction.

"Peach," I said. "I want you to close your eyes. You too, Juliet."

"Is it gross?" Juliet asked. They were the first words she'd spoken.

I recalled the way I'd plunged the blade into Padgett's belly. The brutal *shnick*ing sound. The gush of blood.

"Yes," I said. "It's gross."

Against my hip Juliet shivered. But she closed her eyes.

I checked Peach's.

Shut also.

We drew closer to where I believed the body would be. I was proud of myself for taking the machete with me. In a horror movie, the good guy would be too relieved after killing the villain to do something as logical as confiscating his weapon.

We inched through the tunnel, the girls huddled against my hips.

Still no sign of Padgett.

I frowned.

"Are we past it yet?" Peach asked.

"Hush," I said, squinting into the gloom.

Nothing.

Had Padgett escaped?

It was possible, I realized. I had only stabbed Padgett in the belly.

But what about Brad's body? I had no doubt he was dead, so unless he'd become a zombie or something...

A faint cone of light appeared ahead. We were nearing the entrance of the cave.

I listened for screams, shouts, the sounds of a struggle. But either the struggle with Padgett had already occurred or the others were simply out there waiting.

It didn't make sense.

"What's wrong, Will?" Peach asked.

"Shut it, Peach," I said.

She didn't protest, but her body against me was as rigid as a plank.

The cone of light grew brighter. I estimated we were maybe twenty yards from the mouth of the cave, but I still didn't see Padgett. Had there been a branching off in the tunnel I hadn't noticed? There had to have been. Otherwise, where could Padgett have taken Brad? Where—

Something slammed against me.

There was a small indentation in the tunnel wall, the space just recessed enough to remain in shadow, and it was out of this space that Brad Ralston's corpse lurched.

I screamed, a childlike horror of zombies and other monsters flaring in me. Brad's heavy body drove me against the tunnel wall. I flailed at it, finally managed to thrust it away from me.

It slumped to the floor. Dead, I realized. Despite the stab wound, Padgett had managed to drag Brad's big body into the alcove and shove it toward me at the right moment.

Then the next shock came, and this one was far worse.

Padgett had grabbed Peach.

They were heading toward daylight.

Towing Juliet behind me, I raced after them.

A nightmare reel of images assaulted my light-sensitive eyes as Juliet and I lunged through the cave opening and into the clearing:

Rebecca running toward us, her eyes huge with fright.

Kurt Fisher beside the rusted blue Studebaker, a hand covering his mouth, his eyes as large and alert as I'd ever seen them.

Chris standing horrorstruck, inarticulate, on the rim of the clearing.

Mia gesticulating toward a pair of figures who'd emerged from the cave just ahead of us.

In the center of the clearing, the two figures.

Carl Padgett and my sister.

Padgett holding a gun to Peach's head.

"Let her go!" Mia was shouting.

Rebecca was only ten feet away from the pair when Padgett spun toward her, my little sister's feet actually leaving the ground.

"*Freeze!*" Padgett ordered.

I cursed myself for my ineptitude, my sloppiness. I could see my mistake even now. The wound in Padgett's midsection wasn't in the center of his belly, but nearer his side. I'd given him a nasty but non-fatal stab wound.

No wonder he'd been able to lug Brad's body into the shadows and thrust it at me. I was a fool, and now Peach was paying for it. Numbly, I took a step in Padgett's direction.

"Get back!" Padgett shouted. His eyes glowed a dull green.

I had to get him away from Peach.

Lightning strobed in the dreary twilight, the growl of thunder continual now. The rain had diminished slightly, but it was still coming down hard enough to affect vision.

"Come here, Rebecca," I said.

Rebecca started toward me.

Padgett bared his teeth. "I said don't *move!*"

"She's not going to touch you," I said.

Rebecca reached me, and I said, "Take Juliet. Get her somewhere safe."

"No one's going anywhere," Padgett said. "Not unless you want me to put a hole in your sister's head."

I took a breath, tried to ignore the pinched, doomed look on Peach's face. "You're not going to kill her, Padgett."

"That's right," he said, "as long as everyone behaves."

I took a step in his direction. "That's not what I mean." I nodded toward the gun. "That thing is empty."

He smiled at me. "You'd bet your sister's life on that?"

I took another step. "Why didn't you use it before?"

"I had to be quiet. And I didn't feel like killing you."

Another step. Only about ten paces between us now. "Then why would you shoot Peach? She's only a kid."

Something unspeakable seeped into Padgett's eyes. "Kids are my favorite."

I hesitated. *Jesus*, I thought. What if the gun really was loaded?

Peach whimpered.

"Let her *go*," I said.

"What for?" he asked. "She's no child of mine."

"Let go of her!" Chris shouted. We all turned that way. Chris's eyes were red-rimmed and wet. "Come after me, you bastard—"

"Wait, Chris," I breathed.

"—I'll take you on—"

Something appeared behind Chris.

"—but leave Will's sister—"

Oh God, I thought. *No!*

"—alone!"

I took a step toward my best friend. "*Chris, look out!*"

But it was too late.

The beast had already leapt at him.

◆

Mia screamed. So did the girls.

Kurt took off running.

Padgett hopped up and down, his grin maniacal. "Sweet Jesus! I told you they were real!"

He'd turned toward Chris and the creature, who were now tangled up on the sparse grass. I knew Padgett would only be distracted for a moment, and deep down I knew something else.

I could only save one of them.

Chris or Peach.

My best friend or my sister.

Correction, I told myself in that split second. *Chris is more than your best friend—he's like a brother. You can't just leave him to die!*

I glanced at Peach, who looked up at me, her brown eyes full of terror and hope. I had always been her protector, and now she was looking to me to save her from this monster.

Yet Chris was even now pinned beneath an even more lethal monster. The beast was gigantic, its sparse black hair whipping around as it toyed with Chris, my friend fighting valiantly but only just able to stay alive. Any moment now...

I stood immobile, the moment drawing out. I whimpered, my body racked with anguish. I had to save one or the other *right now*, or I wouldn't be able to save either.

I glanced at Padgett's glowing green eyes, my sister's hopeful brown ones.

With tears already flowing down my cheeks, I made my decision.

I lunged behind the Studebaker so Padgett wouldn't spot me in his periphery, then I rushed toward him. He was still spellbound by the sight of the creature, a rapturous gleam in his bestial eyes. That momentary sense of awe was what I was counting on. If Padgett spotted me before I got to him, he'd be able to shoot me, and then Peach would be dead too.

Ten feet away. Five.

I raised the machete.

Padgett whirled at the last second, started to raise the gun.

I buried the machete in his forehead.

Padgett's arms splayed out as he crumpled, the gun landing softly on the moist soil.

Peach threw herself into my side.

At the same moment, Mia shouted, *"Leave him alone!"*

I turned, knowing what I'd see even before I saw it.

Mia was sprinting toward Chris and the creature in a desperate attempt to intervene. But she was too late.

The creature was already devouring my best friend.

"NO!" I bellowed.

My heart stuttered in my chest, the rest of my body going numb. I wanted Chris to be alive, but I could see the ruin of his torso, the creature already scooping up gobbets of flesh to dine on. In that moment a hundred memories unspooled in my head. Chris and I sitting together on our carpet squares, our kindergarten teacher shushing us as she read *Green Eggs and Ham*. Me stepping on a nail in the woods behind Chris's house and Chris telling me jokes in the waiting room before my tetanus shot. The two of us playing video games, telling each other secrets. The fight we had over a game of one-on-one, me kicking Chris's basketball down the street in anger. Sleepovers. Looking at naked women on the Internet.

Chris was the best friend I ever had.

My brother.

And this monster had killed him.

"Stay with Rebecca," I muttered to Peach, my voice dry.

Rebecca grasped both little girls protectively to her sides, said to them in a thick voice, "Close your eyes."

I bent down and scooped up Padgett's gun. I had little hope it would do us any good. But like a bad dream, Mia was heading straight for the creature, and I wasn't going to be able to stop her.

"Get away from him!" she screamed at the creature. She gave it a convulsive kick in the face. Snarling, the creature seized her by the arm and dragged her down. *Please God no!* I thought. *I can't lose her and Chris both!*

"Hey!" I shouted, striding toward them.

The creature looked up at me. I was sure I saw recognition in its huge green eyes. And hunger.

I had the gun aimed at the creature's face. It showed no fear at all.

Please work, I begged. *Please still have bullets.*

Ignoring me, the creature jerked Mia's body closer, opened its mouth to bite her. My breath clotted in my throat. *Oh God.* My finger tightened on the trigger.

But I didn't shoot it yet. I had to be sure.

Mia was flailing at the beast, fighting it with a ferocity I admired.

Ten feet away, I stopped, aimed.

The creature's jaws widened to take a bite out of Mia's screaming face.

I fired, expecting to hear a sad clicking sound.

Instead, the gun roared and the back of the creature's head disappeared in a messy haze.

I'd seen the monsters get up before, so I aimed, fired again, and took off the side of its face. I squeezed the trigger again, but this time there was no concussion. My ammo was gone.

I dropped the gun and stared at the creature's twitching body.

My eyes shifted to Chris. My lips trembled, a high-pitched moan sounding in the back of my throat.

"Will?" a voice said.

I fell to my knees. Rain pattered on my face, dripped from my chin. But the tears, hot and salty and bitter, burned through the raindrops.

"Will?" the voice asked again. I finally identified it.

Mia. I couldn't face her, couldn't look away from Chris.

My best friend.

"I'm so sorry," she said, coming toward me.

I couldn't speak, couldn't think, couldn't stop looking away from Chris's ruined body, his bloody face, the mouth that would never smile again, the eyes that would never see again.

Chris is dead, I thought. *My best friend, my brother. He's dead.*

A small pair of hands twined around my neck.

I looked and saw Peach staring at me. "I'm so sorry, Will," she said, crying too. She kissed me hard on the temple. Her lips were warm and trembly. "Thank you for getting me," she whispered.

My chest started to hitch, a molten heat blistering my lungs. I realized I was sobbing, but at that moment I didn't feel any embarrassment at crying in front of these people. Mia held one side of my body,

Peach the other. Rebecca came around to stand in front of us, Juliet Wallace on one hip. Rebecca was weeping, but she looked brave. She was stroking Juliet's light hair, protecting her.

I had to protect Peach.

Be strong, I told myself. *Be strong for Peach, for the others.*

Be strong for Chris.

I squeezed my eyes shut, pushed unsteadily to my feet.

We're alive, I told myself. That was something. We were alive, and though Chris was dead, it seemed that the nightmare was finally over. I'd murdered Carl Padgett. The Moonlight Killer would never kill again.

Then I heard it. A dull, thumping noise, as though the earth were being pounded by mallets.

My heartbeat quickening, I hurried up the short incline to glance at a hill in the distance.

"Run," I said.

"Will?" Rebecca said. "What's wrong?"

But I never answered her.

Because that was when the creatures flooded over the hill.

◆

"Get Juliet!" I shouted.

I grabbed Peach, and careful not to slice her with the machete, slung her over my shoulder like a sack of potatoes. I took off with her and from the corner of my eye glimpsed Rebecca running with Juliet hand-in-hand, Mia running abreast of them.

I bolted straight into the woods. Peach bounced on my shoulder, but she didn't protest at all. I couldn't blame her. She'd probably been struck dumb by the sight of the creatures.

A weird, screeching war cry sounded behind us, and I knew the beasts were closing. I was a fast runner, but with Peach on my shoulder, I was a good deal slower.

I shot a glance back. The creatures had closed the distance, and they were approaching from several different directions. A few had followed my exact path, only they were navigating it a hell of a lot faster than I had. Others were setting off at a diagonal, perhaps thinking to head me off.

Four of the creatures were closing on the girls.

Rebecca and Mia were doing their best, but I could see Juliet had just about run out of steam. They were gamely dragging her along, but it was no use. The creatures were only thirty yards away now, and soon they'd be on them. I kept moving, but the machete in my hand felt suddenly heavy. How could I keep the weapon for myself and permit Mia, Rebecca, and Juliet to fend for themselves?

"Look out!" Rebecca shouted, and I turned in time to see her throw herself between Juliet and the nasty uprooted stump she'd almost plowed into. Rebecca was able to redirect Juliet, the little girl stumbling but being saved from falling by Mia, who steadied her with an arm.

But in preventing Juliet from an ugly fall, Rebecca had tumbled, her foot twisting at an unnatural angle. Rebecca pushed to her feet right away, but I saw with a sinking stomach that she was moving with a severe limp.

I compressed my lips. I had to help her. Had to help Mia and Juliet, who were faring little better.

The monsters would overtake them within moments.

Your responsibility is to your sister, a voice in my head declared.

No, I thought, grinding my teeth. *My responsibility is to do what's right.*

My windpipe constricting, I doubled back.

Mia was laboring to keep moving, to keep Juliet moving, but she knew the distance between them and the creatures was dwindling.

But it was Rebecca who shouted. "Give me the knife!"

I was nearly to them, would enter the trail they were on about twenty feet ahead of them. I had no idea what Rebecca had planned, but I felt I owed it to her to do as she asked. I lobbed the machete toward her.

"What's she doing, Will?" Peach asked.

I realized Mia and Juliet had paused, Rebecca already having fallen behind them.

"You can't!" Mia shouted to Rebecca.

"I can't run anymore," Rebecca answered. "You have to move...get the girls somewhere safe."

Mia shook her head. "Rebecca—"

"*Now*, dammit!" Rebecca yelled. "I have to do this. It's the only way!"

Mia looked like she was about to argue, but it happened then. One of the creatures—the biggest one, the monster who'd killed Rebecca's parents—sprang onto the trail between Mia and Rebecca. It ignored Mia completely, its odious figure stalking toward the injured girl.

Mia didn't budge. "Rebecca, we can't just—"

"Would you please *listen?*" Rebecca shouted, but her voice broke, and as she raised the machete, the other four creatures who'd been following her materialized out of the rainy forest.

I noticed that Rebecca wasn't looking at the creatures.

She was looking at Peach and Juliet.

It wasn't your fault! I wanted to scream. *Emmylou's death wasn't your fault. You were only in the fifth freaking grade!*

"We have to go," Peach said into my ear.

The creature who'd cut Rebecca off stalked closer to her. Astonishingly, Rebecca didn't look terrified. As her eyes flitted from Peach to Juliet, her expression was almost placid.

At peace.

Save her! I told myself.

"*Go!*" Rebecca shouted.

The creatures closed in.

"Now, Will," Peach urged. "We have to go *now.*"

She was right, I knew. Rebecca was well beyond the point of being saved. As horrible as that sounds, it couldn't have been more obvious. Not only were there five creatures in her immediate vicinity, but the others who'd been pursuing me and Peach had stopped to watch the proceedings as well.

No, I quickly corrected myself, not just *watch* the proceedings. They were moving forward too, the hunger clear in their pitiless green eyes.

Mia and Juliet started toward us. I could see Juliet was tugging Mia along, but Mia seemed to have come to the same conclusion I had. That as awful as it was, Rebecca was going to die. Rebecca seemed to know it too. She was weeping, but she kept the machete raised high, determined to fight until her last breath.

She's buying us time, I thought, amazed.

Peach rocked against me. "Please, Will. They'll get us too."

"Okay," I said.

Peach pushed out of my arms and seized my hand. "I'll run for a few minutes to give you a break."

I nodded absently, my gaze still fixed on Rebecca and the herd of white beasts. They were taking playful swipes at her now. Rebecca glanced over at us, and for a moment, our eyes locked.

"Keep them alive," Rebecca said.

Mia and Juliet pulled even with us. "Come on," Mia said in a choked voice.

I nodded. We all four started down the trail. We'd only gone about thirty feet when we heard it, a horrible, high-pitched yowl of pain. The beasts had gotten Rebecca.

Tears were streaming down Mia's face, but she and Juliet were still moving. Peach was about ten feet ahead of me, the little lunatic moving with a swiftness I could scarcely believe.

Rebecca's scream cut off abruptly.

It was replaced by the horrid sounds of the creatures feeding.

◆

We'd sprinted in silence for maybe three minutes when Mia asked, "Where are we going?"

I pumped my legs faster, not wanting Peach to get too far ahead. "My house," I called back.

"Why there?"

"At the very least, we can hide there."

Mia was quiet for a time, the only sounds our footfalls, our tortured breathing, and the diminishing patter of raindrops. I kept casting nervous looks around the forest, hoping against hope I wouldn't catch sight of the beasts.

Then Peach screamed.

The monster was maybe sixty yards to our left, and nothing more than a flitting white shape. But the moment it heard Peach's scream it veered toward us and began hurdling whatever objects lay in its path.

"Do you have anything else?" Mia asked, her voice laced with dread. "A knife or anything?"

I didn't bother answering. Because from our right more beasts were approaching. I realized they'd never really lost track of us, were merely finishing off Rebecca before they returned to the hunt.

We were moving faster now, the adrenaline sluicing through our bodies. Even Juliet was scampering along at a good clip, so that Mia and I only had to check our speed a little.

The beast to our left was trying to cut us off.

"Go!" I barked to my sister. I knew she was doing her best, but it just wasn't good enough. The creature was going to hit the trail at about the same time we were.

I accelerated, reached out, and without breaking stride, scooped my sister off the ground.

She uttered a frightened little yelp, then she actually giggled at herself. "You *scared* me, Will."

I wanted to kiss her cheek then, but I couldn't. Because the beast was almost even with us. I thought we were going to make it, but Mia...Juliet...

I glanced back at them. They were too far behind. "Hurry!" I shouted.

Mia threw me a desperate look, dragged Juliet ahead, but Juliet was flagging now, the child weeping openly. She wasn't stupid. Just really young and really scared. She'd seen what had happened to Chris, to Rebecca.

I turned and saw we were almost to the treehouse. Not that it would offer any kind of safety. But at least it might prolong our lives.

If we could make it there.

With a last burst of speed, I got Peach and me clear of the beast.

But it bounded onto the lane behind us, cutting off Mia and Juliet.

Juliet screamed. Mia called my name.

I skidded on the wet trail, nearly fell, and glanced about for something with which to fend off the creature. The only thing I spotted was a slender but solid-looking branch, about three feet long. The kind you'd use for a walking stick.

I set Peach down, brought an index finger to my lips when she started to whimper, and approached the creature, which was looming over Mia and Juliet, its shoulders rising and falling in vicious anticipation. I raised the branch like it was a Louisville Slugger.

It whirled and snarled at me.

Swung at me.

Had I not dropped to the ground, I have no doubt that swipe would have ripped my face off like a Halloween mask. More likely it would have torn my head from my body, the whole thing tumbling end over end and coming to rest on its side the way severed heads did in horror movies.

But it missed me. And I saw my chance. I brought the branch up again, and though I was on my knees this time, I still knew I could get a lot of power in my swing. These creatures had very few weaknesses, but I suspected I knew how to hurt one. As long as it was male, like this one.

I swung the branch and connected with the beast's genitals with such force that the branch actually snapped in half.

The beast's bellow resounded through the forest. It dropped to the earth, its gnarled hands cupped to its balls.

Mia and Juliet scuttled by. I spun, suddenly sure that Peach had been taken while my back was turned. But she was right where I'd left her.

We started down the trail again, the treehouse swiftly coming into view.

I had a mind to keep going, to bust it all the way to my house. After all, it was the only way for us to survive, wasn't it? The treehouse was as surely a death sentence as the rest of the forest was. I was about to explain this to Mia when I saw something that made my legs liquefy.

A dozen creatures had surrounded us.

They'd formed a wide, misshapen ring around the treehouse clearing. The closest ones were about thirty yards away, but I'd seen how fast they could move. We'd be lucky to make it halfway up the rungs before they ripped us to shreds.

We were trapped.

Mia pushed closer to me. "What do we do?"

I looked at her. "Take Peach and Juliet."

"Take them *where*?"

"Up," I said. "Get them up to the treehouse."

I figured she'd argue with me. But she only asked, "You'll be right behind us?"

I nodded. "I don't want to die either."

She had a hand on each of the girls' backs when I said, "Hey, Mia."

She glanced at me over her shoulder.

I swallowed. "You remember when I dropped my chemistry set?"

She stared hard at me, but I couldn't tell whether she remembered or not. After all, it had happened back in the second grade.

"I wanted to thank you," I said. "I forgot to say it when we were younger."

She might have smiled a little, but it was getting dark. With a last glance at me, Mia hurried the girls over to the ladder and began the job of helping them up the rungs. It was a long climb, especially for such little girls, but their terror was lending them speed.

I performed a slow revolution, my gaze taking in all twelve of the beasts. So far they'd opted to withhold their assault. Maybe they wanted some sport out of it. Maybe slaughtering us here on the ground was simply too easy for them.

Regardless, it wasn't until Peach and Juliet were most of the way up the ladder that the first creature began to stride toward us. It came slowly, leisurely, like it knew we had nowhere to go.

The others began to follow.

I glanced up, saw that Peach was almost there. The trapdoor was shut, but that often happened when there was a wind, and today the wind was blowing hard enough to airlift a cow.

"It's stuck," she called.

"Push it," Mia said.

"I *am*," Peach answered.

The creatures were approaching, their green eyes reveling in the impending kill.

"Push it harder," I growled.

"I can't," Peach said. "Help me!"

Annoyed, I turned and looked up at her, and I realized it was as she said. She was shoving up on the wooden door as hard as she could, and it did seem like there was something encumbering it. In fact, I had a sudden, acute worry that she'd struggle too hard against the door and lose her tenuous footing on the wet rung she was standing on. I was about to tell her to let me do it when her efforts jolted the trapdoor just enough to afford a glimpse of what was holding it down. I couldn't be positive about what I'd seen when the door had swung up, but I was pretty sure I knew where Kurt Fisher had gone.

He was keeping us down here with the monsters.

Chapter Fourteen

Endgame

"Will, it won't open!" Peach called.

I dashed toward the oak tree. "Climb down a few rungs!" I called. The creatures were approaching, but they didn't seem to be accelerating. Not yet at least.

The rungs, thank God, were long enough that I could climb up beside Mia without her having to climb down. A good thing too, as Mia was already about twenty-five feet off the ground. For the first time since we'd constructed the thing, I questioned the logic of building the treehouse so damned *high*. Yeah, it might seem cool to sit so far above the forest floor, but now, with two little girls and Mia in a life-threatening situation, I was afraid one of them would go plummeting downward toward a broken neck.

I couldn't lose another person I cared about.

I made it to where Juliet was clinging to the side of the tree like a petrified squirrel. I said, "You okay?"

She didn't answer. Or move, for that matter.

But her hold on the rungs seemed strong enough to last a couple more minutes.

I climbed higher until I passed Peach.

I pounded on the trapdoor. "Kurt? You up there?"

No answer.

I got a good hold on the rung, lowered my head, and rammed the trapdoor with my shoulder. It jounced, but it didn't open.

It wasn't locked, but there was definitely someone holding it down.

"*Kurt,*" I said. "Unless you want to be responsible for the deaths of four people, you better get the hell off the door right now!"

I heard a faint scraping sound, tested the door with my free hand. But it still held fast.

"Dammit," I muttered.

"Will?" Mia said, her voice tight with fear.

I glanced down and saw what she was looking at. The creatures had halved the distance to the oak tree.

They were coming.

I punched the wood above me. "Kurt, you stupid, selfish prick, open the door!"

Nothing.

Peach's voice was strained. "Will, I can't hold on much longer."

I ground my teeth, agonizing. I didn't need to look down to know the creatures were closing in on us. I remembered the way one of them had shimmied up the arm of the bucket lift. Compared to that, this tree would be a cinch. We were dead unless we got through the trapdoor. But there had to be another way...

I shot a glance at the bottom of the treehouse. Some of the branches were bowed, which left room for handholds. I could climb out to the edge of the structure, find gripping places on the boughs that cradled the structure, then climb into the treehouse through the window. Accomplishing this would require me to dangle over a freefall of maybe forty feet, and there was no guarantee I'd be able to scale the outside of the treehouse. But Kurt had the trapdoor pinned, and if I kept trying to dislodge him, the beasts would have us in no time.

I started to climb an outcropping branch.

"What are you doing?"

It was Mia's voice, but I didn't bother answering her. I knew if I stopped to contemplate it, I'd lose my nerve. I climbed farther, farther, nearly to the edge of the treehouse.

My left hand slipped.

For an endless, ghastly moment, I was swinging out over dead space. The creatures weren't below me yet, but they soon would be. If I fell, I might die right away, but if I didn't, the beasts would feast on me the way they had Larry the Utility Worker. The only thing left would be a cruddy pair of sneakers and a few bones.

Groaning, I got hold of the branch again.

Near the edge of the treehouse, I discovered a good-sized bough that protruded out about eight feet. Carefully, I climbed onto the bough, rocked, and looped my legs over the big branch. I'm afraid I must've jerked on the tree a little too violently, because footsteps sounded within the treehouse. As I climbed onto the bough and leaned on the plywood façade, Kurt's wide-eyed face appeared in the window opening. He was grasping something.

He'd found our hatchet.

I hesitated, knowing the creatures had to be right below the treehouse now. Mia and the girls were down there, exposed. Once the beasts started climbing, it would be over for them. Over for all of us.

Then I heard a creaking sound and a muted thump. His expression bemused, Kurt turned away from me.

I realized what had happened. When Peach had heard the footsteps above her, she'd known there was nothing holding the trapdoor closed. She'd climbed inside.

And was now inside the treehouse with Kurt and the hatchet.

With a cry of rage I vaulted toward the window.

The blade came whooshing down at me the moment my fingers clamped onto the open window frame. I jerked my face aside, the hatchet missing me entirely, the bottom of the blade bouncing harmlessly off my shoulder rather than sinking into my flesh. I hauled myself toward the aperture, my feet scrabbling on the wet plywood façade.

Kurt grinned, cocked the hatchet back. In that moment I knew I was dead. If I didn't defend myself, the hatchet would split my skull. But if I did try to fend off the blow, there was no way I'd be able to maintain my perilous hold on the slippery window frame.

Kurt swung the hatchet, but his fingers lost hold of the blade halfway to my face. The hatchet clattered against the inside of the treehouse. Kurt threw back his head and howled in agony. Utterly confused but knowing it was my only opportunity to climb inside, I thrust myself through the opening and tumbled onto the floor. I glanced to the left and saw Kurt grasping the back of his leg.

Peach had stabbed him with a pencil. Not only that, she had buried the damned thing at least two inches deep. Kurt was bellowing in pain and scooting around the treehouse like a dog with his butt on fire.

I waited for him, leaned back, and unloaded on him with my fiercest roundhouse right fist. His head snapped back, his feet flying out from under him. The back of his head cracked against the unforgiving floor, and he lay without moving.

Man, it felt good.

But my elation only lasted for a moment.

Because that's when Mia started screaming.

◆

I scrambled over to the trapdoor, saw Juliet still wrapped against the side of the tree like cellophane, but now she was shrieking, her voice loud and indescribably shrill, and as I leaned out a little I realized why.

One of the creatures had latched onto Mia's ankle.

Mia was about ten feet below me, Juliet right above her. I had to climb over Juliet to get to Mia, and I had no idea how to do that without knocking all three of us off the tree and into the mass of waiting beasts.

And they *were* waiting for us now. I could see that despite the darkening evening. Their iridescent eyes were upturned, their grim stares advertising plainly that the moment Mia or anyone else fell, they'd whir into action and rend their prey to shreds.

I realized with dim fury that the creature grasping Mia's ankle was laughing. No, not laughing— *chortling.* It knew it had her, knew it could pry her off her perch at any time. So it was playing with her, deliberately amplifying her terror for cruel sport.

"*No,*" I breathed. But how to get to her?

Mia kicked and the beast's hand came loose. It swung away from the rungs for a moment, its face a mask of surprise. Then it glowered up at Mia, who was clambering toward Juliet.

"Come on!" I shouted at Juliet. Mia reached her and began shoving her bodily up the ladder. Below them the creature recovered its hold and started climbing again. It looked mad now. Like, *really* mad. And no longer in the mood for games.

Mia's time had almost run out.

I got down on my stomach, called to Juliet, "Move!"

She did, but not nearly fast enough. Of course, she was six and gripped by mortal terror, so maybe I should have cut her a little slack.

I reached through the trapdoor and groped for her hand. Her fingers grasped mine. Using all my strength, I hauled her up. I deposited her on the floor beside Kurt's unmoving form and lunged back toward Mia.

The thing had her again. Only this time it was worse. Its entire upper body was even with Mia's calves, and its noxious fingers were pawing Mia's hips. Its long black tongue slithered over its lips, its green eyes alight with depraved lust.

A bright spire of outrage seared through me, and I shot a desperate look around the treehouse. I saw the many objects we'd collected up here, but other than the hatchet, none of them looked like they'd help Mia, and anyway, I had to climb over Mia in order to use the hatchet, and unless I could also locate an anti-gravitational suit, I knew I wouldn't be able to accomplish that.

"What about the rope, Will?" Peach asked.

I gaped at her and realized she was right.

I snatched the rope out of her hands, tied it around one of the overhead joists as quickly as I could, thinking as I did so how lucky I was that we were crappy carpenters. Otherwise I'd have never been able to slip the rope around the wooden two-by-six above me. Without pause, I tied the other end of the rope around my waist and crossed to the trapdoor opening.

The beast was embracing Mia, a revolting leer etched on its face.

I clamped the hatchet between my teeth. I probably looked like a prepubescent pirate, but I wasn't fighting one of those monsters without a weapon.

I lowered myself through the hole. I had to be extremely careful. If my rescue mission went awry, I'd knock Mia off the tree, killing us both and leaving Peach and Juliet exposed to the beasts' insatiable appetites.

I let myself fall.

As I slipped through the opening, I pushed away from the tree, plummeting, my body angling where I wanted it to, but at that moment a new fear assaulted me—what if the rope was too long? My God, what if I kept right on dropping all the way into the crowd of Children?

But the rope jerked taut. It wrenched my neck something awful, but I couldn't have scripted my fall any better. I was at eye level with the creature's lower back, the rope having permitted me to swing out about eight feet from the tree. Even more astonishingly, the creature didn't seem to have noticed me yet, was apparently too enchanted by the sight of the girl in its arms to worry about someone crashing his party.

I arced toward the beast, raised the hatchet.

Quicker than I would have dreamed possible, the beast whirled and sprang at me. Suddenly abandoned, Mia nearly lost her hold on the rungs. But now I was in far worse shape, for as the beast's wiry body hit me, the hatchet missing its mark and nearly slipping out of my hand, the length of rope groaned as though it were about to snap. With one slimy arm the creature clung to me. The stench of rancid hamburger and soiled diapers bored into my nostrils. But I had bigger things to worry about. The creature had raised its free arm for an attack.

The beast's talons flashed toward me.

Impulsively, I shot up a wrist, thinking to deflect the blow, but in doing so I'd raised the hatchet. There was a *shink*ing sound, then the creature squalled. The meat of its forearm had lodged on the sharp blade.

The creature jerked its arm free and nearly took the hatchet with it. We were dangling a foot or two away from the tree, and I knew if I lost my weapon I'd be dead.

The creature's face darted at mine. I jerked aside, but I only partially evaded the thing's lethal jaws. Blazing heat scorched my ear, and blood splashed down my neck.

The beast's head bounced, and pain bloomed in its face.

Then anger. I glanced up and saw Mia raising her foot to stomp on the creature again. The beast reached up, battened on to her ankle. Mia gripped the rungs above us, fighting and struggling, but the beast wouldn't relinquish its hold. It was more interested in her than it was in me—most of the creatures seemed to be male, and I got the impression they were driven largely by horniness—which allowed me to lean away from it, the hatchet cocked.

When its arm lay against the tree, I shouted at Mia, "Hold still!"

She frowned like I was insane, which I probably was, but she listened. Before the creature could chomp her calf, I hammered down with the hatchet, the blade sinking right through the thing's arm at the elbow. A black jet of ichor sprayed us both, but the creature, shrieking and grasping its severed arm, forgot to hold on. In the next moment it was plummeting toward its waiting brothers and sisters. By the time it hit the ground with a bruising thump, Mia and I were already clambering into the treehouse. We made it inside, and Peach slammed the door shut. I scrambled to the medicine cabinet, fetched the padlock, and slid it into place.

Not that it would make any difference.

Because now we were trapped. Mia and I, two little girls, and an unconscious asshole.

Below us were a dozen monsters.

In other words, we were completely fucked.

♦

The storm's fury had diminished.

For more than a minute, the only sound we detected was the occasional thunk of a raindrop on the sheet metal roof.

The waiting was unbearable. There were tiny chinks in the floor planks, places where the wood had warped and we could glimpse the creatures if we put our faces down and peered through. Peach and Juliet volunteered for this duty, which was fine by me. I needed to think, needed to come up with a plan, because without one we stood no chance.

I sucked in breath. It was like someone had walloped me with a sledgehammer. I couldn't believe I hadn't thought of it before.

"Mia," I said in a harsh whisper. "Get up for a minute."

Frowning, she did, and I wished I had spoken to her a little more delicately. But we didn't have time for apologies now. Any second those monsters would be scaling the tree to kill us and eat us, not necessarily in that order, and I knew I had to work fast.

I gripped the bucket on which she'd been sitting and lifted it.

It rose from the floor, but it was heavy.

Heavy was good.

At my ear, Mia asked, "What's in there? Paint?"

I shook my head. "Kerosene."

She squeezed my arm so hard it made me wince. "Do you have something to light it?"

I nodded. "Over there. By the lamp."

I couldn't believe I'd forgotten it. The kerosene controversy had taken place last summer. Chris had a lazy streak and constantly complained about having to replace the fuel for the old-fashioned lamp we used for illumination up here. The lamp had belonged to Chris's grandmother, and since neither his mom nor his dad were much on family heirlooms, Chris had been permitted to commandeer it for our treehouse.

The problem was, the thing burned through fuel so fast, it got so we were toting the lamp down every week and refilling it from the five-gallon bucket of kerosene at Barley's dad's store. Then Chris had gotten the bright idea to lug the entire five-gallon bucket up to the treehouse. We told him the idea was nuts, but once it got lodged in his head, he wouldn't let it die. He brainstormed strategies, sketched out numerous diagrams, and finally settled on a complicated system of ropes and pulleys.

The amazing part was that it had actually worked. At the time, the bucket had been completely full, Chris arguing that it was pointless to expend all that energy on an insufficient load. Now, after having used the bucket for almost a year, some of it was gone.

But there was still plenty left. Maybe three quarters of it.

Would it be enough to incinerate the monsters beneath us? I didn't know. But it was certainly enough to do some damage. *If* we could both spray the creatures with the kerosene and light them on fire.

But how?

I knew I couldn't just request that they stand still while I doused them. And even if I could, how would I ignite the kerosene? The long red butane lighter we used up here was our only means of starting a fire, and yes, there was a button on the lighter that allowed it to remain lit. But I couldn't just drop it forty feet and hope it would set the creatures ablaze.

Mia asked, "What are you thinking?"

I blinked at her, realized I'd been a million miles away. "I'm just..." I bit my lip, wishing I were smarter.

"How much is in here?" she asked, tapping the bucket lid.

"Four gallons?" I guessed. "A hair less?"

"So the first thing we do is figure out how to deliver the kerosene," she said.

I nodded, liking the way her thoughts synched up with mine. I was also grateful to have someone else working on the problem. After all I'd been through, my brain felt like mush.

For something to do, I went over, put a hand on Peach's back. She was on her belly, squinting through a gap in the floor. "Any movement yet?" I asked.

"I don't think so," she said quietly. "I can only see a few of them, but they're all just waiting. Looking up at me."

Her words chilled me. I wanted to tell her it was her imagination. That she was only imagining those accursed green eyes directed at her, but I suspected she was right. The creatures *were* waiting. For what, I didn't know. But they were undoubtedly planning on taking us by force. The one whose arm I'd lopped off would certainly want revenge.

"He's climbing," Peach said in a thin voice.

I stared down at her a moment, and it wasn't until she looked up at me, tears already welling in her big eyes, that it hit me.

The creatures were coming to get us.

"That's what they were waiting for," she said. "The biggest one. He must've been busy eating Rebecca, but now he's here, pointing up at us."

Mia hustled over to the trapdoor, waved the girls closer. "Sit beside me. Yes, *right beside* me. We need to hold the door down."

We're dead, I thought. The extent of our plan was to try to keep the trapdoor closed, as if that would do any good. I'd seen what these monsters could do, watched them shimmy up wet surfaces, seen them leap fifteen feet with ease. Soon they'd be swarming over the treehouse from all directions, and then it'd be a smorgasbord. Leg of Peach here. Arm of Mia there. With some tasty Will guts for dessert.

The trapdoor under Mia jounced.

"Will?" she said. "We can't hold them."

As if to confirm this statement, the door jarred violently, this time actually bouncing Mia and the girls into the air.

"Do something!" Juliet cried.

I took a step toward them, thinking to climb onto the door too, but that would only delay the breaching of the treehouse. The beasts wouldn't stop until they could feed. That was the only thing that had stopped the biggest one from killing us earlier. The beast had been occupied, it had been stationary…immersed in its feeding. But there was nothing left to eat, other than us.

I toyed with the idea of making a break for it, luring them away from the treehouse so the others could escape.

But they'd catch me for sure. Then they'd kill the girls.

It was hopeless.

Mia looked up at me. "I don't think we can—" Her eyes shuttered wide. "Will, look out!"

I turned just in time to see Kurt Fisher's fist zooming toward my face. He caught me right in the nose, my head snapping back. The pain was so quick and intense I think I lost consciousness for a moment. But I was aware enough to know I'd crashed down onto Mia, both of us tangled in a snarl of limbs. There was a tussle, then Mia was shouting at Kurt to give her the keys back. Something blurred past my face—Kurt's fist, I realized—and then Mia grunted with surprise and pain.

Even after all that had happened, I was astounded that Kurt would punch a girl.

But I was too groggy from the blow Kurt had dealt me to defend Mia. I swiveled my head around, saw Kurt, his eyes bright with what might have been insanity, shoving Peach and Juliet away from the trap door. Kurt seized my forearm, began dragging me toward the trap door. He undid the padlock.

He opened the trap door. The creature that had been pushing up on it lost its grip and tumbled away from the tree with an indignant screech.

I stared at the open trap door. Kurt yanked me closer.

What fogginess had come over me was whipped away by an icy gust of terror.

Kurt was sacrificing me.

"They'll be too busy with you to worry about the rest of us," Kurt said through gritted teeth. He hauled me toward the square opening, the sight of the approaching Children swimming into focus. They were halfway up the rungs, their emerald eyes blazing with anticipation.

"Don't do this," I said, marshaling whatever energy I had to resist Kurt. I started pushing to my feet, but before I could stand he whipped an elbow into my gut and kneed me in the forehead when I doubled up.

He forced me to the floor, my upper body leaning precariously over the opening. "You'll be giving your sister a chance, Burgess. Be a man for once in your life."

"*NO!*" Peach shouted, and in the next moment her little shape was hurtling across the opening and battening onto Kurt's leg like a feral cat. She was punching him, scratching at the arm that was pushing me toward the opening.

Then it happened.

Kurt slapped Peach.

She went flying toward the wall, her little feet rising into the air and jolting when she struck plywood. The sight of her half-conscious body lying there twisted and beaten enraged me like nothing in the world could. Kurt seized my shoulders, began stuffing me downward toward the opening. The creatures were only ten feet away now. In seconds they'd be feasting on me.

"Leave him alone!" Juliet screamed.

I reached up, grabbed Kurt's hands, and pushed them apart. Though I couldn't see his face, I knew he'd lost balance, was falling on top of me. I swung my head up, hoping to head butt Kurt in the face.

His nose crushed like a robin's egg.

He squalled, let go of me, but his momentum brought him down on top of me, sent us both dropping toward the trapdoor opening. I shot out my arms to prevent us both from falling through. I looked down in terror, saw the first creature was nearly to the opening. Five feet away and climbing.

And Kurt and I were sinking through the trapdoor.

"*Kurt,*" I grunted, fighting to support our combined weight. "*Get...off...me.*"

His bloody nose gushed over my neck, poured in runnels over me, dripped through the trapdoor opening.

Pattered on the beast's upturned face.

Its green eyes flashed, its maniacal bloodlust enflamed. I watched in numb horror as its long black tongue wormed out and licked Kurt's blood off its lips.

I strained against Kurt, bucked against his weight, but it was too late, too late. The creature was upon us, reaching up, ravenous for more blood. It reached up, up, its hateful talons growing ever nearer, and I knew this was it, the monsters were finally going to claim me. I only hoped Mia would have the courage to take Peach and Juliet and make a break for it while the beasts were devouring me.

The talons drew even with my face, moved higher.

Then several things happened at once.

Kurt gasped. Something grabbed my ankles. And then the world was twisting, limbs flailing. Kurt began to shriek. My body was yanked upward, Kurt's body scraping over mine, Peach commanding anyone who would listen to help her brother. I realized Peach, Mia, and Juliet were dragging me away from the opening, but the beast was hauling Kurt toward it. I glanced over my shoulder in time to see a gout of blood splash into the air. Kurt's blood.

Kurt's bloody nose had saved me, I realized. It was blood that the creature wanted. That's why it had reached past me and seized hold of Kurt. Inside the treehouse, I pushed to my knees and gazed down at the scene below.

The creature at the top of the rungs was clutching Kurt in one arm and tearing at him with its razor-like teeth. My stomach clenched when I saw what the beast had done to Kurt, how his savaged throat had hinged sideways.

He was dead already.

Below them the other beasts roared, no doubt frantic to get at Kurt's body too.

Another creature clambered over them, its movements impossibly quick. I made to shut the trapdoor but it was too late. One moment I was glancing at Kurt's ruined throat. The next I was flying backward, the creature exploding through the opening, lifting me and pinning me to the flimsy plywood walls. My feet hung two feet off the ground. The creature opened its maw, prepared to rip my throat out.

Its head jerked, something having smacked it from behind. Snarling, it whirled and let me fall. I landed in a heap and saw Mia, her thin leather belt dangling from her fingers like a whip. Before the creature could spring, Mia struck again, the silver buckle lashing the creature in the face and apparently blinding it. It stumbled sideways, howling in fury, its fingers pressed to its bleeding eyes.

I heard more monsters clambering upward. I looked down, saw them swarming over Kurt's dead body. The beast grasping Kurt roared in fury, but the weight of the other beasts was too much. They lost hold of the rungs and tumbled downward in a writhing ball. Watching them fall was like witnessing an avalanche, only instead of snow and rock, this one was comprised of white limbs and bestial faces.

And, of course, Kurt Fisher.

Staring at the glob of beasts, I was seized by a desperate idea.

I tried to blot out the echo of snapping bones and snarling creatures as I dragged the bucket of kerosene to the edge. I had to hurry—the beasts wouldn't remain in place forever.

And there was the small matter of the beast still *inside* the treehouse for me to worry about. Mia was circling the wounded beast, lashing out again and again with the belt. Peach and Juliet were throwing objects at it, batteries and baseballs and *Playboy* magazines Chris and I had smuggled up here in the past couple years.

The thought of Chris made my throat burn, so I shook it away, focused on the kerosene bucket. I used the hatchet for a pry and worked the edges of the lid loose. We'd taken off that lid many times, so the metal tongues holding it in place bent easily.

Mia dropped down next to me. "Hatchet," she breathed.

I handed it to her without thinking. It was a good thing too. The creature had recovered. And was stalking toward us.

Mia swung the hatchet at the creature's foot. At the last moment, the creature sidestepped the blow. The hatchet embedded in the floor. The creature bent forward, cupped Mia's jaw, and leered at her. I started to intercede, but before I could do anything, the beast squealed, its head thrown back in agony. I looked down and saw the carpet cutter finishing its swipe, the hooked, silver blade and the thick wooden handle already painted with black blood.

The creature backpedaled but its legs failed and it landed on its side, its mouth still stretched open in that unearthly wail.

Peach had severed its Achilles tendon.

Peach didn't pause to admire her handiwork, instead rushed over to the creature and swung the carpet cutter again. The creature brought a hand up, and then three of its fingers were clipped off, the ichor spewing all over my sister. It growled at her, and I knew she'd be dead if she didn't get away soon. But she was possessed, gone berserker in defense of us, and my love for her, if it was possible, grew even stronger.

I slung an arm around her waist and yanked her toward me. I didn't know how to finish the creature off, but as foolish as it sounds, the beast in the treehouse wasn't my first priority. It wasn't incapacitated, but it was badly injured and howling in pain.

I returned to the bucket, tilted it. The odor of kerosene filled the treehouse. It began to lap over the rim of the bucket, then to gush. It sluiced through the trapdoor opening and sailed toward the pile of creatures, who had indeed swarmed all over Kurt. The kerosene splashed over the Children, the foul-smelling stuff going everywhere.

A couple of the creatures froze, but the majority of them kept right on rending and tearing and chewing. The mass of white, salamander-thin bodies was so tightly clustered that I could scarcely see the body they were feasting on. But the occasional glimpse was more than enough.

Kurt was a crimson ruin.

Fighting down my gorge, I moved the bucket around more vigorously, tipping it farther and farther as I did. When I thought I'd drenched all of the Children, I tilted the bucket all the way, the vertical position allowing the last dregs of kerosene to drool out onto the creatures directly under me.

The creatures returned to their feeding, a development that surprised me. I'd been sure the moment they smelled the fuel they'd scatter or attack me, but it was obvious they didn't realize how much danger they were in. Or maybe, I mused, their own putrid stench was so overwhelming they couldn't even scent the kerosene.

More likely, they were abandoning themselves to the blood frenzy Kurt's corpse had created.

"What now, Will?" Mia asked.

Coincidentally, this was the same question I was asking myself. Truth was, I had no idea what was next. Mia was immersed in kicking the downed creature in the head, but she kept shooting glances at me, the terror plain in her eyes.

I grimaced, casting about for the butane lighter. There was a horrible moment in which I was sure I'd lost the thing. Then Juliet came to me, extended an arm. "Do you want this?"

With an audible sigh, I accepted the lighter and looked around for something I could light.

There was the rope, but I'd have to untie it, douse it with kerosene, and drop it. All of that would take too long, and now I realized I'd made a catastrophic mistake—perhaps a fatal mistake. I'd neglected to save any kerosene, so even if I could get the rope ready before the Children ceased devouring Kurt, I didn't have the means to light it on fire.

"Will this work?" Juliet asked.

She was grasping the kerosene lamp.

"Oh my God," I breathed and rushed over to her. How had I missed something so obvious? I grabbed it and had started to move toward the trapdoor when something slammed into me from behind. The lamp flew out of my hand, the glass shell that covered the wick exploding in a hail of shards.

"*No!*" I screamed.

The thing had me pinned, glass shards from the lamp piercing my chest, my arms. I tried to roll over but the beast only leaned on me. Lasers of pain shot down my back. It was digging at me, its vicious talons ribboning my flesh. I writhed beneath it, reached back to protect my torn skin, but the talons were merciless, implacable. They ripped through me again, this time slashing sideways, just above my buttocks. The pain was so intense I worried I might faint. Mia was attacking it, I saw with a backward glance. She had ahold of its sparse hair, was wrenching and shaking the creature with all her might.

I finally managed to roll over beneath it. I saw, lying against the plywood wall, the red glass base of the kerosene lamp.

Completely intact.

Full of kerosene.

"Peach!" I yelled. "Grab that lamp!"

Unhesitatingly, Peach hurried over and picked it up. She looked at me for further direction.

"Now smash it," I grunted. The beast's weight pressed down on me as it battled with Mia.

Peach lifted it above her head, prepared to dash the red glass on the floor.

"*No!*" I said quickly. "*On the monster's head!*"

Peach got behind the creature and walloped it in the skull. Fragments of scarlet glass sprayed everywhere, the kerosene dousing the beast.

Bellowing with fury, the creature thrust Mia away and spun toward Peach. It bent to grab her. I snatched up the lighter. Depressed the fuel button. Clicked the starter.

Shoved the bluish flame into the beast's dripping hair.

A crown of fire enveloped its head.

The beast's cry transformed into shocked anguish as a sheet of flame spread over its body. A nine-foot-tall candle, the creature staggered away from Peach.

I shoved it toward the trapdoor.

One instant it was slapping at its fiery face; the next it was disappearing through the opening, its entire body a flapping, shrieking torch. I dropped to my knees in time to see the flaming creature crash into the pile of feasting monsters. I was afraid the other creatures wouldn't catch fire, that the kerosene I'd poured on them wouldn't ignite.

But it did.

Almost at once, the base of the tree was a shifting, jittering kaleidoscope of glowing beasts. Several took off screaming as the flames wrapped around them; others had been so thoroughly soaked in the kerosene that their pallid bodies became scorched, blackened skeletons within twenty or thirty seconds. All four of us gathered around the opening and watched the creatures being consumed.

Then, a lone creature began to scale the rungs, its body only on fire from the waist down. This one, I realized with mounting dread, was the biggest beast of all, the one they'd waited on before they attacked.

Trembling with rage, I pushed away from the opening, went over and scooped up the hatchet.

"Will, no!" Mia shouted, interposing herself between me and the trapdoor.

"I'm not letting it hurt you," I said. "Now *move*."

"It's okay," a voice said.

We all looked down at Juliet, who hadn't ceased her vigil at the trapdoor. Rejoining her, we saw what she meant. The largest beast had stopped climbing, was slumped against the tree, the fire having spread all the way to its armpits.

It glared up at me, its green eyes shot through with rage and loathing.

Then, it tumbled backward and landed with a dull *whump*.

◆

I only watched the creature roast for a few seconds. Then I stood.

"Let's go," I said.

"Wait," Mia said, putting my forearm in a death grip. "What are you—"

"We have to get out of the woods," I said. "There'll be more of them."

She shook her head. "How do you know that?"

"I don't know anything," I said. "But we can't assume we got them all."

She searched my eyes a moment longer. Then she nodded.

Her face molded into a frown when she beheld the burning bodies beneath us. "But how do we…"

"We'll be careful," I said. "I'll go first, you second. Then the girls. I'll help you guys down."

It was difficult going, especially near the ground. But I finally managed to leap clear of the bodies. I kept expecting one of the charred corpses to reanimate. In fact, that was one of my chief motives for getting away immediately. I'd seen the Eric-thing mend and wondered if these monsters could do the same thing. I helped Mia off the ladder, then told the girls to leap toward me one at a time. They did, and despite the terrible wounds in my back, I was able to catch them.

I didn't dare think about my injuries and what they might mean. Was it possible I would change like Eric Blades? Like Padgett?

It was while I was helping Peach to the ground that Mia noticed my wounds. "*Will*," she said, "you'll bleed to death."

"Better than being eaten," I said. "Come on."

She wasn't appeased, but I was too antsy to stick around longer. There were only nine corpses I could see in the vicinity of the tree, which meant there were three more beasts who'd dashed off into the forest after being set aflame. I hoped all three of them had died, but I knew it was folly to count on that. Besides, Mia had a point about my blood loss. I'd begun to grow dizzy, my vision graying around the edges. And I didn't like our chances of making it to civilization if the girls had to drag me.

So we set off down the trail. I led the way, Mia took the rear, and the girls stayed between us. I kept Peach as close as humanly possible. If I hadn't been so torn up by that creature, I would've carried her piggyback.

We'd been walking for a couple minutes when we saw it, the shape huddled a few feet from the edge of the trail. When I first spotted movement, I immediately thought of the creatures. One of the beasts had, my racing thoughts proclaimed, managed to extinguish itself and was now in the process of regenerating. I was raising the hatchet when the figure shifted, and I realized who it was.

Mr. Watkins was down on his knees, his body curled into the fetal position. He tremored with silent sobs.

I rushed over to him, disbelief flooding through me. "Are you hurt?"

His shoulders shook, but he didn't answer.

"Let's keep going, Will," Peach said.

I waved her away, knowing deep down she was right, but still too shocked to heed her advice. Besides, I'd witnessed too much carnage already. I wanted to save anyone I could, even if Mr. Watkins was a coward and a jerk.

Or maybe I felt subconsciously guilty for murdering my biological father.

The evening was well advanced, and it was growing harder to see. In the muted violet twilight I made out Mr. Watkins's light blue shirt, his khaki pants ripped and tattered below the knees. He looked pitiful, broken.

"Come with us," I said. "We're only a couple minutes from my house."

Mr. Watkins didn't look at me. He seemed to be studying his hand.

"Mr. Watkins?" I said. I put a hand on his shoulder, thinking to comfort him.

I froze. The skin beneath the light blue fabric felt…different. Tauter.

"Will?" Mia said in a tight voice. "Look."

But I was already looking. Now I knew why he was studying his hand. And I knew how he'd gotten away from the beasts on River Road.

Mr. Watkins turned and leered at me, his eyes huge and green and absolutely insane with hunger.

Sucking in breath, I backed away, pushing the girls behind me as well as I could. Mr. Watkins stood. He seemed to go on and on, his figure gaunt and tall and ripping through his clothes. Leering, he strode toward us, loomed over us, and though I still had the hatchet, I doubted it would do much good. Because this creature was new, fresh, and we were about to become its first kills. We were—

"GET DOWN!" a voice bellowed.

The Watkins-thing whirled, snarling, and I saw them then, five policemen. All of them with their guns drawn.

Diving, I buried the girls beneath me. Juliet shrieked. Peach grunted as my weight bore down on her. Mia didn't say anything, but I felt her body pinned under mine. We heard a roar, the beast preparing to attack the police.

Then the woods erupted with gunfire. Bullets whizzed over our heads, punched holes in the wet leaves.

Please let us survive, I prayed. *Please don't let this all have been in vain.*

In moments the explosions stopped. Then a tall, pale figure thumped down on the soil beside us.

I glanced over and saw the Watkins-thing staring sightlessly at the purple sky.

A hand fell on my shoulder.

Hissing, I whirled and raised the hatchet.

And saw the female cop with her hands up. "Take it easy," she said. "Just take it easy."

"It's all over," another female cop said.

"It's *not* over," I said, lowering the hatchet. "Those things are still out there. At least three more of them."

A third cop, this one a skinny guy with a dark complexion: "You mean like this one?" He nodded toward the Watkins-thing.

I nodded.

"How do you know that?" one of the female cops asked.

"Because we cremated nine of them. Three more got away."

There was a thick, unbelieving silence.

"What's your name?" the first female cop said to Mia.

Mia told her.

The woman exchanged a glance with her fellow officers.

"I'm Officer Manalo," she said. "Your parents have been worried to death about you."

Mia got shakily to her feet. "But they're..."

Officer Manalo smiled ruefully. "Poor choice of words. Your folks are fine."

The other female cop introduced herself as Officer Lopez. She helped Peach and Juliet to their feet. Both female cops, I decided, were far prettier than any policemen I'd ever seen. They looked like cops from a movie, not real life. Of course, now was probably not the time to be noticing things like that.

"What about you?" one of the male cops said. He was fortyish, square-jawed.

"I'll live," I said and winced.

He frowned, put a hand on my shoulder, and turned me half-around. "You're cut up really badly. Jesus, kid, what's your name?"

I told him.

Something changed in his expression then, but I was too dazed to identify it. He said, "I'm Officer Kosarich. You can lean on me if you need to."

"I've got him," Mia said, slinging my arm over her shoulder.

"Wait a second," a skinny blond cop said. "Are there any other survivors out there?"

Mia looked at me. I could only lower my head.

"Jesus," the blond cop whispered.

"We need to get you four out of the woods," Officer Manalo said.

"Sounds good to me," Mia agreed.

A ruddy-faced cop spoke up. "Maybe one of us should go on ahead, notify the rest that we've found the kids."

Kosarich shook his head. "We can't spare anybody. If what they're saying is true, there are more of these things out there. With Will injured and the two little girls, we're not going to make good time anyway."

Peach scowled at him. "I can run faster than you can."

Officer Lopez grinned and took Peach by the hand, and Officer Manalo took charge of Juliet. The three male cops murmured to one another, and then the whole procession began making its way down the path.

"Look!" Kosarich shouted.

We all turned and saw the rail-thin form loping away into the underbrush.

The Watkins-thing.

"Hell," an officer said. His ruddy face had gone pale.

"That's not possible," Officer Lopez whispered.

"One of you should've shot it," Juliet said.

I had to admit, it was a good point.

"Let's go," I said, unable to suppress my anxiety any longer. Plus, I really was starting to feel woozy. Like, bad enough that if Mia weren't propping me up, I'd faint dead away.

"The kid's right," Officer Manalo said. "Let's get moving."

We got moving.

♦

It was full dark by the time we reached my backyard. I could see figures standing at the rear of the house.

More policemen.

With a surge of horror I remembered my mom.

Please let her be alive, I thought.

I pushed away from Mia and began lurching up the short hill to my yard. I'd only gone a few strides before a blanket of dizziness settled over me. Mia was by my side in an instant, her hands on my shoulders. She was imploring me to take it easy, to wait for the doctors, but there was a low, buzzing dread eating away at me, reminding me of a chainsaw's insectile roar, like a billion cicadas droning at once.

"Is he okay?" a voice asked, and as the little hands embraced me I realized it was Peach. But that only made me feel worse, because as much as I loved her and was thankful she'd survived, I remembered she had no idea how much danger our mom had been in, had no reason to suspect the nightmare wasn't over.

I looked up at Officer Manalo. "Where's my mom?"

Her face changed, became masklike.

"Where's my *mom*?" I growled.

The mask slipped a little, and I saw real remorse there, something so sensitive and sympathetic that I longed to scream at her, to shove her away from me, because I didn't need sympathy. I needed my *family*, needed a chance to put the fragments of our life back together, even if the life we'd had before was pathetic. If Mom was dead, we'd have nothing. I remembered what Padgett had said about siblings who were taken away from their families. They seldom ended up together. And if Mom was dead…if something had happened to her…

…it would be my fault.

I pushed up on my knees, the effort awakening terrible pain in the flayed skin of my back.

Mia put a steadying arm around me. "Will, please—"

"Is she dead?" I asked.

Everybody was looking at Officer Kosarich, who, I noticed with black foreboding, wouldn't meet anyone's eyes.

Officer Lopez swallowed thickly, took Peach and Juliet by the hands. "Come on. Let's get you two dry."

Juliet came willingly, but Peach didn't budge. "What's wrong with Mommy?" she asked.

Officer Lopez stood indecisively for a moment, then escorted Juliet toward the house.

My heart skipped a beat when I realized that Juliet's parents were dead.

Were butchered.

And Juliet had no idea.

But we didn't know about Mom, not for sure. Not yet.

Officer Manalo crouched in front of me. "Look, Will, the rain's starting to pick up again. We've gotta get you to a doctor right away. Plus..." She nodded at the forest. "...that thing might come back."

This last remark hardly registered, though Mia tightened visibly at mention of the Children. What did register was the pair of paramedics dashing toward me, a stretcher bouncing between them.

I glowered at Officer Manalo. "Where's my mom?"

Again, one of those thick silences fell. The paramedics had almost reached us, and now there were four other figures moving swiftly in our direction. Two of them were state troopers. The other two were Bill Stuckey and Chris's mother.

Oh God, I thought with a fresh pang of grief.
Chris.

"Is he with them?" Mrs. Watkins was asking one of the cops. The man didn't look at her.

But Mrs. Watkins had spotted me. "Will!" she said. "Will! Where's Chris?"

My throat went dry. I regarded Officer Kosarich, who looked like a man awaiting the firing squad. "Please," I said. "I need to know if my mom is dead or alive."

Kosarich and Manalo glanced at each other. Then Kosarich nodded almost imperceptibly.

Officer Manalo held out a hand to my sister. "Come here, honey."

"Peach," I said. "Her name is Peach."

Officer Manalo nodded. Reluctantly, Peach came over and stood where Officer Manalo was kneeling.

"What is it?" Mia asked, her voice barely a whisper.

Officer Manalo took a deep breath, steeling herself. I knew what would come out of her mouth before she spoke. But that didn't make it any easier.

"Officer Stuckey was dispatched to your house at approximately 6:15."

I nodded impatiently. "I know that. I was there. He was supposed to get my mom out of that cistern. So did he save her or not?"

I noticed then that Bill Stuckey was trailing the other cops and Mrs. Watkins by a goodly distance, which I also took for a very bad sign. Stuckey kept his eyes down, seemingly riveted by the sight of my wet, overgrown backyard.

Mrs. Watkins broke away from the cops. "Where is Chris?" she demanded.

I stared at Officer Manalo. "Did Mom make it?"

Officer Manalo sighed, glanced at Peach, then at me. She shook her head. "I'm sorry."

I'm sorry. Her words echoed in my brain. *I'm sorry. I'm sorry. I'm sorry.*

I'm sorry.

My mom was dead.

Gone forever.

It felt like my heart exploded. *No!*

My hands balled into fists. Dammit, I should have gone home the moment I escaped Padgett. If I hadn't gone with Cavanaugh, I could've saved my mom. I imagined her down there in that hole, the water lapping over her chin, her frightened eyes gazing up at me. It had seemed impossible at the time. Ludicrous. How could she drown that way? The water rising, that had seemed like an empty threat from Padgett. Surely it was impossible. Surely this couldn't be happening.

But it was. This was real. My mom was dead.

And it was my fault.

A sob rose in my throat. I tried to choke it down, but there was no denying it, no suppressing the geyser of heartbreak gushing through my body. Someone touched my shoulder, but I shoved the hand away, dropped to my knees. I was weeping openly, but I didn't care now. I was the worst person in the world, worse even than those damned monsters. I had failed to save my mother, failed to save the woman who had given me life. I was barely conscious of the voices, barely conscious of anything save my clenched fists, buried in my hair, yanking, jerking until the roots came loose, my teeth bared, the convulsive sobs rocking my body. I knew I should be holding Peach right now, but I couldn't. Could only hate myself and miss my mom and curse myself for not protecting her.

I became aware of a loud wail. I looked over, saw my little sister crumpled on the ground, her mouth stretched in a heartbroken bray. Mia was crying too, but her eyes were on me, and what could I say to her? What could I say to Peach? That I was sorry? That I'd screwed up royally, and my mom had perished because of it? That I despised myself and wished that I had died instead? And in some remote corner of my consciousness I was aware of Mrs. Watkins's jagged voice screaming at me, at the cops, at everyone. *Tell me!* she screamed. *Tell me where Chris is!* But Chris was dead. My best friend, my brother. I'd failed him, failed everyone. I was sprawled out on the ground, my body quaking, the dirt under my face turning to mud. I wanted to scream but I couldn't stop crying, couldn't even breathe. My mom was gone. Forever. And if Mom was dead

(*drowned in that hole*)

that meant I'd lose Peach too. Child Protective Services would swoop in like a carrion crow and

(*the black water closing over her lips, bubbling in her nostrils*)

snatch us and scatter us and then we'd never see each other

(*gasping and sobbing and taking in more water*)

and my sister and I would be strangers and Peach would forget me. Hell, she was only six, and that was

(*and wondering where her son was, wondering if he would save her, her face disappearing in the black water*)

old enough to block most of it out, to move on and have a new life as long as the old pieces, the dark ones, were hidden away, left to rot in cardboard boxes on mildewed shelves and Mom was dead and Peach was leaving me and Jesus Christ why did it have to end this way, why did I have to fail and lose everyone and everything and...and...and...

Chapter Fifteen

After

...and now I'm here. I've been in this place over a
year now. Thirteen months, to be exact. If this were a
novel, I'd talk about the food here (disgusting), how
grumpy everyone is (especially most of the workers),
how poorly I sleep (many nights not at all), or how I've
already gotten into fistfights with the other patients
(four times). And I might tell you about all that later. If
I have time.

But first I want to tell you about The Great
Whitewash. Or at least that's how I think of it.

See, I've never been much on conspiracy theories.
Frankly, they usually strike me as absurd. Just the
bizarre ravings of people with too much time on their
hands.

But you know what they did about Savage
Hollow? The government?

Think about how many people died. If you count
Padgett's victims—Kylie Ann Lubeck, Detective David
Wood, Mr. and Mrs. Wallace, Brad Ralston, and my
mother—there were twenty-two deaths last summer.
Twenty-two deaths, and most of them at the hands of
the Children.

But they blamed it all on Carl Padgett.

Now don't go thinking I feel bad for the man—I
don't. At all. Padgett was a monster; everything that
happened to him, he had coming. In fact, he got off
easier than he should have. I know I should be more
forgiving than that, but I'm sorry, I'm just not there yet.
Who knows if I'll ever be? If you lost your best friend,

your mom, and saw a good many other people butchered, you'd be bitter too.

But I know what happened. I know what I saw. I was *there*, dammit, and I know it wasn't an accident that overturned that utility truck, know it wasn't Padgett that broke Mrs. Ralston's neck on River Road and impaled her husband with a fist.

I know it wasn't Padgett who devoured my best friend.

So I told the police the truth. I told the doctors the truth. I *still* tell the doctors the truth.

And for that, they keep me locked up.

Thirteen months without a visit from Mia. From Barley.

I don't even know where Peach is.

The doctors here acted like I was demented when I told them my story.

But after what happened last month, some of them are starting to wonder.

You remember the Peaceful Valley Nature Preserve? The state park that was going to open this summer?

Well, it did. But before the grand opening ceremony, something happened there. Something horrific.

Reports are still scattered and conflicting, and I don't hear much where I am. They don't let me watch TV or read newspapers, but I still catch bits and pieces from the nurses and orderlies, the few who don't treat me like I'm about to transform into a werewolf or something.

They say there was a massacre at Peaceful Valley.

Over *two hundred people* slaughtered.

Most of the bodies are missing, but the ones that have been found are...

Are not all there.

Earlier, one of the nurses—a guy named Pierre—was walking me down to the courtyard so I could get some exercise. Pierre, who's a skinny black man maybe fifty years old, he says, "Will, there's something you need to know."

Side-by-side with Pierre in the long, stark corridor, I say, "Did someone call me?"

"Wait a minute," he mutters, looking supremely uncomfortable. He keeps shooting sidelong glances at the black glass orbs protruding from the ceilings, the surveillance cameras that remind me of Orwell's *1984* and seem to pepper every nook and cranny of this hellhole they call a rehabilitation center.

Rehabilitation. What a load of crap.

What this place really is, it's a sleek-looking landfill where the authorities store their human garbage. A receptacle for problematic people.

First floor for the elderly.

Second story for grown men.

Third floor for grown women.

Fourth floor for girls.

Fifth story for boys.

The troubled boys, we're the biggest problems for them, so they keep us the farthest from the ground. At least that's how I see it.

Maybe I'm just paranoid.

A guy like Barley, he'd love a place like this. Or rather, he'd love knowing a place like this *exists*. As for actually living here, he wouldn't last a week. Hell, I don't know how I've lasted this long. A kid died earlier this year. He killed himself.

From the government's perspective, that's another problem child eliminated.

Or at least that's how I see it.

Pierre pushes the Down button, waits for the elevator.

He says, "This is a safe place. Listen."

I listen. Pierre is one of the few people who doesn't treat me like a communicable disease.

"The thing at the state park," he says. "The thing I told you about?"

"You mean the massacre?" I ask.

He makes a face. "Yeah, that. Anyway, that's got everybody squeamish. They're thinking you might not be so crazy after all."

"Really?"

He sighs. "But they still think you're dangerous."

Of course they do. My fatal mistake had been telling them not just the story, but the *whole* story.

Because that convinced them I was insane. Because that gave them the justification they needed to lock me up and sever all my ties with the outside world.

We enter the elevator. Pierre pushes the *1* button.

"So that's what you needed to tell me?" I say. "That a few of my captors believe my story?"

Pierre's eyes, ordinarily warm and jovial, go unusually flinty. "Stop with the self-pity, Will. It doesn't do any good."

I look away, trying not to show how stung I am.

"I was telling you about the stuff at the park," Pierre says. "The state police, they're in a lot of trouble with the Feds. Even the CIA."

"How do you know about that?" I ask.

Pierre glances around uncomfortably. "Man, would you shut up for a minute? Who *cares* how I know about it? I know, all right?"

I fall silent. I don't know how Pierre is connected or who he's been talking to, but it's obvious he's telling the truth. Besides, what does he have to gain by talking to me? Nothing, as far as I can see. But he has a lot to lose.

"What I'm telling you," he mutters as we reach the first floor, "is that you're finally gonna have some leverage."

"Leverage?"

"Push the Hold button," he says. "I gotta tie my shoe." He takes a knee beside me.

I glance down at him. "Your shoes are both tied."

He glares at me. "Boy, are you that stupid?"

I wince. Pierre is trying to stall for more time, I realize. Maybe I really am that stupid.

"They're gonna come in here and ask you about what happened last summer. In the woods?"

I nod.

He pretends to tie his shoe. "Don't tell them everything. In fact, hold some stuff back. Let on there's more you never told the doctors. Or the cops. The more they think you know, the more they'll be willing to give you."

I roll my eyes. "Like what? Another trip to the courtyard every day? Extra helpings of blue Jell-O at supper?"

He stands abruptly, glowers at me. "Man, don't you wanna see your sister? Or your friends?"

"They've all forgotten me," I say, striving and failing to keep the hurt out of my voice.

"Come on," he says. "They'll get suspicious, we don't get out of this elevator soon."

We walk in silence to the courtyard.

Once outside, I see we're the only ones here. It's really sunny, and my eyes ache from the glare. We start walking through the nicely manicured grass, the outside air warm on my skin.

Pierre doesn't move his lips much as he talks. His eyes keep darting about, as though a SWAT team might descend on us at any moment.

I think maybe I'm not the only believer in conspiracy theories.

Pierre says, "You're the most popular patient we've got."

"I like you too, Pierre."

He rolls his eyes like I'm a moron. "Not *us*, Will. I mean the folks who keep trying to get in contact with you."

I stare at him, dumbstruck. "I thought no one's tried to...I mean, the doctors said—"

"I *know* what the doctors said," Pierre snaps. He looks around, then lowers his voice. "I talk to the girls at the front desk. One of them's my niece. Anita?"

I have no idea who Anita is because I've never seen the front desk. When they brought me here, I was heavily sedated.

"Anyway, Anita says there've been about fifteen hundred calls for you—that's an actual figure, Will, not an exaggeration—and half as many letters since you arrived."

I could only gape.

"A lot of them have been from that girl you told me about...Mya something?"

My heartbeat quickened. "Mia Samuels?"

"That's the one. And a boy. Someone named—"

"Barley?"

"Yeah," he says and frowns. "What the hell kind of a name is Barley anyway?"

"Never mind," I say. "What else?"

"Anita tells me there's a little girl, name of Peach, who calls at least three times a day wanting to talk to you."

My eyes fill with tears. I can hardly breathe. "That's my little sister, Pierre. I told you about her."

The old kindness returns to his face. In a soft voice, he says, "I know you did, Will. You talk about her all the time."

I wipe a tear away, but several more spill over my cheeks. Peach *has* been trying to reach me. And here I'd believed she'd forgotten me, was too young to remember her big brother.

Pierre puts a hand on my shoulder. "It's okay, Will."

But it isn't. A sudden anger takes hold of me. I rub a hand over my wet nose. "How long have you known about this?"

Pierre looks sheepish. "Truthfully?"

I give him my best *What-do-you-think?* look.

He sighs. "I knew she'd been trying to get ahold of you. I just had no idea how much. When Anita told me the Feds were gonna come calling, I asked her some questions about your case. See, even though she's my niece, we don't talk that much. I got her the job a few years ago, but then she married this dude—he's a real loser—and she knows *I* think he's a loser, and, well..."

"Why didn't you tell me before?"

He sighs. "I probably should have. I just worried what it would do to you. I mean, you're in here, and there's nothing you can do about it. Why worry you with things you have no control over? I figured it would drive you crazy."

"Feeling forgotten has driven me crazy."

Pierre makes a pained face. "I'm sorry, okay? I guess I made a mistake."

I take a steadying breath. "What should I do?"

"Not much, other than hint at big things with the Feds. Get them thinking."

We walk through the courtyard in silence. I chew on what Pierre has told me. At length, I say, "So I'm stuck here. There's nothing I can do."

"Of *course* there's something you can do," he says. Then he catches himself, wipes a frustrated hand over his mouth. "Okay, Will. I'm gonna tell you one more thing, but if you say something—and I mean *anything*, to anybody—my ass is gonna be in big trouble."

"They'll fire you?"

"*Fire* me?" he asks, eyebrows raised. "Hell, that'll be the easy part. I don't mind telling you, I don't relish the idea of losing my pension now, ten years away from retirement. And my wife sure as hell wouldn't be happy."

"I won't tell anyone."

He eyes me for a good while. We walk toward the center of the courtyard, which is about fifty yards across. Now, that might sound plenty large, but I'm here to tell you, when that's all the open space you get, fifty yards isn't much. When I'm out here, I feel like I'm in a kennel. I'd kill to spend some time in the open, or even better, a baseball field. I'd kill to breathe some fresher air.

Figuratively speaking, of course.

When we stop, he looks up, studies the sky for a long moment. I do too. There are big cumulus clouds today, fluffy white ones. Though I can't feel much breeze down here, the clouds are positively racing overhead.

"Pierre?" I say.

Still looking up, he says, "Were you telling me the truth about those things?"

I swallow. I know perfectly well what *those things* are. So I say, "What about them?"

"You say they were tall and pale, right? Really skinny?"

"But strong," I add. "The kind of creature that can rip you in half."

He nods. "They didn't have wings?"

I frown. "Pierre, what are we talking about here?"

He chuckles a little, as if embarrassed. He shakes his head. "After that...whatever you want to call it at the state park. Massacre? Bloodbath?"

I nod.

"There've been all sorts of reports about creatures in the area. Shadeland, I mean. We're on the other side of the county from them, but we still hear a lot of what goes on there." Pierre shrugs. "A couple of the nurses even commute from Shadeland."

I wait, the worm of dread in my belly wriggling and wriggling.

"Some of the reports," Pierre says, "they jibe with your account. Tall, white. Green eyes."

I try to swallow, but my mouth and throat have gone dry. "The Children," I say.

"Whatever, man. You ask me, that's a sick name to call a creature like that."

"I didn't choose it."

He looks around. "There've been other reports too. Ones that talk of creatures that're totally different than yours. Ones that..." He breaks off, shakes his head. "But it's *insane* stuff, you know? I feel funny even mentioning it."

"Try me," I say.

He scowls at the ground for a moment, says, "Remember that niece I told you about?"

"You mean Anita?" I say. "The one with the jerk for a husband?"

He smiles at that, relaxing a little. "That's the one. She lives between Lafayette and Shadeland, but closer to Shadeland. Which means she drives about twenty minutes to work each day and twenty minutes when she's done. She usually pulls the day shift, but after what happened in Shadeland...you know, the Peaceful Valley thing? Several of the workers here have relatives in Shadeland. So she's had to cover extra shifts because employees have been missing so much time comforting their loved ones. Or mourning them."

I wait, wondering where this is going.

Pierre goes on. "She had the late shift a couple nights ago. Not the graveyard shift, but the one ends at midnight? She was driving the highway back to her house—her husband owns a few acres in the country, where he raises alpacas—"

"Alpacas?"

"—tall hairy things. Long necks, sort of cute if you look at them sideways? Anyway, she's heading back to Alpaca Land and not really paying attention because it's really late and she's just trying to make it home before she falls asleep." He pauses, massages his forehead. "See, this is where it gets weird. And I don't really believe it since she was so sleepy and all...she probably just imagined it, you know?"

I try to conceal my impatience. "What happened, Pierre?"

"She says this shape came swooping toward her out of the woods. But it was nothing like the things you've been talking about. This...whatever it was, was black and winged, like some sort of mythological creature. She said it had scarlet eyes. Eyes that glowed. Came at her car at sort of a diagonal, the thing's powerful legs and long tail actually smacking the roof as it swept over her."

I thought of the crude drawings I'd glimpsed in Padgett's cave. The black-winged creatures with red eyes. The coincidence was too great to be ignored.

"But you don't believe it," I say slowly.

He laughs without humor. "I *didn't* believe it. Not until she had me examine the roof."

I can feel my heart squeezing in my chest. "What did you see?"

"Scratch marks," he answers. "Two sets of scratch lines, from the front of the roof to the back. Deep grooves, in some places so deep the metal was torn up in jagged flaps."

Pierre laughs again, but there's nothing pleasant about the sound. "Her husband, he's too pissed off to listen to her story. He's just thinkin' about all the extra alpacas he's gonna have to sell to pay for a new roof. But Anita, she's scared now. She's thinking maybe the reports she's heard from her Shadeland friends are true." Pierre looks at me. "She's thinking maybe you aren't so crazy after all."

"Do you think I'm crazy?" I ask in a quiet voice.

He glances at me. "I never said you were crazy, Will. But you have to admit, your story's pretty outlandish."

I sigh, rub my eyes. "So why are you telling me this? You said there was something else I could do."

"Man, why do you think?" he asks. "I'm telling you because some of the reports from Shadeland have mentioned these winged creatures too. If you talk about them—nothing overt, mind you, just alluding to them in a vague way—it might give you more bargaining power with the authorities."

"Enough to get out of here?"

"I wouldn't go that far, but you never know, right?"

I fall silent.

Pierre is watching me. "Hey, Will?"

I look up at him.

"There is one last thing," he says. "I left it under your mattress a few minutes ago. While you were eating lunch."

"What is it?"

His expression is unreadable. "You'll see. Just don't let anybody else know about it, all right? And if anybody was to find out, you wouldn't mention me. Got that?"

I nod.

We head back inside. It takes every ounce of self-control I possess not to take off sprinting when we reach my hallway. But soon I'm in my room, and the door behind me is locked. With one more glance at the window near the top of the door, I hurry over to the mattress and lift it up.

And see the envelope. Just a simple white one.

I snatch it off the box spring and tear it open. There's a letter inside. It's handwritten, but the words are legible:

Dear Will, it says.

Darcy is writing this letter for me. You taught me how to make my letters, but I'm too slow, and Darcy gets annoyed with me. She's my foster sister. She's fifteen and the one I like the best. There are six of us at the Westfalls—that's the name of the family I'm staying with—but Darcy is the only one I talk to. Oh, Benny is okay, but he's my age, and we fight a lot. But I don't like any of them as much as I like you.

I miss you, Will. They won't let me talk to you where you're staying, and Mr. and Mrs. Westfall won't let me call you anymore even though it's a local call. I want Darcy to drive me over to the hospital but she doesn't have her license yet and she says the Westfalls will kill her if she takes their Mercedes (HI, WILL. THIS IS DARCY. WHAT PEACH SAYS IS TRUE. THE WESTFALLS AREN'T BAD PEOPLE, LIKE VILLAINS FROM A MOVIE, BUT THEY ONLY HAVE US FOSTER KIDS FOR THE MONTHLY STIPEND. THEY TREAT THEIR REAL CHILDREN LIKE PRINCES AND PRINCESSES, BUT THEY MAINLY JUST ACT POLITE TOWARD US. ANYWAY, IT'S NICE TO MEET YOU. I'LL LET YOU GET BACK TO YOUR SISTER NOW). I told Darcy not to put anything else in the note, but she said you wouldn't mind. As if she knew you.

Anyway, Darcy is the only one who calls me Peach. The rest call me Audrey, which you know I hate. I miss Mom sometimes, but not as much as I miss you. Every day I miss you. Since I got kicked off the phone, Darcy lets me call you on hers, but she's only got the kind of phone where you have a certain amount of minutes (TRACK PHONE) and she says I'll use up her minutes calling the hospital. But she lets me call anyway. It makes me feel better just knowing you're alive. Do you think about me? I hope you do because I cry all the time wishing you were with me.

Mia emails me through Darcy's account a lot, and Barley emails me too. I think Barley has a crush on Darcy (PEACH IS ONLY SPECULATING. BARLEY AND I HAVE NEVER EVEN MET FACE TO FACE). Mia and Barley really miss you and keep hoping they'll be allowed to see you. I want to see you too. I should be allowed to see you. I'm your sister! It's not fair what they're doing, Will. Are they ever going to let you out?

Anyway, Darcy says I have to wrap this up (SORRY). Mia and Barley want you to know they're both okay, but they're really scared. Something bad happened in Shadeland a couple weeks ago, and they think more bad things are going to happen. I'm worried about them. But I'm more worried about you. I want to give you a big hug and watch movies with you and have you push me on the goon-goon (WHAT'S A GOON-GOON? PEACH KEEPS ASKING THE WESTFALLS FOR ONE, BUT NO ONE CAN FIGURE OUT WHAT SHE MEANS). I love you, Will. You know that already, but I hope you remember it. I love you more than anyone, even Darcy. Sorry about that, Darcy (NO PROBLEM! WILL SOUNDS LIKE A GREAT BIG BROTHER ☺). But I love you, and I hope I get to see you soon. Don't be sad, okay? I'm fine. I just miss you.

Love,

Peach

I finish reading the note, and with tears blurring my eyes, I re-read it. Then I read it again and again and again. And the tears keep coming. And some of the time I'm laughing, and at other times I'm balling my hands into fists and shaking so badly I almost rip the note. But I don't. I keep reading it. And crying and thinking of my amazing little sister.

◆

That was yesterday.

I didn't sleep last night, and today I'm edgier than usual. Now that I know Mia and Barley and Peach have been trying to contact me, I feel better in a lot of ways, but now my incarceration here feels even more unfair.

There's something else, though. Something I try not to think about, but every time I strive to escape the thought, it comes right back.

Eric Blades and Mr. Watkins turned into monsters. Padgett got scratched, and he claimed the infection is what transformed him into a serial killer.

I got scratched too. Multiple times.

Is that why my temper has gotten worse? Am I imagining things, or am I becoming more like the Children?

I think of the fights I've had since I've been here. I think of the nightmares I've been having on those rare occasions when I can sleep. I hear voices in my dreams. Do they belong to the Children? And if the Children and black-winged creatures are real, does that mean the gigantic versions of them are real too?

Are those the beings who've been trying to speak to me?

I don't know. I only know I need to sleep, even if my dreams are terrifying.

I've been lying here tonight, thinking my insomnia has to end some time. But after three hours of lying awake, I get out of bed knowing I'm going to be up all night again. I go over to the wire mesh window and stare out. The window is one thing I like about my cell. I also have it to myself, and it's surprisingly big. They permit me to have books, but they're pretty strict about violence, language, and sensuality. I keep asking for a Stephen King novel and they tell me not yet.

Assholes.

Anyway, I'm staring out the window and considering all that Pierre told me. I run through Peach's letter, word-by-word, in my head. I get choked up again thinking about my sister.

So when the huge shape swoops by my window, I'm completely unprepared.

I gasp, stumble backward, and nearly end up on the floor. Then I scramble to the window, press my face against the wire mesh, and peer into the night.

And see it. Winging its way back around, the creature is huge, almost prehistoric, its wings maybe twenty feet across. It circles around a big elm tree, hovers above the hospital, and hangs there in the air, its vast wings flapping slowly to keep it aloft. It has lurid red eyes, its flesh a glittering obsidian. The creature reminds me of a dragon, except for the face, which is more sinister than any movie dragon could ever be. Triangular, its mouth crammed with long, curving teeth, the face sweeps slowly over the windows of the fifth floor, searching, searching—

—until they get to mine. At which point the eyes flare red, their eerie light glowing like hellfire. The creature lets out a bloodcurdling screech—one of recognition?—and wings its way into the night.

And here I am, an hour later, still sitting beside the window. I can't believe what I've seen, but I know I've seen it nonetheless. It wasn't imagination. It wasn't a byproduct of my insomnia. It was real.

Which means Anita's story was real.

Padgett's cave drawings were things he'd seen, or images that had been communicated to him telepathically.

I think of Peach, here in Lafayette, only a few miles away.

I think of Barley and Mia, still in Shadeland. Still within walking distance of Savage Hollow and Peaceful Valley.

All the people I care about within reach of the beasts.

I have to get out of here.

Some way, somehow, I have to get to them. To Mia. To Barley.

To Peach most of all.

The Feds are coming tomorrow. I have to convince them to let me go. I'll say anything, *do* anything to get out of this place.

I'll even return to Savage Hollow if it means I'll be released.

I think of the winged beast hovering outside my window.

I think of the Children, of the massacre at Peaceful Valley.

Most of all, I think of my friends. My little sister.

I have to get back to them.

They're all I have left.

About The Author

Jonathan Janz grew up between a dark forest and a graveyard, which explains everything. Brian Keene named his debut novel The Sorrows "the best horror novel of 2012." The Library Journal deemed his follow-up, House of Skin, "reminiscent of Shirley Jackson's The Haunting of Hill House and Peter Straub's Ghost Story." Horror legend Edward Lee proclaimed House of Skin to be "The Quintessential Haunted House Novel."

2013 saw the publication of his novel of vampirism and demonic possession The Darkest Lullaby, as well as his serialized horror novel Savage Species. Of Savage Species Publishers Weekly said, "Fans of old-school splatterpunk horror--Janz cites Richard Laymon as an influence, and it shows--will find much to relish." Jonathan's Kindle Worlds novel Bloodshot: Kingdom of Shadows marked his first foray into the superhero/action genre.

Jack Ketchum called his vampire western Dust Devils a "Rousing-good weird western," and his sequel to The Sorrows (Castle of Sorrows) was selected one of 2014's top three novels by Pod of Horror. 2015 saw the release of The Nightmare Girl, which prompted Pod of Horror to call Jonathan "Horror's Next Big Thing." His newest release is Wolf Land, which Publishers Weekly called "gruesome yet entertaining gorefest" with "an impressive and bloody climax." He has also written four novellas (Exorcist Road, The Clearing of Travis Coble, Old Order, and Witching Hour Theatre) and several short stories. Three of Jonathan's novels have become audiobooks, and Jonathan recently signed an eleven-book hardcover deal with Thunderstorm Books.

His primary interests are his wonderful wife and his three amazing children, and though he realizes that every author's wife and children are wonderful and amazing, in this case the cliché happens to be true. You can learn more about Jonathan at www.jonathanjanz.com. You can also find him on Facebook, via @jonathanjanz on Twitter, on Instagram (jonathanjanz) or on his Goodreads and Amazon author pages.

Coming Soon

Blister by Jeff Strand

Undertaker's Moon by Ronald Kelly

Mayan Blue by Michelle Garza and Melissa Lason

Find these and other horrific books at

sinistergrinpress.com

CPSIA information can be obtained at www.ICGtesting.com
Printed in the USA
LVOW08s1638280416

485768LV00002B/441/P